HEIRS OF THE FORCE

In the jungle outside the academy, the twins make a startling discovery—the remains of a crashed TIE fighter. The original pilot, an Imperial trooper, has been living wild in the jungles since his crash, waiting for a chance to return to duty . . .

SHADOW ACADEMY

Thanks to the Dark Jedi Brakiss—Luke Skywalker's former student—the dark side of the Force has a new training ground . . . the Shadow Academy . . .

THE LOST ONES

Jacen and Jaina could lose an old and dear friend. Zekk is wild and free in the underground mazes of Coruscant—and a perfect candidate for the Shadow Academy . . .

D1398831

YOUNG JEDI KNIGHTS

JEDI SHADOW

KEVIN J. ANDERSON
and REBECCA MOESTA

BERKLEY JAM BOOKS, NEW YORK

STAR WARS: YOUNG JEDI KNIGHTS: JEDI SHADOW

A Berkley Jam Book / published by arrangement with
Lucasfilm Ltd.

PRINTING HISTORY
Berkley Jam edition / September 2003

Copyright © 2003 by Lucasfilm Ltd™. Used under authorization.
Heirs of the Force ®, ™ and copyright © 1995 by Lucasfilm Ltd.
Shadow Academy ®, ™ and copyright © 1995 by Lucasfilm Ltd.
The Lost Ones ®, ™ and copyright © 1995 by Lucasfilm Ltd.
Cover design by Rita Frangie.
Cover illustration by Dave Dorman.

For information address: The Berkley Publishing Group,
a division of Penguin Group (USA) Inc.,
375 Hudson Street, New York, New York 10014.

ISBN: 0-425-18683-0

BERKLEY JAM BOOKS®
Berkley Jam Books are published by The Berkley Publishing Group,
a division of Penguin Group (USA) Inc.,
375 Hudson Street, New York, New York 10014.
BERKLEY JAM and its logo
are trademarks belonging to Penguin Group (USA) Inc.

PRINTED IN THE UNITED STATES OF AMERICA

10 9 8 7 6 5

CONTENTS

Heirs of the Force

To our parents
—Andrew & Dorothy Anderson
and Louis & Louise Moesta—
who taught us to love books

acknowledgments

We would like to thank Vonda N. McIntyre for helping to create the kids, Dave Wolverton for his suggestions with Tenel Ka and Dathomir, Lucy Wilson and Sue Rostoni at Lucasfilm for all their ideas and for giving us the opportunity to do this new series, Ginjer Buchanan and Lou Aronica at Berkley for being so enthusiastic about the project, and Brent Lynch, Gregory McNamee, Skip Shayotovich, and the entire STAR WARS FidoNet Echo computer bulletin board for helping out with the jokes. And special thanks to Lil Mitchell for helping with so much of the typing and to Jonathan MacGregor Cowan for Qorl's name.

1

JACEN SOLO HAD stayed at Luke Skywalker's Jedi academy for about a month before he managed to set up his room the way he wanted it.

Within an ancient temple on the jungle moon of Yavin 4, the student quarters were dank and dim, cold every night. But Jacen and his twin sister Jaina had spent days scrubbing the moss-covered stone blocks of their adjoining rooms, adding glowpanels and portable corner-warmers.

The son of Han Solo and Princess Leia stood now in the orangish morning light that spilled through the slit windows in the thick temple walls. Outside in the jungle, large birds shrieked as they fought for their insect breakfasts.

As he did every morning before going to Uncle Luke's lessons, Jacen fed and took stock of all the bizarre and exotic creatures he had collected out in the unexplored jungles on Yavin 4. He liked to gather new pets.

The far wall was stacked with bins and cages, transparent display cages and bubbling aquariums. Many of the containers were ingenious contraptions invented by his mechanically inclined sister. He appreciated Jaina's inventions, though he couldn't understand why she was more interested in the cages themselves than the creatures they contained.

One cage rattled with two clamoring stintarils, tree-dwelling rodents with protruding eyes and long jaws filled with sharp teeth. Stintarils would swarm across the arboreal highways, never slowing down, eating anything that sat still long enough for them to take a bite. Jacen had had a fun time catching these two.

In a damp, transparent enclosure tiny swimming crabs

used sticky mud to build complex nests with small towers and curving battlements. In a rounded water bowl pinkish mucous salamanders swam formlessly, diluted and without shape, until they crawled out onto a perching shelf; then they hardened their outer membranes to a soft jellylike form with pseudopods and a mouth, allowing them to hunt among the insects in the weeds.

In another cage strung with thick, tough wires, iridescent blue piranha-beetles crawled around with clacking jaws, constantly trying to chew their way free. Out in the jungle a wild swarm of piranha-beetles could descend with a thin deadly whine. When they set upon their prey, the beetles could turn a large animal to gnawed bones in minutes. Jacen was proud to have the only specimens in captivity in his menagerie.

Often Jacen's most difficult job was not keeping the exotic pets caged but figuring out what they ate. Sometimes they fed on fruit or flowers. Sometimes they devoured fresh meat chunks. Sometimes the larger ones even broke free of their confinement and ate the *other* specimens—much to Jacen's dismay.

Unlike Jacen and Jaina's strict tutors at home on the city-covered planet Coruscant, Luke Skywalker did not depend on a rigorous course of studies. To be a Jedi, Uncle Luke explained, one had to understand many pieces of the whole tapestry of the galaxy, not just a rigid pattern set by other people.

So Jacen was allowed to spend much of his free time tromping through the dense underbrush, pushing jungle weeds and flowers out of the way, collecting beautiful insects, scooping up rare and unusual fungi. He had always had a strange and deep affinity for living creatures, much as his sister had a talent for understanding machinery and gadgets. He could coax the animals with his special Force talent, getting them to come right up to him, where he could study them at his leisure.

Some of the Jedi students—especially spoiled and troublesome Raynar—were not pleased about the small zoo Jacen kept in his room. But Jacen studied the creatures, and took care of them, and learned much from the animals.

From a small cistern Jaina had installed in the wall, Jacen

ladled cool water into trays inside the cages. His motion disturbed a family of purple jumping spiders so that they hopped and bounced against the netting of the cage roof.

He ran his fingers along the thin wires and whispered to them. "Calm down. It's all right." The spiders stopped their antics and settled down to drink through their long, hollow fangs.

In another cage, the whisper birds had fallen silent, possibly hungry. Jacen would have to collect some fresh nectar funnels from the vines growing in the stones of the crumbling temple across the river.

It was almost time to go to morning lessons. Jacen tapped the sides of the containers, saying good-bye to his pets. Just before turning to leave, though, he hesitated. He peered into the bottommost container, where the transparent crystal snake usually sat coiled in a bed of dry leaves.

The crystal snake was nearly invisible, and Jacen could see it only by looking at the creature in a certain light. But now, no matter which way he looked, he saw no glitter of glassy scales, no rainbowish curve of light that bent around the transparent creature. Alarmed, he leaned down and discovered that the bottom corner of the cage had been bent upward . . . just enough for a thin serpent to slither out.

"I've got a bad feeling about this," Jacen said, unconsciously echoing the words his father so often used.

The crystal snake was not particularly dangerous—at least Jacen didn't think so. He did know from firsthand experience that the bite of the snake brought a moment of piercing pain, and then the victim fell into a deep sleep. Even though after an hour or so one would wake up and feel no ill effects, this was the sort of hazard someone like Raynar might use to cause trouble and perhaps force Jacen to move his pets to an outside storage module.

And now the crystal snake was loose.

His heart started racing with fear, but he remembered to use one of his uncle Luke's Jedi relaxation techniques to keep himself calm, to help him think more clearly. Jacen knew immediately what he had to do: he would have his sister Jaina help him find the snake before anyone noticed it was gone.

He slipped out into the dim hall, his dark round eyes flicking from side to side to check for anyone who might notice him. Then he ducked into the next rounded stone doorway and stood blinking in the shadows of his sister's room.

One entire wall of Jaina's quarters was filled with neatly stacked containers of spare parts, cyberfuses, electronic circuit loops, and tiny gears taken from dismantled and obsolete droids. She had removed unused power packs and control systems from the old Rebel war room deep in the inner chambers of the temple pyramid.

The ancient temple had once been headquarters for the secret Rebel base hidden in the jungles on this isolated moon, long before the twins had been born. Their mother, Princess Leia, had helped the Rebels defend their base against the Empire's terrible Death Star; their father, Han Solo, had been just a smuggler at the time, but he had rescued Luke Skywalker at the end.

Now, though, most of the old equipment from the empty Rebel base lay unused and forgotten by the Jedi trainees. Jaina spent her free time tinkering with it, putting the components together in new ways. Her room was crammed with so much large equipment that Jacen barely had enough space to squeeze inside. He looked around, but saw no sign of the escaped crystal snake.

"Jaina?" he said. "Jaina, I need your help!" He looked around the dim room, trying to find his sister. He smelled the sharp, biting odor of scorched fuses, heard the clunk of a heavy tool against metal.

"Just a minute." Jaina's voice echoed hollowly inside the barrel-shaped hulk of corroded machinery that took up half of her quarters. He remembered when the two of them, with the help of their muscular female friend Tenel Ka, had somewhat clumsily used their Force powers to haul the heavy machine along the winding corridors so Jaina could work on it in her room far into the night.

"Hurry!" Jacen said, feeling the urgency grow. Jaina squirmed backward out of an opening in the intake pipe. Her dark brown hair was straight and simple, tied back with a string to keep it away from her narrow face. Smudges of grease made hash marks on her left cheek.

Though her shoulder-length hair was as rich and thick as her mother's, Jaina never wanted to take the time to twist and tangle it into the lovely, convoluted hairstyles for which Princess Leia had been so famous.

Jacen extended his hand to help her to her feet. "My crystal snake's loose again! We have to find it. Have you seen it?"

She took little notice of his words. "No, I've been busy in here. Almost finished, though." She pointed down at the grimy pumping machinery. "When this is all done we'll be able to install it in the river next to the temple. The flowing water can turn the wheels and charge all of our batteries." Her words picked up speed as she began to talk. Once Jaina got started, she loved to explain things.

Jacen tried to interrupt, but could find no pause in her speech. "But, my snake—"

"With phased output jacks we can divert power to the Great Temple, provide all the light we need. With special protein skimmers added on, we could extract algae from the water and process it into food. We could even power all of the academy's communication systems and —"

Jacen stopped her. "Jaina, why are you spending all your time doing this? Don't we have dozens of permanent power cells left over from the old Rebel base?"

She sighed, making him feel as if he had missed some deeply important point. "I'm not building this because it's *useful*," she said. "I'm doing it to see if I *can*. Once I know I can do it, I won't have to waste time anymore wondering whether anything I learn here is useful or not."

Jacen was still not sure he understood. But then, his sister never could grasp his fascination for living creatures. "In the meantime, Jaina, could you help me find my snake? It's loose. I don't know where to look for it."

"All right," Jaina said, brushing her dirty hands on her stained work overall. "If the snake escaped from your room, it probably moved down the corridor."

The two of them stepped out into the long hall. Side by side, they scanned the shadows and listened.

Jacen's room was the last chamber in one of the temple passages leading to a cold, cracked stone wall. But none of the cracks was wide enough for the crystal snake to hide in.

"We'll have to check from room to room," Jaina said.

Jacen nodded. "If something's wrong, we should be able to sense it. Maybe I can use the Force to track the snake, wherever it might be hiding."

They heard the other Jedi students in their quarters dressing, washing up, or maybe just catching a few extra minutes of sleep. Jacen cocked his ears and listened, half-hoping to hear someone scream out loud, because then he would know where the snake had gone.

They slipped from room to room, pausing at closed doors. Jacen touched his fingers to the wood, but he caught no tingling sensation that might indicate his escaped pet.

But when they came to Raynar's half-open door, they immediately sensed something out of the ordinary. Peering inside, the twins spotted the boy sprawled on the polished stone tiles of the floor.

Raynar wore fine garments of purple, gold, and scarlet cloth, the colors of his noble family's house. Despite Uncle Luke's gentle suggestions, Raynar rarely took off his fancy costume, never allowed himself to be seen in drab but comfortable Jedi training clothes.

Raynar's bristly blond hair shone like flecks of gold dust in the morning sunlight spilling into his room through the window slits. His flushed cheeks sagged in and blew out as he snored softly in an awkward position on the cold tile floor.

"Oh, blaster bolts!" Jacen said. "I think we've found my snake."

Jaina slid the door closed and stationed herself by the crack so the crystal snake couldn't get past her.

Jacen knelt beside Raynar's form and let his eyelids flutter closed. He stretched his fingers into the air, and his knuckles cracked. He let his mind flow, imagining what a snake's thoughts might be like. As usual he felt many things at once through the Force, but he focused down, looking for his snake.

He sensed a slim, languid line of thought, an easily satisfied mind that right now felt cozy and safe. Its only thoughts were *warm, warm . . . sleep, sleep . . .* and *quiet.* The coiled-up crystal snake dozed beneath Raynar in the folds of his purple under-robes.

"Here, Jaina," Jacen whispered. She left the door to crouch beside him. The fabric of her stained overall hissed like another snake as she dropped to her knees.

"I suppose it's directly *under* Raynar's body?"

Jacen nodded. "Yes, where it's warmest."

"That's a problem," Jaina said. "I could roll him over, and you grab the snake."

"No, that would disturb it," Jacen said. "It might bite Raynar again."

Jaina frowned. "He'd sleep through a week's worth of classes."

"Yeah," Jacen said, "but then at least Uncle Luke could finish a lecture without getting interrupted by Raynar's questions."

Jacen sensed the coiled snake with his mind, saw it resting peacefully; but just then, as if Raynar had heard them talking about him, the boy snorted and stirred in his sleep.

The snake surged with alarm. Jacen quickly sent out a calming message, using Jedi relaxation techniques Luke had taught him. He sent peaceful thoughts, quieting thoughts, that calmed not only the serpent but Raynar as well.

"Working together, we could use our Jedi powers to lift Raynar up," Jacen suggested. "Then I'll pull the snake out from underneath him."

"Well, what are we waiting for?" Jaina said, looking at her brother with raised eyebrows.

Closing their eyes, the twins concentrated. They touched the fringes of Raynar's colorful robes with their fingertips as they imagined how *light* he could be . . . that he was merely a feather wafting into the air . . . that he weighed nothing at all, and they could make him drift upward. . . .

Jacen held his breath, and the still-snoring Jedi student

began to rise from the tiled floor. Raynar's loose garments dangled like curtains underneath him, freeing the sleepy snake.

Suddenly deprived of its warm hiding place, the crystal snake woke up in anger, instinctively wanting to lash out. Jacen sensed it uncoiling and seeking a living target, ready to strike.

"Hold Raynar!" he shouted to Jaina as he flashed forward to snatch the slithering crystal snake. His fingers wrapped around its neck, grasping it behind the compact triangular head. He sent focused claming thoughts into the small reptilian brain, quelling its anger, soothing it.

Jacen's quick movement and release of the Force startled Jaina, and she managed to hold Raynar up for only a second or two. As Jacen worked to calm the serpent, Jaina's grip on the floating boy weakened and finally broke.

Raynar tumbled to the hard stone floor in a pile of arms and legs and garishly colored cloth. The thud of impact was enough to wake him even from a snake-drugged sleep. He sat up with a grunt, blinking his blue eyes and shaking his head.

Jacen continued to calm the invisible snake hidden in his hand. He sent tingling thoughts into its mind until the serpent fizzed with pleasure. Content, it wrapped itself around Jacen's wrist, resting its flat, transparent head on his clenched fist. Even in the best of light it barely shimmered. Its scales were like a thin film of diamonds, its black eyes like two bits of charcoal.

Groggy, Raynar looked at the dark-haired twins standing next to him. He scratched his head in confusion. "Jacen? Jaina? Well, well, well, what are you—hey!" He sat up straighter and shook his left arm as if it had gone numb. Then he glared at Jacen.

"I thought I saw one of your . . . your *creatures* in here, just for a minute. And that's the last thing I remember. Is one of your pets loose?"

Embarrassed, Jacen slid his snake-covered hand behind his back. "No," he said, "I can honestly say that all of my pets are completely accounted for."

Jaina bent down to help the other Jedi boy to his feet.

"You must have just fallen asleep, Raynar. You really should have gone to your sleeping pallet if you were so tired." She brushed his clothes off. "Now look, you've got dust all over your pretty robes."

Raynar looked in alarm at the smudges of dust and dirt on his gaudy garments. "Now I'll have to put on a whole new outfit. I can't be seen in public like this!" He brushed his fingers over the cloth in dismay.

"We'll let you get changed then," Jacen said, backing toward the door. "See you at the lecture."

Jacen and Jaina ducked out of Raynar's room. Feeling suddenly bold enough to joke, Jacen waved good-bye with the hand that still carried the invisible crystal snake.

Together, the twins raced back to their quarters so they could put on their own robes in time to hear Luke teach them how to become Jedi Knights.

2

JAINA DUCKED BACK into her quarters to change into fresh clothes as Jacen ran to stash the crystal snake in its cage. She splashed cold water on her face from the new cistern in her bedroom wall.

Her face still damp and tingling, she stepped out into the corridor. "Hurry, or we'll be late," she said as Jacen ran to join her.

Together, the twins dashed to the turbolift, which took them to the upper levels of the pyramid-shaped temple. They entered the echoing space of the grand audience chamber. The air was a bustling hum of other Jedi candidates assembling in the huge room where Luke Skywalker spoke every day.

Shafts of morning light glinted off the polished stone surfaces. The light carried an orange cast reflected from the or-

ange gas giant hanging in the sky—the planet Yavin, around
which the small jungle moon orbited.

Dozens of other Jedi trainees of varying ages and species
found their places in the rows of stone seats spread out across
the long, sloped floor. To Jaina, it looked as if someone had
splashed a giant stone down on the stage, sending parallel
waves of benches rippling toward the back of the chamber.

A mixture of languages and sounds came to Jaina's ears,
along with the rich open-air smell that came from the uncharted jungles outside. She sniffed, but could not identify
the different perfumes from flowers in bloom—though Jacen
probably knew them all by heart. Right now, she smelled the
musty body odors of alien Jedi candidates—matted fur, sunbaked scales, sweet-sour pheromones.

Jacen followed her to a set of empty seats, past two stout,
pink-furred beasts that spoke to each other in growls. As she
sat on the slick, cool seat, Jaina looked up at the squared-off
temple ceilings, at the many different shapes and colors
mounted in mosaics of alien patterns.

"Every time we come in here," she said, "I think of those
old videoclips of the ceremony where Mother handed out
medals to Uncle Luke and Dad. She looked so pretty." She
put a hand up to her straight, unstyled hair.

"Yeah, and Dad looked like such a . . . such a pirate,"
Jacen said.

"Well, he *was* a smuggler in those days," Jaina answered.

She thought of the Rebel soldiers who had survived the attack on the first Death Star, those who had fought against the
Empire in the great space battle to destroy the terrible super-
weapon. Now, more than twenty years later, Luke Skywalker
had turned the abandoned base into a training center for Jedi
hopefuls, rebuilding the Order of Jedi Knights.

Luke himself had begun training other Jedi back when the
twins were barely two years old. Now he often left on his
own missions and spent only part of his time at the academy,
but it remained open under the direction of other Jedi
Knights Luke had trained.

Some of the trainees had virtually no Force potential, content to be mere historians of Jedi lore. Others had great tal-

ent, but had not yet begun their full training. It was Luke's philosophy, though, that all potential Jedi could learn from each other. The strong could learn from the weak, the old could learn from the young—and vice versa.

Jacen and Jaina had come to Yavin 4, sent by their mother Leia to be trained for part of the year. Their younger brother Anakin had remained at home back on the capital world of Coruscant, but he would be coming to join them soon.

Off and on during their childhood, Luke Skywalker had helped the children of Han Solo and Princess Leia to learn their powerful talent. Here on Yavin 4 they had nothing to do but study and practice and train and learn—and so far it had been much more interesting than the curriculum the stuffy educational droids had developed for them back on Coruscant.

"Where's Tenel Ka?" Jaina scanned the crowd, but saw no sign of their friend from the planet Dathomir.

"She should be here," Jacen said. "This morning I saw her go out to do her exercises in the jungle."

Tenel Ka was a devoted Jedi who worked hard to attain her dreams. She had little interest in the bookish studies, the histories and the meditations, but she was an excellent athlete who preferred action to thinking. That was a valuable skill for a Jedi, Luke Skywalker had told her—provided Tenel Ka knew when it was appropriate.

Their friend was impatient, hard-driven, and practically humorless. The twins had taken it as a challenge to see if they could make her laugh.

"She'd better hurry," Jacen said as the room began to quiet. "Uncle Luke is going to start soon."

Catching a movement out of the corner of her eye, Jaina looked up at one of the skylights high on a wall of the tall chamber. The lean, supple silhouette of a young girl edged onto the narrow stone windowsill. "Ah, there she is!"

"She must have climbed the temple from the back," Jacen said. "She was always talking about doing that, but I never thought she'd try."

"Plenty of vines over there," Jaina answered logically, as

if scaling the enormous ancient monument was something Jedi students did every day.

As they watched, Tenel Ka used a thin leather thong to tie her long rusty-gold hair behind her shoulder to keep it out of her way. Then the muscular girl flexed her arms. She attached a silvery grappling hook to the edge of the stone sill and reeled out a thin fibercord from her utility belt.

Tenel Ka lowered herself like a spider on a web, walking precariously down the long smooth surface of the inner wall.

The other Jedi trainees watched her, some applauding, others just recognizing the girl's skill. She could have used her Jedi powers to speed the descent, but Tenel Ka relied on her body whenever possible and used the Force only as a last resort. She thought it showed weakness to depend too heavily on her special powers.

Tenel Ka made an easy landing on the stone floor, her glistening, scaly boots clicking as she touched down. She flexed her arms again to loosen her muscles, then grasped the thin fibercord. With a snap from the Force she popped her grappling hook up and away from the stone above and neatly caught it in her hand as it fell.

She reeled the fibercord into her belt and turned around with a serious expression on her face, then snapped the thong free from her hair and shook her head to let the reddish tresses fall loose around her shoulders.

Tenel Ka dressed like other women from Dathomir, in a brief athletic outfit made from scarlet and emerald skins of native reptiles. The flexible, lightly armored tunic and shorts left her arms and legs bare. Despite her exposed skin, Tenel Ka never seemed bothered by scratches or insect bites, though she made numerous forays into the jungle.

Jacen waved at her, grinning. She acknowledged him with a nod, made her way over to where the twins were sitting, and slid onto the cool stone bench beside Jacen.

"Greetings," Tenel Ka said gruffly.

"Good morning," Jaina said. She smiled at the Amazonian young woman, who looked back at her with large, cool gray eyes, but did not return her smile—not out of rudeness, but because it wasn't in her nature. Tenel Ka rarely smiled.

Jacen nudged her with his elbow and dropped his voice. "I've got a new one for you, Tenel Ka. I think you'll like it. What do you call the person who brings a rancor its dinner?"

She looked perplexed. "I don't understand."

"It's a joke!" Jacen said. "Come on, guess."

"Ah, a joke," Tenel Ka said, nodding. "You expect me to laugh?"

"You won't be able to stop yourself, once you hear it," Jacen said. "Come on, what do you call the person who brings a rancor its dinner?"

"I don't know," Tenel Ka said. Jaina would have bet a hundred credits that the girl wouldn't even venture a guess.

"The appetizer!" Jacen chuckled.

Jaina groaned, but Tenel Ka's face remained serious. "I will need you to explain why that's funny . . . but I see the lecture is about to start. Tell me some other time."

Jacen rolled his eyes.

Just as Luke Skywalker stepped out onto the speaking platform, a flustered Raynar emerged from the turbolift. Puffing and red-faced, he bustled down the long promenade between seats, trying to find a place where he could sit up front. Jaina noticed the boy now wore an entirely different outfit that was as bright as the one before, and of colors that clashed just as much. He sat down and gazed up at the Jedi Master, obviously wanting to impress the teacher.

Luke Skywalker stood on the raised platform and looked out at his mismatched students. His bright eyes seemed to pierce the crowd. Everyone fell silent, as if a warm blanket had fluttered down over them.

Luke still had the boyish looks that Jaina recalled from the history tapes, but now he carried calm power in his lean form, a thunderstorm bottled up in a diamond-hard gentleness. Through many trials Luke had somehow emerged bright and strong. He had survived to form the cornerstone of the new Jedi Knights that would protect the New Republic from the last vestiges of evil in the galaxy.

"May the Force be with you," Luke said in a soft voice that nevertheless carried the length of the grand audience chamber. The words in the often-repeated phrase sent a tingle across Jaina's skin. Beside her, Jacen flashed a smile. Tenel Ka sat up rigidly, as if in homage.

"As I have told you many times," Luke said, "I don't believe the training of a true Jedi comes from listening to lectures. I want to teach you how to learn action, how to *do* things, not just think about them. 'There is no try,' as Yoda, one of my own Jedi Masters, taught me."

From the front row, in a flash of bright color, Raynar raised his hand, waggling his fingers in the air to get Luke's attention. An audible groan rippled through the chamber; Jacen heaved a heavy sigh, and Jaina waited, wondering what question Raynar would come up with this time.

"Master Skywalker," Raynar said, "I don't understand what you mean by 'There is no try.' You must have tried and failed at some time. No one can always succeed in what they want to do."

Luke looked at the boy with an expression of patience and understanding. Jaina never understood how her uncle could maintain his composure through Raynar's frequent interruptions. She supposed it must be the mark of a true Jedi Master.

"I didn't say that I never fail," Luke said. "No Jedi ever becomes perfect. Sometimes, though, what we *succeed* in doing is not exactly what we *intended* to do. Focus on what you accomplished, rather than on what you merely hoped to do. Or what you failed to do. Yes, recognize what you have lost—but look in a different way to see what you have gained."

Luke folded his hands together and walked with gliding footsteps from one side of the speaking platform to the other. His bright eyes never left Raynar's upraised face, but somehow Luke seemed to look at all of the students, speaking to every one of them.

"Let me give you an example," he said. "A few years ago I had a brilliant trainee named Brakiss. He was a talented student, a voracious learner. He had a great potential for the Force. He seemed kind and helpful, fascinated by everything I had to teach. He was also a great actor."

Luke took a deep breath, facing an unpleasant memory

from his past. "You see, once it became known that I had founded an academy to teach Jedi Knights, it's not surprising that the remnants of the Empire would have their own students infiltrate my academy. I managed to catch their first few attempts. They were clumsy and untalented.

"But Brakiss was different. I knew he was an Imperial spy from the moment he stepped off the shuttle and looked around at the jungles on Yavin 4. I could sense it in him, a deep shadow barely hidden by his mask of friendliness and enthusiasm. But in Brakiss I also saw a real talent for the Force. Part of him had been corrupted long ago. He had a deep flaw surrounded by a beautiful exterior.

"But rather than reject him outright, I decided to keep him here, to show him other ways. To heal him. Because if there could be good even in the heart of my father, Darth Vader, there must also be goodness in someone as fresh and new as Brakiss." Luke gazed up at the ceiling, then returned his glance to the audience.

"He stayed here for many months, and I took special interest in teaching him, guiding him, nudging him toward the light side of the Force in every way. He seemed to be turning, softening . . . but Brakiss was colder and more deceptive than even I had suspected. During one part of his training, I sent him on an illusionary quest that would seem real to him, a test that made him face himself. Brakiss had to look inward—to see his very core in a way that no one else could ever see.

"I had hoped the test would heal him, but instead Brakiss lost that battle. Perhaps he was simply not prepared to confront what he saw inside himself. It broke him somehow. He fled from this jungle moon, and I believe he went straight back to the Empire—taking with him everything that I had taught him of the Jedi Way."

Many students in the grand audience chamber gasped. Jaina sat up and looked at her twin brother in alarm. She had never heard this story before.

Raynar again had his hand up, but Luke looked at him with narrowed eyes so full of power that the arrogant student flinched and put his hand back down.

"I know what you're thinking," Luke continued. "That I tried to bring Brakiss back to the light side, and that I failed. But—just as I told you a few moments ago—I was forced to look at how I had succeeded.

"I *did* show Brakiss my compassion. I *did* let him learn the secrets of the light side, uncorrupted by what he had already been taught. And I *did* make him look at himself and realize how broken he was. Once I accomplished that much, the task was no longer mine. The final choice belonged to Brakiss himself. And it still does."

Now he raised his eyes and looked across the gathered Jedi. As Luke's gaze passed over them, Jaina felt an electric thrill, as if an invisible hand had just brushed her.

"To become Jedi," Luke said, "you must face many choices. Some may be simple but troublesome, others may be terrible ordeals. Here at my Jedi academy I can give you tools to use when facing those choices. But I cannot make the choices for you. You must succeed in your own way."

Before Luke could continue, sudden screeching alarms rang out, sounding an emergency.

Artoo-Detoo, the little droid Luke kept near his side, rushed into the grand audience chamber, emitting a loud series of unintelligible electronic whistles and beeps. Luke seemed to understand them, though, and he leaped down from the stage.

"Trouble out on the landing pad!" Luke said, sprinting for the turbolift. He continued to speak to his students as he ran, his robes flapping behind him. "Think about what I've told you and go practice your skills."

The students milled about in confusion, not knowing what to do.

Jacen, Jaina, and Tenel Ka looked at each other, the same thought in each of their minds. "Let's go see what's going on!"

JACEN SAW THAT other Jedi students, who now rushed to the winding internal staircases or crowded into the turbolifts, had the same idea.

Tenel Ka, though, leaped to her feet and grabbed Jacen's arm, yanking him off the stone bench. "We can do it faster my way. Jaina, follow!"

Tenel Ka raced back to the stone wall below the skylights, weaving between two short lizardlike students who seemed baffled by the commotion and cheeped to each other in high-pitched voices. Already Tenel Ka had unreeled the light-weight fibercord from her belt and removed the sturdy grappling hook.

"We'll go up the wall, out the skylights, and down the outside," she said, twirling the grappling hook in her hand. The muscles in her arm rippled. At precisely the right moment she released the hook.

Jacen and Jaina helped it with the Force, guiding the hook so that it seated properly in the moss-covered sill. Its sharp durasteel points dug into a crack in the stone blocks and held there.

Tenel Ka grasped the fibercord in both hands, tugged backward, and began to climb up the rope. She dug the toes of her scaled boots against the wall, hauling herself up, somehow finding footing on the polished stone blocks.

Jacen grabbed the rope next, holding it steady as Tenel Ka ascended like a lizard up a sunbaked cliff face. As he climbed, his arms ached. He used the Force when he needed to, raising his body up, catching himself when his feet slipped. He would have preferred to show off his physical prowess, especially with Tenel Ka watching.

At last he pulled his wiry body to the top of the Great Temple, squirming out the windowsill to stand on the broad rough-hewn platform left by the ancient builders.

Jacen reached behind him to grab his sister's arm and pulled her up. The humid air of the jungle clung to the top of the pyramid, making it hot and sticky, unlike the cool mustiness of the temple interior.

Before they could catch their breath, Tenel Ka had retrieved the fibercord and was picking her way rapidly along the narrow stone walkway. Pebbles crumbled under her feet, but she didn't seem the least bit concerned about falling.

"Around to the side," she said, not even panting. "We can get down faster that way."

Tenel Ka ran with light footsteps around the perimeter until she stopped, looking down at the cleared landing field where all ships arrived and departed. She stood stock still, like a warrior confronted with an awesome opponent.

Jacen and Jaina came up behind her and stared in amazement and horror at what they saw down in front of the temple.

A battered supply ship, the *Lightning Rod*, had landed in the jungle clearing. Their normal supply courier and message runner—long-haired old Peckhum—stood transfixed beside the open jaws of his cargo bay. His eyes were wide and white. He looked as if he had screamed himself hoarse, and could now make no sound.

He stared at a huge, unnatural-looking monstrosity that loomed out of the jungle as if ready to attack, snarling at him . . . waiting for Peckhum to make the next move.

"What *is* that thing?" Jaina asked, looking to her brother as if he would know.

Jacen squinted at the behemoth. As enormous as a shuttlecraft, its huge squarish body was covered with shaggy, matted hair tangled with primordial moss. It stood on six cylindrical legs that were like the boles of ancient trees. Its massive triangular head sat like a Star Destroyer on its shoulders, but instead of eyes inset in its skull, it had a cluster of twelve thick, writhing tentacles, each one glistening with a round, unblinking eye. Curved tusks sprouted from its mouth, long and sharp and wicked enough to tear a hole through a sandcrawler.

"It's not like anything I've ever seen in my life," Jacen said.

Tenel Ka glared down at the monster with a grim expression. "Working together, we can fight it," she said. "Follow!"

She dashed down the wide-cut stone steps outside the tall temple.

The monster let out a bellow of challenge so loud and so horrendous that it seemed to make the ancient stone blocks tremble. The three young Jedi Knights hurried to the ground level, careful not to slip and fall from the steep steps.

"Help me!" Peckhum cried, his voice tinny with fright.

At the jungle's edge, the hideous monster turned, as if distracted by something. Jacen felt his heart leap, thinking at first that perhaps the wild creature had seen the three of them approaching. But he saw that its attention was fixed instead on another figure walking alone, emerging from the lower levels of the temple pyramid, confidently gliding over the clipped grasses and weeds.

Luke Skywalker wore only his Jedi robe. Jacen expected to see him holding his lightsaber, but both of Luke's hands were empty.

Luke stared at the creature, and the creature stared back with a dozen eyes waving at the ends of tentacles covering its face.

The Jedi Master continued to walk forward, directly toward the monster, as if he were in some sort of trance. He took one step, then another. The beast bristled, but held its ground, bellowing loudly enough to make the trees swish. Jungle birds and creatures fled from the horrifying sound.

While the beast was momentarily distracted, old Peckhum dove to the ground, scuttling on all fours through the open cargo doors of his battered shuttle. Jacen was glad to see the supply runner safe inside the shielded metal walls.

The monster roared upon losing its prey. But Luke spoke in an oddly calm and clear voice that was not at all muffled by the distance. "No, here! Look at me," he said.

Tenel Ka reached the ground by leaping down the last four steps and landing in a crouch. Puffing and red-faced, Jacen and Jaina dashed down beside her, then all three teens stood rigid, watching Luke Skywalker face the jungle beast. They had no weapons of their own.

Suddenly, unexpectedly, old Peckhum charged back out of the open bay doors of the *Lightning Rod*. In his hands he held an old-fashioned blaster rifle. "I'll get him, Master Sky-walker! Just stay there." He ducked down and aimed.

But Luke turned to him and motioned with his hand. "No," he said.

The blaster rifle went flying out of Peckhum's grip. The old supply runner stared in astonishment as Luke continued to stroll toward the monster, seemingly without a care in the world.

"This creature means no harm," Luke said, his voice quiet but firm. He never took his eyes off the beast. "It's just frightened and confused. It doesn't know where it is, or why we are here." He drew a deep breath. "There's no need for killing."

Jacen's stomach knotted with unbearable tension as Luke approached the monster. The thing's long eyestalks waved at him, and its six tree-trunk legs took ponderous steps like an Imperial walker.

The beast lowered its triangular head, shaking it from side to side so that the pointed tusks seemed to scratch holes in the air. It let out a strange, soft *blat* of puzzlement.

Jacen hissed with fear, and his sister's entire body clenched. He had used his own talents with the Force to confront many strange animals out in the jungle, but never anything as powerful as this monster, never such a boiling mass of anger and confusion.

But Luke stepped right up to the shaggy, angry thing, within touching distance. The Jedi Master looked incredibly small, yet unafraid.

Beside the battered freighter, Peckhum fell to his knees. The discarded blaster rifle was at hand, but he didn't dare pick up the weapon again. He looked from the monster to Luke, then to the three watching teens—then off into the jungle, as if terrified that another one of the creatures might appear.

Luke stood in front of the nightmarish beast and took a deep breath. He didn't move. The monster held its ground and snorted. Its eyestalks waved unblinking, pointing slitted pupils down at him.

Luke raised his hand, palm out.

The monster snuffled and waited, motionless, its wicked tusks less than a meter away from Luke Skywalker.

The jungle fell silent. The breeze died away. Jacen held his breath. Jaina gripped his hand. Tenel Ka narrowed her cool gray eyes.

The silence seemed so overwhelming that when Luke at last broke the frozen moment, his whisper sounded as loud as a shout.

"Go," Luke told the creature. "There is nothing you need here."

The monster reared up on its hind set of piston legs, its eye tentacles thrashing in a frenzy. Then it let out another high-pitched trumpet before it spun around and crashed off into the thick undergrowth. Branches cracked, trees bent to one side as it plowed a wide path back to the mysterious jungle depths from which it had come.

Like a snapped string, Luke's shoulders slumped with exhaustion. He seemed barely able to keep himself from trembling as Jacen, Jaina, and Tenel Ka rushed toward him, calling his name. "Uncle Luke!"

Luke turned and looked at the three friends with a smile.

Old Peckhum stumbled up, clutching the antiquated blaster rifle. His eyes glittered with unshed tears. "I can't believe you did that, Master Skywalker!" he said. "I thought I was dead for sure, but you faced that monster with no weapons at all."

"I had enough weapons," Luke said with calm conviction. "I had the Force."

"I wish I could do that, Uncle Luke," Jacen said. "That was really something."

"You will be able to do anything you want, Jacen," Luke said. "You have the potential—as long as you have the discipline."

Luke gazed off into the jungle, where they could still hear trees crashing and shrubs snapping as the monster continued to blunder its way through the forest.

"There are many mysterious things in the jungles," Luke said, then he smiled at the twins and Tenel Ka. He nodded toward Peckhum's ship, the *Lightning Rod*, which still sat open, filled with crates and boxes of supplies and equipment.

"I think our friend Mr. Peckhum is having a rough day," Luke said. "He's got a lot more to unload, and he's probably eager to get back up into orbit, where it's safe." He flashed a smile at the old supply runner, who nodded vigorously.

"Why don't you three consider it a Jedi training exercise to help him. Besides, we need to get ready because tomorrow—" He looked at Jacen and Jaina, eyes sparkling. "Your father and Chewbacca are bringing us another Jedi trainee."

"Dad's coming here?" Jaina said with a yelp.

"Hey, why didn't you tell us before?" Jacen added. His heart leaped at the thought of seeing his father again after a full month.

"I wanted it to be a surprise. He's flying in on the *Millennium Falcon*, but he had to stop at Chewbacca's planet first. They've already left Kashyyyk, and they're on their way here."

Filled with excitement, the young Jedi Knights eagerly helped unload Peckhum's supply ship. It was hard work, demanding more concentration and control of their Jedi lifting abilities than they were used to, but they finished in less than an hour. Jaina and Jacen chattered to Tenel Ka about all the adventures Han Solo had experienced. Jaina groaned about how much work it would be to clean up their quarters in time, so they could impress their father.

Finally, the battered old freighter flew off into the misty skies toward the orangish gas-giant planet of Yavin.

Jacen smiled and looked wistfully at the trampled clearing. The next ship to arrive on the landing pad would be the *Millennium Falcon*!

4

"THERE," SAID JAINA, mentally relaxing her hold on a large mass of tangled wires and cables. It came to rest in a more or less contained jumble atop one of the newly tidied stacks of electronic components in her room. "That should do it," she added with a satisfied nod.

"Does that mean we can go to morning meal now?" Jacen said. "You've been at this half the night."

"I want Dad to be impressed." Jaina shrugged.

Jacen laughed. "He never stacks *his* tools this neatly!"

"Guess I did get a little carried away," Jaina replied, matching his grin. "We've still got a few hours before they get here."

Jacen snorted and stood up from the floor, where he'd been sitting next to his sister while they worked. He brushed the dust off his jumpsuit and ran long fingers through his dark brown curls. "Well, how do I look?"

Jaina raised a critical eyebrow at him. "Like someone who's been up all night."

He hurried over to peer anxiously into the small mirror that Jaina had hung above her cistern. She realized that her brother was just as nervous and excited about seeing their father again as she was.

"It's actually not too bad," she assured him. "I think raking the twigs and leaves from your hair really helped. Here, put this on." She pulled a fresh jumpsuit from a chest by her bed. "You'll look more presentable."

When Jacen went into the next room to change, Jaina took his place at the mirror. She wasn't vain, but, as with her room, she preferred to keep her personal appearance neat and clean.

She ran a comb through her straight brown hair and stared at her reflection. Then, with a quick peek over her shoulder to be sure her brother wasn't looking, she pulled back a handful of strands and worked them into a braid. Jaina would never have gone to this much trouble for an ambassador or some silly dignitary—but her father was worth the effort. She hoped Jacen wouldn't notice or comment on it.

Finished, she stepped through her doorway and poked her head into Jacen's room. "All the animals fed?" she asked.

"I took care of that hours ago," he said, emerging in his clean, fresh robe. He heaved a long-suffering sigh. "At least *someone's* had their morning meal."

Jaina gnawed her lip, anxiously scanning the sky for any glimmer that might herald the arrival of the *Millennium Falcon*. She and Jacen stood at the edge of the wide clearing in front of the Jedi academy, where the hideous monster had appeared the day before. The area's short grasses had been trampled down by frequent takeoffs and landings.

Jaina smelled the rich green dampness of the early morning in the jungle that surrounded the clearing. The foliage rustled and sighed in a light breeze that also carried the trills, twitters, and chirps that reminded her of the wide profusion of animal life that inhabited the jungle moon.

Beside her, Jacen shifted impatiently from one foot to the other, a frown of concentration etched across his forehead. Jaina sighed. Why did it seem like everything took forever when you were looking forward to it, and things that you didn't want to happen arrived too soon?

As if sensing her tension, Jacen suddenly turned to her with a mischievous look in his eye. "Hey, Jaina—you know why TIE fighters scream in space?"

She nodded. "Sure, their twin ion engines set up a shock front from the exhaust—"

"No!" Jacen waved his hand in dismissal. "Because they miss their mothership!"

As was expected of her, Jaina groaned, grateful for a chance to get her mind off waiting, even if only for a moment.

Then a comforting hum built and resonated around them, as if the sound of their mounting excitement had suddenly become audible. "Look," she said, pointing at a silver white speck that had just appeared high above the treetops.

The glimmer disappeared for a few moments and then, with a rush of exhaled breath that she hadn't realized she'd been holding, Jaina saw the *Millennium Falcon* swoop across the sky toward the clearing.

The familiar blunt-nosed oval of their father's ship hovered tantalizingly above their heads for a moment that seemed to stretch to eternity. Then, with a burst of its repulsorlifts, it settled gently onto the ground in front of them. The *Falcon*'s cooling hull buzzed and ticked as the engines died down to a low drone. The scent of ozone tickled Jaina's nostrils.

Jaina knew the shutdown procedures for the Corellian light freighter, but she wished that just for today there was some way to speed things up. When she thought she could wait no longer, the landing ramp of the *Falcon* lowered with a whine-thump.

And then their father bounded down the ramp, gathering the twins into his arms, ruffling their hair, and trying to hug both of them at once, as he had done when they were small children.

Han Solo stepped back to take a good look at his children. "Well!" he said at last, with one of those lopsided grins for which he was so famous. "Except for your mother, I'd say this is the finest welcoming committee I've ever had."

"Dad," Jacen said, rolling his eyes, "We are *not* a committee."

As her father laughed, Jaina took a moment to study him, and was relieved to note that he had not changed in the month that they had been gone from home. He wore soft black trousers and boots that fitted him snugly, an open-necked white shirt, and a dark vest—a comfortable, serviceable set of clothes that he sometimes jokingly referred to as his "working uniform." The battered, familiar shape of the *Millennium Falcon* was unchanged as well.

"How do we look, Dad?" Jaina asked. "Any different?"

"Well, now that you mention it . . ." he said, turning his gaze to each of them in turn. "Jacen, you've grown again—bet you even caught up with your sister. And Jaina," he said with a wicked grin, "if I didn't think you'd throw a hydrospanner at me for saying so, I'd tell you that you're even prettier than you were a month ago."

Jaina blushed and gave an unladylike snort to demonstrate what she thought of such compliments, but secretly she was pleased.

A loud, echoing roar from inside the ship saved her the embarrassment of having to come up with a response. A large form thundered down the boarding ramp. Huge heavily furred arms reached out to grab Jaina and threw her high into the air.

"Chewie!" Jaina shrieked, laughing as the giant Wookiee caught her again on the way down. "I'm not a little kid anymore!" After Chewbacca had repeated this greeting ritual with her brother, Jaina finally said what she and Jacen were thinking. "It's good to see you, Dad, but what brings you to the Jedi academy?"

"Yeah," Jacen added. "Mom didn't send you to check if we had enough clean underwear, did she?"

"Nah, nothing like that," their father assured them with a laugh. "Actually, Chewie and I needed to come out this direction to help my old friend Lando Calrissian open up a new operation."

Jaina had always had a great fondness for Lando, her father's dark and dashing friend, but she also knew him well enough to realize that her adopted "uncle" Lando was always involved in some crackpot moneymaking scheme or another. She held up a hand to stop her father.

"Wait, let me guess. He's—he's starting a new casino on his space station and he needed you to bring him a shipload of sabacc cards."

"No, no, I've got it," Jacen said. "He's opening a new Nerf ranch and he wants you to help him build a corral."

At this Chewbacca threw back his head and bleated with Wookiee laughter.

"Not even close." Han Solo shook his head. "Corusca gem mining deep in the atmosphere of the gas giant." He pointed up to the great orange ball of the planet Yavin in the sky overhead. "He asked us to come and help him set up the operation."

"Oh, blaster bolts!" said Jacen, snapping his fingers. "That was going to be my next guess."

Another faint Wookiee-sounding bellow came from inside the *Millennium Falcon*. Chewbacca turned and strode back up the ramp.

"What was that?" Jaina asked.

"Oh, I forgot to mention," Han said. "When Luke found

out we had to come here anyway, he asked us to stop by Chewie's homeworld of Kashyyyk and pick up a new Jedi candidate. He's going to be your fellow student."

As Han spoke, Chewbacca thumped back down the ramp, closely followed by a smaller Wookiee, who was still taller than Jacen or Jaina. The younger Wookiee had thick swirls of ginger-colored fur, with a remarkable swirling black streak as wide as Jaina's hand that ran from just above his left eye up over his head and down to the middle of his back. He wore only a belt woven of some glossy fiber that Jaina could not identify.

"Kids, I'd like you to meet Chewie's nephew Lowbacca. Lowbacca, my kids Jacen and Jaina."

Lowbacca nodded his head and growled a Wookiee greeting. He was thin and lanky, even for a Wookiee, with gangly fur-covered arms and legs. The young Wookiee fidgeted. Chewbacca barked a question to Han and waved one massive arm in the direction of the temple.

"Sure," Han said. "Go ahead—take him to Luke for now. The kids can get to know each other later."

As the two Wookiees headed off to find Luke, Han said, "Wait here, I have something for you," and ducked back into the *Falcon*. He returned in a few moments, his arms laden with a strange assortment of packages and greenery.

"First," he said, tossing each of them a small message disk, "your mother recorded these personal holo letters for you. There's another one from your little brother Anakin. He can't wait to come here himself."

Jaina looked at the glittering message disks, anxious to play them. But she slipped them into one of the pockets of her jumpsuit.

"And now . . ." Han said, holding up a large bouquet of green fronds sprinkled with purple and white star-shaped blossoms. Grinning, he waggled the flowers.

"Oh, Dad, you remembered!"

Jacen ran forward ecstatically. "My stump lizard's favorite food." He took the leafy bundle gratefully and said, "I'll feed 'em to her right away. See you later, Dad." Then he ran off in the direction of the Great Temple.

Jaina stood alone with her father, looking expectantly at the last bulky package he held in his arms. He set it on the weedy ground of the landing clearing and stepped back so that Jaina could pull aside the rags that covered it.

"Great wrapping job, Dad," she said, smiling.

"Hey, it works." Han spread his hands.

Jaina gasped as she removed the coverings, then looked up at her father, who grinned and shrugged nonchalantly. "A hyperdrive unit!" she said.

"It's not in working condition, you understand," he said. "And it's pretty old. I got it off an old Imperial Delta-class shuttle they were dismantling on Coruscant."

Jaina remembered fondly the times she had helped her father tinker with the *Falcon*'s subsystems to keep it running in peak condition—or as close as they could get. "Oh, Dad, you couldn't have picked a better present!" She jumped up and hugged him, wrapping her arms around his dark vest. She could tell that her father was pleased—and maybe even a little embarrassed—by her enthusiasm.

Her father looked down at her and raised one eyebrow. "You know, there's a couple more components on the ship. If you wanted to help me bring 'em out here, your dad could show you how they all go together."

She ran after him into the ship.

5

IT WAS LATE that morning when Jacen and Jaina finally caught up with their father, Chewbacca, and his nephew Lowbacca. The twins, who had spent hours at their respective assigned duties and Jedi training exercises, arrived back at the students' quarters just as they saw the threesome emerge from a formerly empty room.

"Hi!" Jacen called, hurrying up to Lowbacca with his sister in tow. "Are you tired from your trip? If not, I could show you my room. I have some really unusual pets. I collected most of them from the jungles here and Jaina made some cages for them—you should see those cages—and Jaina could show you her room too. She's got all sorts of broken-down equipment that she uses to build things out of." In his enthusiasm, Jacen never even paused to take a breath.

The much taller Lowbacca looked down at the human boy as Jacen rattled on. "Do you like animals? Do you like to build things? Did you bring any pets or equipment with you from Kashyyyk? Do you like—"

His father chuckled into the stream of questions. "There'll be time enough for that later, kid. We spent most of the morning with Luke, and then we got Lowbacca settled in his room. You two want to take him on a tour of the academy, get him familiar with the place? By now, you probably know your way around better than Chewie or I do."

"We'd love to," Jaina answered before their father had finished his sentence.

"We're the perfect tour guides," Jacen added with a confident shrug. "Jaina and I came to the Jedi academy for the first time when we were only two years old." He smiled a cocky, lopsided grin—the one their mother always said made him look just like his father.

Lowbacca gave an interrogative growl. "He asked how many times you've given this tour," Han translated.

"Well," Jacen sputtered, his face reddening slightly, "if you mean in an *official* capacity, as opposed to, er, um . . ." His voice trailed off.

"What he means is," Jaina put in firmly, "this is our first time."

Lowbacca exchanged a glance with his uncle. Chewbacca raised a furred brown arm, indicated the long corridor with a flourish of his hand, and gave a short bark.

"Right," Han said. "Let's go."

The twins led the group down a set of mossy, cracked stairs to the main level and out onto the grassy clearing in front of the Great Temple. Jacen was eager to prove himself

a good tour guide and pointed to each squarish level of the
gigantic pyramid as he spoke.

"At the very top is an observation deck that gives one of
the best views of the big planet Yavin overhead—unless of
course you climb one of those huge old Massassi trees in the
jungle," he said with a laugh. "The top level of the pyramid
has only one enormous room—the grand audience chamber—that can hold thousands of people."

"That's where the Jedi trainees gather when Uncle
Luke—I mean Master Skywalker—gives his lessons," Jaina
said.

Jacen went on to explain that the lower levels had been re-
modeled in recent years. The larger level directly below the
grand audience chamber housed those who lived at the academy—trainees, academy staff, and Master Skywalker himself—and also contained rooms for storage or meditation, as
well as chambers for guests and visiting dignitaries.

The pyramid's huge ground level held the Communications Center, the main computers, meeting areas and offices,
and common rooms in which meals were prepped and eaten.
It also held the Strategy Center—the chamber that had been
known as the War Room in the days when the temple had
housed the Alliance's secret base. Underground, and completely invisible from where they stood, was a gigantic
hangar bay that stored shuttles, speeders, fighters, and other
aircraft.

On two sides of the Great Temple and along the landing
area flowed broad rivers, and beyond them lay the lush and
mostly unexplored jungles of the fourth moon of Yavin. "The
temples were built by the Massassi, a mysterious ancient
race. There are actually lots of structures scattered throughout the jungles," Jacen said. "Some of them are just ruins, really—like the Palace of the Woolamander across the river
there."

He described the power-generating station next to the
main temple, a series of plate-shaped wheels, twice as tall as
Jacen himself, standing on edge and connected through the
center by a long axle.

"So you see," Jaina said, picking up the narration where

her brother had left off, "with the power station, the river, and the jungles, the Jedi academy is fairly self-sufficient. Come on, let's go inside."

The tour concluded at the twins' quarters, where Jacen and Jaina delighted in showing their father and the two Wookiees their respective treasure troves of pets and salvaged bits of machinery. Han Solo beamed with fatherly pride. Lowbacca displayed a gratifying if subdued interest in the creatures in Jacen's menagerie.

When the group moved into his sister's room, Jacen quickly slid the crystal snake he had been showing off back into its cage and hurried after them. By the time he bounded through the door, Lowbacca was already engrossed in an assortment of gadgets and wiring that he had spread out across Jaina's floor. He was far more interested in the electronics than in the wild jungle creatures.

"Do you like working on machines, Chewie—uh, I mean, Lowbacca?" Jaina asked, bending next to the gangly Wookiee.

The hairy creature expressed his fascination with such a long series of grunts, growls, and rumbles that Jacen was at a loss to understand how a simple yes-or-no question could produce such an animated answer.

As usual, their father translated. "First of all, Lowbacca would take it as a great sign of friendship if you would call him Lowie."

Jacen gave a pleased nod. " 'Lowie,' huh? I like that."

"And for the rest . . ." Han continued, "well, I'm not sure I followed it all. The thing he really gets excited about is computers."

Jaina patted the young Wookiee on the shoulder. "We can do a lot of things together, then, Lowie." Chewbacca chuffed in agreement.

But Jaina's forehead furrowed with sudden concern. "Uh, Dad?" she said. "It's obvious that Lowie has studied our language and understands us as well as Chewie does. But we can't understand *him*. After all, it took you years to learn the

Wookiee language. How is he going to get by here at the Jedi academy where nobody can understand him?"

Jacen nodded agreement, looking at the young Wookiee. "who'll translate for us?"

They were interrupted at this point by a triumphant bark from Chewbacca.

"We have just the answer for you," Han said, clapping his hands and rubbing them together. "A little something that See-Threepio and Chewie cooked up."

Chewbacca turned and held out a shiny metallic device for everyone to see. The sidewise-ovoid apparatus was silvery, slightly longer than Lowie's hand and about four fingers thick, flat on the back and rounded on the front. It looked like a face, with two yellow optical sensors unevenly spaced near the top, a more or less triangular protrusion toward the center, and a perforated oblong on the lower portion that Jacen took to be a speaker.

Chewbacca fiddled with something at the back of the device, and the yellow eyes flickered to life. A thin metallic voice, careful and correct, issued from the tiny speaker. "Greetings. I am a Miniaturized Translator Droid—Em Teedee—specializing in human-Wookiee relations. I am fluent in over *six* forms of communication. My primary programmed function is to translate Wookiee speech into other humanoid languages." It paused expectantly and then added, "Might I be of assistance?"

Jacen laughed. "It can't be!"

Jaina gasped. "Sounds just like Threepio!"

"Almost," their father replied, his mouth twisted in wry amusement. He scratched under his collar with one lazy finger. "A little *too much* like Threepio, for my money. But since he did most of the programming on Em Teedee, I couldn't talk him out of it." He shrugged apologetically.

"Why don't you kids try it out during the midday meal? Chewbacca and I still have some business to discuss with Luke; then we'll take off in the *Falcon* later this afternoon. We've got to see Lando at his mining station."

*   *   *

The common room the Jedi trainees used as a mess hall was filled with wooden tables of various heights. The seats—chairs, benches, nests, ledges, cushions, and stools—came in a broad variety of shapes and sizes to accommodate the differing customs and anatomies of human and alien students.

The plantlike members of the Jedi academy had gone outside to the bright sun-washed steps of the Great Temple, where they could soak up light from Yavin's white sun and photosynthesize for nutrients, adding small packets of minerals into their digestive orifices. Inside the mess hall, though, dozens of unusual species sat together eating exotic foods particular to their own kind.

Jacen followed a step behind, still chattering about the old Massassi temples, as Jaina found a table at one end of the large hall that had a chair appropriate for Lowbacca. So far Jacen had been unable to elicit more than a few nods and gestures from the Wookiee, who seemed deep in thought, intent on absorbing the smells, sights, and sounds around him.

Determined to start a real conversation with the new trainee, Jacen cast about in his mind for a good question. *So, Lowie, how much stuff do you need to move in?* Naw, that was a stupid question.

How about, *How old are you?* No, that would get him only a short answer. And anyway, their father had told them that earlier this morning. Lowie was nineteen, barely an adolescent by Wookiee standards. Maybe something like, *How did you know you wanted to become a Jedi?* Yes, that was good.

But before he could pose the question, the solid, muscular form of Tenel Ka swung into the seat next to him, across from Lowbacca.

"New student," she said, acknowledging Lowbacca in the brief, direct way that was so characteristic of her.

"Lowie," Jacen said, "this is our friend Tenel Ka, from the planet of Dathomir."

"And this," Jaina responded, making the introductions for her side of the table, "is Lowbacca, nephew of Chewbacca, from the Wookiee homeworld of Kashyyyk."

Tenel Ka rose formally and inclined her head, tossing her

red-gold hair. "Lowbacca of Kashyyyk, I greet you," she said, and resumed her seat. Lowbacca nodded in return and uttered three short growls.

Jacen waited for a moment, looking at the little translator droid clipped to Lowie's belt, but nothing happened.

"Well?" Jaina said expectantly. "You going to translate for us, Em Teedee?"

"Goodness me, Mistress Jaina, I *am* sorry," the tiny droid replied in a flustered, mechanical voice. "Oh, how dreadful! My initial opportunity to perform my primary function for Master Lowbacca, and I've failed him. I assure you, masters and mistresses all, that from now on I will endeavor to make each translation as speedily and as eloquently as possible—"

Lowbacca interrupted the translator droid's self-reproach with a sharp growl.

"Translate?" the little droid replied. "Translate what? Oh! Oh, I see. Yes. Immediately." Em Teedee made a noise that sounded for all the world as if it was clearing its throat, and then began. "Master Lowbacca says, 'May no sun rise upon a day, nor any moon rise upon a night, in which he is not as honored to see you, and to be in your presence, as he is at this very moment.'"

Jaina rolled her eyes. Jacen shook his head in disbelief. But Tenel Ka's face remained expressionless.

From the corner of his eye, Jacen caught sight of the troublesome young student Raynar in his colorful robes, snickering at them from a nearby table. Automated servers carried generous bowls of food from the kitchen and placed them in front of each trainee.

But Jacen's attention was brought back to his own table when Lowie growled down into the optical sensors of the translator droid.

"Well, so what if I *did* embellish a bit?" the droid asked defensively, as a plate of steaming, blood-red meat was placed in front of the Wookiee. "I was only attempting to make you sound more civilized."

Lowbacca's threatening growl left no doubt as to whether he was grateful to the droid.

"Very well," Em Teedee huffed. "Perhaps a better translation of Master Lowbacca's words would have been, 'The sun has never shined so brightly for this humble Wookiee as on this day we meet.'"

Jacen accepted a hot cup of soup that his sister passed across the table to him. He shot a questioning look at Lowie, who growled again at Em Teedee.

"Well, have it your way then," the droid said haughtily, but in a more subdued voice. "But I assure you that my translations were much more refined. *Ahem*. What Master Lowbacca *actually* said was, 'I am pleased to meet you.'"

When the Wookiee finally grunted in satisfaction, Tenel Ka replied gravely, as if she had not heard any of the other translations, "It is a pleasure shared, Lowbacca."

As an automated tray trundled past toward Raynar's nearby table, Tenel Ka reached out and snagged the last jug of fresh juice. She poured the rich ruby liquid into each of their cups and then set the jug with a gentle *thump* on the table before them. She blinked her cool gray eyes and solemnly held out her cup.

"Jacen and Jaina are already my friends. I offer you friendship, Lowbacca of Kashyyyk."

The Wookiee hesitated, unsure of what to do. Jaina pressed a cup into his hand. Jacen raised his and said, "Friendship."

"Friendship," Jaina echoed.

Nodding, Lowie lifted his glass high in the air, threw his head back, and let out a roar that rang through the hall.

The small voice of Em Teedee broke the silence that followed. "Master Lowbacca most emphatically accepts your offer of friendship and extends his own." To everyone's surprise, the Wookiee did not correct the translator.

"Accepted," Tenel Ka said, taking a drink. When everyone had followed suit, she said, "And now we are friends."

"That means you can call him Lowie now," Jaina said.

Tenel Ka considered this for a moment. "I choose to honor him by using his complete name."

At another table, three short reptilian Cha'a sat around a trayful of warm, rocking eggs, staring fixedly at them like the predators they were. When the eggs cracked and opened, the

Cha'a lunged for the bright pink furry hatchlings as they emerged fresh from the shells.

Two whistling avian creatures shared a plateful of thin, writhing threads covered with fluffy blue hair—tantalizing ropy caterpillars which they slurped one at a time through their narrow, horny beaks.

As Jacen sat at the table spooning his soup, trying to think of something amusing to say to Tenel Ka, or at least to continue the conversation with Lowie, he caught a glimpse of movement out of the corner of his eye—something slithering toward the table beside them. A glassy glitter. A serpentine flash.

Jacen's heart leaped into his throat. He suddenly wondered if he had fastened the cage of the crystal snake when his father and the Wookiees had finished their tour of his chambers.

"Hey," Raynar said, leaning over the table beside them, his flashy robes so brilliant that they made Jacen's eyes ache. "Would you mind giving our juice jug back?" Raynar used his own Jedi powers to snatch the jug from their table and carry it through the air back toward himself. "Next time please ask before you just take it." He leaned back and crossed his arms over his chest with a self-satisfied expression.

Just then, light fell on the crystal snake, and Jacen saw it with perfect clarity. It reared up on Raynar's lap and hissed at him, its flat triangular head staring the boy right in the face.

Raynar saw it and shrieked, losing his Force concentration. The jug wobbled, then fell, spilling deep red juice all over his bright robes.

Jacen leaped to his feet and jumped for the snake. He had to catch it before it wreaked more havoc. He tackled Raynar, trying to grab the serpent from the other boy's lap. Raynar, thinking he was being attacked from all sides, screamed in terror at the top of his lungs.

As he and Jacen struggled, their entire table toppled over, spilling dark brown pudding, knocking other beverage containers right and left, spraying food on Raynar's companions at the table.

Tenel Ka, not understanding the problem but always ready to defend her friends, jumped into the fray. She picked up Jacen's hot soup and hurled it toward Raynar's companions, who, seeing the attack coming from a new front, decided to retaliate.

A platter of honeyed noodles sailed across the dining hall toward Jaina, but she ducked. The noodles instead splattered and clung to the bristly white fur of a Talz—a bearlike creature that stood up and blatted a musical note of dismay. When Jaina saw the noodles sticking to the alien's white fur, she couldn't stop herself from laughing.

The crystal snake slithered out of Jacen's grasp as Jacen crawled across Raynar's squirming lap. The young Jedi screamed as if he were being murdered, but Jacen scuttled under the dining tables after the serpent. Bumping one of the tables over while grabbing for the snake, he felt smooth, dry scales against his fingertips—but the snake slid through them, and he could not hold on.

Another table was knocked over as Lowie came to help. With a flurry of feathers, the avian creatures squawked and fought over their plateful of squirming, fuzzy blue threadworms.

More food flew through the air, levitated by Jedi powers, and tossed from one table to another. The Jedi students were laughing, seeing it now as a release from the tension of the grueling studies and deep concentration required of them during their training.

Steamed leaves flew in the faces of the reptilian Cha'a, interrupting their predatory concentration. All three of them stood up and whirled to meet the attack, back-to-back, standing in a three-point formation, hissing and glaring. The milky tan eggs on their eating platter continued to hatch, and the pink fuzzy hatchlings chose that moment to escape.

Lowie let out a stone-rumbling Wookiee roar, and Em Teedee squeaked with a high-pitched alarm. "I can't see a thing, Master Lowbacca! Comestibles are obscuring my optical sensors. Do please clean them off!"

Artoo-Detoo trundled into the dining chamber and let out an electronic wail, but his droid cries were drowned out by the laughter and the tumult of flying food. Before Artoo could wheel around and sound the alarm, a large tray of creamy dessert pastries splattered across his domed top. The astromech droid beat a hasty, whirring retreat.

As the crystal snake slithered toward the cracked stone walls to escape, Jacen desperately plowed forward. He reached out with one hand and grabbed the pointed tail. The serpent rippled around invisibly in a fluid motion, lashing its fangs toward Jacen, ready to bite down on the hand holding it. But Jacen held out his other hand, pointing with his finger and the Force, touching the snake's tiny brain.

"Hey! Don't you dare," he said aloud. Then, as the crystal snake hesitated, Jacen grabbed it around the neck and lifted it into the air. The lower part of its long body whipped and thrashed. Jacen coiled the snake around his arm and sent soothing thoughts into its mind. He stood up, grinning and relieved.

"I got it!" he cried in triumph—just as three overripe fruits splashed against his face and chest, bursting their thin skins and spilling rich purple pulp all over him. Jacen sputtered and then allowed himself to giggle, still maintaining his hold on the crystal snake.

"Stop!" A booming voice enhanced by the Force echoed through the dining hall.

Suddenly everything froze as if time itself had paused. All the flying food hung suspended in the air; each drip of liquid dangled motionless above the tables. All sound ceased, save for that of the trainees' gasps.

Master Luke Skywalker stood in the entrance to the dining hall wearing a stern expression as he surveyed the suspended food fight. Jacen looked at his uncle's expression and thought he saw anger, but also a concealed amusement.

Luke said, "Was this the best and most challenging way you could find to put your powers to use?" He gestured to all the motionless food and seemed very sad for a moment. Then he turned to leave—but not before Jacen noticed a smile spreading across his face.

As he departed, Luke called, "Instead, perhaps you can use your Jedi powers . . . to clean up this mess." He gestured briefly with his right hand, and the suspended food platters, bowls of soup, desserts, fruits, and messy confections were released, tumbling down like an avalanche. Practically everyone was splattered all over again as sticky gobbets sprayed into the air.

Jacen looked at the aftermath of the food war. Still holding the crystal snake, he wiped a smear of frosting from his nose.

The other Jedi students, though subdued, began to chuckle with relief, then set to work cleaning up.

6

THE WARM AFTERNOON sun sparkled in the heavy, moist air as Lowbacca accompanied his uncle and Han Solo back to the *Millennium Falcon*. Beside him the Solo twins chattered gaily, apparently oblivious to the thick jungle heat. He could sense an underlying tension, though: Jacen and Jaina would miss their father every bit as much as he would miss his uncle Chewbacca, his mother, and the rest of his family back on Kashyyyk.

Lowbacca's golden eyes flicked uneasily about the clearing in front of the Great Temple. He was still uncomfortable with wide-open spaces so close to the ground. On the Wookiee homeworld all cities were built high in the tops of the massive intertwining trees, supported by sturdy branches. Even the most courageous of Wookiees seldom ventured to the inhospitable lower levels of the forest—much less all the way to the ground, where dangers abounded.

To Lowbacca, height meant civilization, comfort, safety, home. And although the enormous Massassi trees towered up to twenty times as high as any other plant on Yavin 4, compared with the trees of Kashyyyk they were midgets. Lowbacca wondered if he would ever find a place high enough on this small moon to make him feel at ease.

Lowie was so lost in thought that he was startled to see that they had arrived at the *Falcon*.

"Never have the chance to do a preflight when we're under fire," Han Solo said, "but it's a good idea when we do have the time." Standing at the foot of the entry ramp, he smiled disarmingly at them. "If you kids aren't too busy, Chewie and I could use some help doing the preflight checks."

"Great," Jaina said before anyone else could respond. "I'll take the hyperdrive." She rushed up the ramp, pausing for only a millisecond to brush a kiss on her father's cheek. "Thanks, Dad. You're the best."

Han Solo looked immensely pleased for a long moment before bringing himself back to business with a shake of his head. "So, kid, you got any preferences?" He looked at Lowie, who thought briefly, then rumbled his reply.

Although Han Solo had doubtless understood him very well, the pesky translator droid piped up. "Master Lowbacca wishes to inspect your ship's computer systems in order that he might tell it where to go."

Han Solo gave Chewbacca a sidelong glance. "Thought you said you fixed that thing," he said, indicating Em Teedee. "It needs an attitude adjustment."

Chewbacca shrugged eloquently, gave a menacing growl, and administered emergency repair procedure number one: he held the silvery oval with one huge hand while he shook the little droid until the circuits rattled.

"Oh, dear me! Perhaps I *could* have been a bit more precise," the droid squeaked hastily. "Er . . . Master Lowbacca expresses his desire to perform the preflight checks on your navigational computer."

"Good idea, kid," Han Solo agreed, briskly rubbing his palms together. "Jacen, you take the exterior hull; see if anything's nested in the exterior vents in the last couple of hours. I'll start on the life-support systems. Chewie, you check the cargo bay."

This last was said with a lift of the chin and a twinkle in

Han Solo's eye that Lowbacca knew must have meant something to the older Wookiee—but Lowie hadn't a clue. He wondered dispiritedly if he would ever understand humans as well as his uncle did.

The navicomputer was an enjoyable challenge. Lowie ran through all the preflight requirements twice—not because he thought he might have missed something the first time, but because the two places he felt most at home were in the treetops and in front of a computer.

By the time Lowie completed his second run-through, Han Solo had already finished with the life-support systems and was now checking out the ship's emergency power generator. When he saw Lowbacca, Han wiped his hands on a greasy rag, tossed it aside, and held up one finger as if an idea had just come to him. "Why don't you give your uncle a hand in the cargo hold while I finish up here." His roguish grin was even more lopsided than usual.

Lowbacca wondered what the smile meant and why his uncle should still need his help with the cargo. Sometimes humans were very difficult to understand. With a shrug, he headed toward the cargo bay.

"Excuse me, Master Lowbacca," Em Teedee piped up, "but will you be needing my translating services at this time?"

Lowbacca growled a negative.

"Very well, sir," Em Teedee said. "In that case, would you mind if I put myself into a brief shutdown cycle? If you should require my assistance for any reason, please do not hesitate to interrupt my rest cycle."

Lowie assured Em Teedee that the miniature droid would be the first to know if he needed anything from him.

He found his uncle clambering across a mountain of crates and bundles, checking the securing straps. Apparently Lando Calrissian needed a good many supplies for his new mining operation.

Even in the crowded cargo hold, he breathed deeply, enjoying the mix of familiar smells: speeder fuel, machined metal, lubricants, space rations, and Wookiee sweat—

enough to make him homesick for the treetop cities of Kashyyyk. He would have little access to speeders or computers while he studied at the Jedi academy—with the exception, of course, of Em Teedee. But perhaps he could console himself occasionally by climbing the jungle trees and thinking of home.

Maybe he would do that after the *Falcon* took off, but for now there was work to do.

Lowie asked his uncle what still needed to be done, and began to check the webbing on a pile of cargo that Chewbacca indicated. The straps and webbing were loose, and so was the cloth that covered the pile—so loose, in fact, that as Lowbacca began to work, the covering slid away entirely. His jaw dropped, and he stepped back to admire what he had accidentally uncovered.

The air speeder, dismantled into large components, was still recognizable. It was an older model, a T-23 skyhopper, with controls similar to the X-wing fighter, but with trihedral wings, and a passenger seat and cramped cargo compartment at the rear of the cockpit. The blue-metallic hull had been battered and stained with age, but the engine mounted between the wings looked in serviceable condition.

He glanced up to find his uncle staring at him expectantly. Then, to his great surprise, Chewbacca asked Lowie what he thought of the craft.

The skyhopper was compact and well constructed. It wouldn't take much to put all the pieces together again. He complimented the vintage speeder's lines and ventured a guess as to its range and maneuverability. Of course, the onboard computer probably needed a system overhaul, and the exterior could use a bit of body work, but those were only minor drawbacks. The dings and scars on the hull only served to add character.

With a satisfied growl, Chewbacca spread his arms wide and shocked Lowie by telling him the T-23 was a going-away gift. The speeder belonged to Lowbacca, if he could assemble it.

*   *   *

Lowbacca stood next to his T-23 in the clearing with Jacen and Jaina and waved good-bye. After a flurry of hugs, exchanged thanks, and last-minute messages, they watched as Han and Chewbacca climbed back aboard the ship.

Now as the *Millennium Falcon* cleared the treetops and angled into the deep blue sky, the three young Jedi trainees continued waving, each lost in thought for a long moment as they gazed after the departing ship.

At last Jaina heaved a sigh. "Well, Lowie," she said, rubbing her hands together with a look of gleeful anticipation as she looked at the battered T-23. "Need any help getting this bucket of bolts up and going?"

Realizing that even though Jaina was younger, she probably had more experience tuning speeder engines than he did, he nodded gratefully.

They spent the next few hours preparing the T-23 for its first flight on Yavin 4. Jacen occupied himself by telling jokes that Lowie didn't understand, or fetching tools for the two enthusiastic mechanics. Jaina smiled as she worked, glad of the rare chance to share what she knew about speeders and engines and T-23s.

When at last they finished and Lowbacca leaned into the cockpit to switch on the engine, the T-23 crackled, sputtered, and roared to life. It lifted off the ground on its lower repulsorlifts, and a bright glow spluttered from the ion afterburners. The three friends let out two cheers and a bellow of triumph.

"Need anyone to take her for a test flight?" Jaina asked hopefully.

Lowie stumbled over a tentative answer. "What Master Lowbacca is trying to say," said Em Teedee, who had long since finished his rest cycle, "is that, as kind as your offer is, he would vastly prefer to pilot the first flight himself."

Lowbacca grunted once.

"And?" the little droid replied. "What do you mean, 'And?' Oh, I see—the other thing you said. But, sir, you didn't mean . . ."

Lowbacca growled emphatically.

"Well, if you insist," Em Teedee said. "*Ahem.* Master

Lowbacca also *says* that he would be honored to have you as his passenger, Mistress Jaina. However," he rushed on, "let me assure you that last statement was made with the utmost reluctance."

Lowbacca groaned and hit his forehead with the heel of one hairy hand in a Wookiee expression of complete embarrassment.

"Well, it's certainly the truth," Em Teedee said defensively. "I'm *certain* I didn't get the intonation wrong."

Jaina, who had at first looked disappointed at Lowbacca's reluctance, now seemed amused at his chagrin. "I understand, Lowie," she said. "I'd want to take her out on my own the first time, too. How about giving us a ride tomorrow?"

Relieved that the twins were not upset, Lowbacca loudly agreed, jumped into the cockpit, and strapped himself in. The whine of the engines drowned out Em Teedee's attempt at translating. Lowie raised a hand in salute, waited until Jacen and Jaina were clear, brought the engines to full power, and took off, heading out toward the vast jungle.

The T-23 maneuvered well, and Lowbacca reveled in the feeling of height and freedom as he streaked away. But still he found himself yearning for one more thing, something that he had been thinking of all day.

The trees. Tall, towering, *safe* trees.

Scarcely half an hour later, far away from the Jedi academy and the Great Temple, he landed the T-23 on the sturdy treetops, settling the craft in the uppermost branches of the Massassi trees. The tree canopy was not as high as he was used to. The air was thinner, and the jungle smells, though not unpleasant, were different from those of Kashyyyk. Even so, Lowbacca felt more at peace now than he had at any other moment since landing on Yavin 4.

Jacen had said that the huge orange gas giant overhead was best viewed from a Massassi tree—and the human boy was definitely right. Lowie looked around in all directions—at the sky and the trees, at the crumbling ruins of smaller temples visible through breaks in the canopy. He stared at the languid rivers, at the strange vegetation and animals around him. He sighed with relief. He *could* find a place of contentment and solitude on this moon, a place where he could think of family and home while he studied to be a Jedi.

As the late-afternoon sunlight slanted through the thick branches, a distant glint caught Lowbacca's eye. He wondered what it could be. It was not the color of any vegetation or temple ruins. The light reflected from a shiny and evenly shaped object stuck partway up a tree. Lowie leaned forward, as if that could help him see more clearly. He wished he had brought a pair of macrobinoculars.

Curiosity and wonder struck a spark of excitement in him. He wanted to get closer, but caution intervened. It was getting dark. And after all, if the object was important, wouldn't someone have seen it long ago? Perhaps not. He doubted it could be seen from the jungle floor, and it was unlikely that many students came out and climbed to the top of the canopy, this far away from the Great Temple. He was almost certain that no one knew about this discovery.

Heart pounding, Lowie made a mental note of the shiny object's location. He would come back the very first chance he got—he *had* to find out what it was.

7

"I WONDER WHY Lowie never made it to evening meal," Jacen said. Jaina and Tenel Ka sat next to him in the grand audience chamber, where Luke Skywalker had summoned them all for a special announcement. Dusk light shone like burning metal through the narrow windows overhead, but the clean white glowpanels dispelled shadows in the large, echoing room.

"Maybe he was having too much fun flying his T-23," Jaina whispered. "I probably wouldn't have made it back either."

"Perhaps," Tenel Ka said in a low voice, as if giving the matter serious consideration, "he was not hungry."

Jacen flashed her a look of disbelief. "Hey, a Wookiee not hungry? Hah! And you say *I* make dumb jokes."

Tenel Ka shrugged. "It is a thought."

"Okay, well," Jacen said, "I'm not kidding now—what if something went wrong with the skyhopper? What if Lowie crashed in the jungle?"

"Impossible," Jaina replied. Though she whispered, her tone was clearly firm. "I checked all those systems myself."

Tenel Ka's eyebrows raised a fraction. "Ah. Ah-hah. So because you checked them, the systems could not malfunction?" She nodded, and Jacen could have sworn that he saw the shadow of a smile lurking at the corners of her lips.

"Never mind—there's Lowie," Jacen said with relief, waving his arms to attract their Wookiee friend's attention.

"See?" Jaina said smugly. "Told you nothing could happen."

Jacen pretended not to notice. "You're just in time," he said as the Wookiee joined them. "Master Skywalker should be here anytime now."

No one really knew why this special twilight meeting had been called, but it was fairly unusual. Everyone who lived, worked, or trained at the Jedi academy had arrived, filling the chamber with a hushed excitement.

Jacen whispered, "Where were you, Lowie?"

Lowbacca responded in a low rumble, quieter than any Jacen had ever heard a Wookiee use. Without warning, Em Teedee announced in a clear metallic voice, "Master Lowbacca wishes it known that he had a most successful expedition and—" The translator droid cut off in midsentence as Lowbacca clamped a ginger-furred hand over the droid's mouth speaker.

"Shhh!" Jaina hissed.

"Can't you turn it down?" Jacen whispered.

Curious eyes turned to stare at them from every section of the grand audience chamber. Lowbacca hunched down in his seat with a chagrined look that needed no interpreter. He craned his neck forward to stare at the droid clipped to his webbed belt. He issued a series of soft, sharp mutters.

"Oh! Oh, dear me," Em Teedee replied in an enthusiastic though much quieter voice. "I *do* beg your pardon. I did not fully comprehend that you didn't intend to share your discovery with everyone present."

"Discovery?" Jacen said. "What did you—"

But Master Skywalker chose that moment to make his entrance. A hush fell over the crowd, putting an end to all hope of Jacen satisfying his curiosity before the meeting began. Luke mounted the steps to the wide raised platform, closely followed by a slender woman with flowing silvery-white hair and huge opalescent eyes.

"Thank you for gathering here on such short notice," Luke began. "I received news this morning of a pressing matter that calls me away."

As if from a pebble tossed into a pond, a series of surprised murmurs rippled through the room. Jacen wondered if his uncle's imminent departure had anything to do with the messages brought by his father on the *Falcon*.

The blue eyes that looked out over the audience—kind eyes that seemed wise beyond their years—gave no hint of what the Jedi Master's mission might be.

"I don't know how long I will be gone, so I've asked one of my former students, the Jedi Tionne"—he gestured to the slender, shimmering-eyed woman beside him—"to supervise your training while I'm away. Not only does Tionne know my teachings almost as well as I do, but she has a rich knowledge of Jedi lore and history. As you are about to find out, she's well worth listening to."

This intrigued Jacen. He remembered hearing that she was not a particularly strong Jedi, but from the warm smile that passed between Luke and Tionne, he could tell that they understood each other well, and that Master Skywalker must have complete trust in his former student.

As Luke withdrew from the platform, leaving the students alone with Tionne, the silver-haired Jedi retrieved a curiously shaped stringed instrument from somewhere behind her. It consisted of two resonating boxes, one at either end of a slender fretted neck. The strings stretching across the instrument flared out in a fan pattern at both ends.

Seating herself on a low stool, Tionne began to strum. "I will tell you about a Jedi Master who lived long ago," she said. "This is the ballad of Master Vodo-Siosk Baas."

As she began to sing, Jacen agreed with his uncle: Tionne was indeed worth listening to. Her song rang clear and true. Its pure tones carried easily to the farthest corners of the great hall and transported them all to a time they had never witnessed. The music flowed around them, sweeping them along on currents of excitement and courage and triumph and sacrifice.

She sang of dire events that had taken place four thousand years earlier—how the strange, alien Jedi Master had been destroyed by Exar Kun, one of his own students who had turned to the dark side. Master Vodo had begged the other Jedi Masters not to do battle with Exar Kun, and had tried to reason with him alone—though his gentle hopes had ended in tragedy.

In the silence that followed her song, a flood of insight washed through Jacen as he realized that this Jedi was worth listening to for more than just her voice.

Tionne stood, to a collective sigh from everyone present. Jacen hadn't even realized he'd been holding his breath.

"I trust my first lesson to you hasn't been too painful," she said with a merry twinkle in her pearly eyes. "Tomorrow I will give another lesson, after morning meal."

With that, the evening meeting ended. Some listeners remained seated, transfixed, as if trying to absorb the last trickles of music lingering in the room. Others left singly or in whispering groups, while still others stayed behind to talk with Tionne.

Jacen, Jaina, Tenel Ka, and Lowbacca found themselves free at last to talk. They huddled together and discussed Lowie's find. Em Teedee—carefully modulating his voice to an appropriate, secretive level—provided translation.

They speculated by turns about the strange glinting object that Lowbacca had seen out in the jungle. They came to only one conclusion: at the earliest possible opportunity, they would go out together and investigate.

*   *   *

Tionne's morning ballad fell in a fine musical mist, drenching its listeners with wonder and ancient lore. Jacen sat in the second row with his brandy-colored eyes closed, concentrating on her words, trying to absorb everything the music had to teach him. It was just as well that his eyes were shut, since his view was completely blocked by the colorful bulk of Raynar wearing his finest robes.

As the last notes drained away, Jacen opened his eyes to find his sister staring at him in silent amusement. Neither Lowbacca nor Tenel Ka, who sat beside him, gave any indication that they had noticed Jacen's apparent absorption in the music. Then Tionne spoke, drawing Jacen's attention back to the silver-haired Jedi on the raised platform.

"A Jedi's greatest power comes not from size or from physical strength," she said. "It comes from understanding the Force—from trusting in the Force. As part of your Jedi training you will learn to build your confidence and belief through practice. Without that practice we may not succeed when it is most important. This is true of many skills in life. Listen to a story.

"Once, a young girl lived by a lake. Simply by watching others, she learned much about how to swim. One day when her family was busy, the girl jumped into the deep water. Although she moved her arms and legs as she had seen other swimmers do, she could not keep her head above the water.

"Fortunately a fisherwoman jumped in and rescued her. The woman, a practiced swimmer, had not needed to think about how to swim, but the little girl—who had only learned by watching—did not have the skill even to stay afloat. After they were safely out of the water, the fisherwoman took the girl's hand and said, 'Come to the shallows, child, and I will teach you to swim.'"

Tionne paused as if lost in thought, her pearly eyes glittering. "So it is with the Force. Unless we practice what we learn, and unless we are tested, we never know we can trust in the Force if the need arises. That is why this Jedi academy is also called a *praxeum*. It is a place where we not only learn, but we put the learning to use. As with swimming, the more we practice, the more confidence we have. Eventually, our skill becomes second nature.

"The next several days I would like the beginning and intermediate students to practice one of the most basic skills: using the Force to lift. For today, practice lifting only something small—no bigger than a leaf."

Raynar interrupted in a blustery voice, "How can you expect us to *strengthen* our skills if you take us back to a child's level?"

Jacen rolled his eyes at Raynar's rudeness, but he had to admit that he had been wondering the same thing.

Tionne smiled down at Raynar without annoyance. "A good question. Let me give you an example. If you wanted to strengthen your arms, you might lift many stones one time, or you might lift one stone many times. It is the same with your Jedi skills. For today, practice just as I have asked you. It is not the *only* way to strengthen your skills, but it is *one* way. There are always alternatives. I promise you will learn more than just how to lift a leaf."

Tionne dismissed the students. As they left the grand audience chamber and started down the worn stone stairs, Jaina pulled the other three young Jedi to a halt, her eyes dancing. "Are you thinking what I'm thinking?" she asked.

Jacen who did not know what she was thinking, nonetheless sensed her excitement and her eagerness to investigate Lowie's mysterious discovery.

Jaina shrugged. "What better place to practice lifting leaves than out in a jungle?"

8

"YOU SURE THIS is safe?" Jacen asked as he squeezed himself into the cargo well behind the T-23's passenger seat.

"Of course it is," his sister replied automatically as she

climbed into the front. "You like crawling into cramped spaces anyway."

"Only to catch bugs," he grumbled. "There's no cushioning back here."

The cargo well was much too small to accommodate Tenel Ka, who was taller and more solidly built than either of the twins. Jacen would have to settle for the back or be left behind; his sister would take her turn there on the return trip. He squirmed and settled in as the T-23's engines started with a roaring purr.

Lowie called a command over the sound of the warming repulsorlifts. Em Teedee said, "Master Lowbacca requests that you please be certain that your restraints are secure. He is interested in your utmost safety. We shall be departing momentarily."

Lowbacca's voice barked out again, and the droid amended his translation. "Actually, Master Lowbacca *might* have said something closer to, 'Hold on, everyone. Here we go!'"

"Oh, blaster bolts. No crash straps either," Jacen observed as Jaina and Tenel Ka buckled themselves in up front.

The rebuilt T-23 lifted off with a small jerk. The wind howled past the rattling window plates as they picked up height and speed. Jacen felt the thrill of being airborne as the ion afterburners spluttered behind them. Even cramped in the back, he was glad he hadn't stayed behind.

Jacen looked out through the scratched port as Lowbacca let the skyhopper skim just above the treetops, arrowing away from the Jedi academy into unexplored territory. Soon there were nothing but trees as far as Jacen could see through the scratched port, as lush and green as the sky above him was blue.

Though he enjoyed the lovely foliage below him, Jacen's legs began to cramp. By the time the T-23 dove down and came to rest in a small clearing, he could feel the engine vibrations all the way to his teeth.

Up front, Jaina and Tenel Ka unbuckled their restraints and scrambled nimbly out of the T-23. Jacen dragged himself from the cargo well, stretching his stiff legs as he stepped out into the tangled underbrush. He rubbed the seat of his jump-suit with both hands to get the circulation going again. "I think a leaf is about all I *could* lift right now!"

Lowie rushed to the edge of the clearing, beckoning the others. "Master Lowbacca says the tree holding the artifact is over here," Em Teedee called. "It has several broken branches, so he was able to locate it easily from the air."

Jaina looked in the direction that Lowbacca was pointing. "Well, what are we waiting for?" she said. Tenel Ka marched over to the young Wookiee, as if ready to carve a path through the jungle. Jacen took a long and wistful look at all the strange new plants he saw around him, but followed the others into the deep green shadows.

Lowbacca gestured up into the distant branches of an enormous Massassi tree. The trunk seemed as big around as one of the skyscrapers on city-covered Coruscant, and even the lowest branches were well out of Jacen's reach. But Lowie wanted them to climb up after him!

"Oh," said Jaina, a crestfallen look on her face, "I wouldn't get very far climbing that."

Lowbacca assured them, via Em Teedee, that the climb would be easy for a Wookiee. He offered to go up alone for the first investigation and report his findings so they could decide the next step.

"We can explore down here," Jacen suggested. "We might find some other pieces of . . . of whatever it is." *Or maybe some interesting animals or fungus or insects,* he thought hopefully.

Jaina and Tenel Ka readily agreed. Lowbacca swiped a hairy hand along the thick black streak that ran through the fur above his left eyebrow. He swarmed up the trunk, swung into the lower branches, and soon disappeared from sight.

Jacen's stomach rumbled with hunger, and he hoped that Lowbacca would hurry. The three young Jedi trainees poked around in the underbrush, spiraling out from the T-23 in a wandering search pattern. Taking turns, they practiced their leaf-lifting assignment, fluttering leaves in the shrubbery, lifting dry forest debris from the damp and mossy ground.

* * *

Before long, Lowbacca came crashing back down through the thick branches. He dropped to the ground near them and let out a loud Wookiee cry.

Jaina ran toward him, eager and interested. "Did you find it, Lowie?"

Lowbacca nodded vigorously.

"What was it?" Jaina asked. "Can you describe it?"

"Master Lowbacca believes it to be some sort of solar panel," Em Teedee translated as the Wookiee replied. Then the droid launched into a complete description.

Jaina felt her skin prickle with goose bumps. "Hmmmm," she said. "If I'm right, there should be a lot more to that artifact than what Lowie saw. Let's keep looking."

Tenel Ka dug into a small supply pouch she carried with her and withdrew a pack of carbo-protein biscuits. "Here. Nourishment as we search."

Jacen chomped hungrily on his biscuit. "Just what are we looking for, Jaina?" he asked, speaking around a mouthful of crumbs.

"Scrap metal, machinery, another solar panel." Jaina shaded her eyes, scanning deeper into the thick jungles around them. "We'll keep widening the circle of our search until we find something. What we're looking for shouldn't be too far away."

Jacen retrieved a flask of water from the T-23, took a gulp, and handed it to his sister. Jaina took a few mouthfuls of water and passed the flask on to Lowbacca. Then she set off at a trot for the base of the big tree. Jaina didn't look back to see if the others were following, and bit her lip, feeling a brief pang of guilt.

At times like this Jaina always seemed to assume leadership, just like her mother. But how could she help it? Her parents had raised all three of their children to assess a situation, weigh the alternatives, and make decisions.

"Let's spread out," she said.

"Great!" Jacen said, walking around the massive trunk toward a clump of dense undergrowth.

Jaina smiled, knowing full well that her brother's excitement came not from a desire to find the mysterious artifact, but from the opportunity to explore the jungle and examine its creatures more closely.

She was about to head into the underbrush herself when Lowbacca stopped her with a questioning growl. Em Teedee translated. "Master Lowbacca says—and I personally am inclined to agree with him—that the jungle floor is *not* a safe place to split up. Even to speed up a search."

As impatient as she was to continue looking, Jaina stopped to consider. Tenel Ka caught her eye, placed her hands on her hips, and nodded. "This is a fact."

Jaina gnawed at her lower lip again, thinking, and came to a decision. "All right. We spread out a little bit, but only as far as our line of sight. Good enough?"

The other's murmurs of agreement were interrupted by a loud squawking as a flock of reptile birds took flight from the bushes near where Jacen had been exploring. Jacen emerged from the bushes on his hands and knees, looking startled, but not displeased.

"No big discoveries," he reported, "but I did find this." He held out his palm. In it was a plump, furry gray creature, quivering in a small nest of glossy fibers.

Another animal. Jaina sighed with resignation. She might have guessed.

"Ah. A-hah," Tenel Ka said. Lowbacca bent forward to run a shaggy finger along the tiny creature's back.

"Look, Jaina," Jacen said, turning the fluffy nest in his hand. He pointed to a dull, flat loop of metal that was firmly attached to the mass of fibers.

"A . . . buckle?" Jaina said, finally comprehending.

Her brother nodded. "Like the kind in crash webbing."

"Good work," Tenel Ka said with solemn approval.

"Well, what are we waiting for?" Jaina asked. "Let's keep going."

By midafternoon, though, Jaina began to get discouraged. Jacen, on the other hand, was intrigued by every crawling creature or insect they encountered.

"Do please try to be a bit more cautious!" Jaina could hear Em Teedee saying. "That's the third dent today. And I've lost count of how many scratches I've received while you've been exploring. Now if you would only be more attentive to—"

Em Teedee's admonishments were drowned out as Lowie gave a sharp bark of surprise behind a tangle of vines and branches. "Oh! Oh, my. Mistress Jaina, Master Jacen, Mistress Tenel Ka!" Em Teedee's voice was loud enough to startle not only Jaina but a number of flying and climbing creatures. "Do come quickly. Master Lowbacca has made a discovery."

Needing no further encouragement, all of them rushed to see what Lowbacca had found. Jaina felt her heart pounding in her chest, knowing and dreading what they would find.

They worked quickly, scratching and cutting their hands as they pulled away the thick plant growth from the heap of metallic wreckage. Jaina gasped as they finally exposed it—a rounded, tarnished cockpit large enough only for a single pilot, one squarish black solar panel crisscrossed with support braces. The other panel was missing, stuck up in the tree where Lowie had found it. But still the ship was unmistakable.

A crashed Imperial TIE fighter.

9

"BUT WHY WOULD such a craft be here in the jungles of Yavin 4?" Tenel Ka asked, narrowing her eyes in concern as they worked to remove the debris from the ruined craft. "Is it an Imperial spy ship?"

Jaina shook her head. "Can't be. TIE fighters were short-range ships used by the Empire. They weren't equipped with hyperdrive, so there aren't many ways it could have gotten here."

Jacen cleared his throat. "Well, I *can* think of one way," he said, "but that would make this ship—let's see . . ."

"Over twenty years old . . ." Jaina breathed, finishing his sentence for him.

Lowbacca made a low, questioning noise, and Tenel Ka continued to look perplexed.

Jaina explained. "When the Empire built the first Death Star, it was the most powerful weapon ever made. They tested it by destroying Alderaan, our mother's homeworld. Then they brought it here to Yavin 4, to destroy the Rebel base."

As she spoke, Jaina pulled the last bit of brush away from the top canopy of the TIE fighter and looked inside. There were no bones. She slid into the musty cockpit.

"A lot of Rebel pilots died in one-on-one combat with the TIE fighters that protected the Death Star, and a lot of Imperial fighters were shot down too," Jacen said, picking up the story.

Jaina wrinkled her nose at the mildewy smell, the mold-clogged controls. She ran her fingers over the navigation panels in the cockpit, closing her eyes and wondering what it must have been like twenty-some years ago to be a fighter pilot in the Battle of Yavin 4. She envisioned an enemy fighter swooping toward her in a strafing run, her engine hit, her tiny ship careening out of control. . . .

Jacen's voice broke into her thoughts. "But then in the end, our dad flew cover for Uncle Luke's X-wing fighter while he took his final run. Uncle Luke made the shot that blew up the Death Star."

Tenel Ka nodded gravely, her braided red-gold hair like a wreath around her head. "And why is it called a TIE fighter?" she asked.

Jaina answered, speaking up from the cockpit, "Because it has twin ion engines. T-I-E, see?"

Ducking her head, she wormed her way to the engine access panels at the rear of the cockpit and pried open the tarnished metal plate. A squeaking rodent, disturbed from its hidden nest, scampered away, vanishing through a small hole in the hull.

Jaina tinkered with the engines, checking integrity, noting the rotted hoses and fuel lines. But overall, the primary motivators seemed intact, though she would have to run numerous diagnostics. She had plenty of spare parts in her room.

She stood up slowly in the cockpit and poked her head out again, then ran her calloused hands along the side of the crashed TIE fighter. "You know, I think we could do it," Jaina said.

All eyes turned toward her, questioning.

"I think we could fix the TIE fighter."

Her brother stared at her in stunned silence for a moment, then clapped a palm to his forehead. "I've got a bad feeling about this."

As the whine of the T-23 skyhopper faded into the jungle distance, the frightened forest creatures settled back into their routines. They scuttled through the underbrush, chasing each other across the branches, predator and prey. The leaves stirred and flying creatures sent their cries from treetop to treetop, forgetting the intruders entirely.

Far below on the forest floor, the branches of a dense thicket parted. A worn and tattered black glove pushed a thorny twig aside.

The pilot of the crashed TIE fighter emerged from his hiding place into the newly trampled clearing.

"Surrender is betrayal," he muttered to himself, as he had done so many times before. It had become a litany during his years of rugged survival on the isolated jungle moon of Yavin.

The pilot's protective uniform hung in rags from his gaunt frame, worn to tatters and patched with furs from an incredible number of years living alone in the jungle. His left arm, injured in the crash, was drawn up like a twisted claw against his chest. He stepped forward, cracking twigs under his old boots as he made his way to the crash site that was no longer secret. He had camouflaged the wrecked Imperial craft many years ago, hiding it from Rebel eyes. But now, despite all his work, it had been discovered.

"Surrender is betrayal," he said again. He stared down at his fighter, trying to see what damage the Rebel spies had caused.

OVER THE NEXT few days, Tionne increased the complexity of the young Jedi trainees' assignments, and the four companions practiced fine-tuning their control of the Force.

Jaina, Jacen, Lowie, and Tenel Ka found excuses to return again and again to the site of the crashed TIE fighter. With Jaina as the driving force, they took on the repair project as a group exercise—but they always managed to work in any assigned practice sessions during their jungle expeditions.

Although the idea was not flattering, Jaina was forced to admit that part of her motivation for this work was her envy of Lowbacca's personal T-23—she wanted her own craft to fly over the treetops. But she was also drawn by the challenge the wrecked TIE fighter represented. Its age and complexity offered a unique opportunity for learning about mechanics, and Jaina could not turn it down.

But the strongest reason for taking on the project—and perhaps the one that kept them all working without complaint—was that it forged a bond among the four friends. They learned to function as a team, to make the most of each person's strengths and to compensate for each other's weaknesses. The strands of their friendships intertwined and wove together in a pattern as simple as it was strong. This bond included even Em Teedee, who learned to make verbal contributions at appropriate times and was gradually accepted as a member of their group.

Jaina spent most of her time overseeing the mechanical repairs, while Lowbacca concentrated on the computer systems. Jacen had ample opportunity to explore and to observe the local wildlife as, officially, he "searched" through the nearby underbrush for broken or missing components; he also made quick supply trips back to the academy in the T-23 for parts that Jaina or Lowbacca needed. Tenel Ka worked with quiet competence on any task that needed doing and was especially valuable in lugging new metal plates to patch large breaches in the TIE hull.

"Hey, Tenel Ka!" Jacen said. "What goes ha-ha-ha . . . *thump!*"

Her gray eyes looked at him, as lustrous as highly polished stones. "I don't know."

"A droid laughing its head off!" Jacen said, then started giggling.

"Ah. A-hah," Tenel Ka said. She considered this for a moment, then added without the slightest trace of mirth, "Yes, that is very funny." She bent back to her work.

From time to time Lowie climbed to the top of the canopy to meditate and absorb the solitude; the young Wookiee enjoyed his time alone, sitting in silence. Tenel Ka occasionally took short breaks to test her athletic skills by running through jungle undergrowth or climbing trees.

But Jaina preferred to stay with the downed TIE fighter, examining it from every angle and imagining possibilities. She considered no bodily position too difficult or undignified to assume while repairing the craft.

Jaina tucked her head under the cockpit control panel, with her stomach supported by the back of the pilot's seat. Her backside was sticking high in the air and her feet were kicking as she worked, when she felt a playful poke on the leg.

She extricated herself from the awkward position. Lowie handed her a datapad into which he had downloaded the schematics and specifications for a TIE fighter, taken from the main information files in the computer center back at the Great Temple. Jaina studied the data and looked over the list of computer parts Lowbacca needed.

"These should be pretty easy for Jacen to find," she said. "I have most of them right in my room."

Em Teedee spoke up. "Master Lowbacca wishes to know which systems you intend to concentrate on next."

Jaina's brow furrowed in judicious concentration. "We've already decided we won't be needing the weapons systems. I think the laser cannons work fine, but I don't intend to hook them up. I suppose the next step might be to work on the power systems. I haven't done much with them yet."

Jacen and Tenel Ka trotted up to join the discussion. "You

will need the other solar panel," Tenel Ka said. "Up in the tree."

Jacen cocked an eyebrow at her, using Tenel Ka's own phrase. "This is a fact?" Tenel Ka did not smile, but nodded her approval.

Jacen folded his arms across his chest and looked pleased with himself. "Does anyone remember the assignment Tionne gave us for today?"

"Cooperative lifting with one or more other students," Tenel Ka stated without hesitation.

Jaina clapped her hands and rubbed them together, scrambling out of the cramped cockpit. "Well, then, what are we waiting for?"

The process was much more difficult than they had anticipated, but in the end they managed it. Lowie and Tenel Ka climbed up into the tree to clear away the moss and branches that held the panel in place. Tenel Ka secured it with the thin fibercord from her belt, while Lowbacca added sturdy vines to help support the heavy slab. Jaina and Jacen watched from the lower branches of the tree, craning their necks to see.

"Everyone ready?" Jaina asked. "Okay—now concentrate," she said. She gave them a moment to observe the solar panel glittering in scattered light from the sky. They studied the piece of wreckage, grasping it with their thoughts.

"Now," Jaina said.

With that, four minds pushed upward, nudging. In a gentle, concerted motion they lifted the panel free of the branch where it had rested for decades. The large, flat rectangle wobbled in midair for a moment and then began to slowly descend. Tenel Ka kept her fibercord taut, easing the Force-lightened object down.

Together, they brought it to rest a few branches below where it had been. Tenel Ka and Lowbacca untied the vines and the fibercord from the higher branch, climbed down, and retied the strands to the branch on which the panel now rested.

The process was not perfect. Mental coordination among the four friends proved difficult, and they each lost their grip more than once. But the vines and fibercord held, preventing a disaster.

By the time the exhausted companions brought the panel to the jungle floor and carried it to the crash site, all of them were panting and perspiring from the mental exertion.

Jaina sank down beside the TIE fighter with a weary groan. She flopped backward in the dirt and leaves, not caring for the moment that her hair would become as disheveled and full of twigs as her brother's usually was.

Lowie tossed them each a packet of food from the basket of supplies they brought with them every day. Jaina's packet landed on her stomach, and she rolled onto her side with a mock growl of indignation. As she faced a hole in the side of the broken TIE fighter, a sudden thought occurred to her.

"You know," she said, chin in hands, "I'd be willing to bet there's enough room in there to install a hyperdrive."

"You said that TIE fighters were short-range crafts," Tenel Ka said.

Lowie responded with a contemplative sound as he thought this over. Jacen merely moaned at the mention of more work.

"They were *designed* to be short-range," Jaina said. "Never equipped with hyperdrives because the Emperor didn't want to sacrifice the maneuverability."

Jacen snorted. "Or maybe he didn't want any of his fighter pilots making a quick escape."

Jaina turned toward him and grinned. "I guess I never thought of it that way." Her face lit with enthusiasm as she looked at her friends. "But there's nothing to stop us from equipping *this* TIE fighter with a hyperdrive, is there? Dad gave me one to tinker with."

"It is a possibility," Tenel Ka said, without much enthusiasm.

They were all tired, Jaina knew. But her mind raced with the excitement of this new thought. She made a quick decision. "Okay, let's go back to the academy. I want to make some measurements. We'll call it a day."

Jacen sighed with relief. "I think that's been your best suggestion in hours."

* * *

Back again the next afternoon, Jacen lay flat on his stomach, his chin resting on one clenched fist as he surveyed the moist ground beneath a tangle of low, thick bushes. He left his feet sticking out from beneath the bushes so that the others could locate him easily should they look up from their work—though there was little chance of that. From behind him he could hear thumping and clinking as Jaina labored to install the hyperdrive in the TIE fighter.

A thick *splat* told him that Tenel Ka and Lowbacca were applying sealant over the hole patch at the base of the re-attached solar panel. The others were all busy, leaving Jacen free to hunt for "missing parts" again.

He watched, fascinated, as a leaf-shaped creature that matched the blue-green color of the foliage around him attached itself to a branch. It extended a long mottled brown tongue that flattened against the twig in a perfect camouflage. Jacen could sense the leaf creature's anticipation. Soon a crowd of minute insects, drawn by a smell Jacen could not discern, landed on the "branch" and became stuck fast. Jacen chuckled and shook his head as the leaf creature retracted its tongue with an audible *fwoookt*.

With nothing interesting to be seen on the ground, he gave the bush a small shake once the leaf creature departed. He was rewarded with a hissing rustle as a dislodged object fell near his elbow. He picked it up.

It was an Imperial insignia.

He turned the metallic object over in his hand, but then he saw a familiar shimmer at the edge of his gaze, and he reflexively grabbed for it. Jacen wriggled backward out of the bushes, stood, and bounded over to the TIE fighter.

"Look what I found!" he crowed. His sister's lower half protruded at an awkward angle from the cockpit, while she was apparently attempting to connect some part of the hyperdrive behind the pilot's seat.

Her muffled voice drifted out to him. "Just a moment. I need a flash heater."

Tenel Ka passed a small tool in from the other side of the

open cockpit. She and Lowbacca, wiping sealant from their hands, came around to see what Jacen had discovered.

"A brooch of some sort?" Tenel Ka asked, examining it closely.

Jacen shook his head. "An Imperial insignia. Came off a uniform of some kind."

"There," Jaina said, extracting herself from the cockpit of the TIE fighter and jumping down beside them. "That should do it."

Jacen handed her the insignia, and she nodded absently. "Look what else I found," he said, holding up his left arm, which was wrapped in a glowing shimmer.

Jaina made a sound somewhere between a growl and a laugh, and backed away. "Great. Just what we need—another crystal snake that can get loose."

Jacen used a tactic he knew his sister couldn't resist. "Oh," he said, letting disappointment show. "It's just that you've always been so *good* at designing things—I thought you could come up with a cage that the snakes couldn't escape from. But if you really don't think you can . . ."

He saw Jaina's face light at the challenge, but then her brandy-brown eyes narrowed shrewdly, and he knew that she had caught on. "That," she said, "is a dirty trick. You *know* I could—" She shook her head, sighed in mock exasperation, and seemed to resign herself to the inevitable. "Oh, all right! I'll build you a new cage for your crystal snakes—"

"Thanks," a grinning Jacen cut her off before she could change her mind. "You're the best sister in the whole galaxy!"

Jaina huffed indelicately. "But don't bring this new snake back to your quarters until I have the cage ready."

"Okay," Jacen said, "I'll keep it someplace safe—maybe in the cargo compartment. Can I have the Imperial insignia back, please?" Jaina tossed it to him, and he began to polish it against the sleeve of his jumpsuit. "I wonder if it belonged to the pilot."

Lowbacca looked at the crashed TIE fighter and then back at Jacen and rumbled a question. "Master Lowbacca suggests it is unlikely that the pilot survived the crash, even if his fall was cushioned by the Massassi trees," Em Teedee said.

Tenel Ka looked around the site with unblinking eyes. "No bones."

Jacen shrugged. "After twenty years, that's not surprising. Lots of scavengers in the jungle. I've been assuming he was thrown clear."

Tenel Ka's cool eyes looked troubled, but she nodded. "Perhaps."

The four worked in companionable silence as they attached the final hole patch to the damaged hull. Then, while the other three applied the slow-drying sealant, Jacen hunted around in the underbrush. He knew he shouldn't be out of sight for more than a few seconds, but he had already searched all of the thickets in clear view of the crash site.

Promising himself that he wouldn't be gone long, Jacen pushed through a particularly thick tangle of dense, dark-leaved plants and emerged into a small clearing no wider than his outstretched arms. The dirt was completely devoid of plant life, as if some animal trampled it so often that vegetation no longer grew there. It extended deeper into the jungle—a path! It was narrow, but the hard-packed trail was unmistakable.

Forgetting his earlier promise to stay close, Jacen plunged through the bushes and followed the trail. The grove of Massassi trees was younger, their branches lower to the ground. Perhaps that was why none of the companions had seen this path from up above.

The jungle grew darker around him as he trudged on. The chitters, growls, and screeches of forest animals seemed more menacing.

Just as he began to realize that he was much too far away from the others, he came upon a clearing beside a small stream.

Some creature had built a dam across the stream, diverting some of the water into a depression beside it to form a wide, shallow pool. Against the burn-hollowed trunk of a huge Massassi tree at the water's edge leaned a number of long, fat branches covered with moss and ferns to form a crude shelter—perhaps the lair of the creature whose path Jacen had been following.

Jacen reached out toward the little hovel with his mind, but sensed nothing larger than insects living around it. Skirting the small pond, he approached the low shelter, his heart pounding loudly in his chest. He knew he should be more cautious. But what was this place?

What if the beast that lived here was a predator? What if it returned as he was investigating?

Jacen jumped as he heard a loud *crack*—but it was only a twig snapping under his own foot. He bent forward to look into the branchy opening of the shelter, and gasped at what he saw there.

Fully a third of the Massassi tree's trunk had been hollowed out to form a sturdy, dry cave, tall enough for a man to stand in. A makeshift wooden chair stood beside a low mound of leaves that might have been a bed, partially covered by a ragged piece of cloth. A cache of equipment, vines, fruits, and dried berries lay piled against the back of the cave. Perched atop the pile was a nightmarish black helmet with triangular eyeplates and a breathing mask connected to a pair of rubber hoses that Jacen figured had once been linked with an air tank.

An Imperial TIE fighter pilot's helmet.

Jacen stumbled backward, away from the shelter, his breath coming in shallow gasps. He tripped and fell, and found himself inside a ring of low stones and ashes. A fire pit. He scooped away some of the dirt that covered the pit and felt around with trembling fingers. The ground was still warm.

Jacen jumped to his feet and raced toward the little trail at full speed. He ran along the narrow path, heedless of the branches that slapped his face or the thorns that tore at his jumpsuit, oblivious to the animals he startled from their hiding places. He didn't slow as he approached the bushes that surrounded the crashed TIE fighter.

He burst into the tiny clearing and ran up to the wreck, yelling, "Jaina! Tenel Ka! Lowie! He's here. He's alive. The TIE pilot isn't dead!"

The three of them looked up in astonishment just as Jacen heard a rustling in the bushes behind him. He turned to see a haggard, grizzled-looking man step through the bushes. The stranger's face was deeply lined, and he wore a tattered flight suit. His left arm was bent at an awkward angle, and was wrapped in an armored gauntlet of black leather. But in his glove he held an ugly, old-model blaster. And the weapon was leveled directly at the young Jedi Knights.

"Yes," said the Imperial fighter pilot. "I am very much alive. And you are my prisoners."

11

WHEN THE IMPERIAL TIE pilot turned his eyes from her for a split second, Tenel Ka reacted with lightning speed, just as she had been taught by the warrior women on Dathomir.

"Run!" she shouted to the others, knowing exactly what to do. She turned and bolted for the nearest tangled undergrowth, dodging expected blaster fire.

Tenel Ka reacted so quickly and so smoothly that even her most rigid battle trainers would have been proud of her. Their tactics had been drilled into her:

Confuse the enemy.
Do the unexpected.
Take your opponent by surprise.
Don't waste time hesitating.

Tenel Ka tore through the tangled thorns and blueleaf shrubs, clawing with her hands to clear a path that closed behind her as she moved through the thicket. She gasped and panted, bolting ahead, ignoring the scratches and stinging pain of the thorns against her bare arms and legs. The scaled armor protected her vital parts, but her red-gold hair flew around her, snagging loose leaves and twigs. Branches caught at her braids and yanked strands of her hair out by the roots. She hissed with pain, but clamped her teeth together, plunging ahead.

Why couldn't she hear the others running?

"Get help!" It was Jacen shouting behind her, still in the clearing. Why didn't they run?

Then an explosion of flames ripped into the underbrush just to her left. The TIE pilot was firing his blaster at her! The smell of singed leaves and burnt sap stung her nostrils. Tenel Ka dove to the ground, rolled sideways, then ran at full speed in a different direction. If she gave up now, he would kill her. She had no doubt of that—not anymore.

Intent only on distancing herself from the TIE pilot, she fled, changing directions at random to confuse the enemy. Branches cracked underfoot, and Tenel Ka paid no attention whatsoever to where she ran . . . deeper into the densest jungle of Yavin 4.

Lowbacca hesitated only a fraction of a second longer.

Tenel Ka seemed to evaporate as she shouted "Run!" and ducked into the thick forest.

The TIE pilot whirled and pointed his blaster at the place where Tenel Ka had disappeared, and Lowbacca used the instant of distraction. The young Wookiee let out a bellow of surprise and anger, then instinctively surged up the ancient bole of the nearest Massassi tree, climbing higher, *up*, where it was safe.

He grabbed branches and vines, hauling himself up toward the thick, spicy-smelling canopy. Behind him, the Imperial fighter began shooting wildly. Explosions and bright flames from burning foliage ballooned out from where the blaster bolts struck the branches under Lowie's feet. He smelled the ozone of energy discharge, the steam of disintegrated vegetation.

With Wookiee strength, Lowbacca climbed higher and higher, finally reaching thick, flat branches that allowed him to make his way across the treetops toward where he had landed the T-23.

He had to get help. He had to rescue his friends. Tenel Ka

had gotten to safety—or so he hoped—but Jacen and Jaina had not been able to react as quickly or move with such practiced wilderness skills.

"Oh my!" Em Teedee wailed from the clip on his waist. "Where are we going? That person was trying to kill us! Can you imagine that?"

Lowie continued to scramble across the thick branches, loping with great agility, moving farther away from the still-firing pilot.

"Master Lowbacca, answer me!" Em Teedee said, his tinny voice echoing from the speaker-patch. "You can't simply leave me hanging here doing nothing at all, you know."

Lowbacca grunted a reply and kept moving.

"But surely, that's beside the point," Em Teedee quibbled, "since I'm doing everything I can. Just because I have no functional arms or legs doesn't mean I don't *want* to assist you."

The sounds of blaster fire from the clearing below had ceased, and Lowbacca feared that meant Jacen and Jaina were captured—or worse. His thoughts churned it in panic and turmoil. He knew he had to rescue them. But how? He had never done anything like this before. He didn't think Tenel Ka could do it alone, so he had to offer whatever help he could manage.

The branches thinned up ahead, spreading out around the clearing where Lowbacca had settled the T-23. The small ship sat where he had landed it, and he scrambled back down the thick branches, clinging to vines until he reached ground level again. The T-23 was his best chance.

Lowbacca had been so proud of the small craft when his uncle Chewie had given it to him, but now it seemed so small and battered, all but useless against an armed Imperial pilot. He trudged across the weed-covered ground over to the little skyhopper. He would have to use it to make the rescue. He had no better options.

The low, simmering music insects and jungle creatures filled the air. He could hear no sound of blaster fire, no shouts of challenge or pain. It was quiet. Too quiet. Lowbacca hurried.

"Oh, excellent idea!" Em Teedee said as they approached the T-23. "We're going back to the Jedi academy to get reinforcements, aren't we. That's by far the wisest thing to do, I'm sure.

But Lowie knew it would be too late for the twins by then. He had to do something *now*. He told Em Teedee what he intended to do, and the miniature translating droid squawked in dismay.

"But, Master Lowbacca! The T-23 has no weapons. How can you fly it against that Imperial pilot? He is a professional fighter—and he's desperate!"

Lowie had the same fears as he powered up the T-23's repulsorlift engines. He made an optimistic comment to the translating droid.

"Tricks? What tricks do you have up your sleeve?" Em Teedee said. "Besides, you don't even *have* sleeves."

The craft sounded strong and powerful, thrumming and roaring in the jungle stillness. Lowie smelled the acrid exhaust, and snuffled. His black pilot seat vibrated as the ship prepared to take off.

He would need to do some fancy flying to get the craft through the trees to the crash site—but he had to save his friends, offer whatever help he could. Perhaps his noisy approach would startle the TIE pilot enough to make him flee for cover. And then the twins could jump aboard and make their escape.

Lowbacca nudged the throttles forward and lifted the T-23 off its resting place in the trampled undergrowth. The ion afterburners roared as the small ship arrowed through the forest, dodging branches and hanging moss, heading toward his friends—directly into the path of danger.

Back in the clearing, Jacen and Jaina froze for only a moment, then turned and ran, trying to escape—but the bulk of the almost-repaired TIE fighter got in their way. Jaina grabbed Jacen's arm, and the two of them ran together, frightened but knowing they needed to move, *move*.

The Imperial pilot fired his blaster, shooting twice into the thicket where Tenel Ka had vanished. Burning brush and splintered twigs flew into the air in a cloud. For an instant Jaina thought their young friend from Dathomir had been killed—but then she heard more leaves rustling and branches snapping as Tenel Ka continued her desperate flight.

The TIE pilot fired into the trees next, blasting the lower branches—but Lowbacca had gotten away. The twins ran around the end of the wrecked fighter, and suddenly Jacen stumbled over a rectangular box of hydrospanners, cyberfuses, and other tools they had gathered for the repair of the crashed ship—and fell headlong.

Jaina grabbed her brother's arm, trying to yank him to his feet to run again. The ground screeched with an explosion of blaster fire. Three high-energy bolts ricocheted from the age-stained hull of the crashed ship.

Jaina froze, raising her hands in surrender. They couldn't possibly hide fast enough. Jacen climbed to his feet and stood next to his sister, brushing himself off. The TIE pilot took two steps toward them, encased in battered armor and wearing an expression of icy anger.

"Don't move," he said, "or you will die, Rebel scum."

His black pilot armor was scuffed and worn from his long exile in the jungles. The Imperial's crippled left arm was stiff like a droid's, encased in an armored gauntlet of black leather. He had been severely hurt, but it appeared to be an old injury that had long ago healed, though improperly. The pilot was a hard-bitten old warrior. His eyes were haunted as he stared at Jaina.

"You are my prisoners." He motioned with the old-model blaster pistol that was gripped in his twisted, gloved hand.

"Put down the blaster," Jaina said quietly, soothingly, using everything she knew of Jedi persuasion techniques. "You don't need it." Her uncle Luke had told them how Obi-Wan Kenobi had used Jedi mind tricks to scramble the thoughts of weak-minded Imperials.

"Put down the blaster," she said again in a rich, gentle voice.

Jacen knew exactly what his sister was doing. "Put down the blaster," he repeated.

The two of them said it one more time in an echoing, overlapping voice. They tried to send peaceful thoughts, soothing thoughts into the TIE pilot's mind . . . just as Jacen had done to calm his crystal snake.

The TIE pilot shook his grizzled head and narrowed his haunted eyes. The blaster wavered just a little, dropping down only a notch.

Why isn't it working? Jaina thought desperately. "Put down the blaster," she said again, more insistently. But inside the Imperial fighter's mind she ran up against a wall of thoughts so rigid, so black-and-white, so clear-cut, that it seemed like droid programming.

Suddenly the pilot straightened and glared at them through those bleak, haunted eyes. "Surrender is betrayal," he said, like a memorized lesson.

Jacen, seeing their chance slipping away, reached out with his mind and yanked at the weapon with mental brute force.

"Get the blaster!" he whispered. Jaina helped him tug with the Force, reaching for the old weapon in the pilot's grip. But the armored glove was wrapped so tightly around it that the black gauntlet seemed fastened to the blaster handle. The handgrip of the obsolete weapon caught on the glove, and the TIE pilot grabbed it with his other hand, pointing the barrel directly at the twins.

"Stop with your Jedi tricks," he said coldly. "If you continue to resist I will execute you both."

Knowing that the pilot needed only to depress the firing stud—much more quickly than they could ever mind-wrestle the blaster away from him—Jacen and Jaina let their hands fall to their sides, relaxing and ceasing their struggles.

Just then a buzzing, roaring sound crashed through the canopy above—a wound-up engine noise, growing louder.

"It's Lowie!" Jacen cried.

The T-23 plunged through the branches overhead in a

crackling explosion of shattered twigs, plowing toward the crash site at full speed, like a charging bantha.

"What's he trying to do?" Jacen asked, quietly. "He doesn't have any weapons on board!"

"He might distract the pilot," Jaina said. "Give us a chance to escape."

But the armored Imperial soldier stood his ground at the center of the clearing, spreading his legs for balance and assuming a practiced firing stance. He pointed his blaster at the oncoming air speeder, unflinching.

Jaina knew that if the blaster bolt breached the small repulsorlift reactor, the entire vehicle would explode—killing Lowbacca, and perhaps all of them.

Lowbacca brought the T-23 forward as if he meant to ram the TIE pilot. The desperate Imperial soldier aimed at the T-23's engine core and squeezed the firing stud.

"No!" Jaina cried, and *nudged* with her mind at the last instant. Using the Force, she shoved the TIE pilot's arm and knocked his aim off by just a fraction of a degree. The bright blaster bolt screeched out and danced along the metal hull of the repulsorlift pods. The engine casings melted at the side, spilling coolant and fuel. Gray-blue smoke boiled up. The sound of the T-23 became stuttered and sick as its engines faltered.

Lowie pulled up in the pilot's seat, swerving to keep from crashing into the Massassi trees. He could barely fly the badly damaged craft.

"Go, Lowie!" Jacen whispered. "Get out while you can."

"Eject! Before it blows!" Jaina cried.

But Lowbacca somehow managed to gain altitude, spinning around the huge trees and climbing toward the canopy again. His engines smoked, trailing a stream of foul-smelling exhaust that curled the jungle leaves and turned them brown.

"He won't get far," the Imperial pilot said in a raw monotone. "He is as good as dead."

Although the T-23 was out of sight now, far above them in the jungle treetops, Jaina could still hear the engine coughing, failing, and then picking up again as the battered craft limped away. The sounds carried well in the jungle silence.

The repulsorlift engine faded in the distance, its ion afterburners popping and sputtering—until finally, there was silence again.

The TIE pilot, his expression still stony, gestured with the blaster pistol. "Come with me, prisoners. If you resist this time, you will die."

12

LOWBACCA WRESTLED WITH the T-23, trying to control its erratic flight as it lurched across the treetops.

Thick, knotted smoke trailed in a stuttering plume from his starboard repulsor engine. Lowie risked a quick glance to his right again to assess the damage. No flames, but the situation was grim enough. The late-afternoon air currents were turbulent and threatened to capsize the skyhopper.

The T-23 jolted and dipped. Once, it bounced against some upraised branches, which scraped like long fingernails against the ship's lower foils and bottom hull, but Lowbacca managed to wrench the T-23 back on course. He was a good pilot; he would make it back to the academy and bring help, no matter what it took. He didn't know what had happened to Tenel Ka—if she was all right, or if the TIE pilot had captured her by now as well. For all he knew, Lowbacca was the only hope for rescue for his three friends.

His heart pounded painfully and his eyes stung from the chemical smoke that leaked into the cockpit. He noticed a sour, noxious smell, and his head began to swim.

"Master Lowbacca," Em Teedee said, "my sensors indicate that significant quantities of fumes have entered the cockpit."

Lowbacca gave a growl of annoyance. Did the little droid think that his sharp sense of smell hadn't picked that up?

"Well, no," Em Teedee rushed on, "it may not be dangerous *yet*, but if we begin to lose airspeed, less smoke will be drawn away. The airborne toxins could reach potentially lethal levels"—the droid raised his volume slightly for emphasis—"*even for a Wookiee.*"

The speeder gave a shuddering jolt, scraping against branches again. With grim determination Lowbacca pulled up. The T-23 was even harder to manage now. He wasn't sure how long he could last.

But he *had* to make it. He couldn't leave his friends in danger.

The T-23 shuddered and dipped. Lowbacca wheezed, laboring to pull air into his lungs. As if in response to his effort, the starboard engine coughed and sputtered.

And died.

Using all of his piloting skills, Lowie fought to steady the craft in its wobbling descent. The thick, deceptively soft-looking canopy rushed up at him, and the T-23 came to a crunching halt in a blizzard of leaves and twigs. Like a wounded avian, it lay nestled on the treetops, its right lower wing buried in the foliage. The left engine still chugged, but smoke billowed up from the damaged engine below, pouring into the cockpit now.

Lowbacca's head reeled with the impact, but he knew he had to get out. He fumbled with his crash restraints, trying to unfasten them. His vision was blurred from the acrid smoke, and he gagged at the stench. Confusion made his fingers clumsy.

Finally, with a burst of determination, he yanked on the straps until, loosened by the crash, they tore away. Two of the restraints came free in his hands, and he wriggled out of the remaining webbing.

Still no flames, Lowbacca noted with relief as he scrambled from the cockpit and distanced himself from the smoking T-23. Lowbacca gasped in deep lungfuls of the fresh, humid air of Yavin 4. As he worked his way across the treetops in the gathering dusk, one knee ached from where it had banged against the controls during the crash.

But he had no time to think about that. His first rescue attempt might have failed, but *he* had not failed yet. There were always options. He had to get back to the academy.

In his hurried scramble through the upper branches, Lowbacca did not notice when Em Teedee's clip broke at his waist.

The tiny droid fell with a thin wail into the forest below.

Dusk deepened into the full darkness of the jungle night. Swarms of nocturnal creatures awakened, beginning to hunt—but still Lowbacca pressed on.

Common sense had forced him to travel below the canopy, descending to a level where all of the branches were of a sufficient length and sturdiness to support him as he transferred his agile bulk from one tree to the next. Sometimes when he began to tire, or when his injured knee threatened to give way beneath him, Lowbacca relied on his powerful arms instead, swinging from branch to branch, using his keen Wookiee night vision in the murky shadows.

But he never stopped to rest. He could rest later.

Right now all of his senses were as finely tuned as a medical droid's laser beam. The pads of his feet and his acute sense of smell helped him to avoid decaying patches or slippery growths on the tree branches as he walked. His sharp hearing could distinguish between the sounds of wind through the leaves and the rustling of nocturnal animals as they stalked the jungle heights. For the most part, he managed to stay clear of them.

Lowbacca did not fear the darkness or the jungle. The jungles of Kashyyyk held far greater dangers—and he had faced those and survived. He remembered playing late-night games in the forest with his cousins and friends: races through the upper trees, jumping and swinging competitions, daring expeditions to the dangerous lower regions to test each other's courage, and the usual rites of passage that marked a Wookiee youth's transition into adulthood.

As he pushed through a dense clump of growth, a twig snagged Lowie's webbed belt, and he yanked it free. The feel of the intricately braided strands beneath his fingers reminded him of the night when he had won his belt, of his dangerous rite of passage.

He remembered. . . .

He felt his heart race with excitement as he descended toward the jungle floor that night long ago. Lowie had been down that far only twice before, when he had attended the rites of other friends, as was customary; there was strength in numbers when they sought to harvest the long, silky strands from the center of the deadly syren plant.

But Lowbacca had chosen to go alone, preferring to meet the challenge of the voracious syren plant using his own wits rather than borrowed muscles.

The night on Kashyyyk had been cool and dank. The profusion of screeches, chirps, growls, and croaks had been overwhelming. When he'd reached the lowest branches, Lowie had cinched the strap of his knapsack tighter and began his hunt.

With every sense fully alert, Lowbacca had moved stealthily from branch to branch until he caught the alluring scent of a wild syren plant. With sure instinct he'd followed the distinctive odor, feeling a mixture of anticipation and dread, until he squatted on the branch directly above the plant. He leaned over to study his stationary, but incredibly vicious, quarry.

The huge syren blossom consisted of two glossy oval petals of bright yellow, seamed in the center and supported by a mottled, bloody red stalk, twice as thick around as the sturdy tree limb on which Lowbacca sat. From the center of the open blossom spread a tuft of long white glossy fibers that emitted a broad spectrum of pheromones, scents to attract any unwary creature.

The beauty of the gigantic flower was intentionally deceptive, for any creature lured close enough to touch the sensitive inner flesh of the blossom would trigger the plant's lethal reflexes, and the petal jaws would close over the victim and begin its digestive cycle.

Alone, Lowbacca intended to harvest the glittering strands of the plant from the center of the flower—without springing the trap.

Traditionally, a few strong friends would hold the flower open while the young Wookiee scrambled to the treacherous center of the blossom, harvested the lustrous strands of sweetly scented fiber, and quickly made an escape. But even this assistance was no guarantee. Occasionally young Wookiees still lost limbs as the carnivorous plant clamped down on a slow-moving arm or leg.

Performing the task by himself, though, Lowie had needed to be extra careful. He had removed the knapsack from his hairy back and extracted its contents: a face mask, a sturdy rope, a thin cord, and a collapsible vibroblade. He'd placed the mask over his nose and mouth to filter out the syren's seductive scents. He knew that the pheromones could produce an almost overpowering desire to linger or to touch—and he could afford no mistakes.

Working quickly, enveloped by sinister night sounds, he had fashioned a short length of thin cord into a loose slip-knot, then formed a loop to make a sort of seat for himself in the sturdy, longer rope. Passing the free end of the long rope over a branch directly above the syren plant, he'd gathered up the slack in one hand, slid off the limb, and lowered himself with muscular arms.

Lowie had positioned himself as close as he dared to the gently undulating petals of the hungry syren blossom, an arm's length from the tantalizing tuft. He'd gripped the end of the long rope in his strong jaws to hold himself in place and free his hands. Then, using the loop of thin cord to lasso the tuft of precious fibers, he'd pulled himself close enough to slice them loose with his vibroblade. With a triumphant growl he'd jerked his prize toward himself, trapped the bundle against his body with one hairy arm, and stuffed the fiber into his knapsack.

In his excitement, however, the rope had slipped from his teeth. The trailing end uncoiled, dangled precariously, and then brushed one glossy petal of the deadly flower below. With a surge of gut-wrenching terror, Lowbacca had grabbed the tied end of the rope and hauled himself upward as the syren's jaws snapped shut. The petals just grazed one foot as they closed with an ominous slurp and a backwash of wind.

He had earned this fiber, Lowie thought, every strand of it, enough to make a special belt, which he always wore afterward.

Exhaustion sank its claws into every muscle as Lowbacca made his way from one Massassi tree to the next, hour after hour, all through the night.

Distance held no more meaning for him; he had to get to the Jedi academy. He could hear nothing but his own ragged breathing. His injured leg wobbled unsteadily at each step. Fatigue blurred his vision, and twigs and leaves matted his fur. He pushed forward, always forward, arm-leg, arm-leg, hand-foot, hand-foot—

Lowie looked around, confused and disoriented. He had reached for the next branch, but there were no more branches. Raising his head, he looked across the clearing— the landing clearing!—and saw the Great Temple, its majestic tiers outlined in the predawn darkness by flickering torches.

Lowbacca never remembered afterward climbing down out of the tree or crossing the clearing. He noticed only the awesome, welcoming sight of the ancient stone pyramid as he bellowed an alarm. He roared again and again, until a stream of robed figures carrying fresh torches rushed out of the temple and down the steps toward him.

The night and the desperate journey had taken their toll on Lowie. The numbness imposed by his own determination had worn off, and his knee refused to hold him any longer. His gangly legs gave way, and he collapsed to the ground, moaning his message.

When he rolled onto his back, a circle of concerned faces filled his vision. Tionne bent over him and brushed the tangle of matted fur away from his eyes.

"Lowbacca, we were concerned for you!" Tionne said gravely. "Are you hurt?"

Lowie groaned an answer, but Tionne didn't seem to understand. She leaned closer to him, her silvery hair glowing in the torchlight.

"Were Jacen and Jaina with you? And Tenel Ka?" She

paused as he tried to moan another answer. "Did something happen?" she persisted. "Can you tell me where they are?"

Lowbacca finally managed to say that the others were in the jungle and needed help. Tionne's brows knitted together in an expression of worry. She blinked her mother-of-pearl eyes. "I'm sorry, Lowbacca. I can't understand a word you're saying."

Lowie reached toward his belt to activate Em Teedee— but found nothing. The translator droid was gone.

13

TENEL KA RAN through the cool near-darkness of the jungle floor, trying to come up with a plan. She held her bent arms in front of her to protect her eyes and to push obstacles from her path. Branches whipped her face, tore at her hair, and clawed mercilessly at her bare arms and legs.

Her breath came in sharp gasps, not so much from the effort of running—to which she was well accustomed—but from the terror of what she had just experienced. She hoped she had made the right decision. Her pulse pounded in her ears, competing with the symphony of alien noises as the jungle creatures welcomed nightfall. Though she searched her mind, no Jedi calming techniques would come to her.

When the loud squawk of flying creatures sounded directly behind her, Tenel Ka glanced back in alarm. Before she could turn again, she fetched up sharply against the trunk of a Massassi tree. Stunned, she fell back a few paces and sank to the ground, putting one hand to the side of her face to examine her injury.

No blood, she thought as if from a great distance. *Good.* Beneath her fingertips, she felt tenderness and swelling from her cheek to her temple. There would be bruises, of course, and perhaps a royal headache. She cringed at the thought.

Royal. Although no one could see it, her cheeks heated with a flush of humiliation.

Tenel Ka pulled herself to her feet and took stock of her situation. In her newfound calmness she admitted to herself that she was completely lost. Jacen and Jaina—and by now perhaps even Lowbacca—were counting on her to return with help. She had always prided herself on being strong, loyal, reliable, unswayed by emotion. She had been level-headed enough during her initial escape, but then she had panicked. She shook off thoughts of her stupid headlong flight.

Well, she thought, pressing her pale lips together into a firm line, *I am back in control now.* She decided to push on until she found a safer place to spend the night. When morning came, she would try to get her bearings again and return to the Jedi academy.

As she trudged along, searching in the fading light of day, the ground began to rise and become more rocky. The trees grew sparser. When she saw a jagged shadow loom out of the darkness ahead of her, she slowed. Ahead was a large outcropping of rough, black stone, long-cooled lava mottled with lichens.

Tenel Ka tilted her head back and looked up, but she could not see how high the rock went; the jungle dimness swallowed it up. Cautiously exploring sideways, she encountered a break in the rock face, a patch of deeper darkness—a small cave. Perhaps she could spend the night here, in this defensible, sheltered place. The opening was no wider than the length of one arm and extended only to shoulder height, forcing her to stoop to explore further. She needed only to find a comfortable, safe place to rest.

She shivered as she hunched down on the sandy, cool floor of the cave. Her every muscle ached, but for now nothing could be done about her pain; she could bear it as well as any warrior. But she had not eaten since midday. She felt in the pouch at her waist, finding one carbo-protein biscuit remaining. As for the cold, she could light a fire with the finger-sized flash heater she carried in another pouch on her belt.

Dropping to her hands and knees, she scrabbled along the ground near the mouth of the cave, searching for twigs, leaves, anything that would burn. Back on Dathomir she'd had plenty of practice in rugged camping and outdoor endurance.

As she thought of the cozy warmth of a fire and a soft bed of leaves, Tenel Ka's spirits rose. The nightmarish events of the afternoon began to settle into perspective. This was an adventure, she assured herself. A test of her will and determination.

When she had collected kindling and some thicker branches, Tenel Ka began to build her fire against the velvety shadows of gathering night. She fumbled in her belt pouches for her flash heater and groaned as she remembered that Jaina had borrowed it that afternoon. She rubbed her cold, bare arms and blew on her hands to warm them.

Tenel Ka thought longingly of the cheery warmth of a crackling fire, of drinking hot, spiced Hapan ale with her parents. A rare smile crossed her lips as she thought of them, Teneniel Djo and Prince Isolder. If she were at home, she would only have to lift a hand to bring a servant of the Royal House of Hapes running to do her bidding. . . .

Tenel Ka grimaced. She had never known poverty or hardship, except by choice. *Well, you chose this, Princess,* she reminded herself savagely. *You wanted to learn to do things for yourself.*

Her father, Isolder of Hapes, had always said that the two years he spent in disguise working as a privateer had done more to prepare him for leadership than any training the royal tutors of Hapes could provide. And her mother, raised on the primitive planet of Dathomir, was proud that her only daughter spent months each year learning the ways of the Singing Mountain Clan and dressing as a warrior woman—a practice that Tenel Ka had enjoyed all the more because it annoyed her scheming Hapan grandmother.

Teneniel Djo had been even more pleased when her daughter had decided to attend the academy and take instruction to become a Jedi. She had enrolled simply as Tenel

Ka of Dathomir, not wanting the other trainees to treat her differently because of her royal upbringing.

At the academy, only Master Skywalker—who was an old friend of her mother's, and the man Teneniel Djo most admired—knew Tenel Ka's true background. She had not even told Jacen and Jaina, her closest friends on Yavin 4.

Jacen and Jaina. The twins trusted her. They needed her help now. She shivered in the cave. She had to stay safe for the night and then get back to the academy in the morning to bring reinforcements.

Tenel Ka heard a faint rustling, slapping and hissing in the darkness behind her. She looked back into the undulating shadows, blinking to clear her eyes. Had the shadows really moved? Perhaps she had been foolish to spend the night in an unexplored cave, but cold and fatigue had overruled her natural caution. She looked up and thought she could discern glossy dark shapes clinging to the ceiling, moving like waves on an inverted black sea.

Don't be a child, she chided herself. She had always tried to show her friends how self-sufficient and reliable she was. Right now, she was cold and bruised and miserable. What would Jacen say if he could see her? He'd probably tell some dumb joke.

Tenel Ka gritted her teeth. She would just have to build a fire without the flash heater, using skills she had been taught on Dathomir.

It took an agonizingly long time for her strong arms to produce enough friction twirling one smooth stick of wood against a flat branch. Finally, she managed to coax forth a glowing ember and a tendril of smoke. Working quickly, she touched a dried leaf to it and blew. A tiny golden flame licked its way up the leaf. With mounting excitement she added another and then another, and then a few twigs.

A gust of wind threatened to extinguish the struggling flame, so she encircled her fire with a tiny earthen berm to protect it. She added more tinder, and soon the snapping blaze was large enough to warm her and cast a comforting circle of light.

Tenel Ka soon realized that the restless sounds of scratching and stirring she had heard earlier had grown louder—much louder.

Suddenly, a shrieking reptilian form plummeted from the ceiling, its leathery wings outstretched. Twin serpentine heads snapped and a scorpion tail lashed, razor-sharp claws outstretched. Tenel Ka raised an arm to protect her face as the thing drove directly at her. Talons raked her arm as she pushed herself backward toward the cave wall. Sharp fangs opened a gash in her bare leg, and she kicked fiercely, striking one of the creature's two heads with her scaled boot. In the flickering light from the tiny fire, Tenel Ka watched in horror as an entire flock of the hideous creatures—each with a wingspan wider than she was tall—dropped from the shadowy recesses of the cave and swarmed toward her.

She struggled for purchase on the sandy cave floor and pushed her feet against the stone wall. Tenel Ka propelled herself toward the mouth of the cave on her hands and knees.

She kicked the embers of her fire at the flapping beasts as she scrambled past, hardly noticing the bits of charred wood and leaf that singed her own legs. One of the reptilian creatures shrieked in pain.

Tenel Ka smiled with grim satisfaction and launched herself through the cave opening, back out into the pitch blackness of the jungle night.

The monsters followed.

14

AT GUNPOINT, THE TIE pilot led his captives back to the clearing with the small, crude shelter where he had lived for some time.

"So this is why you came running," Jaina said to her brother. "You found where he lives." Jacen nodded.

"Silence!" the Imperial soldier said in a brusque voice.

Jaina, her throat tight and dry, swallowed hard and looked

around at the small, cleared site in the gathering evening shadows. Beside them a shallow stream trickled past. She couldn't imagine how the TIE pilot had survived all alone, without any human contact, for so many years.

The climate of Yavin 4 was warm and hospitable, placing few demands on the home the TIE pilot had created for himself. He had carved out a large shelter from the bole of a half-burned Massassi tree, in front of which he had lashed a lean-to of split branches. Altogether, it provided him with a simple, but comfortable room, like a living cave. Jaina tried to imagine how long it had taken the Imperial, scraping with a sharp implement—possibly a piece of wreckage from his crashed ship—to widen the area under the gnarled overhang.

The TIE pilot had rigged a system of plumbing made from hollow reeds joined together, drawing water from the nearby stream into catch basins inside his hut. He had made rough utensils from wood, forest gourds, and petrified fungus slabs. The man had maintained a lonely existence, unchallenged, simply surviving and waiting for further orders, hoping someone would come to retrieve him—but no one ever had.

The Imperial soldier stopped outside the hut. "On the ground," he said. "Both of you. Hands above your heads."

Jaina looked at Jacen as they lay belly-down on the ground of the clearing. She could think of no way to escape. The TIE pilot went to the thick foliage and rummaged among the branches with his good hand. He wrapped his fingers around some thin, purplish vines that dangled from dazzlingly bright Nebula orchids in the branches above his head. With a jerk he snapped the strands free.

The vine tendrils flopped and writhed in his grip as if they were alive and trying to squirm away. The TIE pilot rapidly used them to lash Jaina's wrists together, then Jacen's. As the deep violet sap leaked from the broken ends of the vines, the plant's thrashing slowed, and the flexible, rubbery vines contracted, tightening into knots that were impossible to break.

Jacen and Jaina looked at each other, their liquid-brown

eyes meeting as a host of thoughts gleamed unspoken between them. But they said nothing, afraid to anger their captor.

Marching clumsily through the humid jungle had made them hot and sticky, and Jaina was still covered with grime from her repairs on the TIE fighter's engines. Now the cool jungle evening chilled her perspiration and made her shiver. Her hands tingled and throbbed, as the tight vines cutting into her wrists made her even more miserable.

In the hour or so since their capture, neither of the twins had heard any further sign of Lowie or Tenel Ka. Jaina was afraid that something had happened to them, that her two friends were even now stranded and lost somewhere in the jungle. But then she realized that her own situation was probably a lot more dangerous than theirs.

Without a word, the TIE pilot nudged them to their feet, then over to the large lava-rock boulders near the fire pit he used outside his shelter. They squatted there together. The stone chairs had been polished smooth, their sharp edges chipped away slowly and patiently over the course of years by the lost Imperial.

The last coppery rays of light from the huge orange planet Yavin disappeared, as the rapidly rotating moon covered the jungle with night. Through the densely laced treetops, thick shadows gathered, making the forest floor darker than the deepest night on Jacen and Jaina's glittering home planet of Coruscant.

The Imperial pilot walked over to the splintered chunks of dry, moss-covered wood he had painstakingly gathered, one-armed, and stacked near his shelter. He carried them back and dropped one branch at a time into the fire pit, stacking the wood in formation to make a small campfire.

The pilot withdrew a battered igniter from a storage bin inside his shelter and pointed it at the campfire. Its charge had been nearly depleted, and the silvery nozzle showered only a few hot sparks onto the kindling; but he seemed accustomed to such difficulties. He toiled in silence, never cursing, never complaining, simply focused on the task of getting the campfire lit. And when he succeeded, he showed no satisfaction, no joy.

With the fire finally blazing, the TIE pilot ducked back inside his hut, rummaged in a vine-woven basket, and returned with a large spherical fruit. The fruit was encased in an ugly, warty brown rind. Jaina did not recognize it. It was nothing they ate at the Jedi academy.

Holding it in his injured, gauntleted hand, the pilot used a sharpened stone to split open the rind, then peeled the fruit with his fingers. The flesh inside was pale yellowish-green, speckled with scarlet. He broke the fruit into sections, shuffled over to the two captives, and pushed one of the fruit sections in Jaina's face. "Eat."

She clamped her lips together for a moment, afraid that the Imperial soldier might be trying to poison her. Then she realized that the TIE pilot could have killed either of them at any time—and that she was extremely hungry and thirsty.

Her hands still bound by the drying vine, she leaned forward and opened her mouth to bite into the bright fruit. The explosion of tart citrus-tasting juice proved surprisingly invigorating and delicious. She chewed slowly, savoring the taste, and swallowed.

Jacen also ate his. They nodded their thanks to the TIE pilot, who fixed them with a stony gaze.

Sensing an opening, Jacen asked, "What are you going to do with us, sir?" He tried to rub his chin against his shoulder to wipe off the juice dribbling from his lips.

The TIE pilot stared unnervingly at him for several moments before he turned his face toward the bushes. "Not yet determined."

Jaina's chest muscles constricted. All of this had been an accident, a mistake. From the thick bushes, the TIE pilot had probably watched them tinker with his ruined ship for days. But Jacen's accidental discovery of his primitive shelter had forced him to react.

What could the Imperial soldier do with them? He didn't seem to have many options.

"What's your name?" Jaina asked.

The TIE pilot snapped upright and looked down at the black leather glove covering his twisted arm. He turned slowly toward her, like a droid with worn-out servomotors. "CE3K-1977." He rattled off the numbers as if he had memorized them. Service rank and operating number only.

"Not your number," Jaina persisted. "Your name. I'm Jaina. This is my brother Jacen."

"CE3K-1977," the TIE pilot said again, without emotion.

"Your *name*?" Jaina asked a third time.

Finally her question seemed to perplex him. He looked at the ground, looked at his tattered uniform. His mouth opened and closed several times, but no sound came out, until finally he said in a croaking voice, "Qorl . . . Qorl. My name is Qorl."

"We're staying at the academy in the old temples," Jacen said, wearing a small grin—the kind that always disarmed their mother when she was angry at him. But it didn't seem to be working with the TIE pilot.

"Rebel base," Qorl said.

"No, it's a school now," Jaina said. "Everyone's there to learn. It's not a base any longer. It hasn't been a base for . . . twenty years or so."

"It is a Rebel base," Qorl insisted with such finality that Jaina decided not to pursue the subject any further.

"How did you get here?" she asked, leaning closer on the smooth rock. The campfire crackled between them. "How long have you lived in the jungle?" The tight vines constricting her circulation made her hands numb. She flexed her fingers as she bent toward the fire. The smoke smelled rich and sweet from the fresh jungle wood.

The TIE pilot blinked his pale eyes and stared into the crackling flames. He looked as if he had been transported back in time and was watching a newsloop of his own buried memories.

"Death Star," Qorl said. "I was on the Death Star. We came here to destroy the Rebel base after Grand Moff Tarkin blew up Alderaan. This was our next target."

Jaina felt a pang as she remembered her mother talking of the lovely grass-covered planet Alderaan, the peaceful windsongs and tall towers rising above the plains. Princess Leia's home had been the heart of galactic culture and civilization—until it was wiped out in a single blow by the incredible cruelty of the Empire.

"We must obliterate the Rebels at all costs," Qorl continued. "Rebels cause damage to the Empire."

He recited a litany of what seemed to be memorized phrases, thoughts that had been brainwashed into him. "The Emperor's New Order will save the galaxy. The Rebels want to destroy that dream, and so we must eradicate the Rebels. They are a cancer to peace and stability."

"You were on the Death Star," Jacen prompted. "That was over twenty years ago. What happened?"

Qorl continued to stare deeply into the fire. His scratchy voice was barely more than a whisper. "The Rebels knew we were coming. They fought. They sent their defenses against the battle station. All TIE squadrons were launched.

"I flew with my squadron. All my companions were destroyed by X-wing defensive fire. I was damaged in the cross fire . . . one solar panel out of commission. I spun away from the Death Star, out of control.

"I needed to get back to effect repairs. All comm channels were jammed, filled with dozens of requests for assistance. My orbit was decaying, and I spun toward the fourth moon of Yavin. I kept trying to hail someone on the comm channels. When I finally got through, I was told I would have to wait for rescue. They instructed me to make a good landing if I could—and to wait."

"So you crashed," Jaina said.

"The jungle cushioned my fall. I was thrown out of my craft into the dense brush . . . when one of the solar panels caught and lodged in the trees above. I limped over to my TIE fighter. Stayed as close as I dared, afraid that it might explode. My arm—" He held up his left arm in the black leather gauntlet. "Badly injured, ligaments torn, bones broken.

"I looked up into the sky just in time to see the Death Star blow up. It was like another sun in the sky. Flaming chunks of debris fell through the air. It must have started dozens of forest fires. For weeks, meteor showers were like fireworks as the wreckage rained down onto the moon.

"And I stayed here."

The firelight bathed Qorl's face with a dancing, yellowish glow. The jungle sounds burred in a hypnotic hum all around them. The TIE pilot gave no sign that he realized his two captives were listening. Only his lips moved as he continued his tale.

"I have waited here, and waited, as ordered. No one has come to rescue me."

"But," Jaina said, "all those years! This place has been abandoned for quite some time, but people have been at the Jedi academy for eleven years now. Why haven't you turned yourself in? Don't you realize what's happened in the galaxy since you crashed?"

"Surrender is betrayal!" Qorl snapped, glaring at her as anger flickered across his weathered face.

"But we're not lying," Jacen said. "The war is over. There *is* no more Empire." He took a deep breath and then plunged ahead. "Darth Vader is dead. The Emperor is dead. The New Republic now rules. Only a few remnants of old Imperial holdouts are still buried in the Core Systems at the center of the galaxy."

"I don't believe you," Qorl said flatly.

"If you take us back to the Jedi academy we can prove it. We can show you everything," Jaina said. "Wouldn't you like to go home? Wouldn't you like to be free of this place? We could get your arm treated."

Qorl held up his glove and stared at it. "I used my medikit," he said. "I tended it as best I could. It is good enough, although there was much pain . . . for a long time."

"But we've got Jedi healers!" Jaina said. "We've got medical droids. You could be happy again. Why stay here? There's nothing to betray: There is no more Empire."

"Be quiet," Qorl said. "The Empire will always rule. The Emperor is invincible."

"The Emperor is dead," Jacen said.

"The Empire itself can never die," Qorl insisted.

"But if you won't let us take you back to get help, then what do you *want*?" Jaina asked.

Jacen nodded, chiming in. "What are you trying to accomplish?"

"What can we do for you Qorl?"

The TIE pilot turned away from the campfire to stare at them. His haggard, weather-beaten face held new power and obsession, springing from deep within his mind.

"You will finish repairs to my ship," he said. "And then I shall fly away from this prison moon. I'll return to the Empire as a glorious hero of war. Surrender is betrayal—and I *never* surrendered."

"And what if we won't help you?" Jacen said with all the bravado he could manage. Jaina instantly wanted to kick him for provoking the TIE pilot.

Qorl looked at the young boy, his face coldly expressionless again. "Then you are expendable," he said.

15

IT TOOK EM Teedee several moments to recalibrate his sensors after he dropped from Lowbacca's fiber-belt. He had fallen, bouncing, crashing, and bonking through the canopy until he finally came to rest on a dense mat of leafy vines that tied together the lower branches.

"Master Lowbacca, come back!" he said, amplifying his voice circuits to their maximum volume levels. "Don't leave me! Oh, dear. I *knew* that was a bad idea."

He adjusted his optical sensors so he could see better in the dim light of the lower levels. He was surrounded by thickets that were nearly inaccessible to anyone as large as even a young Wookiee.

"Help! Help me!" Em Teedee shouted again. He decided it would be most effective to continue shouting every forty-five seconds, because he calculated that was the minimum amount of time necessary for anyone nearby to come within earshot.

Unable to move and scout out his location, Em Teedee's best guess was that he was still twenty meters above the ground. He hoped that no slight jarring of the branches would cause him to break free and tumble down again. If he fell that far to the ground, he might strike one of the rough lava outcroppings and split open his outer casing. With his circuits spilled across the jungle floor, no one would ever be able to put him back together again in the proper fashion. His circuits buzzed at the thought.

Forty-five seconds had passed. He called out again for help, then waited. He shouted repeatedly for the next hour and eleven minutes, hoping desperately to attract some sort of attention, someone to come rescue him.

But when he finally did attract a curious investigator, Em Teedee wished he had kept his vocal circuits switched off.

A large pack of chattering woolamanders scurried through the lower canopy, stirring up leaves and cracking twigs in their hectic passage. The arboreal creatures were loud and agile, able to clamber from thin branches to thick ones and back again without losing their balance. They seemed to be engaged in a contest to see who could yowl and chatter the loudest in the jungle silence as twilight deepened.

Somehow, over all the ruckus, they managed to hear Em Teedee's cries for help.

Em Teedee knew from his limited database of Yavin 4 that woolamanders were curious, social creatures. Now that they had heard him, they began to search. In only moments, with their sharp, slit-eyed vision, they had spotted the translator droid's shiny outer casing in the jungle shadows. The pack of colorful, hairy creatures swarmed toward him.

"Oh, no," Em Teedee cried. "Not you. Please—I was hoping for someone *else* to rescue me."

The woolamanders came closer, rattling branches, rustling leaves. Their bright purple fur bristled with suspicion and delight.

"Go away! Shoo!" Em Teedee said.

The woolamanders let out a loud, shrieking celebration of their discovery. A large male snatched Em Teedee from his resting place in the vines.

"Put me down," Em Teedee said. "I *insist* that you let go of me at once."

The large male tossed Em Teedee to his mate, who caught the translator droid and turned him over and around, poking at the shiny circles. She dug her grimy finger into the gold circle of his optical sensors.

"That's my eye—get your finger away from it! Now I'm upside down. Straighten me out . . . . put me down!"

The female shook and rattled him to see if he would make other noises. When she went to a thick branch and made ready to smash him down on it, as she would crack open a large fruit, Em Teedee set off his automatic alarm sirens, shrieking and whooping at such volume and at such a painful pitch that the female dropped him. He bounced on another leafy branch, then came precariously to rest.

"Help!" Em Teedee wailed.

One of the smaller woolamanders rushed in to snatch him from his resting place. With loud chattering and squeals of delight, the young woolamander dashed along the lower branches, holding his prize high as Em Teedee continued to howl for assistance. The other young woolamanders chased after the youngster, clamoring for the prize.

Em Teedee, in such a panic that he could no longer stand it without overloading his circuits, shut down so he wouldn't have to see what was about to happen to him.

Sometime late in the night he powered back on again to find that he could see nothing: His optical sensors were covered with thick fur.

He detected a gentle motion . . . breathing, snoring. Then the young woolamander stirred in its sleep. It shifted, allowing Em Teedee to discover that the small creature now lay sleeping in the crotch of a tree branch, contentedly hugging his new toy to his fur-covered chest.

Around them, the other family members of the large arboreal group sighed and dozed, resting peacefully. Em

Teedee had an impulse to cry out again for help, still hoping that someone might come to rescue him.

All the noisy woolamanders were finally asleep, though, and Em Teedee decided to treasure this moment of peace. He could only hope for something better to happen the next day.

16

DAWN CAME FAST and hot, as the distant white sun climbed around the fuzzy ball of Yavin. Jungle creatures awoke and stirred. The air warmed rapidly, thick with humidity that rose from low hollows where mist had collected in the night.

Jacen and Jaina had slept awkwardly, their hands still tied with the resilient purple vines. Jacen fervently wished he had spent more time practicing delicate and precise Force exercises. He didn't have the skill or the accuracy to nudge and untie the thin knotted vines with his mind.

As soon as there was light enough to work, Qorl emerged from his tree shelter and shook the twins awake. He gave them each sips of cool water from a gourd he dipped in the stream, then used a long stone knife to saw off the vines binding their wrists.

Jacen flexed his fingers and shook out his hands. His nerves tingled and stung with returning circulation.

The Imperial soldier pointed the blaster at them, gesturing for the twins to move. "Back to the TIE fighter," he ordered. "Work."

Jacen and Jaina trudged through the jungle, stumbling through vines and shrubs; the TIE pilot followed directly behind them. They reached the site of the crashed ship, where it lay uncovered and glinting in the early morning light. With a knot forming in his stomach, Jacen saw burned patches from where Qorl had shot his blaster at Tenel Ka and Lowie.

"I know you are nearly finished with repairs," the TIE

pilot said. "I have been watching you for days. You will complete them today."

Jaina blinked her brandy-brown eyes and scowled at him. "We can't possibly work that fast, especially with just the two of us. This ship has been crashed for twenty years. We haven't finished cleaning the debris from the sublight intakes. The power converters all need to be rewired."

Jacen watched his sister and knew she was lying.

"Cyberfuses still need to be installed," she continued. "The air-exchange system is clogged; it needs to be—"

Qorl raised the blaster, but did not alter the emotion in his voice. "*Today*," he repeated. "You will finish today."

"Oh, blaster bolts! I think he means it, Jaina," Jacen muttered. "Show me what I can do to help."

Jaina sighed. "All right. Collect the box of tools you tripped over yesterday. Get the hydrospanner. I'll use my multitool to finish some calibrations here in the engines."

Qorl sat down on a lumpy, lichen-encrusted boulder, using his good hand to brush crawling insects from his legs. The Imperial soldier waited like a droid sentinel, unmoving, watching them work. Jacen tried to ignore him—and the blaster.

Gnats and biting insects swarmed around Jacen's face, attracted by the sweat in his tangled hair. He passed tools to his sister, trying to find the components and equipment Jaina needed as she crawled and rummaged in the TIE fighter's engine compartment.

He could sense Jaina's growing anger and frustration. She couldn't think of a plan. Yes, Jacen supposed, they could simply sabotage the ship repairs—but Qorl would realize what they'd done almost immediately, and he would get even with them. They couldn't risk that.

Now Jacen wished that his sister, in all her excitement, hadn't installed the new hyperdrive unit their dad had given her. He wished that they all hadn't worked so hard, made so much progress. Now it was almost too late.

Jacen brushed a hand across his forehead, blinking sweat away. His stomach growled. He turned to the TIE pilot, sitting nearby on the rock, still pointing the blaster barrel directly at him. The threat was getting tiresome.

"Qorl," he said, intentionally using their captor's real name. "Could we have some water and more fruit? We're hungry. We'll work better if we're not hungry."

Qorl nodded slightly and began to stand up. But then he froze, hesitated, and settled back into his rigid position. "Food and water when you are finished with repairs."

"What?" Jacen said in dismay. "But that could take all day."

"Then you will be hungry and thirsty," Qorl said. The TIE pilot looked somewhat anxious, impatient. "You are stalling. Proceed."

Jacen realized that Qorl might be worried that either Tenel Ka or Lowie had managed to get back to the Jedi academy and summoned help. They were a long distance from the Great Temple, across a treacherous jungle . . . but there was always a chance.

Jaina finished adjusting a cooling system regulator. She twisted a knob; a cold, bright blast of supercooled steam screeched up, making feathers of frost on the exposed metal surface. She stepped back and rubbed a grimy hand across her cheek, leaving a dark stain beneath her liquid-brown eyes.

"Qorl?" she said. "Who are you going to see when you get back?"

"I will report for duty," he said.

"Are you going home? Do you have a family?"

"The Empire is my family." His answer was rapid, automatic.

"But do you have a family that *loves you*?" Jaina asked.

Qorl hesitated for the briefest moment, then gestured threateningly with the blaster. "Get back to work."

Jaina sighed and motioned for her brother to help her. "Come on, Jacen. Take those last packages of surface metal sealant," she said. "We need to reinforce the melt spots on the outer hull." She pointed to three stained and vaporized bull's-eye spots on the TIE fighter's outer plating—damage Qorl himself had caused the day before by firing his blaster at the twins.

With a cushioned hammer, Jaina pounded the bent plates back into position. Jacen dug into the toolbox until he found a packet of animated metal sealant. The special paste would crawl across the damaged area, smooth itself, and then seal down with a bond even stronger than the original hull alloy. Jacen applied one packet of the patch material and listened to it hiss and steam as it coated the burn spot. Jaina fixed the second spot.

The third melted area lay high on the cargo compartment, close to the open transpari-steel canopy that protected the cockpit. Jacen took the last pack and crawled atop the small craft. He popped the seal, applied the patch, and waited for the animated sealant to do its work.

As he watched the gooey substance finish its repairs, Jacen heard small creatures stirring around him. He sensed something nearby and, looking down into the cargo space, saw a glimmer of movement, almost transparent, barely noticeable. Jacen's heart leaped. He leaned down, reaching deep into the TIE fighter, and grabbed for it. Hope began to fill him.

"Boy, get out of there!" Qorl yelled. "Come back where I can see you."

Panting, his heart pounding, Jacen pulled himself free. He backed away from the cockpit and jumped to the ground, keeping his hands clearly in sight.

Jaina bent over and whispered to him with concern in her eyes. "What are you doing? What did you find in there?"

Jacen grinned at her, then recovered his expression before Qorl could notice it. "Something that might save us all."

"No more talking," Qorl snapped. "Hurry."

"We're doing the best we can," Jaina replied.

"Not good enough," the pilot said. "Do you need encouragement? If you cannot complete repairs faster, I will shoot your bother. Then you will complete the repairs by yourself."

Both Jacen and Jaina looked at the TIE pilot in shock. "Qorl, you wouldn't do that," Jaina said.

"I received my training from the Empire," Qorl answered. "I will do what is necessary."

Jacen swallowed—he knew the TIE pilot was telling the truth. "Yeah, I'll bet you would," he said.

With a sigh and an expression of disgust, Jaina stood up and tossed the hydrospanner onto a pile of tools on the jungle floor. She brushed her hands down her thighs, wiping grime on the legs of her jumpsuit.

"Never mind," she said. "It's finished. We've done everything we can. The TIE fighter is ready to fly again."

17

INSIDE THE TORCHLIT temples of the Jedi academy, Lowbacca bellowed in confusion and alarm. He waved his lanky, hairy arms to emphasize the urgency of the situation. He didn't know how to make them understand him; he only knew he had to warn them of the TIE fighter, had to get help for Jacen and Jaina and Tenel Ka.

Tionne and the other Jedi candidates around her grew agitated. None of them could speak the Wookiee language. "Lowbacca, we can't understand you," she said. "Where is your translator droid?"

Lowie patted his hip again and made a distressed sound. He'd have never imagined he'd be so upset not to have the jabbering droid at his side.

"Where are Jacen, Jaina, and Tenel Ka?" Tionne asked. "Are they all right?"

Lowbacca bellowed again and gestured out into the jungle, trying to explain everything.

"Was there an accident? Are they hurt?" Tionne asked. Her mother-of-pearl eyes were wide and her silver hair flowed about her as if it were alive. With her long, delicate hands, she clutched Lowie's furred arm.

Her voice had been so calm and silky when she sang Jedi

ballads to the gathered students in the grand audience chamber. Now her words had a hard, crystalline edge, the forcefulness of a true Jedi Knight.

Lowbacca tried to think of how to explain, but his growing frustration made it more and more difficult. He had no words they could understand. Yes, he could gesture back toward the jungle—but how to describe a crashed TIE fighter? A surviving Imperial pilot? The twins taken hostage?

The young Jedi Knights had kept their little project completely secret while they were making repairs to the crashed ship. Jaina had wanted the revamped craft to be a surprise she could show off to the other trainees. But now having kept it a secret was working against them. No one could guess what he was talking about; no one knew about the crash site.

He didn't know what had happened to Tenel Ka, either. Had she been killed, or had she somehow escaped? Was she even now lost in the jungles by herself, being stalked by predators? He moaned in dismay.

Unable to restrain himself, Lowie rattled off the whole story in loud Wookiee grunts and roars. Everyone around him grew agitated, unable to decipher a word he was saying. Finally, his frustration got the best of him; Lowie pounded his fists on one of the stone walls and pushed past Tionne and the other Jedi candidates into the cool shadows of the Great Temple.

"Where are you going, Lowbacca?" Tionne called, but he didn't answer her.

Though Lowie was still tired, the others could not catch up with him. With only the slightest limp, his long, muscular legs carried him down the winding corridors of the ancient stone ruin. Breathless, he reached the room that had been the old command center when the temple served as a Rebel base. Luke Skywalker maintained it to keep contact with the rest of the New Republic.

He knew his uncle Chewbacca was still in the Yavin system, near the orange gas giant where Lando Calrissian had set up his orbiting mining facility for Corusca gems. If only

Lowie could get in touch with the *Millennium Falcon*, speak to his uncle, he could explain everything directly. Chewbacca—along with Jacen and Jaina's father, Han Solo—would know just what to do.

With a loud sigh of relief, Lowie sank into a chair in front of a console. The station was filled with the only things in the Jedi academy that seemed familiar to him at this moment: the computers and electronic equipment. He knew exactly how to communicate with them.

Lowbacca worked the controls with speed and determination, tapping his clawed fingers over the appropriate buttons. He had already established an open channel to the *Falcon* by the time Tionne and the others caught up with him in the Communications Center.

Tionne immediately realized what he was doing, and she nodded. "Good idea, Lowbacca!" She waited beside the young Wookiee as a sleepy-sounding Han Solo answered the call.

"Yeah, this is Solo. Who's calling? Luke? Is this the Jedi academy?" Lowbacca bleated into the microphone pickup, hoping the human pilot would understand him.

Tionne leaned over next to Lowbacca before he could continue and spoke into the voice pickup. "Something has happened here, General Solo. The twins and Tenel Ka have disappeared, and Lowbacca is trying to tell us what happened. But he can't make us understand him. He's lost his translator droid."

With a roar of surprise, Chewbacca came on the line. Excited, Lowie once again explained everything as fast as he could in the Wookiee language. Chewbacca roared back in outrage, and Han broke in.

"Quiet, old buddy. I heard most of that, but a few of the details were sketchy. Something about a crashed TIE fighter and an Imperial soldier taking them hostage?"

Both Wookiees made loud sounds of agreement.

"Okay, sit tight. We're on our way!" Han said. "We can undock from Lando's station in just a few seconds. We were ready to get out of here anyway. The *Falcon*'ll be there in about two hours—middle of the local morning, I think. Just hold on and get ready to help me fight for the kids!"

Lowie and Chewbacca both bellowed in agreement. Tionne looked at the young Wookiee in amazement. "A TIE fighter! Imperials here? Quick, we must get everyone ready in case they attack."

With a searing white flicker from its aft sublight engines, the *Millennium Falcon* cruised through the deep blue atmosphere toward the ancient Massassi structures. Lowie stood in the open landing area in front of the Great Temple, anxious to see his uncle. He waved his shaggy arms for the ship as it approached.

The bright light of morning grew warmer with each passing minute. The two hours it had taken for the *Millennium Falcon* to leave the Yavin gas giant and approach the jungle moon had seemed the longest of Lowie's life.

Now he stepped back into the shade of the temple as the *Falcon* settled to the ground with hissing bursts of its repulsorlift engines. The landing pads settled and stabilized, and then the boarding ramp came down like an opening mouth.

Chewbacca bounded down the ramp, ducking his hairy head to keep from bumping the low ceiling, and headed toward the temple. Lowie ran to meet him halfway, limping slightly. Han Solo charged out and joined them, his blaster already drawn.

"Ready to rescue the kids? Let's go!" Han said. Tionne and several of the other Jedi candidates hurried out. Han looked around. "Where's Luke? Isn't he back yet?"

"Master Skywalker isn't here," Tionne said. "We have to defend *ourselves*."

"We'll take care of it," Han said. "Lando gave us some extra weapons, and all our laser cannon banks are charged. Lowie, can you show us where they're being held?"

Lowbacca nodded his shaggy head.

"If there are any more Imperial TIE fighters around," Han said, "the most important thing you can do is guard the Jedi academy, Tionne. This would be their obvious target. The

Empire doesn't particularly like the New Republic getting another batch of Jedi Knights."

"We'll be here to defend the academy, General Solo," Tionne said. "You find the children."

"All right, Lowie," Han said. "Let's go—no time to waste."

18

THE ROAR OF twin ion engines shattered the deep stillness of the jungle morning as the TIE fighter returned to life. Birds squawked in terror and fled into the high branches. Dust and dry, crumbling leaves scattered in clouds around the Imperial ship.

Encased in the cockpit, Qorl throttled up the power, slowly, gently, as if feeling it grow at his fingertips. Foul brownish exhaust spat out of the clogged vent ports in the rear of the single-fighter craft. The Imperial ship growled, ready for action again after its long retirement.

The TIE pilot emerged from the cockpit, his battered black helmet in hand, the respirator hoses dangling and disconnected from his empty emergency-oxygen supply. Although the glossy blast goggles had been scratched and worn down during the years of his exile, he carried the helmet proudly, like a trophy.

Qorl was ready to report back to duty.

"Propulsion systems check out," he said. "With the addition of the functional hyperdrive motor you installed, I am now able to cross the galaxy and find the remnants of my Empire. This short-range fighter could not otherwise have taken me there."

"Good work, Jaina," Jacen grumbled. She elbowed him in the ribs, and he fell silent.

"What are you going to do with us, Qorl?" Jaina asked the pilot. "Why go away from here? If you'd just come back with us to the Jedi academy, everything would be all right—the war is over."

"Surrender is betrayal!" Qorl shouted, with a surge of emotion stronger than Jacen had seen in him before. The pilot's hand shook as he pointed the ever-present blaster at them. "Your usefulness to me is at an end," he said, his voice a low threat.

Jacen's stomach clenched with sudden dread. Jaina had hoped to make the TIE fighter her own vehicle so she could joyride just like Lowie did in his revamped T-23. But the small fighter could carry only one person: the pilot. Qorl could never take them along as prisoners, even if he wanted to. Would the pilot remove his last obstacles—the only witnesses to his exile—with clean Imperial efficiency? Would he just shoot them both and then fly off in search of his home?

Jacen desperately tried to send calming thoughts to soothe Qorl, as he so frequently did with his crystal snakes. But it was no use: His mind encountered the rigid wall of brainwashing that had locked Qorl's thoughts into unchangeable patterns.

The TIE pilot looked away, and his temper seemed to lessen. Jacen couldn't tell if that was a result of his Jedi powers or if the Imperial soldier had simply been distracted.

"So what *are* you going to do with us?" Jacen asked.

Qorl glanced back at the twins, his face haggard. He looked very old and drained. "You have helped me a great deal. You are the only . . . company I have had for many years. I will leave you here alone in the jungle."

"You're just going to abandon us?" Jaina asked in disbelief. This time, Jacen elbowed *her* in the ribs. He didn't relish the idea of being stranded in the jungle any more than she did, but several less-appealing possibilities had occurred to him.

"You can survive if you are resourceful," Qorl said. "I know, because I did. Perhaps someone will find you eventually. Hope is your best weapon. It may not take twenty years for *you* to get home."

He pondered for a moment, holding his dark helmet in his hands. Behind him, the repaired TIE fighter continued to purr, as if anxious to fly again. "You are lucky to be here, safe," Qorl finally said. "I will rejoin the Empire. But as my last act here on this cursed jungle moon, I am going to destroy the Rebel base."

"No!" Jacen and Jaina both shouted in unison.

"It's just a school now. It's not a military base," Jacen added.

"Please don't do this!" Jaina said. "Don't attack the Jedi academy."

But Qorl gave no sign that he heard them. He carefully placed the battered old helmet on his shaggy head and tightened down the blast shield.

"Wait!" Jaina cried, her eyes pleading. "They have no weapons in the temples!" She reached out with her mind, trying to touch the pilot, but he aimed his blaster at her and backed away.

Qorl climbed into the cockpit of the TIE fighter, eased himself into the ancient, torn seat in front of the controls, and sealed himself in. The twins rushed forward, pounding on the hull with their fists.

The roar of the engines increased and the repulsorlifts sent out a blast that knocked leaves, pebbles, and jungle debris in all directions.

The TIE fighter hummed, shifted from its overgrown resting place, and began to rise.

Jaina tried one last time to grab the hull plates, but her fingers slid along the smooth metal. Jacen pulled her back as the TIE's engine power increased. The exhaust shrieked through the fighter's cooling systems.

The twins staggered back under the protection of one of the overarching Massassi trees, alone and defenseless in the thick jungles.

Qorl's TIE fighter, which had lain hidden and crippled on the surface of Yavin 4 for more than twenty years, finally rose into the air. Its twin ion engines made the characteristic moaning sound that had struck fear into the hearts of so many Rebel fighters.

With surprisingly skillful maneuvering and a burst of speed, Qorl's fighter climbed up through the forest canopy and soared away toward the Jedi academy.

19

IN THE DARKNESS of the jungle night, Tenel Ka plunged through tangled vines and dense, thorny thickets, hoping that the flying reptiles would not be able to follow. She panted from the exertion; breath burned in her lungs, but she did not cry out.

She could still hear the flap of the reptiles' wide, leathery wings close behind her as they swooped in for the kill with their razor talons. The raucous cries of their hideous twin heads chilled her blood. She remembered hearing that such a beast had almost killed Master Skywalker many years ago. *How did the monsters manage to maneuver in the crowded jungle?* she wondered. Why couldn't she lose them?

The bushes beside her hissed and rattled, and a stinger tail narrowly missed her arm. One of the winged monsters was directly above her, then. What could she do?

She pushed through a narrower space between two trees and heard a *thump* above her as the flying creature got stuck in the opening between the trees. *Good*, she thought. The rest would have to go around. That would buy her some time.

Tenel Ka pelted across a clearing toward the shadow of what she hoped was another patch of underbrush, but she had misjudged the speed with which the reptilian creatures could navigate the jungle obstacles. She could feel the menacing wind from their wings as one of them swooped down directly in her path.

She sensed, rather than saw, the outstretched claws, and tried to turn aside, but slipped on rotting vegetation and fell hard against a fungus-covered log. She sensed a second pair of claws rip through the air where her stomach had been only moments before. She shuddered as twin heads cried out in rage and frustration above her, tearing at thick, tangled twigs in the brush.

Why couldn't she remember her Jedi calming techniques when she needed them? Why hadn't she practiced harder? She closed her eyes, *sensed*, and rolled to one side as the flying monster drove down for another attack.

The sound of dozens of wings overhead prodded her back into motion. She rolled onto her bare hands and knees, scrambled through some low thornbushes, pushed herself to her feet, and kept running.

Sense, she told herself. *Use the Force.*

Suddenly, she changed direction, as if by reflex. She didn't quite know why she had, for she couldn't see where she was going in the thick night, but she knew she was right. Over and over, she dodged grasping talons and the thrust of stinging tails, until she came to a thick stand of Massassi trees. At her noisy approach, a chorus of squawks and scolding chitters erupted from the trees ahead.

Woolamanders—an entire pack, from the sound of them. She had probably disturbed their communal sleep. Perhaps they would be a sufficient distraction.

Tenel Ka crouched low and dove into the shelter of the close-growing trees. Surprisingly, not one of the winged monsters followed. Instead, she heard their cries as they circled above and, deprived of their initial prey, hunted the woolamanders instead. The flying creatures screamed their blood lust, and the voices of the terrified woolamanders became fierce and defiant as the battle raged in the branches far overhead.

Sweat, twigs, leaves, and dirt clung to Tenel Ka's red-gold hair. She shook her head to clear it. She was almost certain that through the racket, she had somehow heard a faint, familiar voice.

"Oh please, *do* be careful. My circuitry is extremely complex and should not under any circumstances be—" The voice cut off a moment later with a tiny wail. Then there was a *thud* as something hard landed beside Tenel Ka's foot.

"Em Teedee, is that you?" she said. She groped around on the ground and picked up the rounded metallic form.

"Oh, Mistress Tenel Ka, it *is* you!" the little droid cried. "I shall be eternally grateful to you for this rescue. Why, you have no idea the ordeal I've been through," he moaned. "The poking, the prodding, the shaking, the tossing. And such a dreadful—"

"My night has been no more enjoyable than yours," Tenel Ka interrupted drily.

"Listen!" Em Teedee said. "Oh, thank goodness! Those dreadful creatures are leaving."

Tenel Ka didn't know whether Em Teedee was referring to the woolamanders or the giant flying reptiles, but she realized that the sounds of the overhead battle were moving farther and farther away through the canopy.

"We must make our escape immediately, Mistress Tenel Ka."

"We can't. We'll have to wait until morning. Can you keep a watch out tonight while I sleep?"

"I'd be delighted to keep a watch for you, Mistress, but *must* we spend the night here?"

"Yes, we must," Tenel Ka snapped, defensive now that the worst danger was over. "I need to wait until daylight so I can climb a tree and find out where we are."

"Oh," said Em Teedee. "But whyever should you want to do something like that?"

Tenel Ka growled, "Because we're lost in the jungle. This is a fact."

"Oh, dear—is *that* all that's bothering you?" Em Teedee said. "Why didn't you say so? After all, I am fluent in six forms of communication *and* I am equipped with all manner of sensors: photo-optical, olfactory, directional, auditory—"

"Directional?" Tenel Ka broke in. "You mean you *know* where we are?"

"Oh, most assuredly, Mistress Tenel Ka. Didn't I just say so?"

She groaned and shook her head. "All right, Em Teedee, let's go. Lead on."

*　　*　　*

Tenel Ka's spirits were brighter than the twin beams that shone from Em Teedee's eyes and lit her way along the forest floor. As annoying as the little droid could be, she was glad of his company. Em Teedee seemed genuinely interested in hearing all that had happened to her since the TIE fighter pilot had tried to capture them that afternoon. In turn, she found herself enjoying his descriptions of the T-23 crash and his adventures with the woolamanders. She wondered what had happened to Lowbacca, and to the twins.

They stopped only a few times, so that she could drink or check the dressing on her minor wounds. Using rudimentary first-aid supplies she kept in her belt, she had bound up the claw scratches on her arm and the gash on her leg. The wounds throbbed and burned, but did not slow her down. She jogged much of the way, and kept to a fast-paced march even when she needed to rest.

The distant white sun of the Yavin system was bright in the morning sky when Tenel Ka and Em Teedee finally broke through the last stand of trees into the cleared landing area. The sun-warmed stone of the Great Temple glowed like a welcome beacon in the distance.

"Oh, we made it!" Em Teedee said joyfully. Tenel Ka looked around and saw in the center of the clearing a ship that she recognized well: the *Millennium Falcon*.

Running toward the modified light freighter at full speed were two Wookiees, one large and one smaller, and Jacen and Jaina's father, Han Solo. She guessed immediately what mission they were on and changed her course toward the *Falcon*, waving and shouting as she ran.

Overhead, she heard the bone-chilling howl of a fast-approaching TIE fighter. She put on another burst of speed toward the ship.

But Solo and the Wookiees did not see her. In their hurry to rescue Jacen and Jaina, the three scrambled up the ramp of the *Falcon*. They must have kept the engines idling to keep them warm, she figured, for she could hear their whine.

Tenel Ka wanted to help rescue the twins; she couldn't let them down again. "Call them, Em Teedee," she said, pouring on a last burst of speed, though her legs already trembled with exhaustion.

Em Teedee mused, "Am I to take it that you wish to communicate with them?"

"This is a fact."

"Certainly, Mistress. I would be delighted, but what shall—"

"Just *do* it!" She gritted her teeth and sprinted as fast as she could.

Suddenly Em Teedee's voice boomed at top volume through the clearing. "Attention, *Millennium Falcon*. Please delay departure momentarily to take on two additional passengers."

Tenel Ka didn't even mind the ringing in her ears when she saw the ramp of the *Millennium Falcon* lower. At full tilt, she ran up the ramp.

"Okay," she gasped, collapsing to the floor in the crew compartment. "Let's go!"

Han Solo and the two Wookiees looked at her in amazement for an instant, but no one needed any further urging. Even as she spoke, the hatches sealed, and with a surge of defiance the *Millennium Falcon* took off.

20

QORL FLEW HIS single fighter at top speed over the thick jungle canopy. The rushing air of Yavin 4 screamed around the TIE fighter's rounded pilot compartment and the rectangular solar arrays. He remembered his days as a trainee. He had been an excellent pilot—one of the best in his squadron—soaring through mock battles and enforcing the Emperor's unbending will.

Air currents buffeted him, and the pilot reveled in the sensation of flight. He had not forgotten, not even after so many years. The vibrating power that pulsed through the fighter's engines, along with a sense of freedom and liberation after so long an exile, buoyed him.

Qorl watched the knotted green crowns of Massassi trees flowing beneath him in the storm of his ship's passage. With his thickly gloved, badly healed arm, he found it difficult to control the Imperial craft—but he was a fighter pilot. He was a *great* pilot. He had managed to land his ship, despite grievous engine damage, under heavy enemy fire. He had survived undetected in hostile territory for two decades.

Now, flying low over the trees to avoid notice from any possible defenses at the Rebel base, Qorl felt his memories, his ingrained skill, come flooding back to him.

The Empire is my family. The Rebels wish to destroy the New Order. The Rebels must be eliminated—ELIMINATED!

His greatest advantage was surprise. This attack would come out of nowhere. The Rebels would be expecting nothing. He would streak in with all weapons blazing. He would level the Rebel base structures, blast them into rubble. He would kill all those who had conspired to blow up the Death Star, who had killed Darth Vader and Grand Moff Tarkin. He, a single soldier, would secure vengeance for the entire Empire.

There! Qorl squinted through the scratched goggles of his blast helmet. Protruding from a clearing in the dense jungle, a towering stone temple rose up—a ziggurat, the squarish pyramid that served as the main structure of the base.

Qorl roared low over the facilities of the old Rebel stronghold. A wide, sluggish river sliced through the jungle near the site of the temples. On the opposite side of the brownish-green current lay other crumbling ruins, but they seemed uninhabited. Then he noticed a large power-generating station next to the towering ziggurat and knew for certain that he had not been wrong: This base was still used as a military installation.

As he brought the TIE fighter in on his first attack run, Qorl saw that the jungle had been cleared to make a large landing area in front of the Great Temple. On the flat field he saw only one ship—disk-shaped, with twin prongs in front.

Qorl didn't immediately recognize the make or model of

the lone ship below. It was some kind of light freighter, not a Rebel X-wing or any of the familiar battleships he had learned about during his rigorous combat training.

On the ground, several people ran toward the ship, sprinting away from the stone pyramid. Scrambling to battle stations perhaps? His lip curled in a snarl. He would take care of them.

He flicked the buttons on his control panel, powering up the TIE fighter's weapons systems. Before he could align the victims in his targeting cross, though, all the small figures below managed to climb aboard the light freighter. Its boarding ramp drew up, preparing for launch.

He dismissed the light freighter as a possible target—for now, at least. It was probable, Qorl realized, that the Rebels kept a large force of more powerful fighters in an underground hangar bay. If so, his first task was to prevent those crafts from launching—even if only by damaging the doors enough to keep the ships trapped inside.

He decided his best strategy would be to continue his straight-line course and fire with full-power laser cannons on the main structure of the Great Temple. He would blow the entire building to rubble—perhaps causing it to collapse internally, thus eliminating the Rebels and destroying all their equipment inside.

Then he could swoop around and take care of the single light freighter, even if it managed to get up off the ground. His third target would be the power-generating station.

With the Rebels completely paralyzed by his lightning attack, he would swing back for the last time. He would charge up his laser cannons again and go for the kill, mopping up anything he had missed the first time.

From start to finish, it would take only a few minutes to bring the Rebels to their knees.

Qorl centered the Great Temple in his targeting cross, aiming at the apex of the squared-off pyramid, with its thin banks of skylights and ancient vine-covered sculptures. The TIE fighter zoomed in.

He grasped the firing stick with his good hand. At exactly the right moment he depressed the firing buttons, letting an expression of anticipation light his normally emotionless face.

Nothing.

He squeezed the button again and again—*and nothing happened!* The weapons systems did not respond.

Qorl flicked on the backups as he spun the TIE fighter in the air, barreling down again on his target. Over and over he tried to fire, but the laser cannons were completely dead. His eyes swept the diagnostic panels, but all the readings seemed normal.

With his gloved hand Qorl pounded on the instrumentation panel, as if that would fix anything—and with old Imperial equipment, sometimes it did. But not this time.

He frantically worked with the controls, digging under the panels to restart the weapons systems even as he flew on. He reached down and felt around his seat, searching for anything he could use to jump-start the malfunctioning laser cannons.

Qorl caught the glimmer out of the corner of his eye, reflected against the dark goggles of his helmet. He glanced down and noticed something *moving* . . . sinuous, barely seen, glittering and transparent.

The crystal snake reared up right beside him, its triangular head showing up as a faint rainbow in the glow from the cockpit lights. Qorl, who had seen plenty of the reptilian creatures during his exile on Yavin 4, spotted it immediately and reacted.

He let out a startled cry and tried to brush the snake away. It lunged and bit down as he reached out with his crippled arm to block it. The crystal snake dug its spearlike fangs into the thick leather of Qorl's gauntlet, but was unable to penetrate all the way to his skin.

As he flung his hand back and forth, Qorl could feel the heavy weight of the crystal snake writhing, snapping, though he could see almost nothing at all.

He let the TIE fighter fly itself as he reached with his good hand to grab the long body of the serpent just behind its head. He ripped the fangs free and stuffed the thrashing creature into the cockpit jettison chute. With a cry of disgust he ejected the snake into the air, where it fell toward the treetops of the jungle moon, disappearing instantly in the bright sunlight.

He wrestled for control of his weaponless vessel. The Jedi twins must have done something in their repairs.

He managed to stabilize his erratic flight—but before he could decide on a new course, bright streaks from an enemy laser cannon sizzled through the air, bolts of energy that ionized the atmosphere around Qorl's TIE fighter.

He yanked at the control stick with his good arm, and his fighter lurched into a starboard spin. The Rebel light freighter had taken to the air and was flying after Qorl like a furious bird of prey. And *its* weapons worked just fine.

Qorl punched in full power to the twin ion engines and decided that his only chance for now was to try to escape.

In the heart of the jungle, next to Qorl's primitive dwelling, Jacen and Jaina sat beside each other, deep in concentration. They reached out with the Force to see what was going on back at the Jedi academy. Their powers were only sufficient to bring them shadowy images, distant echoes of thoughts . . . but it was enough.

"He didn't know I never fixed the weapons systems . . . but then, he never asked. I managed to jury-rig the readouts so they would look normal," Jaina said at last. "He can fly, but his ship is defenseless."

"Yes, and I think the crystal snake must have distracted Qorl somehow," Jacen said. "I wonder what happened to it." They smiled at each other.

"I suppose our next step," Jacen said, squinting up at the morning light that filtered through the trees, "is to figure out how to get back home."

Jaina pushed a tangle of her usually straight brown hair back from her face and took a deep breath. "Agreed," she said, then clapped her hands and rubbed them together. "So what are we waiting for?"

"HANG ON!" HAN Solo yelled.

As the *Millennium Falcon* lifted off from the trampled landing area in front of the ancient temple, Tenel Ka struggled to a seat beside Lowbacca and strapped herself in.

"That TIE fighter's coming in, and it looks mean," Han said as he and his Wookiee copilot frantically set switches and calibrated the weapons targeting systems. "Hope Tionne managed to get all the Jedi trainees to safety."

Their seats tilted back as the *Falcon* angled up into the air, its sublight thrusters roaring behind it. The Imperial TIE fighter broke through the sky overhead like a yowling battering ram.

Han Solo looked grim as he gripped the controls. His jaw was set, his shoulders rigid. At the moment he had no way of knowing whether his children were safe, or if this Imperial enemy had killed them both, just as the pilot had tried to blast Lowbacca and Tenel Ka.

Tenel Ka wished she could give him some reassurance, but she knew nothing herself. Still panting with exhaustion from her long run through the jungle, she adjusted the restraints across the reptilian armor on her chest. At her side Em Teedee's thin, warbly voice spoke up. "I beg your pardon, Mistress Tenel Ka, but I can't see a thing! Your crash webbing has blocked my optical sensors."

When Tenel Ka freed the flat, silvery device from its restraints, Em Teedee let out what sounded like a sigh of relief. "Ah, yes, much better. Now I can see perfectly. Oh, dear!" he said in alarm. "I didn't want you to rescue me from that dreadful jungle just so we could all be blown up chasing that TIE fighter."

Lowbacca grunted and looked over at the small translating droid with obvious surprise and relief.

"This is yours, Lowbacca," Tenel Ka said. "I found it in the jungle." She handed Em Teedee to the young Wookiee, who accepted the little droid gratefully, bleating his thanks.

Han Solo spun the *Falcon* around in a tight arc, its engines rumbling behind them as they pursued the TIE fighter. "He's coming in on an attack run," Han said. "But he's not firing his weapons for some reason."

Through the cockpit windows, Tenel Ka watched as the TIE fighter she had helped to repair zoomed low over the Great Temple, seemingly bent on destruction—but its laser cannons did not fire.

"I'm going to get his attention, Chewie," Han said. "You open a comm channel. That guy did something to my kids— and I want to find out where they are."

Chewbacca growled and reached with his long hairy arm to toggle a few switches on the *Millennium Falcon's* control panel.

Han fired two warning shots. Bolts of brilliant light streaked past the squarish planar wings of the Imperial craft—bracketing it, but doing no damage.

"Attention, TIE pilot," Han said. "You're going nowhere if I don't find out where . . ." He paused. ". . . the two young Jedi Knights are. You're in the middle of my targeting cross, so your choices are simple: surrender, or we blow you out of the sky."

A gruff voice came back over the comm systems. "Surrender is betrayal," the pilot said, then broke the connection.

The TIE fighter zoomed upward on an impossibly steep trajectory, climbing into the air above the dense green treetops. Then the Imperial ship wheeled about in an evasive maneuver.

"All right," Han said, his anger evident. "This old ship has taken on plenty of TIE fighters in its day. We can take on one more. Punch it, Chewie."

The *Falcon* lunged forward in another burst of speed as Chewbacca worked the controls.

Em Teedee wailed, "Oh, no! I can't watch. Somebody cover my optical sensors."

Han spared a second to glance back at the droid, and found Lowbacca cradling Em Teedee in his lap. "Just like having See-Threepio with us again. I think we may have to adjust that programming."

"Oh, dear," Em Teedee said.

In the back Lowbacca grumbled a suggestion, which his uncle seconded loudly.

"Good idea," Han said. "Let's try the tractor beam first. Maybe—just maybe—we can bring that ship to the ground without destroying it. That way we can get some information. If we say 'Please,' he might be a little more cooperative."

Chewbacca worked the *Falcon*'s tractor beam generator, casting out the invisible beam like a force-field net to grab the Imperial ship.

The TIE fighter lurched and jerked to one side as the tractor beam snagged a partial hold—but the pilot alternated bursts from his twin ion engines and tore free, spinning upward in a tight corkscrew that made Han whistle with reluctant admiration.

"This guy's good," he said. "After him, Chewie! Full speed."

The TIE fighter, as if seeing it as his one chance for escape, darted back down toward the rough greenery of Massassi trees. It dodged jagged branches that thrust up like blackened witches' fingers where lightning and forest fires had burned the jungle, dipped down to trace the winding courses of rivers, and streaked over lush canyons—all with the *Millennium Falcon* following in hot pursuit.

If it were only a matter of speed, the *Falcon*'s more powerful engines could have outrun the TIE fighter and brought it down, but the small ship's maneuverability among the dangerous treetops gave the Imperial pilot a definite advantage.

Han Solo, however, had greater determination. "What have you done with my kids?" he yelled into the comm channel.

It was obvious he expected no answer, but to everyone's surprise, the pilot spoke back in a calculating voice. "They are your children, pilot? They were alive when I left them—but the jungle is a dangerous place. There's no telling if they will last long enough for you to rescue them."

Tenel Ka marveled at the brilliant strategy. "It's a trick," she said. "He wants you to break off the pursuit."

"I know," Han said, glancing back at her. His face was ashen. "But what if it's true?"

The TIE pilot used Han's brief hesitation to take his last best chance for escape: arrowing upward and bolting straight toward space. The twin ion engines roared through the thinning atmosphere.

Chewbacca yelped in reaction. Without waiting for Han to give the order, the Wookiee copilot pushed the accelerators to maximum. The *Falcon*, white heat rippling from its rear sublight engines, zoomed after the TIE fighter.

The acceleration slammed Tenel Ka back against her seat, and she grimaced as the tug of additional gravities stretched her skin. She squeezed her eyes shut. Beside her, Lowbacca grunted with the strain, but Han and Chewie seemed accustomed to putting such stress on their bodies.

The bright, milky-blue sky grew darker, turning a deep purplish color around them as they soared upward. The stars shone out as the *Falcon* pulled into the night of space. The blurry sphere of the great orange gas giant Yavin filled most of their cockpit windows.

The TIE fighter zigzagged to throw off pursuit, shifting course at random intervals and burning a great deal of energy.

"Maybe we can still wound his ship and pull him in," Han said, his voice strained.

Chewbacca piloted the *Falcon* as Han controlled the weapons systems. "I can't get a target lock," Han said.

The TIE fighter zoomed above the green jewel of the jungle moon.

Arching around in a tight orbit, the *Falcon* clung to it, following closely. Han fired repeatedly with his laser cannons—but the scarlet bolts missed.

Han pounded his fist on the control panel. "Hold still for a minute!" he shouted.

Then, as if obliging, the TIE fighter paused in the middle of the weapons system's aim-point grid. The target lock flashed brightly, and Han gave a whoop of excitement.

"Gotcha!" he said, and depressed both sets of firing studs.

But at the last possible instant, the lone TIE fighter shot

forward with a blaze of astonishing speed, becoming a molten metal point of light. It dwindled in the sudden distance, screaming forward with instant lightspeed—and plunged into hyperspace with a silent bang.

"It's not my fault," Han Solo said, gaping at the vanished target. He let his shaking hands fall away from the firing controls. "A TIE fighter doesn't have lightspeed engines! It's a short-range ship."

Lowbacca grumbled an explanation, and Tenel Ka nodded.

"Jaina did *what*?" Han said in disbelief. "But that hyperdrive was for her to tinker with, not to install. She's got a lot of explaining to do when I see her—" He broke off, suddenly realizing where the twins were.

"Forget the TIE fighter. Let's go get the twins!" he said.

He changed the *Falcon*'s course and arrowed straight back down to the emerald-green sphere of the jungle moon of Yavin.

22

BACK AT THE tiny jungle clearing where the wreck of the TIE fighter had rested for two decades, Jacen and Jaina decided that their best chance for rescue lay in climbing to the treetops—no matter how difficult it might be. From that height, they could spot any incoming ships and set up some sort of signal.

Before leaving, they scrounged at the crash site and at Qorl's old encampment for whatever they could possibly find useful, then stuffed it in their packs. Their Jedi training had taught them to be resourceful.

Remembering how they had used the Force to help them scale the Great Temple with Tenel Ka, the twins found a Massassi tree with plenty of densely interwoven branches and hanging vines. They stared upward, then at each other, before beginning the long, sweaty climb. Jacen and Jaina were scratched up and aching and smeared with forest debris by the time they made it to the top—but to their surprise, they felt invigorated by their accomplishment.

Up in the canopy in a thick nest of tangled branches, they tried to light a leafy fire to send a beacon of smoke into the sky. Jacen collected leaves and twigs and piled them onto a curved piece of plasteel left over from their repairs on the TIE fighter.

Jaina had brought Tenel Ka's flash heater, but the charge was low. When the finger-sized unit sputtered and flashed, sending out a few last sparks, she took the back panel off and used her multitool to tinker with the circuits. By pumping up the power output, she produced one last flash that set the pile of fresh branches on fire.

The lush green leaves burned slowly, and the fire would not gain enough heat to become a bright blaze. But, as they had hoped, a satisfying gray-blue smoke curled upward, a clear signal for anyone who was looking.

Even so, they couldn't be certain that anyone would know where to look. Unless Lowbacca or Tenel Ka had managed to get back to the academy, no one would have any idea where to begin a search.

"Guess it might be a good idea next time if we let someone know where we're going and what we're doing, huh?" Jaina said, staring up at the discouragingly empty blueness.

"Probably," Jacen agreed, settling himself beside her on the branches. Sweat ran down his face as he rested his chin on his grimy hands. "Want to hear another joke?"

"No," Jaina answered firmly. She wiped her damp forehead with the sleeve of her now-ragged jumpsuit, and continued scanning the skies. She shifted beside him, feeling the breeze and listening to the whisper of millions of leaves.

Jacen fed more leaves to the fire.

Suddenly, Jaina sat up straight. "Look!" she said, pointing up. A white starpoint grew brighter, glittering silver. Ripples of sound from a sonic boom echoed like thunder across the sky of Yavin 4. "It's a ship."

Jacen closed his liquid-brown eyes and smiled. Then the

twins blinked and looked at each other. "The *Falcon*," they said in unison.

"Can Dad sense us?" Jacen asked.

"I don't think so," Jaina said. "At least not with the Force. But wait . . ." She closed her eyes again, reaching out with what she knew of Jedi powers. "Lowie's with him!"

"And Tenel Ka, too," Jacen said. "They're all right!"

Jaina laughed with relief. "Did you expect any less from a young Jedi Knight?"

The *Falcon* must have spotted their smoke, and now headed toward them. High in the branches, the twins stood and waved. As it approached, the blaster-scarred light freighter seemed the most beautiful machine they had ever seen.

The big ship hovered over them with a gust of its repulsor-lifts. Branches blew away beneath them, but Jacen and Jaina held their positions, reaching upward as the bottom access hatch of the *Falcon* popped open.

Chewbacca's hairy arm dangled down, grabbing Jacen's hands and pulling him up into the ship as if he were a piece of lightweight luggage. A moment later, Lowie's ginger-furred arms reached out to help Jaina up.

Han scrambled from the cockpit, rushing to scoop up both of his children in a big hug. "You're alive—you're not hurt!" he said, looking them over with anxious relief. "Sorry I'm late."

"It's all right," Jacen answered. "We knew you'd come."

Tenel Ka and Lowie also greeted the twins, with hugs all around and enthusiastic thumps on the back.

"Oh, hooray!" Em Teedee's tinny voice chimed in. "This *is* cause for a celebration."

"Let's get back to the Jedi academy first; I'm sure everyone's been worried about us," Han said. "I think we need to tell about a few adventures."

A few days later, after the *Falcon* carried the T-23 back from where it had crashed in the treetops, Lowbacca and Jaina worked in the shadow-draped courtyard of the Great Temple, tinkering with the damaged skyhopper. Jaina poked her grease-smeared face up out of the engine compartment and looked around.

She watched as Jacen scurried across the landing field out front, low to the ground, trying to catch an eight-legged lizard crab he wanted to add to his collection. Leaves and broken blades of grass were tangled in his tousled hair, as usual. The creature darted left and right, trying to find a hiding place among the close-cropped weeds of the landing field.

Spying a large shady spot, the lizard crab scuttled for shelter out of reach under the T-23. Jaina giggled as Jacen pulled up short just in time to keep from banging his head against the skyhopper's hull.

With a shrug, he leaned against the craft and brushed the dirt from his jumpsuit. "Oh well," he said, grinning. "Next time."

"As long as you're just standing there, could you please hand me a hydrospanner?" Jaina said.

Jacen bent and rummaged in the tool kit on the grass, then handed the tool up.

"You concentrate on the onboard computer systems, Lowie," Jaina said, discussing repair strategies. "That's what you're best at." At the Wookiee's growl of agreement, she added, "Don't worry about these engines. I'll have them running again in no time."

"Mind if I join you?" a calm voice said from behind her.

"Uncle Luke!" Jaina cried, jumping up and turning toward him. "When did you get back?"

"Only this morning," Luke Skywalker said, looking admiringly at the vehicle. "Could you use any help? I'm pretty good with these little air speeders, you know." He smiled as if savoring a fond memory. "I had a ship a little like this once . . . my own T-16 skyhopper when I was growing up on—"

Just then, Tenel Ka emerged from the large lower door of the Great Temple. The cool underlevels had once stored the Rebel base's X-wing fighters.

"Excuse me for a moment," Luke said, and turned to raise his hand in a warm greeting. He strode over to Tenel Ka and spoke to her for a long while as if she were an old friend. Being with the great Jedi Master caused the young girl from Dathomir to look uncharacteristically intimidated.

"Well, what are we waiting for?" Jaina asked the others. She opened an inner access panel with her multitool and began running diagnostics on the T-23's engines. Jacen surreptitiously scanned the cropped grass and weeds, looking for another specimen to catch.

Lowbacca snared a tangle of wires from the cockpit control panels and began sorting them by color and function. He murmured to himself as he worked, and Jacen could hear Em Teedee start to speak. At a *clunk* of something metal hitting the floor plates, Jacen stuck his head into the T-23. Lowbacca had accidentally dropped Em Teedee from his belt again.

The miniature translating droid began scolding the young Wookiee at high volume. "Really, Master Lowbacca, do try to be careful! You've dropped me again, and that's simply careless. How would you like it if *your* head detached and kept falling on the ground? I am an extremely valuable piece of equipment and you ought to take better care of me. If my circuits become damaged I won't be able to translate, and then where will you be? I can't believe—"

With a grunt, Lowbacca switched off Em Teedee, and then made a satisfied sound.

Jacen looked up to see Jaina staring at the deep blue sky. He followed her gaze and knew exactly what she was thinking. "Do you suppose Qorl ever made it back home?"

"If he does, I wonder if he'll find what he expects when he gets there," she answered. "He would have been better off staying with us."

When they noticed Luke Skywalker and Tenel Ka strolling back toward the T-23, Lowie and Jaina climbed out of the dismantled cockpit to stand next to Jacen.

Luke looked at the battered air speeder and ran his fingertips over its smooth hull. "Back on Tatooine I used to roar through Beggar's Canyon in my own T-16, chasing down womp rats."

Jacen and Jaina looked at their uncle, amazed and unable

to imagine the introspective Jedi Master as a hotshot daredevil pilot.

Luke's lips curved in a wistful smile. "That was a whole different life from now." He turned to the young Jedi Knights. "When you get this thing fixed, I'd like to go for a ride with you. If that's all right."

They looked at him in astonishment. Lowie muttered something indecipherable and cleared his throat nervously.

"I hope you're fitting in here, Lowbacca," Luke said, nodding toward the young Wookiee. "I know it's difficult to go away from home and stay in a strange place, but I see you've made some new friends."

He looked at the others. "I'm proud of you all," Luke said. "You did a fine job under very trying circumstances, even when I wasn't here to guide you. You have a lot of potential—but becoming a Jedi Knight takes a great deal of hard work and practice."

The students nodded. "This is a fact," Tenel Ka said solemnly.

"You're young, and there are many things you could do with your lives," Luke said. "Are you certain you still want to become Jedi Knights?"

Their enthusiastic shouts rang out in unison. Lowbacca's loud bellow was so emphatic that even with Em Teedee switched off, none of the others needed a translation.

Shadow Academy

To our brothers and sisters—

Mark—who has been my hero since childhood. A true Jedi Knight, always ready to race to the rescue

Cindy—who always watched out for me. You showed me that effort and determination will get you what wishing and waiting will not

Diane—who broadened my horizons. Thanks for forcing me to watch every monster-and-hero movie ever made

Scott—who tolerated all the books I read to him. Thanks for telling me in May of 1977 that there was a movie I just had to go see—*Star Wars*

Rebecca Moesta

and *Laura*—for never fighting with me, always understanding (just kidding!), and providing a wealth of experiences for me to draw upon in my writing

Kevin J. Anderson

ACKNOWLEDGMENTS

We would like to thank Lil Mitchell for her tireless typing and for urging us to bring her each chapter faster and faster, Dave Wolverton for his input on Dathomir, Lucy Wilson and Sue Rostoni at Lucasfilm for their unwavering support, Ginjer Buchanan and Lou Aronica at Berkley for their continuing enthusiasm, Jonathan MacGregor Cowan for being our test audience . . . and Skip Shayotovich, Roland Zarate, Gregory McNamee, and the entire *Star Wars* ImagiNet Echo computer bulletin board for helping out with the jokes.

1

JACEN GRASPED THE lightsaber, feeling its comforting weight against his sweaty palms. His scalp tingled beneath its unruly tangle of brown curls as he sensed the approach of his enemy. Closer, closer . . . He drew in a slow breath and reached with one finger that trembled ever so slightly to press the button on the handle.

With a buzzing hiss, the cold metal handle sprang to life, transforming into a sword of glowing energy. The deadly lightsaber pulsed and vibrated in his hands like a living thing.

With a mixture of fear and excitement, Jacen's wiry frame tensed for the attack. His liquid-brown eyes fluttered shut for a moment as he visualized his opponent.

Without warning, he heard the hum of a lightsaber slice down from above.

Jacen whirled just in time and caught the blow with his own lightsaber. The deep red of his opponent's weapon throbbed with power, filling his vision as the two glowing blades warred for dominance.

Jacen knew he was far outmatched in size and strength, that he would need all of his wits to get out of this encounter alive. His arms ached with the strain of holding off the blow, so he took advantage of his smaller size, spinning under his opponent's arm and dancing out of reach.

The attacker advanced toward him, but Jacen knew better than to let him get that close again. The ruby glow flashed toward him, and he was ready. He parried the blow and then swept sideways with his own blade before dodging backward and blocking the next thrust.

Attack and counterattack. Thrust. Parry. Block. Light-sabers sizzled and hissed as they clashed again and again.

Though the room was cool and dank, perspiration ran down Jacen's face and into his eyes, nearly blinding him. He saw the arc of red light barely in time and ducked to avoid it. A cocky lopsided grin sprang to his lips, and he realized he was enjoying himself. Stone chips flew around him as the deadly ruby blade gouged the low ceiling just over his head.

Jacen's grin faded as he tried to take a step backward and felt cold stone blocks press into his shoulder blades. He parried another thrust, sprang sideways, and fetched up against another stone wall.

He was cornered. An icy fist of fear clenched his stomach, and Jacen dropped to one knee, flinging up his blade to ward off the next blow. A sound like thunder echoed through the chamber. . . .

Jacen opened his eyes and looked up to see his uncle Luke standing in the doorway, clearing his throat. Startled, Jacen fumbled to turn off the lightsaber and accidentally dropped the extinguished handle to the flagstones with a clatter.

The sandy-haired, black-robed Jedi Master strode into the private room that served as both his office and his meditation chamber at the Jedi academy. He held his hand out toward the lightsaber, and the weapon sprang to his palm as if magnetized.

Jacen gulped as Master Luke Skywalker fixed him with a solemn gaze. "I'm sorry Uncle Luke," Jacen said, his words coming out in a tumbling rush. "I came here to ask you for your help, and when you weren't here I decided to wait, and then I saw your lightsaber just lying on your desk, and I know you said I'm not ready yet, but I didn't see how it could hurt to just practice a little. So I picked it up, and I guess I just got carried away and—"

Luke held up one hand, palm outward, as if to forestall further explanation. "The weapon of the Jedi shouldn't be taken up lightly," he said.

Jacen felt his cheeks flush at the gentle rebuke. "But I *know* I could learn to use a lightsaber," he said, defensive. "I'm old enough, and I'm tall enough, and I've been practicing in my room with a piece of pipe I got from Jaina—I'm sure I could do it."

Luke seemed to consider this for a moment before shaking his head slowly. "There'll be time enough for that when you are ready."

"But I'm ready *now*," Jacen protested.

"Not yet," Luke said, smiling sadly. "The time will come soon enough."

Jacen groaned with impatience. It was always *Later*, always *Some other time*, always *Maybe when you're older.* He sighed. "You're the teacher. I'm the student, so I have to listen, I guess."

Luke smiled and shook his head. "Ah. Be careful—don't assume a teacher is always right, without question. You have to think for yourself. Sometimes we teachers make mistakes, too. But in this case, I am right: You're not yet ready for a lightsaber.

"Believe me, I know what it's like to wait," Luke continued. "But patience can be as strong an ally as any weapon." Then his eyes twinkled. "Don't you have more important things to be worrying about right now than imaginary lightsaber battles—like getting ready for your trip? Don't your pets need to be fed?"

"I'm all packed, and I'll feed the animals just before we leave," Jacen said, thinking of the menagerie of pets he had collected since coming to the jungle moon. "But the trip *is* what I came here to talk to you about."

Luke raised his eyebrows. "Yes?"

"I—I was hoping you could talk to Tenel Ka and convince her to come with us to see Lando Calrissian's mining station."

Luke's brows drew together, and he chose his words carefully. "Why is it important to change her mind?"

"Because Jaina and Lowbacca and I are all going," Jacen said, "and . . . and it just won't be the same without her," he finished lamely.

Luke's face relaxed, and his eyes sparkled with humor. "It's not so easy to change the mind of a Force-wielding warrior from Dathomir, you know," he said.

"But it doesn't make sense that she wants to stay behind,"

Jacen exclaimed. "She made up some dumb excuse that it would be boring—said she was sure Corusca gems weren't any more beautiful than rainbow gems from Gallinore, and she's seen plenty of those. But she didn't *sound* bored; she sounded worried or nervous.

"We must think for ourselves," Luke said, "and sometimes that means we have to make difficult or unpopular decisions." Luke put an arm around Jacen's shoulders and led him toward the door. "Go feed your pets now. Have a safe journey to GemDiver Station—and rest assured, Tenel Ka has good reasons"

Tenel Ka woke with a start, shivering and drenched with perspiration in the cool, stone-walled chamber. Sunset-copper hair hung across her vision in tangles that had once been orderly braids. Her bedsheets were twisted about her legs as if she had been running in her sleep.

Then she remembered the dream. She *had* been running. Running from black-cloaked shadowy figures with purple-splotched faces. Muddled memories of stories her mother had told her as a child swirled through her sleep-fogged brain. She had never seen those terrifying forms before, but she knew what they were—witches from Dathomir who had drawn on the dark side of the Force to work all manner of evil.

The Nightsisters.

But the last of the Nightsisters had been destroyed or disbanded long before Tenel Ka had even been born. Why should she dream of them now? The only Force-wielders left on Dathomir used the powers of the light side.

Why these nightmares? Why now?

She squeezed her eyes shut and flopped back on her bed with a grunt as she realized what day it was. This was the day that her grandmother, Matriarch of the Hapan Royal Household, was sending an ambassador to visit Tenel Ka, heir to the Royal Throne of Hapes. And she didn't want her friends to know she was a princess. . . .

Ambassador Yfra. Tenel Ka shuddered as she thought of her iron-willed grandmother and her ambassadors, women who would lie or even kill to preserve their power—although her grandmother no longer ruled Hapes. Tenel Ka shook her head in wry amusement. The impending visit must be why she had dreamt of the Nightsisters.

Although the inhabitants of her mother's primitive planet of Dathomir and her father's plush homeworld of Hapes were light-years apart, the parallels between the Hapan politicians and the Nightsisters of Dathomir were obvious: All were power-hungry women who would stop at nothing to keep the power they craved.

Tenel Ka levered herself into a sitting position. She did not relish the idea of meeting with Ambassador Yfra. In fact, the only positive thought she could muster about it was that her friends would not be here to observe it. At least Jacen, Jaina, and Lowbacca would be far away on Lando Calrissian's GemDiver Station before the ambassador ever arrived. They would not be here to wonder why their friend, who claimed to be a simple warrior from Dathomir, was being visited by a royal ambassador from the House of Hapes. And Tenel Ka was not ready yet to explain that to them.

Well, she couldn't stay in bed any longer. She would have to get up and face whatever the day had to offer her. The meeting was unavoidable. "This," she muttered, flinging aside the covers and standing, "is a fact."

Jaina and Lowbacca sat in the center of Jaina's student quarters surrounded by a holographic map of the Yavin system.

"That ought to do it," she said. Her straight shoulder-length hair swung forward like a curtain, partially veiling her face, as she hunched over to scrutinize the input pad for her holoprojector. She had built the projector herself, piecing it together from her private stock of used electronic modules, components, cables, and other odds and ends that she kept neatly organized in a bank of bins and drawers that filled one wall of her quarters.

"Pretty impressive, huh, Lowie?" Jaina asked, flashing a lopsided grin at the ginger-furred young Wookiee. She pointed at the luminescent sphere drifting above their heads that represented the gas-giant planet of Yavin.

Lowbacca pointed to the image of a small green moon that hovered just above his left shoulder, in orbit around the big orange planet. He gave an interrogative growl.

"Ahem," the miniature translator droid Em Teedee said from the clip on Lowie's belt, as if clearing its throat. Em Teedee was roughly oval in shape, rounded in the front and flat on the back, with irregularly spaced optical sensors and a wide speaker grill at the center. "Master Lowbacca wishes to know," the miniature droid went on, "if the sphere he indicated represents the moon Yavin 4, where we are now."

"Right," said Jaina. "The gas planet Yavin has more than a dozen moons, but I haven't managed to program them all in yet. What I mainly wanted to see," she continued, "was the trajectory we're going to follow when Lando takes us to his gem-mining station in the upper atmosphere of Yavin."

Lowie growled a comment, and Jaina waited impatiently while the prissy translator droid interpreted for her.

"Of course it's a *bit* dangerous," she responded, rolling her brown eyes in exasperation, "but not much. And this is too good an opportunity to pass up. Lando's going to let us help with some of the mining operations, not just watch," Jaina said, pointing to a spot just above the glowing surface of Yavin.

Lowbacca reached for the holoprojector's input pad and pressed a few buttons. In a moment a tiny metallic-looking object appeared near the surface: GemDiver Station.

"Show-off," Jaina said, chuckling at the speed with which Lowie had programmed the holo map. "Tell you what, from now on I build 'em, you program 'em—fair enough?"

Lowie pretended to preen, rumbling his agreement as he smoothed his hand along the black streak that ran through his fur from his forehead down his back.

Just then Jacen bounded through the door. "They're here," he said breathlessly. "I mean *almost* here. They're on approach. I was in the control room, and I heard that the *Lady Luck* was coming in." Twin pairs of eyes—each the color of Corellian brandy—met in a mixture of excitement and anticipation.

"Well, then," Jaina said. "what are we waiting for?"

* * *

Jaina watched with admiration as Lando Calrissian strode down the ramp of the *Lady Luck*, an emerald-green cape billowing out behind him and a broad smile on his dark, handsome face. His frequent companion, the bald cyborg assistant Lobot, followed him down the gangplank and stood stiffly at his side.

Lando greeted Jaina with a gallant kiss on the hand before turning with a formal bow to her twin brother Jacen and Lowie. Next, he clapped the shoulder of Luke Skywalker, who had come to meet the *Lady Luck*, his barrel-shaped droid Artoo-Detoo following close behind him.

"Take good care of them, Lando," Luke said. "No unnecessary risks, okay?" Artoo added a few beeps and whistles of his own.

Lando looked at Luke, pretending to take offense. "Hey, you know I wouldn't let these kids do anything I didn't think was a safe bet."

Luke grinned and gave Lando's shoulder an affectionate slap. "That's what I'm afraid of."

"You're just worried that once they see my GemDiver Station they'll be so impressed they won't want to come back to your Jedi academy," Lando joked.

Then, with a flourish of his cape, Lando Calrissian motioned Lowie and Jacen up the ramp. He turned to Jaina. "And what can I do to make this field trip more interesting and rewarding for you, young lady?" he asked, offering her his arm to escort her into the ship.

"The first thing you can do," she said, accepting his arm with an enthusiastic smile, "is tell me all about the *Lady Luck*'s engines. . . ."

THE *LADY LUCK* left the jewel-green jungle moon behind
as Lando Calrissian and his trusted companion Lobot piloted
them across space toward the gaseous ball of Yavin.

"You kids should enjoy this," Lando said. "I don't think
you've seen anything quite like Corusca mining before."

As the *Lady Luck* approached the giant planet, the orbiting industrial station came into view. Lando's Corusca-
mining facility, GemDiver Station, was a symphony of
running lights and transmitting grids surrounded by dozens
of automated defensive satellites. The security satellites
homed in on the *Lady Luck*, powering up weapons as the ship
approached. But when Lando keyed in an access authorization code, the satellites acknowledged his signal, then turned
back to their robotic perimeter search for intruders and pirates.

"Can't have too much security" he said, "not when you're
dealing with something as valuable as these Corusca gems."

Lobot, the bald, computer-enhanced human, continued his
cool surveillance of the controls. Lights on the mechanical
apparatus implanted on the back of Lobot's skull flashed and
blinked as he studied the guidance grid and compass. Piloting smoothly, Lobot brought the *Lady Luck* into the main
docking bay on GemDiver Station.

"I'm glad Luke let you come up here," Lando said, glancing back at Jacen, Jaina, and Lowie. "You can't learn everything about the universe just by sitting in the jungle and
lifting rocks off the ground with your mind." He flashed a
grin. "You need to broaden your horizons—learn about the
way commerce works in the New Republic. That'll give you
some useful knowledge, in case your lightsabers ever fail."

"We don't have lightsabers yet," Jacen said dejectedly.

"Then you might as well learn something useful in the
meantime," Lando answered. Seeing Jacen's frustration, he
added, "You know, your uncle Luke is concerned about your
safety. He can be pretty cautious, but I trust his judgment.

Don't worry, you'll get that lightsaber eventually. I bet if you just relax and stop thinking about it, you'll be practicing with a lightsaber before you know it." That said, he helped Lobot finish the landing check as the *Lady Luck* settled down in the empty bay.

Stepping out of the ship, Lando beamed and showed off his station, making enthusiastic gestures. With Lobot trailing silently behind, Lando led the three young Jedi Knights to a transparisteel viewing window that looked out at the tempestuous orangish soup of the gas giant.

Jacen pressed close to the broad window, peering down at the knotted storm systems that chained through the clouds. From this distance Yavin looked deceptively gentle in pastel yellows and whites and oranges. But he knew that even in the upper atmosphere, the winds had crushing strength, and the pressure farther down was enough to squash a ship down to a fistful of atoms.

Beside him, Jaina studied the weather patterns analytically. Lowie stood between the twins, his lanky form towering over them. He growled with amazement.

"I think it's most impressive," Em Teedee said from the clip on Lowie's belt. "And Master Lowbacca thinks so too."

GemDiver Station orbited just at the fringe of Yavin's outer atmosphere. The station's inclined orbit took it high above the planet and then dipped down to graze the gaseous levels so that Lando's Corusca gem miners could delve into the planet's deep, swirling currents.

Lando tapped his fingertip against the transparisteel window. "Far down where the atmosphere ends, the metallic core scrapes against the liquefied air. Pressures are great enough to crush elements together into extremely rare quantum crystals called Corusca gems."

Jacen perked up. "Can we see one?"

Lando thought for a moment, then nodded. "Sure. We've got a shipment ready to go out," he said. "Follow me."

With his emerald cape flowing behind him, Lando strode down the scrubbed-clean corridors. Jacen stared at the metal bulkheads, the chambers, the computer-lined offices.

The walls were smooth plasteel plates painted in soft colors and embroidered with glowing optical tubes in a variety of designs. In the background Jacen heard the faint whispering noises of forests, oceans, rivers. The soothing colors and gentle sounds made GemDiver Station an attractive place, comfortable and pleasant—not at all what he had expected.

As they approached a set of large armored doors, Lando tapped buttons in his wristlink and turned to Lobot. "Request access to security level."

Lobot mumbled something into a microphone at his collar. The sealed metal doors hissed, then slid aside to reveal an airlock chamber, the far side of which was an insulated portal providing access to open space. Four armored, conical projectiles lay on a rack; each module was only about a meter long and bristled with self-targeting lasers.

"These are the automated cargo pods," Lando said. "Because Corusca gems are so valuable, we have to take extra security precautions."

Several multiarmed droids worked busily beside the first cargo pod, an open module padded with thick insulation. The droids' copper exoskeletons gleamed, as if newly polished.

"They're packing up our next shipment. Let's take a look," Lando said.

The companions peered into the small opening of the cargo pod, where a nimble-fingered copper droid had packed four Corusca gems, each no larger than Jacen's thumbnail. Lando reached in and plucked out one of the gems.

The droid flailed its multiple hands in the air. "Excuse me, excuse me!" it said. "Please do not touch the gems. Excuse me!"

"It's all right," Lando said. "It's me, Lando Calrissian."

The copper droid's flailing ceased abruptly. "Oh! Apologies, sir," it said.

Lando shook his head. "I've got to get those optical sensors replaced."

He held the Corusca gem between thumb and forefinger; it glinted like liquid fire in his grasp. It did more than just reflect light from the glow-panels on the ceiling—the Corusca gem seemed to contain its own miniature furnace, its trapped light bouncing around inside the crystalline facets for ages until by sheer probability some of the photons found their way out.

"Corusca gems have been found in no other place in the galaxy," Lando said, "only the core of Yavin. Of course, prospectors keep searching other gas-giant planets, but for now my mining station is where all Corusca gems come from. A long time ago the Empire had a sanctioned station here. It went bankrupt pretty quickly without Imperial price supports, though. Corusca mining is a hazardous job, you know, with a high investment right from the start—but it's really paying off for me."

He let Jacen, Jaina, and Lowie hold the gem and marvel at its beauty. "Corusca gems are the hardest substance known," he said. "They can slice through transparisteel like a laser goes through Sullustan jam."

The nervous packing droid plucked the gem from Lowbacca's hairy hand and replaced it in the cargo pod, packing extra sealant around the stones before it closed the access port. The droid engaged a sequence of controls on the back of the cargo pod, and the bristling spines of self-targeting lasers raised themselves up to their armed position.

"Cargo pod ready for launch," the copper droid said. "Please leave the launching bay."

Lando ushered the three kids out of the room, and the heavy metal doors sealed behind him as the droids scurried about their tasks. "Over here. We can watch through the outer port," he said. "This cargo pod is a hyperspace projectile targeted to my broker on Borgo Prime, who distributes the Corusca gems for a percentage of the profits."

They pressed together at a thick round window that looked away from the planet out into space. As they watched, the cargo pod shot out of the launching bay, then hovered to reorient itself and adjust its coordinates. The bright light of its thrusters traced a line across the blackness of space.

Satellites around GemDiver Station rotated as their sensors tracked the pod, aiming their own weapons; but the cargo pod apparently sent the proper ID signals, and the defensive satellites left it alone. Then, in a blur of motion, the pod streaked forward, flashing into hyperspace with a wealth of Corusca gems in its belly.

"Hey, Lando, can we help you do some of the gem mining?" Jacen asked.

"Yes, we'd like to see how it's done," Jaina added.

"I don't know . . . ," Lando said. "It's tough work, and a little risky."

"So is training to be a Jedi Knight," Jaina pointed out, "as we've already seen. Don't you think learning is worth a bit of risk?"

Lowbacca growled a comment.

"What do you mean you're willing to take the risk?" Em Teedee said. "Dear me, I believe Master Calrissian was actually emphasizing the hazards in the hope that you would *not* want to go."

"Well, we'd like to go anyway," Jacen piped up.

Lando held up a hand, grinning as if he had just thought of something—though Jacen could sense that he had been planning it all along. "Well, maybe it *is* time I got back to doing some real work around here instead of all this management stuff. All right, I'll take you down myself."

To Jacen, the Submersible Mining Environment looked like a large diving bell. Its hull was thickly armored, a dull gray with oily smears of color that reflected weirdly in the lights. The hatch appeared thick and durable enough to withstand turbolaser fire.

"This is called the *Fast Hand*," Lando said, "a little ship we designed exclusively for going to the greatest depths of Yavin 4. It's gone almost all the way to the core, where we can reach the biggest Corusca stones." He ran his fingers over the oily hull plating.

"The *Fast Hand* is covered with a fine skin of quantum armor," Lando said, awe apparent in his voice, "a little something developed by the Empire. But we turned the military applications to our own uses—the ultimate in commercial spin-off technology." Lando sounded as if he were giving a speech to a board of directors, and then he remembered his audience. "Well, never mind. The armor on this baby is strong enough to withstand even the pressures deep in Yavin's core. We'll be lowered down, connected to Gem-Diver Station by an energy tether—like an unbreakable magnetic rope."

"Not even the storms can snap it?" Jaina asked.

Lando spread his hands wide, dismissing her concern. "We might get jostled around a bit, but . . ." He laughed. "The seats are padded. We'll be okay."

Lowbacca stooped, but still banged his head on the low doorway as he climbed into the diving bell. Jacen and Jaina jumped in after him. As Lando followed them into the *Fast Hand*, he pulled the hatch shut.

He rapped his knuckles against the inside wall with a metallic thump. "Safe and sound," he said, then settled into the cushioned seat in front of the piloting controls. Jacen strapped into the copilot's chair beside him, while Jaina and Lowie took the rear seats. Thick, square windows covered the walls and floor, giving them a view no matter which way they looked.

"Oh my, isn't this exciting?" Em Teedee said. Lowie grunted in agreement.

3

LANDO KEYED IN some instructions on the control panel. "I'm telling Lobot we're ready for departure."

Red lights flashed on the bay walls, signaling the *Fast Hand*'s status as it prepared for release into Yavin's atmosphere. Three technicians trotted out of the room, and the airlock doors sealed behind them.

"Hang on," Lando said.

The floor beneath the *Fast Hand* slid away. Jacen's stomach lurched as the armored diving bell fell from GemDiver Station, down into the swirling fury of gases. Lowie yelped in sudden astonishment. Jacen's pulse raced. Jaina gripped the arms of her seat.

The *Fast Hand* hurtled downward, but soon Jacen sensed their descent stabilizing, slowing, becoming more controlled.

"I can feel the energy tether holding us," Jaina said.

Jacen reached out with his Jedi senses and detected a shimmering cool thread that connected them to the orbiting station high above. Eager and interested, he unclasped his crash restraints and looked out the nearest windowport as the roiling clouds rushed closer, slamming toward them.

Jacen saw a fleet of tiny ships like agricultural drones skimming across the tops of the rising gases. The small ships hauled a glowing golden web behind them, like a faint net dragged through the clouds.

"What are those?" Jaina asked, curious as always about how things worked.

"Contractors of mine," Lando said. "Corusca fishermen. They take a fleet of skiffs along the cloud tops, trailing an energy seine behind them. As they fly through the clouds, the energy differential in the net reacts to the presence of tiny Corusca stones. They pick up only smaller stones and Corusca dust. It may not seem like much, but it's still quite valuable and worth the effort.

"I help support their operation, and they give me a percentage of their catch. But the larger Corusca gems are deeper down. The great pressures near the core always made it impossible to mine those big gemstones, but with this new quantum armor, we can take the *Fast Hand* all the way down."

"Well, what are we waiting for?" Jaina asked.

"Right. Let's go," Jacen said, rubbing his hands together. Then he flashed a mischievous grin. "Hey, Lando, I heard two droids talking the other day. The first one said, 'Well, did you beat the Wookiee at sabacc?' and the second one said—"

"—'Yes, but it cost me an arm and a leg,'" Lando finished. "That's an old joke, kid."

Jacen frowned at first, then giggled. "Maybe that's why Tenel Ka didn't laugh at it."

Jaina looked at her brother. "I don't think that's the reason she didn't laugh."

The diving bell continued its descent. Lando plied the controls, unreeling the energy tether. As the dense organic mists and colored aerosols folded around them, the winds became gentle fingers drumming against the walls, growing louder and more insistent.

The storm systems increased in fury. Bolts of blue lightning shot across the murky sky as far as Jacen could see. Static electricity crawled over the outer hull like jagged caterpillars, sparking and snapping against the connecting point of the energy tether.

Lowie uttered a long and concerned-sounding sentence in Wookiee language, and his translator droid piped up. "A good question, Master Lowbacca. What *does* happen if the energy tether is severed? How would we get back?"

"Oh, we've got life-support supplies aboard," Lando said, waving his hand again. "We could survive quite a while down here until a rescue mission was mounted from Gem-Diver Station. We have communications and energy backups—but it won't happen, don't worry"

As if to disagree with him, an unexpected gust of wind slapped them sideways so that Jacen tumbled from his seat. He pulled himself back up and sheepishly refastened his crash webbing.

Suddenly the *Fast Hand* seemed to snap free from its connecting line. They dropped like a cannonball, plunging and plunging for a full ten seconds. Lowie yowled, and Jacen and Jaina cried out. Lando pumped up the energy levels until finally he managed to reconnect the tether.

"See? No problem," he said with a nonchalant grin, but Jacen could see the beads of sweat on Lando's forehead. "You all might want to tighten your crash webbing, though," he said. "These storms make for some hefty turbulence in the lower atmosphere. That's what stirs up the interface level and gives the Corusca gems a nudge. Once we get a little lower, we'll start hunting."

"I'd like to try my hand at it," Jaina said.

"I'll let you each have a turn at the controls, but I should warn you that Corusca gems are very rare, even down here. Don't expect to find anything."

Jacen asked, "If we're at the controls and we find a Corusca gem, can we keep it?"

Lando smiled indulgently. "Well, I suppose . . . but we can't spend a lot of time down here looking for gems."

"Oh, we won't," Jacen said. "But it's still good to have some incentive."

Lando laughed. "Just like your father," he said. Jacen smiled, thinking of all the times Lando Calrissian and Han Solo had worked with each other—or in competition against each other—over the years of their long friendship.

Lando looked at his controls again and opened up more window panels on the floor so they could see the murky gases beneath them, supercharged with energy.

"This is probably good enough," Lando said. "Let's start fishing." He glanced at the chronometer on his wrist. "We really need to head back up soon." He swallowed, and Jacen sensed just how nervous Lando really was to be down this far. Daredevil gem hunters willing to risk their lives for the fabulously expensive Corusca stones usually did all the deep dives.

The *Fast Hand* had gone so far into the planetary atmosphere that by now the winds were dark around them, so dense that even light from Yavin's sun could not penetrate. Lando clicked on the diving bell's spotlights, and cones of creamy light struggled against the battering storms and whirling gases.

"I'm going to deploy our trolling cables," Lando said. "They're electromagnetic ropes that dangle down to catch flying Corusca gems whipped up by the storms. You can each have only a few minutes, because we need to get back up to the station. These storm systems are getting worse."

The storms hadn't seemed to be getting worse at all to Jacen; they had been bad enough to begin with. But the tension apparent on Lando's face made Jacen want to end their expedition quickly as well.

"Lowbacca, why don't you try first?" Lando suggested. "Come up front and take the controls."

The young Wookiee crouched in a seat that was far too small for him and rested his hands on the multiple joysticks of the controls. He directed the dangling, sizzling energy cables that trailed out like magnetic tentacles through the stormy atmosphere.

Jacen unbuckled his crash webbing again and crawled along the floor to peer though the square portholes. He could see the yellow magnetic whips that extended from the *Fast Hand* raking through the gaseous clouds, but catching nothing.

After a few moments, Lowie groaned in frustration. Em Teedee said, "Master Lowbacca wishes to offer someone else a turn." Lowie relinquished the controls to Jaina, who sat down with focused concentration, the tip of her tongue wedged between her lips at the corner of her mouth. Her eyes, golden-brown pools that stared into nothingness, fell half-closed as she worked the controls. Jacen watched the energy lines writhe below, sifting through the clouds, searching.

"Now, don't get disappointed," Lando said. "I told you it's still hard work to find even one gem. They're quite rare. If they weren't, they wouldn't be so valuable."

Jaina continued to search for a few minutes longer, then gave up. Jacen climbed to his feet and came forward, struggling to keep his balance in the gale-force winds. He caught the arm of the chair and pulled himself into it, letting his hands wrap around the controls.

As he tugged on the joysticks he could feel the response from the lashing energy cables, groping about like nimble fingers sifting through sand to find gold. He reached out with his mind, concentrating as Jaina had, using what he knew of Jedi powers to search for the precious gems. He didn't know what a Corusca stone would *feel* like, but he expected he would know if he encountered one. The whirling clouds seemed empty, thick with useless gases and crushed debris, nothing of interest.

His twin sister sat behind him, and he could feel her hoping for his success. Just as he was about to give up, Jacen suddenly felt a flash, a glint in his mind. He nudged the joysticks sideways, stretching out the long electrical fingers, searching, extending them as far as they would reach. With one lightning tip he scratched through the clouds, stretching, *stretching* . . . and finally he snagged the glimmer in his mind.

The control panels lit up. "I got one!" he cried.

Lando looked as shocked as anyone else, "You did!" he said. "Okay, let's bring it in fast. Time to go."

Lando took over and reeled the magnetic tentacles back into the *Fast Hand*, pulling in the catch. As he stabilized the energy tether again, Lando opened a small access port in the floor and pulled up a durasteel cargo box rimed with frost. He withdrew an irregular but beautiful Corusca gem, larger than the one he had shown them earlier. It flashed with trapped fire.

Breathlessly, Jacen took it from Lando, cradling it in the palms of his hands. "Look what I got!" he said.

Jaina and Lowie offered their congratulations. Lando, knowing he had promised to give the prize to the kids, shook his head in grudging admiration. "Keep that safe, Jacen," Lando said. "That's enough to buy half a city block on Coruscant, I bet."

"It's worth *that* much?" Jacen ran his fingers along the smooth, incredibly hard surface of the gem. "What if I lose it?" he said.

"Put it in your boot," Jaina said. "You know you never lose things there."

"I will," Jacen agreed. "I think I'll give it to mother for her next birthday."

Lando slapped his forehead. "Even Han never gave Leia something that valuable! Almost makes me wish I had a couple of kids," he muttered. "All right, let's head back up."

As if to encourage him, another fist of wind slammed the side of the *Fast Hand* and sent them spinning. Jacen fumbled with his Corusca gem, nearly dropped it on the floor, then caught it again and clutched it in his fist. He immediately tucked it into his boot, where he wouldn't have to worry about it falling out.

His forehead still furrowed with anxiety, Lando Calrissian

reeled in the energy tether, hauling the *Fast Hand* back toward the safer levels of Yavin's atmosphere.

The storms tossed them around. Once they heard a loud *spang* against the quantum-armored hull. Lando yelped and looked over at the wall. "Another one! Jaina, get over there and check that seal," he said.

"What happened?" Jacen asked.

On her knees, Jaina scuttled over to check. "Looks like it's okay," she said.

"What was it?" Jacen insisted. He saw the tiniest dent on the inside, but sensed no leaking atmosphere.

"We just got hit by a Corusca gem thrown at high speed by these winds. It's like a projectile weapon striking us, and only the quantum armor saved us. I can't believe this luck." Lando shook his head. "I spend hours and hours looking for those gems on my own and come up empty-handed. But when I bring you down here, Jacen snatches one right away, and then we get hit by another as we're heading back up top."

Lowie bellowed a comment, and Em Teedee said, "I fervently agree with Master Lowbacca: Let's hope we don't encounter any more of them."

Lightning bolts flashed around the hull, sparking blue light into the murky clouds. But as they rose higher toward the safety of GemDiver Station, the storm winds grew calmer, less insistent. Lando relaxed visibly.

When they finally rose back into the glittering GemDiver Station, and the floor sealed beneath them, Lando heaved a sigh of relief and slumped down in the pilot's chair.

The pressure bay refilled with atmosphere, and Lando flicked the controls to unseal the armored hatch. "There. We're back safe and sound," he said, climbing out on unsteady legs. "I think that's enough adventures for now. How about we relax and get something to eat?"

Lando had barely finished making the suggestion, though, when the sudden wailing of station alarms screeched across the intercom systems.

"Now what is it?" Lando asked. "What's going on?"

The three young Jedi Knights jumped out of the *Fast*

Hand and followed Lando as he ran to a comm station on the wall. "This is Lando Calrissian. Give me a status update."

"An unidentified fleet just appeared out of hyperspace," came the tense voice of a station security chief. "They refuse our hails and are heading toward GemDiver Station at great speed, intent unknown." The voice clicked off.

Jacen and Jaina ran toward one of the viewports and looked out into the darkness of space. Then Jacen saw the ships, like a swarm of meteors, streaking in their direction. Somehow he sensed they were powering on their weapons—up to no good. He gulped.

"Looks like an Imperial fleet to me," Jaina said.

4

LANDO RUSHED TOWARD the control bridge of Gem-Diver Station. "Come on, kids. Follow me!" he shouted.

Jaina took the lead while Lowie and Jacen followed at a run. Lowie's long Wookiee legs nearly made him plow over Lando in his haste. "Oh, *do* be careful, Lowbacca!" Em Teedee called.

Taking a turbolift to the upper observation tower, they bustled onto the control bridge, a cylindrical turret that protruded above the main armored body of GemDiver Station. Narrow rectangular windows encircled the control room, allowing a full view in all directions. The glowing diagnostic screens directly below each viewport flashed alarm warnings. Lando's armed guards ran about, strapping additional weapons to their belts, preparing to defend the station.

"We are under attack, sir," Lobot murmured in his quiet, difficult-to-hear voice. The cyborg was a blur of motion, hands darting from keyboard to keyboard, eyes scanning the screens around him and silently assessing details. The lights on the computer implants at the sides of his head flashed like fireworks.

Lando scanned the narrow observation ports and saw the fleet of ships coming in from deep space. "Do you think they're pirates?" he asked. Then to the twins and Lowie, he said reassuringly, "Don't worry. We've got station security on alert. These people don't have a chance against our defenses."

Jaina studied one of the diagnostic screens, pursing her lips. She shook her head. "Not just pirates," she said, recognizing some of the ships by the ellipsoid shape of their main body, engine turrets swept back like jagged wings on top and bottom. "Imperial craft. The four on the outside are Skipray blastboats, each fully equipped with three ion cannons, proton torpedo launcher, concussion missiles, and two fire-linked laser cannons."

Lando seemed startled. "Yeah, that's right."

She looked calmly up at his surprised expression. "Dad had me study a lot of ships. Believe me, these're more than even your security systems could hope to fight."

Lando clapped a hand to his forehead and groaned. "That's not just a pirate fleet, that's an armada! What's the big ship in the middle? I don't recognize it."

In her mind Jaina ran through mechanical specifications of all the ship designs she had learned from her father—but right now she was at a loss.

"Some kind of modified assault shuttle, maybe?" Jaina said. Through the magnification on the screens they stared as the ships came relentlessly in. "But I don't understand that contraption in the bow."

The mysterious assault shuttle had a strange device mounted at its front end, circular and jagged, like the wide-open mouth of a fanged underwater predator.

"Send a distress signal," Lando said to Lobot. "Full spectrum. Make sure *everybody* knows we're under attack here."

With maddening computer-enhanced calm, Lobot shook his bald head. "I've already tried. We're jammed, sir—can't punch a signal through their screens."

"Well, what do they want?" Lando asked in exasperation.

"They've made no demands," Lobot replied. "They refuse to answer our hails. We do not know what they're after."

Jaina stared out the window at the incoming ships and felt cold inside. She shuddered. Jacen squeezed her hand, his forehead wrinkled with anxiety. They had realized the same thing.

"I've got a bad feeling about this," Jacen said. "It's . . . *us* they want, isn't it?"

"Yeah, I can feel it," Jaina said, her voice barely above a whisper. Lowie nodded his shaggy head and groaned in agreement.

"What do you kids mean?" Lando looked at them with disbelief in his large brown eyes. "They *must* be after our Corusca gems—it's the only thing that makes sense."

Jaina shook her head, but Lando was too busy to pay further attention. The four flanking blastboats angled out from the central assault shuttle toward the defensive satellites surrounding GemDiver Station.

"Have you removed the fail-safes from the targeting systems?" Lando asked.

Lobot nodded. "Systems ready to fire," he murmured. High-powered lasers from the defensive satellites lanced out toward the blastboats, but the small satellites could not generate enough power to penetrate the heavy Imperial armor.

Each Skipray blastboat targeted one of the small satellites and unleashed a crackling blur from its ion cannons. The defensive satellites powered up, preparing to fire again, but then all the lights went dead.

"The ion cannons fried the circuits," Lobot announced in his calm voice. "All satellites are off-line."

The Skiprays came in for another strike and fired with laser cannons, this time blasting the defensive satellites into molten metal vapor.

"We've still got the station's armor," Lando said, but now his trembling voice betrayed his lack of confidence.

The modified assault shuttle in the middle of the armada homed in on one of the lower space doors. From the bottom decks of the station came a loud *thump* and *clang* as something large and heavy struck the outer hull—and stayed.

"What are they doing?" Lando asked.

"The modified assault shuttle has attached itself to the outer wall of GemDiver Station," Lobot reported.

"Where?"

The bald cyborg checked readings. "One of the equipment bays. I think they're trying to force their way in."

Lando waved his hand in dismissal. "Well, they can knock but they can't come in." He smiled nervously. "Just keep all the airlocks sealed. Our station armor should hold."

"Excuse me," Jaina said, "but I may have figured out what that modification is. I think they plan to bore through the station walls. The jagged things we saw looked like teeth—so I'm guessing they cut through metal."

"Not *this* metal." Lando shook his head. "The station wall is double-armored. Nothing could cut through it."

Jacen spoke up. "I thought you said Corusca gems could cut through anything."

Lando shook his head again. "Sure, but that would take a whole shipment of industrial-grade Corusca gems." Then he stopped, eyes widening. "Well, uh, we *have* shipped some industrial-grade gems since we upgraded our operations."

He picked up a comlink and spoke into it. "This is Lando Calrissian. All security details go to lower equipment bay number"—he leaned over Lobot's shoulder to look at the screen—"number thirty-four. Full armor and weapons. We're about to be boarded by hostile forces."

Lando took a blaster pistol from the sealed armory case inside the bridge deck. He turned to Lobot. "*Nobody* boards my station without my permission." He started down the corridor, calling over his shoulder as he ran. "You kids find a safe place, and stay there!"

So of course the young Jedi Knights followed him.

Station guards in padded, dark blue uniforms sprinted from corridor intersections. The pastel colors and nature sounds of GemDiver Station seemed oddly out of place, no longer soothing amid the chaos of defensive preparations and the turmoil of screeching alarms.

By the time they reached lower equipment bay 34, a squad of station guards had already set up their position behind storage containers and supply modules, blaster rifles drawn and aimed at the wall.

Jaina heard a whining, gnawing sound that made her teeth vibrate. A circular section of the outer wall glowed, and she could imagine the assault shuttle on the other side, linked to GemDiver Station like a huge battle-ready brine-eel, chewing its way through the station armor.

A bright white line appeared in the circle as a Corusca tooth bit through the thick plate. Jaina hoped belatedly that the attacking ship's seal against the station was airtight.

One of Lando's station guards, keyed up with overwhelming tension, let off two shots from his blaster rifle. The bolts spanged against the wall and left a discolored blotch on the inner hull, but the jaws of the boring machine continued to chew through the plates.

In a flash, with a puff of steam and the *crump* of small, shaped explosives, a large disk of the outer hull fell forward into the equipment bay.

Lando's security forces started firing immediately, even before the smoke cleared, but the enemy on the other side did not pause either. Dozens of white-armored Imperial stormtroopers boiled through the hole like a hive of frenzied lizard-ants that Jacen had once kept in his collection of exotic pets. The stormtroopers fired as they charged—using only the curving blue arcs of stun beams, Jaina was relieved to see.

Four stormtroopers went down with smoking holes in their white armor, but more and more poured out of the assault shuttle. The air in the equipment bay was crisscrossed with bright weapons fire.

Looming behind the armed stormtroopers, cloaked in shadows and rising smoke, stood a tall and sinister woman dressed in a black cape with spines on each shoulder. She had flowing ebony hair like the wings of a bird of prey. Despite her growing terror, Jaina saw that the woman's eyes were a striking color, like the violet of iridescent jungle flowers on Yavin 4. Jaina felt her heart clench as if hands of ice had wrapped around it.

The ominous dark woman stepped through the smoldering hole in the wall of GemDiver Station, oblivious to the weapons fire. A faint electric-blue corona of static lightning clung around her like the powerful discharges that had zapped the *Fast Hand* in the atmospheric storms of Yavin.

"Remember—don't harm the children," the woman shouted. Her voice was slow and heavy, but razor-sharp menace edged every word.

At the mention of the children, Lando whirled to see that the twins and Lowie had followed him. "What are you doing here?" he said. "Come on, we've got to get you to safety!" He waved his blaster pistol toward the entryway. Then, as if in afterthought, he turned and fired three more times, catching one of the white-armored stormtroopers full in the chest.

Jacen and Jaina bolted down the corridor. Lowie, needing no further encouragement, bellowed as he ran along.

Lando came charging after. "I guess you were right," he said, panting. "For some reason they *are* after you."

"I'm just a simple droid," Em Teedee wailed. "I certainly hope they don't want me."

A series of muffled explosions erupted behind them, and a shockwave of heat rippled through the station's metal corridors, making the kids stumble.

Lando caught his balance and steadied Jaina. "Turn right," he gasped. "Up here."

They ran. More blaster fire followed them, then a third explosion. Lando clenched his teeth. "This has *not* been a good day," he grumbled.

"I most heartily concur," Em Teedee chimed from Lowie's waist.

"Here! In the shipping chamber." Lando gestured for the three others to stop outside the barricaded door of the launching room where they had seen the cargo pods and the droids packing Corusca gems for automated shipment.

He punched in an access code, but Lando's fingers were trembling. A red light blinked. "ACCESS DENIED." Lando hissed something, then rekeyed the number. This time the light winked green, and the heavy triple doors sighed open. Inside, the two copper-plated droids continued packing the hyperpods. "Excuse me," one droid said, sounding flustered, "would you please discontinue those explosions? The vibrations make it much more difficult for us to process."

Lando ignored the droids as he pushed the kids inside. "We can't get you away from here—those blastboats would come after you before you knew it—but this is the safest place on the station. I'll stand outside and guard the door." He gripped his blaster pistol, feigning confidence.

Lowie growled, obviously wanting to fight, but before Jacen or Jaina could say anything, Lando slapped the emergency panel. The thick doors clanged shut, locking them inside the chamber.

Jacen placed his ear against the thick door and listened, but he could hear only the muffled noises of battle. Lowie, his ginger-colored fur standing on end with battle-readiness, kneaded his big knuckles. Jaina looked around the room for anything to help them fight.

Jacen yelled to the droids, "Hey, is there an armory in here? Do you have any weapons?"

The droids interrupted their packing and swiveled smooth copper heads toward him, optical sensors glowing. "Please do not disturb us, sir," they said, then resumed their tasks. "We have essential work to do."

Outside the door, the sound of gunfire suddenly increased. Jaina pulled Jacen back from the door as she heard Lando shout. The door vibrated with the impact of energy bolts; then everything went quiet. Jaina waited, backing away and looking into her twin brother's brandy-brown eyes. They both swallowed. Lowbacca let out a thin sound like a whimper. The multiarmed droids continued working, undisturbed.

A shower of sparks ran around part of the door as heavy-duty lasers cut into it, slicing away a section.

"D'you suppose you could invent some sort of weapon for us in the next few seconds?" Jacen said.

Jaina racked her brain for inspiration, but her inventiveness failed her.

The door split open, melted and smoking. The security breach set off yet another alarm, but the sounds were pitiful and superfluous in the already-overwhelming noise of the battle for GemDiver Station.

Stormtroopers muscled their way in.

The two packing droids trundled indignantly toward the stormtroopers. "Intruder alert," one of the droids said. "Warning. No unauthorized entry is permitted. You must return to—"

In response, the stormtroopers fired with all their weapons, blasting both copper droids into shards of smoking components that clattered and sparked on the floor.

Jaina saw Lando sprawled unconscious on the floor outside the door, his green cape pooled around him, his right arm extended forward, still grasping the blaster pistol.

The towering dark woman strode in, her violet eyes flashing at the three companions. The stormtroopers leveled blaster pistols at Jacen, Jaina, and Lowbacca.

"Wait!" Jaina said. "What do you want?"

"Do not let them manipulate your minds," the dark woman shouted to the stormtroopers. "Stun them!"

Before Jaina could say anything else, bright blue arcs shot toward her and the others, and they were overcome by a wave of unconsciousness.

Jaina fell into blackness.

5

ON YAVIN 4 Tenel Ka paced the ramparts of the Great Temple that housed Luke Skywalker's Jedi academy. As befitted a warrior of Dathomir, she wore scaled armor that shone as if it had just been polished . . . which it had. Her red-gold hair was caught up in a multitude of ceremonial braids, each decorated with feathers or beads. Her cool gray eyes scanned the leaden skies for any sign of the ship that would bring the dreaded ambassador from her grandmother.

Wind whipped the ornamented braids about her face, and Tenel Ka pushed them away in annoyance. The humid air felt oppressive, charged with menace. Yavin's dry season had ended.

She sensed an uncomfortable tingling in the depths of her mind that told her something was about to happen, as if lightning were about to strike. She sighed. Her grandmother's messengers and diplomats could be as lethal as lightning. . . .

They were not above killing an enemy, or even a friend, to ensure that the successor to the throne of Hapes was the one they most desired to have in power. It was rumored that her grandmother's assassins had murdered Tenel Ka's own uncle, brother to her father, Prince Isolder.

She started in surprise as a raindrop, warm as blood, landed with a splat on her bare arm. Although the air was not cold, she shivered.

Her feelings toward her grandmother were complex: She both admired and despised the older woman. Tenel Ka preferred to dress in the lizard-skin armor of the warrior women of Dathomir, like her mother, rather than in the fine web-silks of the Royal House of the Hapes Cluster.

So far, Tenel Ka had managed to tread a fine line between pleasing and annoying her grandmother. She knew that if she stepped over that line too far, assassins might someday pay her a visit. . . .

A branch of lightning crackled across the ominous sky, followed by a boom of thunder. Atop the temple, Tenel Ka paced like a caged animal, her agitation increasing as she stalked along the edge of the pyramid and wondered why Ambassador Yfra did not come. So great was her turmoil that she didn't even notice that Luke Skywalker had joined her on the observation deck until he stood directly in front of her.

The Jedi Master placed both of his hands on her shoulders and looked into her eyes. Peace and warmth flowed from him, and Tenel Ka felt herself begin to relax. "There's a message in the Comm Center for you," he said quietly. "Would you like me to be present while you speak with the ambassador?"

Tenel Ka could not suppress a shudder of revulsion as she thought of her grandmother's thin-lipped emissary. "Your presence would"—she paused for a moment, searching for words—"honor me, Master Skywalker."

Tenel Ka stood erect, holding her head high as she faced her grandmother's ambassador in the Comm Center viewscreen—an image that for all its apparent cruelty still held traces of proud beauty. Ambassador Yfra's hair and eyes were the color of polished pewter.

"Our meetings on Coruscant took longer than we anticipated, young one," Yfra was saying in a voice that indicated she was not used to being questioned. "Therefore, our meeting with you must be postponed for two days."

Tenel Ka gave no outward sign of her discomposure, but her heart sank. Jacen, Jaina, and Lowbacca were due back long before then. She sent a pleading glance to Luke.

The Jedi Master stepped forward and spoke in a soft voice. "Perhaps I could bring the Princess of Hapes to meet with you on Coruscant?" he offered.

Ambassador Yfra smiled in what Tenel Ka knew was meant to be a kindly fashion, but there was no kindness or conciliation in her eyes. "I have specific orders to observe the heir of Hapes in her place of study."

Tenel Ka opened her mouth to speak, but was spared the necessity when an emergency beacon flashed next to the screen. Luke reacted instantly. "Ambassador Yfra, we have a priority override communication coming in. Please wait," he said, switching the channel before the ambassador had a chance to reply.

The dark face of Lando Calrissian appeared, his handsome features marred by a worried frown. Confusion haunted his bleary eyes. His hair and clothes were disheveled, and warning sirens whooped in the background.

"Luke, buddy," he rasped, "I'm not sure exactly what happened. They . . . fried our security satellites, boarded the station . . . must've stunned us. We're okay, but—" Lando's troubled eyes closed and his jaw tightened, "Jacen, Jaina, and Lowbacca are gone. They've been kidnapped."

Luke drew in a deep breath. Tenel Ka guessed he was using a Jedi calming technique, but with less success than usual. His body appeared relaxed, but his clear blue eyes carried a laser-sharp look. One hand was clenched into a fist at his side. "Who did this?" he asked, his voice terse.

Lando shook his head. "We don't know who has the kids or why, but I've got all my best people working on it. It was someone connected with the Empire, though—that's for sure."

"I'll be there within the hour," Luke said, reaching for the comlink.

"Wait," Tenel Ka said. "These are my friends. I know how they think. I know what they would do. I cannot cower here while they are in danger. Please. I must go with you."

Luke nodded. "Your presence would . . . honor me," he answered, echoing her earlier words. His eyes went back to Lando's image. "*We'll* be there within the hour," he amended, then switched back to the ambassador's comm frequency.

Ambassador Yfra's mouth was open as if she were prepared to protest such rude treatment, but Luke spoke first. "I'm sorry to keep you waiting, Ambassador, but an emergency has come up. It requires both my presence and that of the princess. I'm afraid we must postpone any plans to meet with you until this situation is resolved. Please convey our respectful greetings to the Royal House of Hapes." With a slight bow, he snapped off the comm channel.

Even though she was worried about her friends, a feeling of satisfaction bubbled up within Tenel Ka at the deftness with which Master Skywalker had handled Ambassador Yfra.

Luke looked at Tenel Ka. "I'm sure the ambassador isn't used to being postponed with so little explanation, but we have more important things to do right now."

Tenel Ka nodded emphatically. "This is a fact."

Tenel Ka tried to be impartial and unemotional as Master Skywalker expertly guided the shuttle toward GemDiver Station. She needed to remain unruffled and alert, to search for any clue that might help them recover the three young Jedi—the best friends she'd ever had.

The multicolored lights of the station winked as the docking-bay doors slid open and Luke brought the shuttle in for a landing. At any other time Tenel Ka might have noted her surroundings, the artistry and craftsmanship that had gone into the station's construction—but the moment the shuttle doors opened, she was assailed by a sense of lingering violence and darkness. Of *wrongness*.

Harried and disheveled, Lando Calrissian met them at the shuttle. Motioning for Luke and Tenel Ka to follow, he led them to the sealed shipping bay where the final struggle had occurred.

Tenel Ka swept the chamber with her eyes, noting the blaster burns on the walls and ceiling of the outer corridor, the congealed rivulets of molten plasteel, the shards of broken metal. Then she watched as Luke sank down on one knee, placed both hands against the floor, and let his eyes flutter closed.

"Yes, it happened here," he murmured. He took a few deep breaths, then fixed Lando with the piercing blueness of his gaze. "Don't blame yourself," he said. "You fought well."

Lando's face was filled with regret, and he shook his head. "But it wasn't enough, buddy. I couldn't save them." A note of anger and self-reproach crept into his voice. "I was too busy trying to defend my station—thinking they were pirates come to steal my Corusca gems. I didn't even realize they were after the kids until it was too late."

Luke neither condemned nor pardoned Lando, Tenel Ka noticed. He simply listened.

At last Lando spoke again in a quiet voice. "If there's anything you need to help find them—my station, a ship, a crew . . . anything at all—"

Lando's offer of help was cut short by the arrival of his assistant Lobot, whose computer headset flashed with an ever-changing array of lights. "We finished patching the hull breach in lower equipment bay thirty-four," he said without preamble.

Lando turned to Luke and Tenel Ka, his forehead creasing into an indignant scowl. "They sliced us open like a disposable can of emergency rations."

The bald cyborg nodded in corroboration. "Their equipment was specially designed to remove a section of hull."

Lando continued, "The only thing I know of sharp enough to slice through durasteel that quickly is—"

"Corusca gems," Luke finished for him.

"Industrial grade," Lobot added.

"Right," Lando said morosely. "They used *our own gems* against us."

"Rare and expensive," Lobot said. "Not just anyone could purchase them."

Tenel Ka saw Luke's eyes light with sudden hope. "Can you tell us where your shipments of such gems were sold?"

Lando shrugged. "Like my friend said, industrial-grade gems are fairly rare. We've made only two shipments since our operation opened." He sent a questioning glance at his cyborg assistant.

Lobot pressed a panel on the back of his head and cocked it to one side as if listening to a voice no one else could hear. A moment later he nodded. "Both shipments were sold through our broker on Borgo Prime."

"Can you find out who he sold them to?" Luke asked.

"I doubt it," Lando said. "Gem brokers are pretty skittish. They pay a good percentage, but they're secretive—afraid that if we know who their customers are, we won't need the middlemen anymore."

"Then we must go to Borgo Prime and find out ourselves," Tenel Ka said with fierce determination.

Luke sent her a warm smile, then turned back to Lando. "What is Borgo Prime anyway?"

"An asteroid spaceport and trade center. It's also a hangout for merchants, thieves, murderers, smugglers . . . the dregs of the galaxy" Lando flashed Luke a grin. "A lot like Mos Eisley on Tatooine. You'll feel right at home."

Tenel Ka waited in silence as Master Skywalker faced the screen in GemDiver Station's Communications Center.

Han Solo stood with one arm around his wife, Leia, who was supported on the other side by Lowie's uncle, Chewbacca.

Tenel Ka studied the images on the screen and decided that at this moment Leia Organa Solo looked more like a concerned mother than a powerful politician.

"But Luke, they're *our* children," she was saying. "We can't simply stand by and do nothing if they're in danger."

"Not on your life!" Han said.

"Of course not," Luke agreed quietly "But as the New Republic's chief of state, you can't afford to put yourself in that same danger. Mobilize your forces. Start an investigation. Send out spies and probe droids. But stay there and act as a central clearinghouse for information."

"All right, Luke," Leia said. "We'll work from Coruscant for now, but once we've done everything we can from here, we'll go looking for them ourselves."

"I'll come get you in the *Falcon*," Han said.

"Give me ten standard days first," Luke said. "I have a lead I'm going to follow right now before the trail gets cold. We need to get going. We'll keep you informed of our progress."

"We?" Han asked. "Is Lando going with you?"

"No," Luke replied. "The heir of Hapes will honor me with her company," he said, gesturing to Tenel Ka.

"We are grateful for your assistance," Leia said formally.

Tenel Ka nodded toward the screen with a brief, stiff bow. "Jacen, Jaina, and Lowbacca have a greater call on me than honor," she said. "They have my friendship."

Leia's face softened. "Then I owe you my gratitude as a mother as well." Chewbacca rumbled what Tenel Ka could only interpret as an agreement.

"Don't worry, we'll find them," Luke said, his voice filled with urgency. "But we need to leave now."

Han lifted his chin and smiled at Luke. "Okay, get going, kid."

Just before the communications link was broken, Leia spoke again. "And may the Force be with you."

JAINA CAME BACK to consciousness with Lowie shaking her shoulders. The lanky Wookiee moaned plaintively until she groaned and woke up, blinking her eyes.

A rush of unpleasant sensations flooded through her: queasy stomach, pounding head, aching joints—aftereffects of the stormtroopers' stun beams. The human body wasn't designed to be knocked out with a blast of energy. Her ears hummed, too, but her instincts told her that the sounds were real—the rumbling vibrations of a big ship in hyperdrive.

Uncertain about whether she dared risk a more vertical position, Jaina cautiously turned her head. She saw that she, Jacen, and Lowbacca were together in a small, nondescript room. Jaina took a deep breath, scratched her straight brown hair, and ran her hands down her grease-smeared jumpsuit to make sure everything was still intact.

Suddenly recalling the attack on GemDiver Station, Jaina sat up so quickly that a fresh wave of nausea washed over her and pain exploded at her temples. She gasped, then forced herself to relax and let some of the pain drain away. "Where are we?" she asked.

Jacen was already sitting up on a narrow pallet, rubbing his brandy-brown eyes and running long fingers through his tousled hair. He wore a look of confusion, and Jaina sensed deep turmoil coming from her brother. "Not a clue," he said.

Lowbacca also made a dismayed, questioning sound.

"Least we're all together," Jaina said. "And they didn't put binders on us." She held up her hands, surprised that the Imperials had not separated their prisoners and tied them up. Water and a food tray lay in an alcove by the wall. From the looks of it, Lowie had already sampled some of the fruit.

"Hey, I wonder what happened to everyone at GemDiver Station. What do you suppose they did to Lando?" Jacen asked.

Jaina shrugged, still feeling queasy. "Saw him lying unconscious just before they stunned us. But I don't think they planned to kill him. They weren't looking for Corusca gems, either. Seems like they only wanted *the three of us*."

"Yeah . . . kinda makes you feel valuable, huh?" Jacen agreed glumly. Lowie growled.

Jaina stood up and stretched, feeling better as she moved. "Guess I'm okay, though. How about you two?"

Jacen smiled reassuringly, and Lowie nodded his shaggy head. The streak of black fur that swept over his eyebrows bristled with uneasiness. He smoothed the fur back and grunted.

It was then that Jaina noticed something else wrong. She looked down at the Wookiee's waist, but the miniaturized translating droid was no longer there.

"Lowie! What happened to Em Teedee?"

Lowie made a strange, sad sound and patted his waist.

"Imperials must've taken it from him," Jaina said. "What do they want?"

"Oh, just to take over the galaxy, cause a bunch of problems . . . hurt a lot of people—you know, the usual," Jacen answered flippantly. He went over to the flat metal door. "Hmmmm . . . it's probably locked, but there's no harm in trying," he said, tapping the controls with his fingers.

To Jaina's surprise, the door hummed sideways to reveal a guard standing at attention just outside. A stormtrooper in a skull-like white helmet turned to face them.

"Whoa!" Jacen cried, then he lowered his voice. "Well, at least the door opens."

"Maybe they just can't figure out how to lock the door," Jaina said. "Remember how clunky and unreliable Imperial technology is." She let sarcasm seep into her voice for the guard's benefit. "And you know how lousy stormtrooper armor is. Probably couldn't even stop a water blaster."

"Just walk past him," Jacen suggested in a stage whisper, seeing that the stormtrooper hadn't moved. "Maybe he won't stop us."

The stormtrooper shouldered his blaster rifle. "Wait here." The filtered voice coming through the white helmet was flat, but somehow menacing. The guard spoke quietly into his helmet comlink, then shut the three young Jedi Knights in their cell again.

They sat in anxious silence for a moment. "We could tell jokes," Jacen suggested.

Before Jaina could think of an appropriate answer, the cell door whisked open again. This time, beside the stormtrooper stood the towering, sinister woman from the assault on Gem-Diver Station. Jaina took a quick breath.

The tall woman's black hair flowed like waves of darkness down her shoulders, and her ebony cape sparkled with bits of polished gems, swirling around her like a starry night sky. Her violet eyes blazed in a face so pale it seemed carved from polished bone. Her lips were a dark wine color, as if she had just eaten an overripe fruit. The woman was beautiful—in a cruel sort of way.

"So, Jedi Knights, you are awake at last," she snapped. Her voice was deep and thick, without the hissing edge Jaina had expected. "I must begin by saying how *disappointed* I am in you. I had hoped for more resistance from such powerful students already trained in the Force. Your Jedi defenses were pitiful! But we shall change that. You will be taught new ways. Effective ways."

The woman spun on one heel, and her black cloak swept around her like trailing smoke. "Follow me," she said, and stepped into the corridor.

"No," Jaina responded. "Who do you think you are? Why have you brought us here against our will?"

"I said *follow*!" the woman repeated. When they made no move to comply, she pointed her polished nails at them and twitched her fingers.

Suddenly, it felt as if a resilient invisible cord had wrapped around Jaina's throat. The woman crooked her finger, yanking at Jaina as if she were a pet on a leash. Jaina lurched as the invisible rope hauled her out of the cell.

Lowbacca and Jacen strained against similar bonds of Force, the Wookiee yowling his defiance. Despite their struggles, all three children were dragged on Force leashes tripping and stumbling into the corridor.

"I can do this all the way to the bridge, if you like," the

woman said, her deep red lips curved into a mocking smile. "Or, you can save your energies for more productive resistance later."

"All right," Jaina croaked, sensing that this woman had dark Jedi powers she could not match—at least not yet.

When the Force bonds dropped away, the companions stood gasping and trembling. They looked at each other in angry humiliation, knowing they were beaten.

Jaina was the first to recover. Swallowing hard, she stood straight, put her chin in the air, and followed the woman in black. Her brother and Lowie fell in behind Jaina. "Who are you?" Jaina asked after a while.

The woman paused in midstep, as if considering, then answered. "My name is Tamith Kai. I am from a new order of Nightsisters."

"Nightsisters? You mean like on Dathomir?" Jacen asked.

Jaina remembered the stories their friend Tenel Ka told when it was her turn to scare them before they practiced Jedi calming techniques—stories of the horrible evil women who had once twisted civilization on her world.

Tamith Kai looked at Jacen, her wine-dark lips set in something between a scowl and a smile. "You've heard of us? Good. My planet is rich in Force-wielders, and the Empire has helped to bring us back. Now perhaps you'll realize you can't resist. Cooperation, on the other hand, will be rewarded."

"We won't cooperate with you," Jaina challenged.

"Yes, yes," Taniith Kai said, as if bored. "All in good time."

"Hey, where are you taking us?" Jacen asked, walking quickly to keep pace with his sister. Lowie strode behind them, grumbling and fumbling at his waist as if he actually missed Em Teedee.

"You'll see soon enough," the Nightsister said. "We are almost ready to leave hyperspace."

All four of them stepped onto a lift platform that carried them up a level and opened out onto the bridge of the fleeing ship. The single pilot sat with his back to them in a padded high-backed chair, hunched over the controls. Ahead, through the bridge viewports Jaina could see the swirling colors of hyperspace.

The pilot reached out with his right hand and grabbed a lever as a countdown trickled to zero. Then he yanked the lever, and hyperspace suddenly unfolded, washing away into the star-studded darkness of normal space.

"We're near the Core Systems," Jaina said immediately, looking out at the rich starfields and the streamers of interstellar gas clotted together near the center of the galaxy

The crowded Core Systems were the last bastions of Imperial power; not even New Republic forces had been able to flush them out completely. But they had arrived nowhere close to any system. They found themselves merely hanging out in the middle of the star-strewn blackness.

"We have reached our destination, Tamith Kai," the pilot said, swiveling in his tall chair.

Jaina's heart leaped as she recognized the weary, hard-bitten face and iron-gray hair of the former TIE pilot who had been stranded on Yavin 4 for so many years.

"Qorl!" Jacen exclaimed.

Lowie roared in anger.

Qorl had attacked them in the jungles when the young Jedi Knights had found his crashed TIE fighter and tried to fix it. The Imperial pilot had shot at Lowie and Tenel Ka, who had managed to escape into the undergrowth, but Qorl had taken Jacen and Jaina prisoner.

"Greetings, young friends. I never did thank you for fixing my ship and allowing me to return to my Empire."

"You betrayed us!" Jaina cried, feeling a surge of anger toward the brainwashed man. While being held captive, the twins had befriended Qorl, exchanging stories with him around the campfire. Jaina had felt sure the TIE pilot was softening, realizing that the ways of the Empire were filled with lies. But in the end, Qorl's military conditioning had been too strong.

"I returned as any soldier would and gave my report," Qorl said in a dull voice. "These people accepted me and . . . reindoctrinated me. I told them of your existence—powerful young Jedi Knights just waiting to be trained to serve the Empire."

"Never," Jaina and Jacen snapped in unison, and Lowbacca agreed with a roar.

Tamith Kai looked down at them mockingly. Standing beside Qorl, the dark-haired woman seemed even taller than before, more intimidating than ever. "Your anger is good," she said. "Fuel it. Let it grow. We will use it when your training begins. But for now . . . we have reached our destination."

Lowie gave a growl of disbelief.

Jaina looked out the front viewports, trying to calm herself. Master Skywalker had said that giving in to anger was a path to the dark side of the Force. She must not lash out, she knew; she must think of some other way to fight back.

"We're in the middle of empty space," Jaina said. "What is there for us to see?"

"Space is not always empty," Tamith Kai said. Her thick voice held a singsong quality, as if her mind was thinking of something else. "Reality is not always what it seems."

At his station Qorl verified the coordinates, then punched in a security code. "Transmitting now," he said.

Tamith Kai turned her sharp violet eyes toward the young Jedi Knights. "You are about to begin a new phase of your lives," she said, pointing to the viewscreens. "Behold."

Space shimmered like a blanket of invisibility peeling away. Suddenly a space station hung in front of them, torusshaped, like a donut. Weapons emplacements ringed the station's entire perimeter, pointing in all directions, making it look like a spiked disciplinary collar for some ferocious beast. Tall observation towers rose like pinnacles on one side of the station.

Jaina swallowed hard.

"Cloaking device off," Qorl announced.

"Take a good look," Tamith Kai said, but she did not glance at the viewscreens. Her eyes glittered with violet fervor at the children. "Here you'll be trained as Dark Jedi . . . for the Empire."

Qorl spoke up, reminding her. "We must commence docking immediately and reactivate the invisibility shielding."

The Nightsister nodded but did not seem to hear, never taking her eyes off the young Jedi Knights. "Welcome to the Shadow Academy," she whispered.

7

TENEL KA SLID a hand under the crash webbing of the copilot's seat and scratched at the rough-woven, unfamiliar material of her disguise. She wished for the dozenth time that she could wear her comfortable reptilian armor, which was as supple as it was protective and never irritated her skin.

She had been silent, intimidated, through most of the journey to Borgo Prime, unable to bring herself to speak. Beside her sat Master Skywalker—the most famous and revered Jedi in the entire galaxy—calmly and competently piloting the *Off Chance*, an old blockade runner Lando had won in a sabacc game and claimed he no longer needed.

Tenel Ka's grandmother had insisted that the girl's royal training include diplomacy and correct methods of addressing individuals of any rank, species, age, or gender. Though not loquacious, Tenel Ka was also not shy; yet somehow, alone with the impressive Jedi Master in the confines of their tiny cockpit, she could find nothing to say. She tried to think, but her sluggish mind would not cooperate. Weariness clung to her like the sweat-damp clothing she wore. She squirmed in her seat and tried to suppress a nervous yawn.

Luke glanced over at her, a smile at the corners of his mouth. "Tired?"

"Not much sleep," Tenel Ka answered, embarrassed that he had noticed her fatigue. "Bad dreams."

Luke's blue eyes narrowed for a moment, as if he was

searching for a memory, but then he shook his head. "I haven't been sleeping well either—but, tired or not, we can't afford to make mistakes. Let's go over our cover story again. Tell me who you are."

"We are traders from Randon. We will avoid using names. But, if we must, you are Iltar and I am your ward-cousin Beknit. We trade in archaeological treasures. We are not above breaking the law to make a profit. We have come from a secret archaeological dig on . . ." She paused for a moment, searching her brain for the name of the planet.

"Ossus," Luke supplied.

"Ah. Aha," Tenel Ka said. "Ossus." She took a deep breath while she etched the name into her mind, then she continued. "On *Ossus*, we discovered a treasured vault, secured with an Old Republic seal. The treasure chamber is set deep into rock and plated with armor so thick that no blaster or laser can pierce it.

"We dare not blast the surrounding rock for fear of destroying the treasure. We've come to Borgo Prime in search of industrial-grade Corusca gems to slice through the armor and open the treasure vault. We are ready to pay handsomely for the right type of gems."

Tenel Ka watched with interest as the dull, lumpy asteroid of Borgo Prime loomed in their forward viewports. The rock had been hollowed out, honeycombed in ages past by generations of asteroid miners who sought one type of mineral, then another as market conditions changed. But more than a century ago, Borgo Prime had been stripped clean of even the least-desirable ore—leaving a spongelike network of interlocked caves, fully equipped with all the life-support systems and transportation airlocks the miners had needed. It had been a simple matter to convert the played-out mine into a bustling spaceport.

Luke transmitted the standard request for clearance to land and received it without difficulty.

"We've been cleared for docking bay ninety-four," Luke said. "Are you ready, uh, Beknit?"

Tenel Ka nodded matter-of-factly. "Of course, Iltar."

Luke studied her for a moment, earnest concern filling his

face. "It could be rough down there, you know. You heard what Lando said: Borgo Prime is filled with people who have no conscience—thieves, murderers, creatures who would just as soon kill you as greet you."

"Ah. Aha," Tenel Ka said, raising an eyebrow. "Sounds like a visit to my grandmother's court on Hapes."

The two Randoni traders, "Iltar" and his ward-cousin "Beknit," left their blockade runner in the dockyard cavern behind an immense hangar door and walked along the causeway that joined Borgo Prime's largest space dock to its business district deep in the core of the asteroid.

In spite of her many rehearsals, Tenel Ka found it difficult to remember that she was supposed to be an experienced trader, used to frequenting such spaceports. She gawked openly at the tall rows of prefabricated dwellings welded up and down the inner walls and all the garish flashing lights of the alien businesses in separate atmosphere domes around them.

This place was so different from the primitive, untamed world of Dathomir. Even Hapes with its serene and stately cities—some of them larger than this entire asteroid—bore no resemblance to the spaceport's seedy, gaudily lit establishments, that hummed with a life of their own. Overhead, through the clear arching plasteel that covered a rift in the ceiling, the stars and space were all but obscured by Borgo Prime's glaring lights.

Luke paused beside Tenel Ka, letting her collect her thoughts. "You've never been anyplace like this, have you?" he asked.

She shook her head and started to walk again, searching for words to describe the unsettling emotions. "I feel . . . foolish. Out of place." She scuffed her toes along a causeway surface that was paved with colorful, glowing advertisements.

She paused to read an ad, then another. The first one announced in phosphorescent script that flared into light as she stepped near it,

BORGO LANDING
SPACE DOCKS BY THE HOUR OR BY THE MONTH.

The next one read simply

INFO TO GO
DISCREET INQUIRIES OF ALL SORTS
COMPLETELY CONFIDENTIAL.

Tenel Ka shook her head. "I do not understand this place," she said. "It both revolts and . . . entices me at the same time."

"You don't have to go through with this, you know," Luke said. "I could handle it myself."

It was completely true, Tenel Ka realized—an uncomfortable thought. She tossed her head and ran a nervous hand over her hair, which she wore loose, in Randoni style, so that it flowed down her back in a cascade of red-gold ripples like a sun-dappled stream. She tried to look confident, but icy fingers of doubt prodded her mind. "I will do what I must to rescue my friends," she said, her voice as brisk and businesslike as she could make it. "Where is this nest or hive that Lando told us to find?"

Luke pointed to another lighted ad at their feet. "I think we just found it," he said with a pleased expression.

SHANKO'S HIVE
FINE DRINKS AND ENTERTAINMENT
ALL SPECIES, ALL AGES.

The flat image showed an insectoid barkeeper proffering a dozen drinks with its multijointed, chitinous arms. A row of blinking beacon lights set into the walkway indicated the direction of the "hive."

A sudden bout of stage fright assailed Tenel Ka, but she knew how important it was for them to stay in character. She straightened her clothing, cleared her throat, and looked at Luke. "You must be very thirsty after your long journey, Iltar," she said.

"Yes. Thank you, Beknit," he answered smoothly. "I could use a drink." Then he leaned toward her and asked in a lower voice, "Are you *sure* you want to do this?"

Tenel Ka nodded firmly. "I'm ready for anything."

"I did not expect an establishment quite so large on an asteroid of this size," Tenel Ka said, tilting back her head to look at the rounded ripples of Shanko's cone-shaped Hive, a gray-green edifice sealed in its own atmosphere field. The edifice rose at least a quarter kilometer above the inner floor of Borgo Prime.

Feathery wings of fear and uncertainty fluttered in her stomach, and she paused to draw in a deep breath. To Tenel Ka's great chagrin, a subtle spark of amusement danced in Master Skywalker's eyes. "You know what waits for us in there, don't you?" he asked.

"Thieves," she answered.

"Murderers," he added.

"Liars, scum, smugglers, traitors . . ." Her voice trailed off.

"Almost like family back on Hapes?" he asked with a gentle, teasing smile.

As heir to the Royal Throne of Hapes, Tenel Ka had faced trained assassins, as had her father, Prince Isolder, before her. If she could do that, surely she could handle a little spaceport cantina.

"Thank you," she said, taking the arm he offered. "I am ready now."

Luke slid a pass chit into a small slot in the door. "Let's try to keep a low profile." The door slid open.

The first thing that caught Tenel Ka's eye when she stepped through the door was the insectoid bartender, Shanko, who stood over three meters high.

The room was filled with indescribable odors she could not begin to identify—not actually pleasant, but not quite offensive either. Particulates hung in the air from a multitude of burning objects: pipes, candles, incense, chunks of peat in blazing bog-pits, even clothing or fur from the occasional customer who got too close to one of the fires.

Without speaking, Luke gestured with his chin toward the bar. Even if he had spoken aloud, Tenel Ka could not have heard him above the noise of at least half a dozen different bands playing hit tunes from as many different systems.

Fortunately, they had decided before entering where they should start their inquiries. Knowing that on Randon the female ward-cousin was highly honored—mainly for her potential inheritance—and was always served first, Tenel Ka stepped up to the bar to place her order.

"Welcome travelersssss," Shanko said, folding three pairs of multijointed arms and bowing until his antennaed head nearly touched the bar.

"Your hospitality is as welcome as the prospect of refreshment," Tenel Ka replied.

"Sssso, you have been well ssschooled," Shanko said. "Are you perhapsss a ssscholar? A diplomat?"

"She is my ward-cousin," Luke put in smoothly.

"Then it iss *indeed* an honor to ssserve you," Shanko said, raising himself to his full three-meter height.

"I would like a Randoni Yellow Plague," Tenel Ka said without hesitation. "Chilled. Make it a double."

"And I would like a Remote Terminator," Luke said.

The covering membranes of the bartender's multifaceted eyes nictated twice in surprise. "Not often requesssted. A ssstrong drink, iss it not?" He seemed flustered for a moment, then made a gurgling buzz deep in his thorax that Tenel Ka could only interpret as a laugh. "Will that be preprogrammed or randomizzzed?"

"Randomized, of course," Luke replied.

"Ah, a rissssk taker," Shanko said, tapping two forelegs on the bartop in approval.

Then his arms became a blur of motion as he pulled levers and pushed buttons, filling cups and vials, mixing their drinks in less time than it had taken to order them.

"There is no profit without risk," Luke said, accepting his drink from one of Shanko's many hands.

Tenel Ka leaned forward and lowered her voice. "We seek information," she said, drawing out a small string of Corusca gems that she had kept hidden under the rough material of her robe until then.

Shanko nodded in understanding. "We have the finessst information brokerss in the Sssector. There iss even a Hutt." He gestured toward an area to the right of the bar. "If you do not find what you ssseek here," he said with obvious pride, "it isss not to be found on Borgo Prime."

They thanked Shanko and headed in the direction he had indicated. The music of the bands faded slightly as they pushed into the milling throng of patrons, each imbibing its favorite form of refreshment. The crowd was so thick, Tenel Ka could not see where they were going.

Beside her, Luke paused and closed his eyes. "A Hutt information broker, huh?" he mused aloud. "They're the best you can get."

Tenel Ka felt a slight tingle as she watched him reach out with the Force to touch the minds around him, searching. She searched, too, but with her gray eyes open. A quick glance revealed nothing of interest. She looked up the open center of the hive's cone and at the curving stairways that climbed its ridged sides, which—judging from the signs on the walls— led to gambling rooms and lodgings.

Luke opened his eyes. "Okay, I have him." He took Tenel Ka's arm and pushed his way through the crowd. They passed a bank of stim lights, where a cluster of photosensitive customers wriggled and bounded to silent strobing "music."

They found the Huttese information broker ensconced behind a low table near the wall of the hive. A small Ranat with gray-brown fur stood at the Hutt's elbow, whiskers twitching. The Hutt was thin by Huttese standards and could not have had much status on his homeworld. Perhaps that was why he did business on Borgo Prime, Tenel Ka thought.

"We have come for information, and we are prepared to pay for it," Luke said without preamble.

The Hutt picked up a small datapad that lay on the table in front of him and punched a few buttons.

"What are your names?" he asked.

"What is *your* name?" Tenel Ka asked, raising her chin slightly.

The Hutt's eyes narrowed to slits, and Tenel Ka had the impression that the broker was revising his opinion of them. "Of course," he said. "Such things are unimportant."

Luke shrugged. "And all information has its price."

"Of course," the Hutt repeated. "Please sit down and tell me what you need."

Luke sat on a repulsorbench, adjusted the height, and motioned for Tenel Ka to sit beside him, next to a planter holding a tall, leafy shrub. Luke took a long gulp from the drink in his hand, but when Tenel Ka raised her cup to her lips, he sent her a warning look. When the Hutt bent to confer with his Ranat assistant for a moment, Luke took the opportunity to whisper, "That drink could knock you from here to the Outer Rim."

"Ah," Tenel Ka said. "Aha." She set the drink down with a small *thunk.*

When the Ranat scurried off on whatever business the Hutt had assigned it, Luke and Tenel Ka began telling their fictional tale, carefully offering only as much information as they thought was needed.

As they rambled on, taking turns embellishing the details, the other patrons in the hive supplied the usual chaos of a busy, seedy bar. Several different blaster battles rang out from dim areas, while huge armored bouncer droids trundled in to bash heads together and eject any customers who did not pay for the messes they made.

A group of smugglers played a reckless game of rocket darts, missing the prominent target on the wall and launching one of the small flaming missiles into the side of a fluffy, white-furred Talz. The creature roared in pain and surprise as his fur ignited, then took out his misery on the drunken Ithorian sitting next to him.

Large customers tried to eat smaller customers, and the bands kept playing, and Shanko kept mixing drinks. The Hutt information broker was distracted by none of it.

As they spoke, Luke continued to sip his drink and Tenel Ka cast about for a way to dispose of hers. When the Ranat returned and conferred again with the Hutt, Tenel Ka reached over to the planter beside her chair and dumped half of her drink into it.

It was only after the stalk began to shudder violently and the leaves curled up that Tenel Ka realized that the shrub was not a decoration but a plant-alien customer! She whispered an apology and turned back just as the Ranat hurried off with the Hutt's datapad and a new assignment.

The Ranat came back in a moment, followed by a heavily bearded man who walked with a limp.

"This Ranat here said 'no names,' and that's fine with me," the bearded man said, sitting down at the table. "Ranat tells me yer in the market for an industrial-grade Corusca gem? Ain't no one else can arrange that fer ya. Industrial-grade gems . . . sooner er later they hafta come through me."

"Are you the purchasing agent, then?" Tenel Ka said without thinking.

The bearded man snorted. "How 'bout we jes say I'm a middleman."

Again, Luke explained as briefly as possible about the treasure vault on Ossus, and before long they had struck a deal to purchase one industrial-grade Corusca gem.

That done, Luke probed the middleman for information about who else might have bought industrial-grade gems. The man's eyes grew wary and distrustful. "No names— that's the bargain," he said stoutly.

Tenel Ka pulled off another string of the fine Corusca gems that hung around her neck and placed them on the table beside the payment she and Luke had already made for the large gem.

"Surely you understand our caution," Luke said. "We must know if there is anyone capable of stealing our treasure from us."

The middleman picked up the string of gems and looked them over carefully "Can't tell ya much," he said in a low voice. "Last shipment o' big industrial gems, one person bought 'em all. Big order."

"Can you describe their ships, tell us what planet they came from?" Luke pressed.

The bearded middleman still did not look up. "Not much, actually. Never saw the ship she came on. All I know's she called herself a . . . a lady of the evenin' . . . er a daughter of darkness, er somethin' like that."

Tenel Ka caught her breath, and she felt Luke stiffen beside her. "You mean a—a *Nightsister*?" Tenel Ka asked with a quaver in her voice.

"Yeah, that was it! A Nightsister," the middleman said. "Goofy name."

Luke's eyes met Tenel Ka's and held.

"Thank you, gentlemen," Luke said slowly. "If you're right, I'm afraid this 'Nightsister' may have taken some of our valuables already."

8

JACEN STOOD BEHIND Qorl's pilot chair, biting his lip. The Nightsister Tamith Kai loomed over them, powerful and threatening. He flashed a glance at Jaina, but he didn't think they could do anything to resist.

Not yet anyway.

Docking doors on the ring of the Shadow Academy eased open in the silence of space, exposing a dark cavernous bay rimmed with flashing yellow lights to guide Qorl's ship in. The Imperial pilot worked the controls with grim proficiency, and Jacen noticed that his damaged left arm—which had never properly healed when his TIE fighter had crashed on Yavin 4—was now bulkier, encased in black leather from the shoulder down, wrapped with straps and battery packs.

"Qorl, what happened to your arm?" Jacen asked. "Did they heal it for you, like we promised we'd do at the Jedi academy?"

Qorl diverted his attention from the docking maneuvers, turning his haunted pale eyes toward the boy. "They did not heal it," Qorl said. "They *replaced* it. I now have a droid arm, which is better than my old one. Stronger, capable of more tasks." He bent his leather-bound arm.

Jacen caught the faint whirring of servomotors. His stomach clenched in sick revulsion. "They didn't have to do that," Jacen said. "We could have healed you in a bacta tank, or a medical droid could have tended you. At worst you would have been fitted with a biomechanical prosthetic that looks just like a real arm—even my uncle has one of those. There was no need to give you a droid arm."

Qorl's face was stony, and he turned his attention back to piloting his craft. "Nevertheless, it is done. My arm is better now, stronger."

The Imperial ship drifted into the docking bay, and lines of pulsing lights continued to illuminate the reflective metal walls. A transparisteel-encased observation bay with angular windows protruded from the inner wall above. Jacen could see small figures running diagnostics, working systems to guide Qorl's ship in.

The ship settled down with barely a bump. The docking-bay doors closed behind them, sealing the prisoners inside the sinister Shadow Academy.

Tamith Kai spoke into the comm channel. "Engage cloaking device," she said, her deep voice as irresistible and compelling as a tractor beam.

Though Jacen could see or feel nothing different, he knew that the large space station had suddenly vanished, leaving the illusion of nothing but empty space, where no one would ever find them.

Flanked by a stormtrooper escort, Tamith Kai ushered the children down the boarding ramp, away from the assault ship that had kidnapped them from GemDiver Station. She took them across the bay, toward a broad scarlet door that slid open as they approached.

On the other side stood a young-looking man dressed in flowing silvery robes. His smooth skin and silken blond hair seemed to glow. He was one of the most *beautiful* humans Jacen had ever seen—perfectly formed, like a holo simulation of an ideal man, or a sculptor's masterpiece chiseled out of alabaster. A contingent of stormtroopers stood behind him, blaster rifles resting on their shoulders.

"Welcome, new recruits," he said in a gentle voice that carried undertones of music. "I am Brakiss, leader of the Shadow Academy."

Jacen heard his sister gasp and couldn't restrain his own exclamation. "Brakiss?" he said. "Blaster bolts! We've heard about you. You were an Imperial spy planted at Master Skywalker's academy, trying to steal our training methods."

Brakiss smiled as if inwardly amused.

"That's right," Jaina continued excitedly "Master Skywalker figured out who you were, but when he tried to turn you to the light side—to *save* you—you couldn't face the ugliness inside yourself."

Brakiss's smile never faltered. "Ah, so that's how he tells it? MasterSkywalker and I did not agree on the . . . particulars of training in the Force. But he had at least one good idea: He was correct to bring back the Jedi Knights. He realized that the Jedi were the preservers and protectors of the Old Republic. They unified the decaying old government and kept it alive long after it should have dissolved into anarchy.

"And now that there is anarchy among the remnants of the Imperial forces, *we* need such a unifying force. We have already found a powerful new leader, a great one"—Brakiss smiled—"but we also need our own group of Dark Jedi Knights, Imperial Jedi, who will cement our factions together and give us the will to defeat the wicked and unlawful government of the New Republic and bring about the Second Imperium."

"Hey, our *mother* leads the New Republic!" Jacen objected. "She's not wicked. And she doesn't torture people, or kidnap them, either."

Brakiss said, "It all depends on your perspective."

"Who's this new leader, anyway?" Jaina interrupted. "Haven't you tried to find a single leader before—and ended up with everyone fighting to run what's left of the Empire? It won't work."

"Silence," Tamith Kai said, her voice thick with menace. "You will not ask questions; you will receive indoctrination.

You will be trained as powerful warriors to fight in the service of the Empire."

"I don't think so," Jacen said defiantly

His sister's face flushed with anger. "We won't cooperate with you. You can't steal us away and just expect us to be diligent little students for you. Master Skywalker and our parents will comb the galaxy to find us. They *will* find us, and then you'll be sorry."

Behind them, Lowie snarled and spread his long arms as if longing to tear something limb from limb, as his uncle Chewbacca was rumored to do whenever he lost a hologame.

The stormtroopers suddenly trained their rifles on the infuriated Wookiee.

"Hey, don't shoot him!" Jacen said, moving between the stormtrooper and Lowie.

Jaina spoke up in an authoritative tone that took Jacen by surprise. "What have you done with Em Teedee, Lowie's translator droid? He needs to communicate—unless of course all of these stormtroopers can somehow speak the Wookiee language?"

"He will be given his little droid back," Tamith Kai said, "as soon as it has undergone . . . suitable reprogramming."

Brakiss clapped his hands at the troopers. "We will go to their quarters now," he said. "Their training must begin soon. The Second Imperium has a great need for Dark Jedi Knights."

"You'll never turn us," Jaina said. "You're wasting your time."

Brakiss looked at her, smiled indulgently, and stood in silence for a long moment. "You may find that your mind will change," he said. "Why don't we wait and see."

The stormtroopers formed an armed escort around them as they marched along the clanking metal deck plates.

The Shadow Academy was not comfortable and soft like Lando's GemDiver Station. The walls were not painted with pastel colors; there were no soothing strains of music or nature sounds over the loudspeaker systems, only harsh status reports and chronometer tones that chimed every quarter hour. Stenciled labels marked the doors. Occasional computer terminals mounted to the walls displayed maps of the station and complicated simulations in progress.

"This is an austere station," Tamith Kai said as Jacen stared at the cold, heartless walls. "We don't bother with luxury accommodations like your jungle academy. However, we have made sure that you each have a private chamber so you can conduct your meditation exercises, practice your assignments, and concentrate on developing your Force skills."

"No!" Jaina said.

"We'd rather stay together," Jacen added.

Lowbacca roared in agreement.

Tamith Kai came to an abrupt stop and looked down at them. "I did not *ask* your preference!" she said, her violet eyes blazing. "You will do as you are told."

They reached an intersection of corridors, and here they split into three groups. Brakiss led the cluster of stormtroopers that surrounded Jaina, taking them down a corridor to the right. A larger group of guards, tense and with weapons at the ready, helped Tamith Kai to escort Lowbacca. The remaining guards closed around Jacen and led him off to the left.

"Wait!" Jacen cried, and turned to look at his twin sister for what felt to him like the last time. Jaina stared back at him, her brandy-brown eyes wide with anxiety, but when she bravely lifted her chin, Jacen felt a surge of courage himself. They would find some way out of this.

The guards hustled him down a long corridor until they stopped at one door in a line of identical-seeming doors. Student chambers, he thought.

The door whisked open, and the stormtroopers herded Jacen into a small cubicle, bare-walled and uncomfortable. He saw no speaker panel on the wall, no controls, nothing that would let him communicate with anybody.

"I'm staying in here?" he said in disbelief.

"Yes," the lead stormtrooper said.

"But what if I need something? How am I supposed to call out?" Jacen said.

The trooper turned his skull-like plasteel mask to look directly at him. "Then you will *endure* until someone comes for you." The stormtroopers stepped back, and the door shut behind Jacen, closing him in, weaponless and alone.

Then, to make things worse, all the lights went out.

9

TENEL KA WOKE to pitch-darkness, cramped and confined, surrounded by a dull vibration. Her heart drummed a rapid cadence, and perspiration prickled her skin. An urgency, a feeling that something was terribly wrong, nudged the back of her mind. She tried to sit up and bumped her head—hard—against the unyielding bottom of the bunk above her. Stifling an exclamation of annoyance, she remembered that she was aboard the *Off Chance*. She relaxed slightly—but only slightly.

When they had finished with the Hutt information broker on Borgo Prime, Luke and Tenel Ka decided their best hope for finding Jacen, Jaina, and Lowbacca lay in going directly to Dathomir, homeworld of the original Nightsisters. Their only clue was the mysterious Nightsister, and they had to find out who she was and whether she had the twins and Lowbacca.

Luke had urged Tenel Ka to get some sleep while they made their journey. It was the first opportunity she had had to rest since her friends had been kidnapped, and Tenel Ka gratefully accepted.

And so she had slept, sealed away from light and sound, in one of the berths aboard the *Off Chance*, but her rest had again been disturbed by shadowy dreams. She touched a switch by her head and winced as bright cabin light flooded the sleeping cubicle. She rolled onto her stomach, swung her legs over the side of the bunk, and dropped a meter and a half to the floor of the cabin. Shaking back her tumble of loose red-gold hair, Tenel Ka stretched to her full height and noted with pleasure the freedom of movement that her tough, supple lizard-hide armor afforded her. She was glad to be dressed as a warrior again.

The uneasy feeling left by her dream persisted as Tenel Ka made her way to the cockpit and lowered herself into the copilot's seat next to Luke. She gazed through the front viewport at the swirling colors that indicated the *Off Chance* was traveling through hyperspace.

Luke looked up from the controls. "Did you get some sleep?"

"This is a fact." She fastened the crash webbing around her, then grabbed a thick clump of her hair and began plaiting it into a braid, adding a few feathers and beads that she kept in a pouch attached to her belt.

"But you didn't sleep *well*?"

She blinked at this, somehow surprised that he had noticed. "This is also a fact."

Luke did not reply. He simply waited, and with growing discomfort she realized he was waiting for her to explain.

"I . . . had a dream," she said. "It is not important."

His intense blue eyes searched her face. When he spoke, it was in a low voice. "I feel fear in you."

She grimaced and shrugged. "It is a dream I have had before."

His eyelids fluttered shut briefly, and he tilted his head as he might have done had he been studying her with his eyes open. ". . . the Nightsisters?" he said at last.

"Yes. It is childish," she admitted as color rushed to her cheeks, staining them with embarrassment.

"Strange . . . I dreamt about them, too," Luke said.

Tenel Ka looked at him in disbelief. "I used to think they were just a story that mothers and grandmothers on Dathomir told to scare children. But the Nightsisters were all destroyed. How could there be any left?"

"The people of Dathomir are often strong in the Force, and it would not be difficult for someone else to train them in the ways of evil," he said. He leaned back in the pilot's seat and stared out at hyperspace as if summoning an old memory. "In fact, many years ago—before you were born—I traveled to Dathomir searching for Jacen and Jaina's parents. Han and Leia. That was when I met your mother and father, and we all joined forces to defeat the last of the Nightsisters."

Tenel Ka looked at him curiously. This was a part of the story her parents spoke little about. "My mother thinks very highly of you," she said, hoping he would elaborate.

Luke slid her a teasing glance. "But did she ever tell you how we met? That she *captured* me?"

"You don't mean—" Tenel Ka began. "She couldn't have expected . . ."

Luke chuckled at her discomfiture. "This is a fact."

"Oh, Master Skywalker!" Tenel Ka gasped in chagrin at the very idea of Luke submitting to the primitive marriage customs she had always viewed as quaint and provincial. On Dathomir, a woman selected and captured the man she wanted to marry. Her mother, Teneniel Djo, had done *that* to Luke Skywalker?

It brought a renewed flush of embarrassment to her face to realize that her mother had captured the greatest Jedi Master in the galaxy and had expected him to marry her and father her children. Then, all at once, the situation struck her as so ridiculous that she let loose with what was, for her, a rare sound indeed—a giggle.

"My mother has always taught me to have respect for Jedi, and most of all for you, Master Skywalker, but . . . please do not be offended"—she gasped, tears of mirth rising to her eyes—"I am certainly glad she did not succeed."

Luke, still smiling, reached over and gave her shoulder an understanding squeeze. "So am I. Your parents belonged together."

"I love my father, you know," Tenel Ka said, sobering, "and my mother."

"And yet you've never told your friends who your real parents are," Luke said. "Why?"

Tenel Ka squirmed uncomfortably in her crash restraints, which suddenly felt too confining. She had often mulled this problem over, and had come to the same decision again and again. "It is difficult to explain," she said. "I am not ashamed of my parents, if that is what you think. I am proud that my mother is strong in the Force and that she, a warrior from Dathomir, now rules the entire Hapes Cluster. And I am proud of my father and what he managed to become, despite the way he was raised—despite the one who raised him."

Luke nodded sagely. "Your grandmother?"

"Yes," Tenel Ka gritted. "Of *that* part of my family, I am not proud. My grandmother is power-hungry. She manipulates. I am not sure she even knows how to love." She felt a bleak bewilderment as she turned to look at Luke. "Yet my father is loving and wise. He is not like her."

"No, he isn't," Luke said. "Long ago your father Isolder did something difficult and very brave. Realizing that your grandmother loved power so much she was willing to kill anyone who threatened her, he rejected her teaching. She is a strong, proud woman, but her lessons were poisonous. He chose instead to value and honor life wherever he found it. Your father's difficult decision was the right one.

Tenel Ka nodded. Her thoughts were bitter. "My lineage is tainted by generations of bloodthirsty, power-hungry tyrants. I am not *proud* that I was born to the royal family of Hapes," she spat. "I do not wish my friends to know that I am heir to the throne, because I have done nothing to earn it, choose it, or deserve it."

Luke's face was thoughtful. "Jacen and Jaina would understand that. Their mother is one of the most powerful women in the galaxy."

Tenel Ka shook her head violently. "Before I tell them, I must prove to myself that I am not like my ancestors. I choose to take pride only in what *I* accomplish, first through my own strength, and then through the Force—never through inherited political power. My parents are very proud that I have decided to become a Jedi."

"I understand," Luke said. "You've chosen a difficult path." He smiled at her warmly. "It is a good start for a Jedi."

THE NEXT DAY, Jaina's joy at seeing her brother again was overshadowed by Tamith Kai's presence and the fact that they were each being shepherded down the corridor by a pair of well-armed stormtroopers.

When Jacen broke away from his guards just long enough to give her a quick hug, she spoke her words in a whispered burst. "I've got a plan. I need your help."

Rough, armored hands pulled the brother and sister apart. One of the armor-clad guards leveled his blaster pistol at the twins and motioned them to move on.

Jaina smiled in wry amusement. Even with Tamith Kai present, Brakiss still wasn't certain of their cooperation. The stormtroopers were here to ensure that they caused no trouble.

A slight nod of Jacen's head told Jaina that he understood her words. "Want to hear a joke?" he asked brightly, purposely changing the subject.

"Sure," Jaina answered with feigned innocence.

Jacen cleared his throat. "How many stormtroopers does it take to change a glowpanel?"

Jaina cringed inwardly. Her brother certainly was brave—or perhaps foolhardy. Nonetheless, she took the bait. "I don't know, how many stormtroopers *does* it take to change a glowpanel?"

One of the guards stepped ahead of Jaina and stopped at the door to a lecture room in which she could see dozens of people seated. She guessed they were probably the other Shadow Academy trainees. The guard with the blaster pistol gestured for them to enter.

"It takes two stormtroopers to change a glowpanel," Jacen said in a voice loud enough for everyone to hear. "One stormtrooper to change it, and the other one to shoot him and take credit for all the work."

Jaina tried unsuccessfully to suppress a snort of laughter. Tamith Kai glared violet daggers at Jacen.

Jacen squirmed under her angry regard and muttered, "I can tell *you're* from Dathomir. Your people aren't exactly known for their sense of humor."

As her two guards took her arms in a bruising grip, Jaina was forced to admit that her brother's small act of bravado had released something inside her, had shown her that her mind—at least for now—was still free, that she still had choices.

She was dragged into the meeting room, where her guards shoved her into a sitting position at one end of a narrow, backless bench. Jacen's guards seated him on the opposite side of the room—no doubt to punish him for his joke. Jaina was delighted to see that Lowie sat less than a meter away from her, with only one student between them. He roared a greeting at her and Jacen.

The other students were all human, clean-cut, and wearing dark uniforms. They seemed eager to learn, glad to be at the Shadow Academy, genuine Imperial youth. She had seen people like this before. She, Jacen, and Lowie might be the only ones resisting the training, she knew.

Jaina frowned when she saw that Em Teedee was still not at Lowie's belt. That would make communication difficult. She wondered what her uncle Luke would do in such a situation. She sat up straight, cleared her mind, and sent a gentle thought probing in Lowie's direction. She did not feel any pain from him. He was unharmed—of that she was certain—but she did sense tension, confusion, and simmering frustration. She tried to send him soothing thoughts. She wasn't sure how much got through, but when Lowie briefly reached a furry hand around to touch her shoulder, she knew he understood.

Jaina wondered if she dared speak openly to her Wookiee friend. She would have to find out what the student next to her was like first. He was about her age, and a little taller. Like all the willing students, he wore a tight, sleek-fitting charcoal jumpsuit beneath a flowing robe of purest black. He had blond hair and moss-green eyes, and he glanced at her without any particular recognition or interest.

She sent her thought probe toward the young man, but caught nothing beyond elusive snatches that blared fleetingly in her mind, like disconnected notes from an orchestra tuning its instruments.

"Why are we here?" Jaina asked in a voice just above a whisper.

"Because we are here," he replied, aloof and a bit defensive. "Because Master Brakiss wishes us to be here." He looked at her with suspicion, as if she had proved herself mentally deficient. "Are we not all here to learn the ways of the Force from Master Brakiss?"

Before Jaina could reply, Brakiss himself strode into the chamber. The silence in the room was instant and complete. Not a cough or a syllable challenged his compelling presence. Brakiss let his piercing eyes rove across the faces of the gathered students. When his eyes met hers, Jaina felt an inexplicable chill creep down her spine.

Without preamble, he began to teach.

"The Force is an energy that surrounds all living things. It flows through us. It flows from us."

As his voice streamed around the students, Jaina felt her mind begin to relax. This wasn't so bad after all. All of it was true. The power in Brakiss's voice urged action, demanded agreement. Jaina saw the heads of many of the students nodding. She nodded too.

Jaina could not remember the words as Brakiss led them smoothly, logically from one concept to another. All she remembered were the thoughts, the feelings, the *rightness* of it all.

Then suddenly, for some reason—perhaps it was the light touch of a furry hand on her back—the words came into focus again, began to penetrate the complacent fog of unquestioning agreement that had blanketed her mind.

"You each have the tools inside you to master yourselves, and to master the Force," the tranquil, confident voice said. "And to draw on the strength of the Force, you must learn to draw on what is strongest in you: strong emotions, deep desires, fear, aggression, hate, anger."

A resounding *No!* rang through Jaina's mind, and she

shook her head to clear it. "That . . . can't be true," she whispered. "It's not true."

The student next to Jaina flicked his eyes at her with a look of disdain. "Of *course* it's true," he said, as if using indisputable logic. "Master Brakiss said it, so it must be true."

"What makes you so sure?" Jaina hissed. "Can't you see that he has a hold on your mind? You should get away from this place and start thinking for yourself."

"I don't *wish* to leave," he said, his expression implacable. "I wish to study with Master Brakiss and become a Jedi."

Jaina seethed at his stubbornness. "Have you even thought about this? You can't just blindly accept whatever he says without bothering to think about it. What if he's wrong?"

"He is the *teacher*." The student's moss-green eyes blinked at her as if her question made no sense. He stood abruptly, begging Brakiss's attention.

Jaina took the opportunity to lean behind him and whisper to Lowie. "I've got a plan! In a couple of days, I'll need you to knock out all the station's power. Be ready." As she sat back up, her mind finally registered the fact that the stubborn blond student was addressing Brakiss.

"—is trying to convince your other students that they should not believe you, that you do not have the true teachings of the Force. And therefore I suggest that this—this *girl* is not a worthy pupil for you, Master Brakiss."

Brakiss's beautiful, piercing eyes narrowed and came to rest on Jaina. She felt the press of his powerful mind against hers. She tried to resist.

"You are new here," he said. "You do not know our ways. Listen to my teachings, then make your judgment. Decide for yourself. But do not encourage others to disbelieve me *ever* again."

In unison, the students murmured their agreement—with three exceptions.

"At this academy we do not learn only one side of the Force," Brakiss went on, resuming his lecture, though his comments seemed directed primarily toward Jacen, Jaina, and Lowie. "This is not a school of darkness. I call this a Shadow Academy, for what does life create by its very nature, if not shadows? And it is only through using the full range of your emotions and desires—the light *and* the dark— that you will become truly strong in the Force and fulfill your destiny. The light side by itself offers only limited power. But when the light is blended with the dark, and you work within the shadows, then you achieve your full potential. Use the strength of the dark side."

Jaina looked across at Jacen, who was slowly shaking his head. Close beside her, Lowie growled deep in his throat. Unable to contain herself any longer, Jaina stood. "That's not right," she said. "The dark side doesn't make you any stronger. It's faster, easier, more seductive. Its also more tenacious. Just as the light side brings freedom, the dark side brings only bondage. Once you enslave yourself to the dark side of the Force, you may never escape."

A collective gasp went up, but no one said a word as Jaina and Brakiss faced each other over the students' heads. Brakiss was silent for a long moment, his mind pressing down on hers with suffocating weight.

With a mental heave Jaina flung aside the influence of his mind on hers and challenged him, her eyes filled with pride, her thoughts free.

At last, Brakiss shook his head sadly. "I did not wish to make an example of you. But you leave me no choice. You have chosen to pit your puny light-side powers against my own. I gave you one warning. You will not receive another."

With that, Brakiss lifted one hand slightly, almost as if to wave a fond farewell. Blue fire danced from his fingertips and surrounded Jaina in a haze of bright agony.

Brakiss's calm cruelty against Jaina launched Lowbacca into an unbridled rage. Unable to control himself, he leaped from his cramped seat, knocking over the blond student. He howled at the top of his lungs and bared long Wookiee fangs. Ginger-colored fur stuck out in all directions as he yanked up the bench he had been sitting on and raised it over his head.

Alerted by the disturbance, the guards charged into the room, their stun pistols drawn, looking for the source of the chaos—and the enraged Wookiee was not difficult to find.

Lowie threw the bench at the incoming stormtroopers. His blow knocked the first cluster of guards backward into each other, tumbling them down like children's blocks. Five more stormtroopers tripped over their fallen companions but still managed to wade into the room.

The other Shadow Academy trainees added to the uproar, trying to shout Lowie down. The Wookiee just roared back at them. From the podium, Brakiss urged everyone to be calm, but no one listened.

Another door whisked open, and a new contingent of stormtroopers rushed in from the far side of the room.

Jacen dashed to his unconscious sister's side and cradled her head and shoulders in his lap. With relief, he sensed that she was not seriously injured from the Force blast. She groaned and blinked her brandy-brown eyes, trying to fight her way back to consciousness.

"Jaina," he called. "Jaina, snap out of it!"

"All right . . . I am," she said, struggling to sit up. Then she seemed suddenly to notice the brawl that Lowie had started on her behalf.

The second set of stormtroopers drew their stun pistols as Lowie yanked a bench out from under another Shadow Academy student, sending her to the floor. The student squealed in outrage. Lowie ignored her and raised the bench to throw at the incoming stormtroopers.

They pointed their stun pistols and fired—but the beam caught the front of the bench, doing no damage. Lowie tossed it, and the troopers scrambled out of the way as the bench crashed against the side wall. Lowbacca ducked to pick up something else to throw—and just as he did, the first set of stormtroopers on the other side of the room, finally climbing back to their feet, fired their stun pistols.

Glowing blue arcs shot over Lowie's back, missing him

and striking full against three of the second set of troopers on the other side, stunning them. They sprawled senseless on the floor in a clattering tumble of white plasteel armor.

"Cease this disturbance!" Brakiss shouted. His normally smooth features had lost their serene composure.

One of the stormtroopers in the first group took two steps forward and aimed his stun pistol directly at Lowie's back as the Wookiee stood up, presenting an easy target.

Jacen watched and—in the moment before the stormtrooper could fire—used his greatest strength with the Force to grasp the trooper's blaster and wrench it halfway around, twisting it in the white-gloved hand so that when the guard squeezed the firing button, the barrel was pointed toward his own chest. The stun beam splashed out, knocking the trooper to the ground, unconscious.

"Lowie, I'm all right," Jaina called, picking herself up and climbing to her feet. "Look, I'm all right!"

More stormtroopers rushed in from both sides of the room, weapons drawn.

"Lowie, calm down," Jacen said.

Lowbacca looked from side to side, fingers spread, arms ready to tear something apart, until he saw he was clearly outnumbered.

Brakiss stood with his fingers outstretched. A shimmering power curled between them, ready to be unleashed.

"We don't want to damage you," Brakiss said, filled with savage intensity, "but you must learn discipline." The master of the Shadow Academy looked to the stormtroopers. "Return them to their quarters, and keep them separated! We have great work to do here and cannot be distracted by unchanneled displays of temper."

Then Brakiss adjusted his handsome features until he looked calm and soothing again. He raised his eyebrows in admiration toward Lowie. "I am pleased to see the strength in your anger, young Wookiee. That is something we must develop. You have great potential"

White-armored guards crushed Lowie's hairy arms in their unfeeling grip. The stormtroopers marched the three young Jedi Knights out into the corridor and toward their cells.

11

DATHOMIR SPARKLED LIKE a rich topaz jewel, welcoming Tenel Ka as Luke piloted the *Off Chance* down into the atmosphere. Anticipation tingled through her. Regardless of the unhappy circumstances that brought them here, Tenel Ka could not help the feeling of pleasure and joy that throbbed through her veins with every beat of her heart. *Home-home. Home-home.*

Turbulence buffeted the blockade runner as they descended. Luke studied the displays on the navigation console and adjusted their course from time to time.

It's been a long time since I made a visit to the Singing Mountain Clan," Luke said. "I don't remember exactly how to get there. I think I can get us close, but unless you happen to know the coordinates—"

Tenel Ka rattled off the numbers before he could finish his thought. At the same time, she leaned forward and entered the coordinates into the navicomp.

"I come here often," she explained. "It is my second home in the galaxy, but it is the first home of my heart."

"Yes," Luke said, "I can understand that."

As the *Off Chance* carried them to the home of the Singing Mountain Clan, they passed over shining oceans, lush forests, vast deserts, rolling hills, and wide fertile plains. Tenel Ka felt strength and energy flow through her, as if the very atmosphere of the planet had the power to recharge her.

"Look," Luke said, pointing down at a herd of blue-skinned reptiles racing at incredible speed across a plain.

"Blue Mountain people," Tenel Ka said. "They migrate every dawn and every dusk."

Luke nodded. "One of them gave me a ride once."

"That is a rare honor, Master Skywalker," she said. "Not even I have had that opportunity"

The pale pink sun was high above the horizon by the time they reached the wide, bowl-shaped valley of the Singing Mountain Clan, Tenel Ka's second home. A green and brown patchwork of fields and orchards spread beneath them in the pinkish sunlight. Small clusters of thatched huts dotted the valley, and morning cooking fires glimmered here and there.

Luke pointed to the stone fortress built into the side of the cliff wall that rose high above the valley floor. "Does Augwynne Djo still rule here?"

"Yes. My great-grandmother."

"Good. We'll go directly to her then. I'd prefer to tell only a few people why we are here and keep our presence as secret as possible," he said, then he brought the *Off Chance* to a smooth landing on the valley floor beside the fortress.

"That should not be difficult," Tenel Ka replied. "My people do not speak unnecessarily."

Luke chuckled. "I can believe that."

Tenel Ka paused halfway up the steep path that led to the fortress. She was not at all fatigued; she was simply savoring the moment.

Luke, who had been following behind her with unwavering steps, halted without a word and waited for her to continue. He did not seem the least bit winded, his breathing slow and regular—no small feat considering the rapid pace Tenel Ka set.

The longer she knew Master Skywalker, the more she admired him, and the better she understood why her mother—who did not often speak highly of any man except her husband, Isolder—had always held Luke Skywalker in high esteem.

Tenel Ka drew in a deep breath. The air was delicious, but not just from the mouthwatering odors of roasting meat and vegetables that wafted from the cooking fires. It was late summer in the valley, and the warm breeze was redolent with the scents of ripening fruit, golden grasses, and early harvest.

Despite the intermingled odors of the lizard pens and the herd of domesticated rancors, there was a freshness to the air that lifted her heart.

Tenel Ka set off again as if there was not a moment to lose. Finally, she stood before the gate of the fortress, where she announced herself as a member of the clan.

The gates were thrown open and Tenel Ka's clan sisters welcomed her with warm embraces and low murmurs of greeting. All were dressed in lizard-skin tunics of various colors, like the one Tenel Ka wore. Some wore elaborate helmets, while others simply wore their hair in decorated braids.

One clan sister with black hair that fell to her waist drew the two travelers inside. "Augwynne told us you would come," she said. Her expression was grave, but Tenel Ka could see the smile that lit her eyes.

"Our mission is urgent," Tenel Ka stated, not bothering to greet the woman. "We *must* see Augwynne alone at once." She had never used such a tone of command in Master Skywalker's presence before, but she knew her clan sister would not be offended. At times like this, pleasantries were an unnecessary luxury among her people.

The woman inclined her head slightly "Augwynne has guessed this much. She waits for you in the war room."

The ancient woman stood as they entered the room. "Welcome, Jedi Skywalker. And welcome great-granddaughter Tenel Ka Chume Ta' Djo." She embraced each of them in turn.

Tenel Ka groaned. "Please," she said, "do not use my full name. And do *not* send word that we are here."

Luke interrupted. "We're following a trail that has led us from Yavin to Borgo Prime to Dathomir. Our need for information has brought us to you."

Tenel Ka took a deep breath and searched for words. She looked directly at her great-grandmother. Augwynne's wrinkle-nested eyes were attentive, cautious. "We are searching for the Nightsisters. Do any remain on Dathomir?"

Augwynne's heavy sigh told Tenel Ka that they had come to the right place. The old woman fixed her gaze on Luke.

"They are not Nightsisters as you and I knew them," she said. "Not wizened crones with discolored skin, who rotted from the nightspells they spoke." She shook her head. "No, they are a newly formed order of Nightsisters, young and fair, and allied with the Empire." She lifted a finger to stroke Tenel Ka's cheek. "Their evil is subtle. They tame and ride rancors as we do. They dress as warriors, if they choose. They are not even all women . . . but they *are* the children of darkness. They are dangerous, with new goals. Do not seek them out."

"We must," Tenel Ka said simply. "It is our best hope for rescuing my closest friends."

Augwynne gave her great-granddaughter a measuring look. "You pledged friendship with these people you must rescue?"

Tenel Ka nodded. "With full ceremony."

"Then we have no other choice," Augwynne said with finality. "You must present your case before the Council of Sisters."

12

BRAKISS HAD A private office on the Shadow Academy, a place where he could go for solitude and contemplation.

Now, as he pondered, he stared at the brilliant images surrounding him on the walls: a waterfall of scarlet lava on the molten planet Nkllon; an exploding sun that spewed arcs of stellar fire in the Denarii Nova; the still-blazing core of the Cauldron Nebula, where seven giant stars had all gone supernova at once; and a vista of the broken shards of Alderaan, destroyed by the Empire's first Death Star more than twenty years before.

Brakiss recognized great beauty in the violence of the universe, in the unbridled power provided by the galaxy or unleashed by human ingenuity.

Standing alone and in silence, Brakiss used Force techniques to meditate and absorb these cosmic catastrophes, crystallizing the strength within himself. Through the dark side, he knew how to make the Force bend to his will. The power stored within the galaxy was his to use. When he captured it and held it with his heart, Brakiss could maintain his calm exterior and not be prone to violence, as his fellow instructor Tamith Kai so often was.

Brakiss eased back in his padded chair; letting his breath flow slowly out. The synthetic leather squeaked as his body rubbed against it, and the warmers inside the chair brought the temperature to a relaxing level. The cushions conformed themselves to his body to give him the greatest comfort.

Tamith Kai refused such indulgences outright. She was a hard woman, insisting on privation and adversity to hone her skills for the Empire that had recognized her potential and taken her from the bleak planet Dathomir. Brakiss, however, found that he could think better when he was at ease. He could plan, mull over possibilities.

Brakiss switched on the recording pad on his desktop and called up the day's records. He would have to make a report and ship it in an armored hyperdrone to their powerful new Imperial leader, hidden deep in the Core Systems.

It had been some time since the encampment he founded in the Great Canyon on Dathomir had provided any strong new students, but the three talented young trainees kidnapped from SkyWalker's Jedi academy were another story, worth the risk of stealing them. Brakiss could sense it.

But their focus was all wrong. Master Skywalker had taught them too much and in the wrong ways. They didn't know how to turn their anger into a sharpened spearpoint for a larger weapon. They contemplated too much. They were too calm, too passive—except for the Wookiee. Brakiss needed to train those three. He and Tamith Kai would employ their separate specialties to work on them.

Brakiss drummed his fingertips on the slick surface of his desk. Occasionally, he felt twinges of sadness for having left the Yavin 4 training center. He had learned much there, though his own mission for the Empire was always uppermost in his mind.

Long ago, the Empire had selected Brakiss because of his untapped Jedi ability. He had undergone rigorous training and conditioning so that he could spy on Skywalker's academy, gathering precious information. No one was supposed to know he was a scout, planted there to learn techniques that he could teach to the Second Imperium. The new Imperial leader had insisted on developing his own Dark Jedi, a symbol that those faithful to the Empire could rally around.

Somehow, though, Master Skywalker had immediately seen through the deception. He had realized Brakiss's true identity. But unlike previous clumsy and unpracticed spies who had come to Yavin 4 with the same mission, Brakiss had not been expelled outright. Skywalker had shown little patience for those others—but apparently he had seen real potential in Brakiss.

Master Skywalker had begun working on him, openly teaching him those things he most needed to learn. Brakiss did have a great talent with the Force, and Master Skywalker had shown him how to use it. But Skywalker had repeatedly tried to contaminate Brakiss with the light side, with the platitudes and peaceful ways of the New Republic. Brakiss shuddered at the thought.

Finally, in a private and supremely important test, Master Skywalker had taken Brakiss on a mental journey within himself—not allowing him to look outward through the rivers of the Force, but turning the dark student inside to see his own heart, so he could observe the truth about what he himself was made of.

Brakiss had opened a trapdoor and fallen into a pit filled with his self-deception and the potential cruelties that the Empire could force him to carry out. Master Skywalker stood beside him, forcing him to look—and keep looking—even as Brakiss scrambled to escape from himself, not wanting to face the lies of his own existence.

But the Imperial conditioning ran too deep. His mind was too far lost in service to the Empire, and Brakiss had nearly gone insane from that ordeal. He had run from Master Skywalker, taking his ship and fleeing into the depths of space.

He had remained alone for a long time before finally returning to the embrace of the Second Imperium, where he put his expertise to work . . . just as it had been planned from the beginning.

Brakiss was handsome, perfectly formed, not at all corrupted as the Emperor had appeared in his last days, when the dark side had devoured him from within. Brakiss tried to deny that corruption—to comfort himself with his outer appearance—but he could not escape the ugliness in the darkness of his heart.

He knew his place in the Empire would be reborn, and he had learned to be content with that service. His greatest triumph was his Shadow Academy, where he could oversee the new Dark Jedi being trained: dozens of students, some with little or no talent at all, but others with the potential for true greatness, like Darth Vader himself.

Of course, the new Imperial leader also recognized the danger in creating such a powerful group of Dark Jedi. Knights who had fallen to the dark side were bound to have ambitions of their own, tempted by the power they themselves controlled. It was Brakiss's job to keep them in line.

But the great leader had his own protective measures. The entire Shadow Academy was filled with self-destructive devices: hundreds, if not thousands, of chain-reaction explosives. If Brakiss did not succeed in creating his troop of Dark Jedi, or if the new trainees somehow staged a revolt against the Second Imperium, the Imperial leader would trigger the station's self-destruct sequences. Brakiss and all the Dark Jedi would be destroyed in a flash.

A hostage to darkness, Brakiss was never allowed to leave the Shadow Academy. By order of the great leader, he would remain there, confined, until he and all his trainees had proven themselves.

Brakiss found that sitting on a huge bomb made it difficult to concentrate. But he had great confidence in his own abilities and in Tamith Kai's. Without that confidence he could never have become a Jedi in the first place—and he would never have dared to touch the teachings of the dark side. But he *had* learned those ways, and he had grown strong.

He would turn these new students. He was sure he could do it.

Brakiss smiled as he finished the report encapsulating his plans. The lanky Wookiee's anger was something to take advantage of, and Tamith Kai was the best at that. The new Nightsister was a born tormentor, and she carried out her duties extremely well. Brakiss would let her train Lowbacca.

He, on the other hand, would work with the twins, the grandchildren of Darth Vader. They were too calm, too well trained, and resisted in subtle ways that would prove far more difficult to deal with.

For them, he had other methods. First, he had to find out what Jacen and Jaina *really wanted*—and he would give it to them.

From that point on, they would be his.

13

THE SHADOW ACADEMY'S training chamber stood large and empty, a yawning, vacant space walled off on all sides. The doors sealed behind Jacen, imprisoning him with Brakiss, leaving him to face whatever the teacher had in store. The walls were a flat gray, studded with a grid of computer sensors. Jacen saw no controls, no way out.

He looked up at the beautiful man, who stood in silvery robes watching Jacen with a calm, patient smile.

Brakiss reached into his shimmering robes and withdrew a black cylinder about half the length of Jacen's forearm. It had three power buttons and a series of widely spaced grooves for fingerholds.

A lightsaber.

"You will need this for today's training," Brakiss said, broadening his smile. "Take it. It's yours."

Jacen's eyes widened. His hand reached forward, but he

drew back, trying to hide his eagerness. "What do I have to do for it?" he asked warily.

"Nothing," Brakiss answered. "Just *use* it, that's all."

Jacen swallowed and did not meet Brakiss's eyes, afraid to show how he longed to have his own lightsaber. But he didn't want to have it in this place, under these circumstances. "Hey, I'm not supposed to," he said. "I haven't completed my training. Master Skywalker and I had this discussion just a few days ago."

"Nonsense," Brakiss said. "Master Skywalker is holding you back unnecessarily. You already know how to use one of these. Go ahead."

Brakiss extended the lightsaber handle to Jacen, moving it closer, tantalizing him. "Here at the Shadow Academy we feel that lightsaber skills are among the *first* talents a Jedi should develop, because strong, able warriors are always needed. If a Jedi Knight is not ready to fight for a cause, then what good is he?"

Brakiss pressed the lightsaber into Jacen's hands, and Jacen instinctively curled his fingers around it. The weapon felt at the same time heavy with responsibility and light with power. The finger grooves were widely spaced for his young hand, but he would grow accustomed to it.

Jacen touched the power button, and with a *snap-hiss* a sapphire beam crackled out, indigo at the core but electric blue on the fringes. He flicked the blade from side to side, and the molten energy sliced through the air, trailing a faint smell of ozone. He slashed back again.

Brakiss folded his hands together. "Good," he said.

Jacen whirled and held the lightsaber up. "Hey, what's to stop me from just cutting you down right here, Brakiss? You're evil. You've kidnapped us. You're training enemies of the New Republic."

Brakiss laughed—not a mocking laugh, but simply an expression of wry amusement. "You won't kill me, young Jedi," he said. "You would not cut down an unarmed opponent. Cold-blooded murder is not part of the training Master Skywalker gives his young trainees ... unless he has changed his curriculum since I left Yavin 4?"

Brakis's alabaster-smooth face seemed exquisitely serene, but he raised his pale eyebrows. "Of course if you do let loose your anger," he said, "and slice me in half, you will have taken a significant first step down the dark path. Even though I won't be here to see the benefits, the Empire will no doubt use your abilities to great advantage."

"That's enough," Jacen said, switching off the lightsaber.

"You're right," Brakiss agreed. "No more talk. This is a training center."

"What are you going to do to me?" Jacen said, holding up the lightsaber handle, alert and ready to switch it on again.

"Just practice, my dear boy," Brakiss said, easing toward the door. "This room can project holo-remotes, imaginary enemies for you to fight, to help you hone your skill with your new weapon. Your lightsaber."

"If they're just holo-remotes, why should I fight at all?" Jacen said defiantly. "Why should I cooperate?"

Brakiss crossed his arms over his chest. "I'm inclined to ask you to indulge me, but I doubt you would do that—at least not yet. So let us put it another way." His voice took on a sudden hard edge, as sharp as razor crystal. "The holo-remotes will be monster warriors. But how do you know I won't slip in an actual creature to fight against you? You would never know the difference, the holo-remotes are so realistic. And if you stand there and refuse to fight, a real enemy might just remove your head from your shoulders.

"Of course, I probably won't do that in the first session. Probably not. Or maybe I will, to show you I'm sincere. You'll be here a long time training in the dark side. You never know when I might lose patience with you."

Brakiss stepped out of the training chamber, and the metal doors shut behind him with a clang.

Alone in the dimly lit chamber with its flat gray walls, Jacen waited, tense. Except for his breathing and his heartbeat, the room was completely silent, as if it swallowed all noise. He shifted, felt the hard Corusca gem still hidden in his boot. He took comfort in the fact that the Imperials had not found it and taken it away from him, but he didn't know how it could help him now.

Jacen turned the lightsaber handle in his hands, trying to decide what he should do. Intellectually, he was certain Brakiss was bluffing, that the man would never send in a real murderous monster. But a part of Jacen's heart wasn't so sure, and the slight twinge of doubt made him uneasy.

Then the air shimmered. Jacen heard a grinding sound and whirled to look behind him. A door he had not noticed before crawled open to reveal a shadowy dungeon from which something large and shambling scraped forward, dragging sharp claws along the floor.

Jacen's hobby back at home had been studying strange and unusual animals and plants. He had pored over the records of known alien races, memorizing them all—but still it took him a few moments to recognize the hideous monster that was now emerging from its cell.

It was an Abyssin, a one-eyed monster with greenish-tan skin, broad shoulders, and long, powerful arms that hung near the ground and ended in claws that could shred trees.

The cyclopean creature plodded out of its cell, growled, and looked around with its one eye. The Abyssin seemed to be in pain, and the only thing it saw—and therefore its only target—was young Jacen, armed with his lightsaber.

The Abyssin roared, but Jacen stood firm. He held up his free hand, palm outward, trying to use the soothing Force techniques that had proven so successful when he'd tamed new animals as his pets.

"Calm down," he said. "Calm down. I don't want to hurt you. I'm not with these people."

But the Abyssin didn't want to be calmed, and stalked forward, swinging its long arms like clawed pendulums. Of course, Jacen realized, if the monster was really just a hologram, then his Jedi techniques would be irrelevant.

The Abyssin pulled out a long, wicked club that had been strapped against its back. The club looked like a gnarled branch with spikes on one end, with a far longer reach than the lightsaber's. The one-eyed monster could pound Jacen and never be touched by the Jedi blade.

"Blaster bolts!" Jacen muttered under his breath. He

flicked on the lightsaber, feeling the power of the energy blade that pulsed in front of him with a blinding blue glow.

The Abyssin blinked its single large eye, then charged forward, its fang-filled mouth wide open. The creature swung its spiked club like a battering ram.

Jacen slashed in front of himself with the lightsaber defensively, instinctively. The glowing blade sliced off the tip of the club as easily as if it were a piece of soft cheese. The spiked end clanged on the metal floor.

The monster looked at the smoking end of its club for just a second, then howled and charged again. Jacen was ready this time—his heart pounding, adrenaline flowing, attuned to the Force and focused on his enemy.

The Abyssin hammered down with the club, too close for Jacen to strike with the lightsaber. He dodged to the side, and the creature swung again, this time with a raking handful of claws.

Jacen made a dive for the floor and rolled, holding the lightsaber at arm's length to keep from harming himself with the deadly blade.

The Abyssin pounced on him, thrusting with the thick end of the club. But Jacen lay on his back and held the lightsaber up, twisting his wrists to slash the remainder of the club down to a smoldering stump in the monster's hands, then rolled sideways to dodge the heavy wood as it fell to the floor.

The Abyssin tossed away the useless stump and yowled again, then lunged to grab Jacen from the floor. But Jacen held the lightsaber in front of himself, pushing it forward like a spear. The glowing tip plunged into the descending monster's broad chest, scorching through until it disintegrated the Abyssin's heart.

With a loud and fading shriek of pain, the creature slumped and fell forward. Jacen winced, knowing he would be crushed by the brute—but in midair the cyclops flickered and dissolved into static, then nothingness, as the hologram projectors shut down.

Gasping and sweating, Jacen turned off the lightsaber.

The hissing energy beam was swallowed into the handle with a descending *thwoop*. He stood up and brushed himself off.

As the door opened again, Jacen whirled, ready to face another hideous enemy. But only Brakiss stood there, quietly applauding.

"Very good, my young Jedi," Brakiss said. "That wasn't so bad now, was it? You show great potential. All you need is the opportunity to practice."

14

LOWIE CROUCHED ATOP the sleeping platform in his own cell, back pressed to the corner, shaggy knees drawn up to his chest. He wallowed in abject misery and self-recrimination; occasionally he let out a groan.

How could he have been so stupid? He had let the riptide of Brakiss's teaching draw him further and further into his sea of anger until he had been immersed in it, swept away by its current.

Jacen had not given in. And seductive as Brakiss's teachings were—Lowie refused to think of him as *Master* Brakiss—Jaina had not succumbed to them either; she had merely stood up and spoken for what she believed.

A growl of self-reproach rumbled deep in his throat. He alone, who had always prided himself on his thoughtfulness—on his dedication to studying, to learning, to understanding—had allowed himself to be influenced by the poisonous teachings. He would have to be more careful in the future. Resist, block out the words.

If Jacen and Jaina could stay strong, then so could Lowie. Jaina had not given up. She said she had a plan, and he would need to be ready to do his part when the time came to escape. Lowie drew comfort from the thought of his friends' strength. He *could* resist giving in to his anger. He pounded a furry fist against the wall at his side and bellowed his defiance. He *would* resist.

As if in response to his challenge, the door slid open and two stormtroopers stepped in, followed by Tamith Kai. Lowie wrinkled his nose, noting something else that had entered his room uninvited: the unpleasant smell that hung about them, an odor of darkness. The stormtroopers each carried an activated stun wand, and Lowie guessed that they expected him to cause further trouble.

"You will stand," Tamith Kai said.

Lowie wondered whether he dared resist. A prod from one of the stormtroopers' stun wands answered the question for him.

Tamith Kai's violet gaze raked up and down Lowie for a moment, and then she blew out a short breath, as if about to start a difficult task that she had set herself.

"You are not yet skilled in the ways of the Force," she said, not unkindly, "yet you have the capacity for great anger." She nodded with approval. "This is your greatest strength. I will teach you now to draw upon that anger, to bring forth your full power in the Force. You will be surprised at how it will accelerate your learning."

She turned to the stormtroopers. "Remove his belt."

Lowie put a protective hand to the glossy braids that encircled his waist and crossed over his shoulder. He had risked his life to acquire these fibers from the syren plant as part of his rites of passage into Wookiee adulthood; then he had painstakingly woven them into a belt that symbolized his independence and self-reliance.

He opened his mouth to snarl an angry objection but stopped short, realizing that this was exactly the response Tamith Kai hoped for—to goad him into anger. He would not be so easily fooled this time. He stood, resolute and passive, while the stormtroopers removed the precious belt.

She motioned for him to precede her from the room. One of the stormtroopers administered an encouraging prod. Tamith Kai's smile mocked Lowie. "Yes, young

Wookiee," she said, "your anger shall be your greatest strength."

They led him to a large, unfurnished chamber. Bright orange and red light glared down from unfiltered glowpanels set into the ceiling. The chilled air stank of metal and sweat. When the door slid shut with a hiss and a clang, Lowie looked around. He was completely alone.

Lowbacca stood waiting for what seemed like hours, alert, prepared for whatever Tamith Kai might use to provoke him. His golden eyes roved the blank walls with suspicion.

Nothing happened.

As he waited, the lights in the room seemed to glow brighter, the air to turn colder. Finally, he sat down with his back pressed to one wall, still wary, still watching.

Nothing.

After a long time, Lowie straightened up with a jerk, realizing that he had been about to doze off. He eyed the walls again, looking for any changes, and found himself wishing for even the annoying Em Teedee to keep him awake—and to keep him company.

Sound exploded in Lowies head, high-pitched and excruciating, awakening him from a fitful sleep. Garish lights flashed overhead, blinding in their intensity. Lowie sprang to his feet.

Trying to focus his eyes, he looked around for the source of the siren and pressed his hands over his ears, groaning in pain. But he could not block out the sound that sliced into his brain as a laser would slice into soft wood.

Without warning, all sound ceased, leaving a vacuum of silence. The glowpanels stabilized, returning to their former level of brightness.

Tamith Kai's face appeared behind a broad transparisteel panel in the wall that Lowie had not noticed before. Still groggy from his interrupted sleep, Lowie threw himself against the panel in frustration. Tamith Kai's pleased chuckle sobered him instantly. "A fine start," she said.

Lowie backed into the center of the room and sat down,

wrapping his long hairy arms around his legs, afraid to make any further response lest he lose his temper again.

Her taunting voice echoed through the empty chamber. "Oh, we are *far* from finished with our lesson, Wookiee. You will stand."

Lowie pressed his forehead to his knees, refusing to look at her, refusing to move.

"Ah," the voice continued, "perhaps it is for the best. The fire of your anger will burn brighter the more fuel I add."

The high-pitched sound drilled into his brain again, and flashing lights assaulted his eyes. Lowie concentrated, focused his mind inside himself. He mutely endured.

The lights and sound ceased as a heavy black object fell from an access hatch onto the floor beside him. Deep in concentration, Lowie didn't flinch, but he looked up to see what it was.

"This is a sonic generator," Tamith Kai's rich, deep voice announced. "It produces the lovely music you've been enjoying today." An undercurrent of cruel amusement rippled through her words. "It also contains the high-intensity strobe relay for the glowpanels. To complete your lesson for the day, all you need do is destroy the sonic generator."

Lowie looked at the boxy object: It measured less than a meter to a side, was made of a dull burnished metal with rounded edges and corners, and had no handholds whatsoever. He reached for it.

"Rest assured," Tamith Kai's voice came again, "even a full-grown Wookiee cannot lift it without using the Force."

Lowie tried to heft the object, found that she was correct. He closed his eyes and concentrated, drawing on the Force, and tried again. The generator hardly budged. Lowie shook his head in confusion. The weight itself, or the object's size, should not have mattered, he told himself. Perhaps, he reasoned, he was just too tired. Or perhaps Tamith Kai was using the Force to hold it down.

"Think, my young Jedi," Tamith Kai chided. "You cannot expect to lift the heaviest object with your weakest muscles."

Lights flashed again, and a dagger of sound pierced his ears. But only for a moment.

"Do not keep your anger pent up," Tamith Kai's voice continued as if there had been no interruption. "You must use it . . . release it. Only then can you set yourself free."

Lowie recognized what she was doing, and the knowledge gave him strength. He closed his eyes, drew a deep breath, and concentrated, prepared to resist the lights and sound.

But he was not prepared for what followed.

From all sides, jets of icy water exploded from the walls, buffeting him with bruising force. He was drenched and shivering, but still the high-pressure streams pummeled him, invaded him. The prying liquid forced itself up under his eyelids, inside his ears and mouth, and streamed down his body, chilling him to the bone.

As unexpectedly as it had begun, the watery attack ended. Shuddering convulsively from the cold, Lowie looked down to find himself ankle-deep in water that was barely warmer than glacial runoff. Anger welled up within him, but he suppressed it, let it flow out of him as the water had streamed down his body. He tried instead to shift the sonic generator again, but to no avail.

As if Lowie's effort had triggered it, the sonic generator began a fresh assault on his senses, strobing the glowpanels and flooding the room with high-pitched wailing until Lowie feared he would drown in it.

Instead, he concentrated on thoughts of his friends Jacen and Jaina. He would be strong.

When the generator paused, more fists of freezing water pounded him again from all sides.

How long these tortures alternated, Lowie could not say. After a time, it seemed his life had always been a litany of lights, sound, water, lights, sound, water . . .

And still he did not give in to his anger.

By the time Tamith Kai spoke to him again, he was curled into a tight, freezing ball of soggy misery, perched directly on the sonic generator in an effort to bring feeling back to his numb legs and feet.

"You have the power within you to end your ordeal," her voice said with mock pity. "Alas, young Jedi, fortitude is only admirable when it gains you something."

Lowie did not raise his head or acknowledge her words.

"You cannot help yourself in this way. You cannot help your friends. Your friends have already learned the truth of my words," she went on.

Lowie's head snapped up, and he voiced a growl of disbelief.

"Ah, but it is true," she said, a note of encouragement in her voice. "Would you like to see them?"

Before he could utter a bark of agreement, a pair of holographic images spun in the air before his eyes. One showed Jacen wielding a lightsaber, a look of fierce enjoyment lighting his young features. In the other Jaina used the Force to toss aside heavy objects, her head thrown back with a challenging grin.

Lowie reached toward the luminescent images with a yelp of stunned disbelief—and fell face-first into the icy water that covered the floor. He hauled himself back to his feet, and the sonic generator resumed its torturous whine.

From deep within him, horror mixed with rage and a sense of betrayal, fanning the embers that had smoldered for so long. Flames of anger sprang up inside him, warming him with their undeniable heat, rising higher and higher until they burst from his throat in a howl of fury.

And he knew no more.

Lowie woke to restful darkness back in his own cell. The room was warm, and he lay on his sleeping platform covered with a soft blanket. His muscles ached, but he felt well rested. He moved a hand to his waist and found that he was once again wearing his webbed belt.

The voice of Tamith Kai spoke next to him. Lowie was not surprised to find the tall, dark-haired Nightsister standing beside him. In the dim light of the cell's glowpanels he saw that she held an irregularly shaped metal object.

"You have done well, young Wookiee," she said.

Lowie gave a sad moan as the memory of what he had done flooded back to him.

"With your anger you succeeded beyond my highest expectations," Tamith Kai said, looking at him with obvious pride. "As a reward, I've brought you back your droid."

Lowie's mind faltered with confusion. Should he feel *proud* of what he had done? Should he be ashamed? He received Em Teedee from Tamith Kai's hands with relief and clipped the little droid to its accustomed place at his belt.

"You will make a fine Jedi," Tamith Kai said. She smiled conspiratorially. "After you unleashed your anger, we were unable even to repair the sonic generator, as we have every time before." And then she swept out of the room, leaving him to his thoughts.

Lowie stood and groaned as his muscles refused to cooperate, and he slumped back onto the sleeping platform.

"Well, if you ask my opinion," Em Teedee's thin voice piped up, "you caused a great deal of your own pain through your needless resistance."

Lowbacca growled a surprised reply.

"Who asked *me*?" Em Teedee said. "Well, I really don't know why you should be so upset. After all, you're here at the Shadow Academy to learn. Why, you're very fortunate that they've taken such an interest in you.

"The Imperials are very perceptive, you know. So perceptive, in fact, that they saw my own potential and have included me in their plans. I am most honored."

With an uncomfortable suspicion. Lowie barked a question.

"Wrong with me?" Em Teedee asked. "Why, nothing. Quite the contrary. As an expression of their complete confidence in me, Brakiss and Tamith Kai have had my programming enhanced. I feel much better now than I ever have. I am to be an integral part of your instruction here. You must realize that they have only your best interests at heart. The Empire is your friend."

Lowie made a thoughtful sound as if accepting Em Teedees words—and reached down to switch the little droid off.

His head had suddenly become clear: Em Teedee's words had crystallized something in his mind. He might have given in, but he had not given up. And if he knew anything about

Jacen and Jaina, the same was true for them—at least that's what he would have to hope.

15

IT WAS MIDAFTERNOON by the time Tenel Ka returned. She found Master Skywalker quietly contemplating in the small slave's quarters Augwynne Djo had offered him to keep him away from curious eyes during the meeting.

"I've spoken with the Council of Sisters," she said. Waves of afternoon heat rippled up the cliffside to the fortress of the Singing Mountain Clan, giving the air a flat, burnt smell. "They expect visitors to come at dusk. At that time all of our questions will be answered."

"Then we wait," Master Skywalker said, looking at her with his intense blue eyes. "It is one of the most difficult things to do—especially at such an urgent time, when we don't know what's happened to Jacen or Jaina or Lowbacca. But if waiting gets us answers where action would not . . . then waiting"—he smiled—"is the action we must choose."

Like a good guest, Tenel Ka busied herself with minor duties to help the Singing Mountain Clan as the hours crawled slowly by.

The sun swung toward the horizon and dusk. Low clouds in the otherwise clear air burned pink and orange, scattering leftover rays into the heated atmosphere. Clicking insects and scuttling lizards began to move about as their world cooled with evening, adding faint rustling noises to the day's silence.

On the lower tier of cliff dwellings, looking down upon the baked rocky plain, Tenel Ka and Master Skywalker watched the lengthening shadows cast by sunset across the desert. Compared with the bright reptilian hides Tenel Ka wore, Master Skywalker's brown robes seemed drab and nondescript—but she knew the strength and skill he harbored within himself.

Tenel Ka noticed something dark and large moving across the plain. She perked up and squinted her gray eyes, studying the creature as it came closer. Some large beast bearing a rider—no, two riders.

Master Skywalker nodded. "Yes, I see it. A rancor carrying two." Tenel Ka squinted again, then realized that Luke was enhancing his vision with the Force, sensing as well as seeing.

Others from the Singing Mountain Clan came to their open adobe windows and stood on the cliff balconies, gazing down in nervous anticipation.

The rancor plodded forward, slow but unstoppable. Tenel Ka could clearly see the hulking monstrosity, whose knobby, tan-gray body seemed nothing more than a vehicle loaded with ferocious fangs and claws. A tall, muscular woman rode in front; behind her sat a dark-haired young man with thick eyebrows, wearing a cloak of silver-shot black, just like the woman's.

"She's a Nightsister," said Tenel Ka. "I can feel it."

Master Skywalker nodded. "Yes, but this new breed seems well trained and even more dangerous. Something is happening here. I can feel we're on the right track."

"But—what is that . . . man doing with her?" Tenel Ka asked. "No ruler on Dathomir would treat a man as her equal."

"Well," Luke said, "perhaps things really *have* changed."

Below, the Nightsister rider pulled the enormous rancor to a halt. The clawed, lumpy-headed beast hissed and reared up, dragging its knobby knuckles across the baked hardpan. The Nightsister dismounted, and her black-robed companion slid down beside her. They stood between two towering bronze rocks that thrust up from the sands.

"Hear me, worthy people!" the woman called up the cliffs. Her shout echoed along the rocks, reflecting her words and making her voice seem louder and broader. Tenel Ka wondered how the dark woman could speak so forcefully.

She felt the Nightsister's tug on her imagination even as she stood and listened.

"She's using a Force trick," Master Skywalker said, "pulling on your emotions, making you interested in what she's about to say."

Tenel Ka nodded. A cool breeze stirred up by the rapidly changing temperatures of evening whipped her red-gold hair about her face.

"Once again, we come to seek others interested in what we have to offer. Yes, we know that long ago evil Night-sisters ruled Dathomir with an iron hand and a cruel will. They were bad people—but that doesn't mean their training was completely wrong, that everything they knew about power is to be despised.

"I am Vonnda Ra, and this is my companion Vilas. Yes—a male. I can sense you are shocked and surprised, but you should not be. From other allies, we have learned that this power we call . . . *the Force* dwells in all things, male and female. Not only can the Sisters use it for their own benefit, but males—Brothers—can also wield such strength."

Many of the people in the cliff dwellings stirred.

"I sense your disbelief," Vonnda Ra said, "but I assure you it is true."

Tenel Ka whispered to Master Skywalker. "I have seen many things in the last few years," she said, "and I believe I know how other societies work—but I fear that some of the more conservative clans on Dathomir are not quite ready to accept such measures of equality."

Master Skywalker nodded, but pursed his lips gravely. "There's nothing in Jedi teachings that favors either male or female—or even human, for that matter. Your people have only been deceiving themselves."

Far below, Vonnda Ra stood beside her tamed rancor and shouted up. "Vilas, my best male student, will demonstrate for you one small thing he has learned, something that will amaze you."

Dark-haired Vilas removed his spangled black cloak and draped it on the patched whuffa-hide saddle across the rancor's back. He began to concentrate, standing off to himself in the flat, baked dirt between the stone columns, his arms at his side, hands clenched into fists.

Even from this far up the cliff, Tenel Ka could hear Vilas humming. Beneath their bushy brows, his eyes were squeezed shut. His black hair began to rise, flickering with static electricity. He rippled with a growing power.

Up in the purple sky, stars had just begun to shine through, bright white lights against the darkening backdrop of the almost-faded sunset. Clouds started to gather, faint wisps at first, like corded shadows across the sky that knotted and drew together. Tenel Ka stood back as the breeze picked up and became colder.

"We are always searching for new trainees," Vonnda Ra shouted up to the gathered crowd. The Singing Mountain people clustered forward to their windows and balconies.

"If any of you would like to learn the ways of the Force, to do what Vilas and I can do—whether you be male or female, noble-born or slave—come join us. Our settlement is at the bottom of the Great Canyon only three days' journey from here by foot.

"We cannot guarantee that we will choose you, but we will test your abilities. Any we find with the right kind of talent, we will adopt as our own. We will teach you to be an important part in the machine of the universe. Your future can be bright, if you are with us."

As Vonnda Ra finished, an ear-shattering peal of thunder drowned out her last words. Violent blue lightning danced in great forks that skittered across the sky.

Vilas had climbed one of the bronze rock pinnacles, scrambling up, light-footed, as if someone were drawing him up on cables. Now he stood on the flat weathered rock, arms raised. Static electricity swirled like a whirlpool around him as the gathering thunderstorm coalesced at his bidding.

More lightning flickered around the desert-scape, striking solitary boulders on the flat plain and sending up showers of dust and sparks. The storm thickened, slashing at them with cold wind. Tenel Ka blinked back stinging tears as her hair thrashed around her.

Vilas stood atop his pinnacle of rock, commanding the storm. The clouds thickened, turning the sky black.

Tenel Ka looked down the cliff face and saw that beside the lone rancor, Vonnda Ra also held her hands outstretched, palms up, fingers spread, calling the storm. Lightning came down across the desert. The rancor snorted and reared, but did not run.

"Come the Great Canyon," Vonnda Ra shouted above the screaming wind. "If you want to touch power such as this, come to the Great Canyon."

Vilas prang down from the stone pinnacle and landed with ease on the windswept desert sands next to the rearing rancor. He and Vonnda Ra scrambled onto the patched saddle.

Vonnda Ra grabbed the creature's reins and yanked it about. The clawed monster loped off into the distance as the storm continued to rage around the cliffs.

Tenel Ka stared after, trying to keep her eyes on the dwindling silhouette of the monster and its two riders. "So now we know. . . ." she said. "What shall we do?"

Luke put his hand on her shoulder, and she could sense his confidence. "We go to this Great Canyon and offer ourselves as candidates," he said. "They *are* looking for new people to train. And now we're sure we're on the right track. Jacen, Jaina, and Lowbacca might be there already."

Tenel Ka bit her lip and nodded. "This is a fact."

16

JAINA LEFT THE lightsaber switched off and pushed it back toward Brakiss, but he wouldn't take it.

"I won't play your games," Jaina insisted.

"We do not *play* at the Shadow Academy," Brakiss said. "But we do practice. Important training for a Jedi."

"Fighting stupid holographic monsters? I won't do it anymore. I've done too much for you already. You may as well just take us home, because we'll never serve your Shadow Academy."

Brakiss spread his hands. "Ah, but you're getting so good with the lightsaber," he said, as if reasoning with a recalcitrant child. "Try it one more time. I'll give you a worthy opponent, someone a bit more challenging to fight."

"Why should I?" Jaina said. "I don't owe you anything. I want to see my brother. I want to see Lowie."

"You will see them soon enough."

"I won't fight unless you promise I can see them."

Brakiss sighed. "Very well. I promise to let you see each other again, during classes. But only"—he held up one finger—"if you agree not to cause more disturbances."

Jaina pressed her mouth into a grim line. For now, this was the best she could hope to accomplish. "Agreed."

Then Brakiss said, his tone disturbingly encouraging, "Think of it this way—the more training you undergo, the better chance you'll have if ever you fight against me. Consider it . . . training for your eventual escape, hmmm?"

She found the calm smile maddening on his smooth, handsome face.

"There will be another change in our session this morning. As you fight, you will be shrouded in a holographic disguise. It will not hinder your movements, but you may find it a bit distracting. You must learn to fight wearing this three-dimensional mask: for the good of the Empire, we may occasionally need to deploy our Dark Jedi in disguise."

Jaina held the lightsaber in front of her. "All right, I'll fight this one training session—then you have to let me see my brother and Lowie."

"That was our agreement," Brakiss answered. "I'll go arrange it now. Meanwhile, good luck." He slipped back out the doorway, and it sealed shut.

The flat gray walls flickered, and Jaina saw shadows wrap

themselves around her—not enough to blind her; just a blur. She realized it must be the holographic costume.

On the other side of the room an imaginary wooden door groaned open, and Jaina rolled her eyes. Just a corny illusion, as everything else had been. Jaina was not amused. Her only challenge was trying to figure out how the equipment on the station worked. Someday she would foil the Shadow Academy, bring its systems crashing down. For now, she would play along with Brakiss, and eventually she would find a way to turn the head teacher's schemes against him.

Her new opponent stepped out of the barred dungeon doorway—a tall, looming figure wrapped completely in black. The black plasteel mask echoed and hissed as Darth Vader breathed through his respirator.

Startled, she caught her breath, instinctively flicking on her lightsaber. Brakiss wasn't playing fair! This went beyond any of the other illusions he had sent against her before. Darth Vader had been killed before the twins were even born, but the Dark Lord of the Sith had been her grandfather; she knew all about him.

Vader's lightsaber was a deep pulsing red, like fresh blood, glowing with light from within. Jaina felt both anger and dismay rise within her, and she stepped forward to confront him. Her holographic costume swirled around her, but she didn't let it distract her.

Jaina hated the evil acts Darth Vader had performed during his alliance with the Emperor—but she also loved the *idea* of what her grandfather Anakin Skywalker could have been, the good man he had become in his last moments when he turned against the Emperor and ended his reign of terror.

Whether it was her own fear or something deeper, Jaina sensed a great uneasiness in the training chamber, a pulsating dread that slowed her movements.

Darth Vader took advantage of her shocked hesitation. He came toward her, scarlet lightsaber sizzling. His breathing echoed all around her. Vader slashed with the weapon, and Jaina countered with her own beam, producing a shower of sparks as the energy blades crossed and struck.

They struck again and again. Thrusting. Parrying. Attacking. Defending.

Jaina swung, trying to land a blow on Darth Vader's chest armor, but the Dark Lord brought his own beam up to crash against hers. She backed away as he attacked with greater strength, slashing, striking with his lightsaber. The shrieks of electrical discharge nearly deafened her. But as Jaina began to falter, she pretended Vader was Brakiss or Tamith Kai—the ones who had kidnapped her and brought all of them to this school of darkness—and was able to defend herself with renewed strength, this time pushing Vader back.

She struck blow after blow. The lightsabers clashed, but Darth Vader seemed to draw strength from Jaina's fury. They fought on for a long time, neither gaining the upper hand. Jaina lost track of how many minutes or hours passed.

They stood with lightsabers crossed and electric arcs flying around them, pressing against each other, straining with all their might. But Vader could not defeat her, and she could not defeat him. They were equally matched.

She gritted her teeth and strained, her breathing heavy, her lungs burning cold. She gasped, but would not let up. Vader also did not stop.

"Enough!" Brakiss's voice came over the intercom.

The training room's holographic simulation faded, leaving her standing in the flat gray room, her lightsaber still crossed with her opponent's. Only now she could see who her adversary really was.

Jacen.

In the control room, looking down at the displayed images from the simulation chamber, Brakiss tapped his fingers together. With great pleasure, he watched the twins battle each other.

Wearing his dark Imperial uniform, Qorl stood beside him, observing the activity. The monitor showed none of the holographic disguises, just the twins fighting, battling to the death—and not even knowing it! Their lightsabers crossed and locked, neither twin overpowering the other.

Qorl remained silent for a long moment, fidgeting with restrained anxiety. Finally he said, "Isn't this dangerous, Brakiss? With one slip, those children could kill each other. You would lose two of your best trainees at the Shadow Academy."

"1 doubt I'll lose them," Brakiss said, dismissing the thought with a wave. "But if one kills the other, then we will know which is the stronger fighter. That is the one we must concentrate our training on."

"But what a waste," Qorl said. "Why would you do this? What is the point?"

Brakiss turned to the old TIE pilot, allowing just a trace of anger to show on his perfect face. "The point is to obtain and develop the strongest fighters for the Empire. The most talented Dark Jedi."

"No matter what the cost?" Qorl said.

"Cost is of no consequence," Brakiss replied. "These young twins are simply tools to be used—as you are, as we *all* are."

Qorl frowned and watched the continuing battle. "Are you saying the twins are expendable?"

"They are ingredients . . . components to be installed in a great machine. If they do not meet our stringent testing requirements, they are no good to us.

"But perhaps you're right," Brakiss said, finally conceding. "They have both fought well and demonstrated their skills with the lightsaber. Now to make a real impact on them."

He turned on the comm. "Enough!" he said, and disabled the holographic disguise generator.

The twins cried out, then sprang apart, astonished to discover they'd been fighting each other.

After a few moments Brakiss switched off the intercom, not wanting to listen to the children's outraged cries anymore. He shrugged and smiled at Qorl. "I did promise to let her see her brother. I don't know why she should be so upset."

Qorl turned away and walked toward the exit, so Brakiss would not see the depth of his uncertainty. The harsh treatment of Jacen and Jaina disturbed him, affecting him against his wishes.

"Their training is coming along quite nicely," Brakiss said as Qorl reached the door. "I am pleased with their progress. They will become great Dark Jedi in our service."

Qorl made a noncommittal reply as he slipped out and closed the door behind him.

17

TENEL KA AND Luke rode astride a young rancor that had not yet been marked to show ownership by any particular clan.

The night air was warm and still heavy with moisture from the unnatural storm Vonnda Ra and her student Vilas had called up. Dathomir's two moons floated in and out of wispy clouds, shedding a diffuse pearly light on their path.

Tenel Ka sat in front of Luke on the whuffa-hide saddle, guiding the rancor steadily in the direction of the Great Canyon. She was a good rider, and she knew it. She had to admit that it felt good to demonstrate to Master Skywalker that she was an expert at something.

A light breeze rustled the leaves of the low bushes around them, so that when Luke leaned forward to whisper in her ear, Tenel Ka hardly heard him at first. "I had to kill a rancor once," he said. "It was a shame—they're such fine creatures."

"Even so," Tenel Ka answered, "they are dangerous to those who are not their friends."

Luke was silent for a while. "I've fought many battles," he said at last, "and yes, I have had to kill. But I've learned from the light side of the Force that it's better to do everything in my power first to . . . *turn* a situation—"

"But surely," Tenel Ka interrupted, "a Nightsister—or

anyone else seduced by the dark side—would not hesitate to
kill *you*."

"Exactly!" Luke's soft exclamation took her by surprise.
"Now you begin to understand," he said. "Those who use the
light side do not believe the same things as those who use the
dark side. But we can only *demonstrate* our differences by
acting on our beliefs. Otherwise . . . we're not so different
after all."

"Ah. Aha," Tenel Ka said. "Just as *I* struggle to show that
I am different from my grandmother on Hapes . . ." Her
voice trailed off. "Yes, I see now."

In spite of the darkness, their surefooted rancor picked its
way steadily down the steep path that led to the floor of the
Great Canyon. During their descent, they spotted a cluster of
more than a dozen campfires, and knew that they had found
the Nightsisters' encampment.

By the time they reached the canyon floor, both Luke and
Tenel Ka were sore and aching and weary. The air was cool,
with a light mist hovering close to the ground, and they were
both glad of the warm cloaks that Augwynne had pressed on
them during their rushed preparations for departure. She had
given them each a change of clothes appropriate to their
cover story, along with a bag of provisions. Then she had
hugged Tenel Ka fiercely. "Daughter of my daughter's
daughter," she said, "go in safety. The thoughts of the
Singing Mountain Clan are with you." She turned to Luke.
"And may the Force be with you."

Augwynne had released Tenel Ka and spoke again to
her. "I am proud of what you do for your friends. You are a
true warrior woman of our clan. Always remember our
most sacred rule from the Book of Laws: 'Never concede to
evil.' "

Now, as they drew closer to that evil, Tenel Ka shivered
and pulled her cloak more tightly about her. She wondered if
they would find Lowbacca, Jacen, and Jaina at the camp of
the Nightsisters, or if that would only be an intermediate step
in their search. Could the Nightsisters be training them in the
dark ways of the Force? Tenel Ka let her eyes drift shut and

cast about with her mind, but she sensed no trace of her three friends.

As if understanding the direction of her thoughts, Luke leaned forward again. "If we don't find them here, the Force will guide us. We are close . . . I feel it."

An ululating cry rang out from the canyon rocks above them. Tenel Ka started in surprise. "A scout sounding the alarm," she said, irritated with herself for having been caught off guard.

"Good," Luke replied. "Then they know we're here."

Tenel Ka hesitated at first, uncertain of whether it was safe to continue, and then urged the young rancor forward. She looked up at the sky, which had lightened from black to predawn grayness, reminding her again of how much time had passed since her friends had been captured.

Rounding the next bend in the trail, the rancor came to an abrupt stop. Tenel Ka looked at the path ahead of her and saw that their way was blocked by three full-grown rancors, each bearing a rider, dressed much as Vonnda Ra and Vilas had been earlier that evening.

The pressure of Luke's hand at her waist was a warning, but she already knew. Even in the dimness she could see that each of the riders held an Imperial blaster aimed directly at them.

Tenel Ka had been raised to take command, and though she rarely exercised that power, it did come naturally. She sat up straighter in the saddle and held one arm high. "Sisters and brothers of the Great Canyon Clan," she said, "we have heard your message as far away as the Misty Falls Clan and have traveled here to join you. We are not without skill in the Force, and we wish to learn your ways, to use *all* of the Force and to become strong."

Leaving the rancors at the well-provisioned stockade, Tenel Ka and Luke followed the guards toward the center of camp. She was surprised to see two Imperial AT-ST scout walkers clanking like mechanical birds around the perimeter on guard duty, near the penned rancors.

Passing between boldly colored tents made of water-repellent lizard hides, Tenel Ka noted roughly ten women and at least as many men going about their early-morning business in eerie silence, as if the warm ground mists swirling up to their knees muffled all sound. She saw no children at all in the encampment, heard no baby's cries, no sounds of young ones playing. In fact, she saw very few in the Great Canyon Clan who were even as young as she was.

Though she had known what to expect, it amazed Tenel Ka that men came and went here as freely as the women, apparently slaves to no one. She wondered if it really was possible on Dathomir that these men and women now thought of each other as equals.

At the center of camp, they came at last to an enormous patchwork pavilion that floated on the mist like a barbaric island made of furs and lizard hides sewn together. It was held up at the center and the corners by spears, three meters long and as thick around as Tenel Ka's wrists.

One of the Nightsisters raised a tent flap and motioned them inside. They entered, but the Sister did not follow. The flap dropped shut behind them, sealing out the wraithlike mists and the morning light. Waiting for her eyes to adjust, Tenel Ka tried to sense her friends; she still found no trace, but the light touch of Master Skywalker's hand on her arm reassured her.

At the center of the tent a tiny pinpoint of light suddenly flared into a bright flame, and Tenel Ka saw that it came from an oil lamp fashioned out of the inverted skull of a mountain lizard. Beside the lamp, on a wide platform covered with furs and cushions made from the hides of a variety of wild beasts, an imposing woman reclined in a massive chair made from a stuffed rancor head. The woman beckoned them forward into the flickering circle of light.

Without so much as a greeting, Vonnda Ra asked, "What is your business here?"

Tenel Ka, who had recognized the dark-haired woman instantly, said, "I have come to join the Nightsisters, and I have brought my slave with me."

"What have you to offer us?" Vonnda Ra looked mildly

interested, but not impressed. "Many come wishing to join us, but they are weak. Women seek us out because their powers are small or they have no status in their clans. Men come here because they have never had power, and our teachings offer them freedom—but they usually have even less to offer. What do you have?"

Vonnda Ra's hand reached out and pointed to the lizard skull filled with burning oil. "Can you do this?" The lamp floated straight upward toward the peak of the tent, casting an ever-wider but dimmer circle of light, and then settled slowly back down onto the platform beside Vonnda Ra.

Tenel Ka nodded. "I have had some training." Deciding against using any theatrical gestures or words, she half-closed her eyes in concentration and grasped the lamp with her mind. She had never enjoyed showing off her skill with the Force, using it only when absolutely necessary, but this performance was not for herself. She would probably never see Jacen and Jaina and Lowbacca again if she could not show these Nightsisters her true potential.

She drew in a deep breath, let it out again. Without a sound the lamp glided off the platform and high into the air over their heads. Tenel Ka thought about the flame, feeding it with her mind and making it brighter, brighter, until its warm radiance reached even to the darkest corners of the pavilion. Then she sent the lamp sailing around the outer edges of the tent; it made the complete circle so quickly that she heard Vonnda Ra gasp with amazement. Through her half-closed eyes Tenel Ka watched the dark-haired woman sit up, one hand outstretched, palm up, as if to ask a question.

Tenel Ka brought the lamp in closer for another circle, and then another, smaller and closer to the central tent post, until at last it spun around the center pole in a dizzy downward spiral, still glowing brightly—all in a matter of a few seconds. Last, Tenel Ka brought the spinning lamp lightly to rest in Vonnda Ra's outstretched hand.

The Nightsister gave a gleeful chuckle. "You are welcome here, Sister," she said. "What is your name?"

Tenel Ka threw her head back. "My name—*our names*—

no longer have any meaning for us. We discarded them when we left our clan."

"Come here," Vonnda Ra ordered. When Tenel Ka did as she was told, the Nightsister stood and took the young girl's chin in her fingers and looked deep into her eyes. "Yes," she said with a satisfied nod. "You have much anger in you. Are you willing to go elsewhere to learn? To a place of instruction among the stars?"

Tenel Ka's heart leaped. Perhaps *this* was where Jacen, Jaina, and Lowbacca had been taken. "Wherever your finest teachers are, that is where I wish to go," she replied.

"But you must leave your slave behind. We will have little use for him," Vonnda Ra said.

"No!"

Vonnda Ra sighed. "What if I were to tell you that men rarely have any talent, and that we have never trained one this old? He would only distract you from what you must learn. There is little hope of teaching him. If you knew all this, then what would you say?"

"Then I would say . . . ," Tenel Ka replied, leveling her best cool gray stare at Vonnda Ra, "that you are a fool."

Vonnda Ra's eyes went wide with surprise, but Tenel Ka did not stop. "This man has watched and learned the ways of the Force since before I was born. Not many—*not many who still live*—have seen his power. But I have seen it."

Vonnda Ra abruptly turned her skeptical gaze toward Luke. "If you can lift this," she said, pointing to her lizard-skull lamp, "*and* bring as much light to this tent as she did"— she nodded toward Tenel Ka— "then you shall accompany her."

The Nightsister looked at Luke and then back down at the lamp. When it did not move, a small contemptuous smile flickered at the corners of her mouth. Then something large and dark floated between them and blocked her view The flame from the oil lamp brightened, and the massive rancor-head chair grinned at her, its lifeless eyes glowing with reflected light. Then the head lifted and glided around the perimeter of the tent like a shuttlecraft.

Tenel Ka could see Master Skywalker standing with

arms crossed over his chest, one knee bent in an apparently relaxed posture, his head cocked to one side, smiling at Vonnda Ra as he sent the rancor head whizzing about the pavilion.

"Since you asked," he said, "I will give you light." Suddenly, in a blur of motion, the stuffed rancor head shot upward with the speed of blaster fire. It disappeared through the ceiling of the tent, leaving a gaping hole in its wake, through which the bright morning sunlight streamed.

Vonnda Ra looked more than a little nervous as she stepped forward and took Luke's chin in her hands. For more than a minute she gazed transfixed into his eyes. "Yes," she hissed at last. "Yes, you understand the dark side."

She backed away from him as if in awe, stared up at the dent in the ceiling of her pavilion, then looked back at Luke and Tenel Ka. "We expect an Imperial supply shuttle at dawn tomorrow," she said. "When it leaves this planet, the two of you must be on it."

18

JACEN, JAINA, AND Lowbacca were at first surprised and delighted that they would be together for the next exercise—but the grim expressions on Brakiss and Tamith Kai soon soured their pleasure. Obviously, Jacen thought, the two Shadow Academy instructors had something difficult and dangerous in mind.

"Because you must move forward in your training," Brakiss said, motioning outward to represent progress, "we have designed exercises to present greater and greater challenges for your abilities."

Lowie groaned in dismay.

"For this next test, the three of you must work *together*. Each trainee must learn to act in concert with others to assist our cause. There are times when we must be unified to provide appropriate service to the Second Imperium."

Em Teedee parroted from his place at Lowie's waist, "Oh, most certainly—appropriate service to the Empire."

Lowie growled at the translating droid to be quiet.

"You needn't take that tone with me! I am simply reinforcing the things you need to know," the reprogrammed Em Teedee replied, miffed.

The three companions found themselves in a new room this time, smaller, more claustrophobic, with numerous round hatches built into the walls on every side.

Tamith Kai went to a control panel in one corner and tapped in a series of commands with her long-nailed fingers. Four of the metal hatches slid open, and spherical remotes floated out on repulsorfields.

The remotes were metal balls studded with tiny lasers. They reminded Jacen of the defensive satellites that had been unable to stop the Imperial blastboats from invading Gem-Diver Station. He felt uneasy, wondering if the floating drones would start firing at them.

"These remotes are your protection," Tamith Kai said. "That is, if the Wookiee can operate them correctly."

Lowie growled a question. "Oh, do be patient, Lowbacca," Em Teedee said. "I'm sure she'll explain everything in good time. She's quite good at this, you know."

Brakiss gestured to the remaining hatches on the wall. "These will open at random," he said, "and they will hurl objects at you."

Brakiss reached into the folds of his silvery robe and withdrew a pair of polished wooden sticks, each about the length of Jacen's arm. He handed them to the twins.

"These are your only weapons: these sticks—and the Force. If the Force is your ally, you have a powerful weapon.

"We know that already," Jaina snapped.

"Good," Brakiss said, his intensely calm smile still in place. "Then you won't object to the other restrictions we place on you." From his sleeve he pulled out two long, black strips of cloth. "You'll be blindfolded. You must use the Force to detect the objects coming at you."

Jacen felt his heart sink.

"When the objects fly at you, you must either nudge them aside with the Force or strike them with the wooden sticks." He shrugged. "That is all. A simple enough game."

Tamith Kai took up the explanation. "The Wookiee will be in an observation chamber, working to protect you as well. He'll have full control of the computer to run these four remotes. They have powerful enough lasers to disintegrate any of the projectiles. Of course, if he misses, and the laser strikes you instead, he could cause serious injury."

"So"—Brakiss rubbed his hands together, a look of anticipation on his beautiful face—"you have your own weapons, and the Wookiee has the remotes. The three of you must work together to keep yourselves alive."

Jacen swallowed nervously. Jaina lifted her chin and scowled at the two teachers. Lowie bristled, clenching and unclenching his hairy hands.

"Let me point out," Tamith Kai said, her voice thick and powerful, "that these are *not* holograms. These are real threats, and if one strikes you, you will feel real pain."

"Just what kind of objects are these, anyway?" Jacen asked. "What're you going to throw at us?"

"There will be three levels to your test," Brakiss answered. "During the first stage we will throw hard balls at you. They may sting, but will cause no permanent damage. In the second round, as the test speeds up, we will throw rocks, which could break bones and cause serious injury."

Tamith Kai's deep red lips wore a broad smile, as if she were savoring some pleasant thought. "The third round will involve *knives*."

Jaina sucked in a shaky breath.

"Glad you have such faith in our abilities," Jacen grumbled.

"I will be greatly disappointed if you are both killed," Brakiss told them, his expression earnest.

"Hey, so will we," Jacen said.

"I think *he'll* get over it before we will," Jaina added in a low voice.

Jacen shifted his weight on his feet and covered a wince

as he stepped down on the hard Corusca gem in his boot. He had kept it hidden there, not knowing what else to do with it—but right now the last thing he wanted was to feel the sharp gemstone under his heel and be distracted. He wiggled his foot until the gem was tucked comfortably off to the side.

Brakiss snugged the blindfold over Jacen's eyes, and everything went black. "The Wookiee will do what he can to protect you."

Jacen gripped the hard stick in his hands and considered dealing the Dark Jedi teacher a good whack on the kneecaps, then claiming he had become disoriented by the blindfold, and it was an accident. But he decided that such an act would only buy them trouble, and they needed their energy for other purposes.

"Good luck," Brakiss said, unseen, close to his ear.

Jacen didn't respond, and he heard Tamith Kai chuckle as they led Lowie out of the chamber. The Wookiee moaned, but Em Teedee's tinny voice snapped back, "Now, Lowbacca, complaining will do you very little good. You must learn to be brave and dedicated, as I am."

Jacen, standing in blackness with nothing to hold on to but his stick, heard the doors hiss shut behind them. "You ready for this, Jaina?" he asked.

"What kind of question is that?" she said.

The room remained silent around them. He could hear himself breathe, his heart pounding in his ears. He sensed Jaina beside him, heard the rustle of her clothes as she moved.

"Might be better if we stand back-to-back," she suggested, "cover each other as much as we can."

They pressed themselves shoulder-to-shoulder and listened and waited. Soon they heard a hum of machinery, a quiet, grinding sound, as one of the metal portholes slid open. Jacen reached out with the Force to see through the blindfold, to detect where the projectile would come from.

Then, with a sudden *whump* of compressed air, one of the objects shot at them like a cannonball. Using his senses, Jacen whirled, swinging the stick like a bat. He tried to smack the ball out of the way, but it struck him on the shoulder. It was hard, and it stung.

"Ow!" he yelped. Then a second ball shot out. He heard the sizzle of the remotes firing, but then Jaina also cried out behind him—not so much in pain as in startled embarrassment.

He tried to visualize where the next missile would come from. The noises came faster now. He heard another metal porthole hissing open, another hard ball shooting toward him. He swung the wooden stick, and this time grazed it with the edge. He felt a surge of triumph, but realized that he had hit the ball more through blind luck than any skill with the Force.

Another hiss of a porthole, another ball, and another, coming from a different direction. Under Lowie's control, the remotes shot tiny blasts at the flying balls. Jacen heard an impact and thought perhaps Lowie had struck one of the targets. He hoped the lanky Wookiee wouldn't misfire.

Brakiss had instructed them to use anger to increase their control over the Force; as another ball hit Jacen in the ribs, the stinging impact did make him want to lash out in retaliation. But Jacen also remembered his uncle Luke's lessons: A Jedi knows the Force best when he is calm and passive, when he lets it flow *through* him rather than trying to twist it to his own purposes.

Jacen heard a loud crack of wood as his sister struck one of the hard balls. "Gotcha!" she cried.

As he let his mind open up, Jacen saw a small, bright blur through the blindfolded darkness; and he *knew* the next ball would come from that direction. He used the Force to nudge it out of the way, and the ball swung wide, smacking the wall instead. Then he saw another bright blur, then another, and another, as more projectiles came, faster and faster!

He used the Force. He swung the wooden stick, trying to keep up with the flying balls. He sensed that Jaina was also doing better, and that the laser bolts from Lowie's remotes seemed to be striking their targets more often. But with the sheer number of projectiles, Lowie had to miss occasionally.

Something hard and rough struck Jacen on the right arm just at the elbow, and the wave of blazing pain took his breath away. His arm went numb, and Jacen shifted the stick to his left hand, realizing that the test had reached its second stage—they were being bombarded with sharp stones.

In the observation chamber, Lowbacca worked frantically at his computer controls, guiding the four defensive drones. He fired their lasers and vaporized a few targets. But then the projectile launches picked up speed, and Lowie knew he didn't dare misfire—because if he struck one of the twins with a laser, it would do at least as much damage as one of the stones.

He missed another one, and a rock hit Jaina on the thigh. He saw her blindfolded face crumple in a wince of sudden agony. Jaina's knees buckled, and she nearly went down; but she managed to keep her balance somehow, swinging automatically with the stick and deflecting another stone that came straight at her head.

More sharp rocks hurtled toward the twins, launched with deadly speed. Lowie began shooting all the remotes at once—targeting, firing, targeting, firing. He had already slagged one of the portholes so it could no longer launch stones. But despite his best efforts, he missed again, and this time a rock struck Jacen in the side.

The twins were both hurt now, badly bruised and reeling, though they kept fighting as best they could. Lowie groaned a quiet apology and kept working at the computer controls.

Em Teedee spoke in a sharp, pestering voice. "Need I point out, Lowbacca, that the Empire will be quite disappointed if you don't perform to the best of your abilities in this test?"

Lowie didn't waste energy telling the translating droid to be quiet. He worked the complex controls, calling up programming, reassigning parameters, hammering instructions with his left hand, controlling the remotes with his right hand, using everything he knew about computers.

Lowie had a desperate plan—but his attempt absorbed part of his concentration. In his moment of distraction more and more of the hard rocks got through to pummel the Jedi twins. But Lowie had no choice, if he was to make his plan come off.

He sensed that in order to demonstrate their power, the teachers at the Shadow Academy were willing to risk hurting their students. As long as they were left with the strongest trainees, they didn't care if someone actually got killed during the exercises. Lowie's only hope was to bring it all down.

He glanced up, tossing ginger-colored fur out of his eyes, as the stones kept flying.

Jacen was on his knees now, dazedly swinging one-handed with the stick. His right arm hung limp at his side. Lowie saw that both of his friends were battered and bruised, and that still the rocks fired at them without mercy.

After a moment's pause, something changed—and long metal knives began flying out.

Lowie worked close to panic, but forced his concentration on the computer. It was his only hope. Jacen and Jaina's only hope.

The twins used their Force abilities to deflect the incoming blades into the walls, where they left long white scars on the metal. Another knife launched out. And another.

Frantically keying in more commands on the control terminal, Lowie let the floating remotes fall silent. He had one last idea. One last chance.

"Master Lowbacca," Em Teedee scolded, "just what do you think—"

Lowie punched in a command string that he hoped would bypass all other informational sequences, then executed it.

Five portholes opened at once, each ready to launch its deadly knife blade—

Suddenly, the entire training room shut down. The lights winked out. The porthole doors slammed shut. Everything went dark.

With a heavy groan of relief, Lowie slumped back in his chair, running a broad hand over the black streak of fur above his eyebrow. At last he had managed to crash the murderous testing routine.

"Oh, Lowbacca!" Em Teedee wailed. "Dear me, you've really botched everything up! Have you any idea how much trouble it will be to fix this mess?"

Lowie smiled, showing fangs, and purred in contentment.

Brakiss and Tamith Kai charged into the observation room. The Nightsister, her black cloak swirling around her like a storm cloud, was furious. Her violet eyes looked ready to shoot lightning bolts. "What have you done?" Tamith Kai demanded.

Brakiss raised his eyebrows, an expression of proud amusement on his face. "The Wookiee has done exactly what I told him to do," Brakiss said. "He defended his two friends. We didn't tell him he had to follow our rules. It seems he accomplished the objective admirably."

Tamith Kai's wine-dark lips formed a sour expression. "You *condone* this, Brakiss?" she said.

"It shows initiative," he said. "Learning to find innovative solutions is an important skill. Lowbacca here will be a fine addition to the defenders of the Empire."

Lowie roared at the insult.

"Oh, Lowbacca, I'm so proud of you!" Em Teedee said.

Stormtroopers brought out Jacen and Jaina, who stumbled as they walked, obviously hurt. Their clothes were ragged and torn. Scrapes and bruises covered their faces, arms, and legs. Blood oozed from a dozen minor cuts, and the twins blinked their brandy-brown eyes in the bright lights of the observation room.

Brakiss commended both of them for their efforts. "A very good test," he said. "You young Jedi Knights continue to impress me. Master Skywalker must be doing a good job selecting his candidates."

"Better candidates than *you'll* ever get," Jaina said, finding the strength to defy him despite her injuries.

"Indeed," Brakiss agreed. "That's why we decided to take some of those that he has already selected. You three were only the first we obtained from the Jedi academy. You've shown such potential that we are now ready to kidnap another group from Yavin 4. From there, we'll have all the Jedi students we could possibly use."

Lowie growled. Jacen and Jaina looked at each other aghast, then at their Wookiee friend. Even without using the Force, the three companions knew they all shared the same urgent thought.

They had to do something—and soon.

19

TENEL KA USED a Jedi relaxation technique, hoping to quell her nervousness before Vonnda Ra could pick up on it. Waiting beside her at the strip of packed dirt the Nightsisters used for a landing field, Luke looked serene, but Tenel Ka caught a trace of curiosity and excitement in him, as if he were embarking on a great adventure.

"There," said Vonnda Ra, stretching an arm toward the horizon where a glimmer of silver flickered. As Tenel Ka watched, the streamlined metallic shape grew rapidly larger.

"You are most fortunate," Vilas said, striding up behind them. Vonnda Ra sent him a questioning look, and he shrugged. "I felt *her* presence, and I could not help but come to greet her." He indicated the approaching craft. "One of our most accomplished young sisters, Garowyn herself, will escort you to your new place of training."

Tenel Ka guessed that Garowyn must also come from Dathomir, since the name was common enough here. Another Nightsister then. *How could so many Nightsisters have come together so quickly?* she wondered. It was not yet two decades since Luke and her parents had eradicated the old Nightsisters, yet here again was a growing enclave of both women *and* men who had been seduced by the dark side of the Force, lured by its promises of power. The Empire had been here as well, seeking new allies.

Tenel Ka gritted her teeth. Were her people truly so weak?

Or was the temptation of great power, once tasted, too strong to resist? She renewed her resolve: She would *not* use the Force unless her own physical powers were inadequate for the situation. She didn't like easy solutions.

Tenel Ka stifled her feelings as a compact, shiny ship settled with effortless precision not far from where they stood. Although she knew it belonged to the Nightsisters—or to whomever had kidnapped Jacen and Jaina and Lowbacca—she marveled at its construction.

The ship was not large, probably built to carry a dozen people, but its lines were clean and smooth, almost inviting Tenel Ka to run her hand along its side. No carbon scoring stained the hull; its surface bore no pits, dents, or evidence of the meteorites commonly encountered in space and atmosphere. The overall design seemed vaguely Imperial, but Tenel Ka could not identify it as any type of craft she had ever seen before.

She heard a low whistle from Luke and a murmured question, as if he were talking to himself. "Quantum armor?"

"Exactly," Vilas said, sounding pleased.

As an entry ramp extended from the sleek underbelly of the small craft, Vonnda Ra stepped forward to greet the woman who emerged, clasping both of her hands in welcome. When the woman stepped off the ramp, Tenel Ka saw that she was half a meter shorter than Vonnda Ra. Though petite, the newcomer was powerfully built. Long, light brown hair streaked with bronze fell to her waist, secured with just enough braids and thongs to keep it out of her way, as befitted a warrior woman of Dathomir.

Without further ado, the woman pilot broke away from Vonnda Ra and came to stand before Luke and Tenel Ka. Her hazel eyes assessed each of them critically. "You are new recruits?"

Before Tenel Ka could answer, Vilas broke in, as if desperately eager to talk to the pilot. "You'll find that they have remarkable potential, Captain Garowyn."

Tenel Ka heard tension and hope—and longing—in his voice. She wondered if Vilas could be secretly in love with Garowyn. Her features were refined, and her creamy-brown skin was set off to perfection by her tight-fitting red lizard-skin armor. The black knee-length cape she wore open at the front seemed to be her only outward concession to the fact that she was a Nightsister, and Tenel Ka guessed from the haughty set of her mouth and her shrewd eyes that Garowyn did not often make concessions.

"Vilas, busy yourself unloading the supplies," Garowyn said dismissively. "I will test these two myself." Vilas cringed and shuffled dispiritedly over to unload the ship, but Garowyn did not notice. She threw Luke and Tenel Ka a challenging look and directed a question at them. "What do you think of my ship, the *Shadow Chaser*?"

"It's beautiful. I've never seen anything like it," Luke replied softly.

"This is a fact," Tenel Ka said in a reverent voice.

"Yes, this is a fact," Garowyn said, apparently satisfied. "The *Shadow Chaser* is state-of-the-art. At the moment she's the only one of her kind." Then, seeming to forget that Vonnda Ra and Vilas even existed, she said, "I do not wish to waste time. Come aboard. When the hold is empty we will get under way."

With that, she turned smartly and headed for the ship. Luke and Tenel Ka followed.

As the *Shadow Chaser* accelerated into hyperspace and the twinkling lights in the forward viewscreen elongated into starlines, Tenel Ka watched Garowyn set her automatic controls and stand up from the pilot seat.

"Our journey will take two standard days," Garowyn said, moving past them and out of the cockpit. "I may as well acquaint you with my ship. No expense was spared for the *Shadow Chaser*."

She showed them the food- and waste-processing systems, the hyperdrive engines, the sleeping cubicles . . . but most of it was a blur to Tenel Ka.

"And these"—Garowyn pointed toward several hatches at the back of the cabin—"are the escape pods. Each is large enough to carry only one passenger, and is equipped with a homing beacon that broadcasts its location on a signature frequency that can only be decoded at the Shadow Academy, where you will learn your true potential."

With that, Garowyn resumed the tour, but Tenel Ka flashed an alarmed glance at Master Skywalker, who met her gaze with equal concern. Her mind whirled at the idea that another Jedi academy existed, an academy for learning the dark powers of the Force. A *Shadow Academy*.

Garowyn decided to test them thoroughly. She questioned Luke and Tenel Ka by turns about their familiarity with the Force. Luke was vague in his answers, but Garowyn—perhaps because she was from Dathomir and considered men to be of little importance—concentrated her efforts on finding out more about Tenel Ka.

When Garowyn asked what experience she had, Tenel Ka answered truthfully. "I have used the Force, and I believe that I am strong. However," she added, her voice growing hard, "I will not rely on the Force so much that I become weak. If there is anything I can do under my own power, I will not use the Force to do it."

Garowyn laughed at that, a harsh, cynical laugh that grated in Tenel Ka's ears. "We will change your mind without too much difficulty," she said. "Why else would you come to us for training?"

Tenel Ka considered this for a moment and phrased her reply carefully. "I have no greater desire than to learn the ways of the Force," she said at last.

Garowyn nodded, as if that closed the issue, and turned to Luke. "I refuse to conduct lightsaber drills aboard the *Shadow Chaser*, but we shall see soon enough how well you sense my intentions using the Force." She picked up a stun staff in each hand and tossed one of them to Luke. Luke stretched out his arm, fumbled slightly, but caught the staff before it touched the floor.

And so it went for most of the day.

Tenel Ka did the best she could at each stage of the testing, but she could see that Luke was holding back, not revealing the full extent of his power—she had observed Master Skywalker enough to know this.

After seeing him weaken or fail in several of the tests, however, a thread of worry began to weave through her mind. What if Master Skywallker had fallen ill? What if he couldn't use his powers? Or what if—it hurt to even think it—what if he had been wrong, after all? What if the dark side really *was* stronger? If so, she and Master Skywalker did not stand a chance of rescuing Jacen, Jaina, and Lowbacca.

Tenel Ka felt weak and drained by the time she had lifted her tenth object to satisfy Garowyn's sense of completeness. The titanium block wobbled and shook as she lowered it to the floor of the cabin.

Garowyn gave a derisive chuckle. "Your pride in self-sufficiency is your weakness." With that, she closed her hazel eyes, flung her head back, and stretched an arm toward Tenel Ka.

Tenel Ka felt the hair on her scalp and her skin prickle as if lightning were about to strike. Her stomach churned, and she felt giddy and disoriented. She bent her legs to sit but found nothing to support her. She was floating a meter above the cabin floor. Tenel Ka stifled a gasp of outrage and attempted to use her mind to wrench herself free.

Garowyn's creamy-brown face was furrowed with cruel lines of deep concentration. "Yes," she said in a guttural, triumphant voice, "try to resist me. Use your anger."

Realizing that this was exactly what she *had* been doing, Tenel Ka went limp. As she did so, Garowyn lost her grip slightly, and Tenel Ka wobbled in midair. So, she mused, *the Nightsister is not as strong as she thinks she is.*

Then, pretending to struggle again to hide what she was doing, she removed the fibercord and grappling hook that she carried at her waist and looked around for an anchor point. She soon found something that would work perfectly: the wheel on an escape pod's pressure hatch.

Garowyn was still amusing herself with Tenel Ka's "struggles" when, with a practiced flick of her wrist, Tenel Ka flung out her line; the grappling hook caught securely on its intended target. Before the Nightsister could notice, Tenel Ka went completely limp again. When Garowyn's grasp wavered again, Tenel Ka jerked on the line and wrenched herself free, falling to the floor and landing painfully on her rear.

She looked up to see Garowyn's petite form towering over her. But instead of an angry rebuke, all she heard from the Nightsister was a short, sharp bark of amazed laughter.

Garowyn reached out a hand to help Tenel Ka up. "Your pride has served you this time, but it may be your downfall yet," she said.

"That is often true of pride," Luke said quietly, seeming to agree. His eyes assessed the Nightsister. "I believe I could do that."

Garowyn's lips twisted in a derisive smile. "What? You think you could fall on your—?"

"No," Luke cut in. "I believe I could lift a person."

"So?" Garowyn chortled, as if rising to a challenge. "Do your best."

She crossed her arms over her chest, and her hazel eyes dared Luke to move her. Suddenly, her eyes grew wide with astonishment and confusion as her feet drifted off the floor, and she rose a full meter and a half into the air.

"I can see that it is time to teach *you* the power of the dark side as well," she snapped haughtily. She closed her eyes and wrenched with all her might.

Tenel Ka sensed that Luke loosened his grip—but only partially. Garowyn still floated above the deck, but he allowed the force of her movement to turn her around and send her into a dizzying spin.

Then, never taking his eyes from the twirling Nightsister, Luke said, "Tenel Ka, if you would be so kind as to open that first escape pod."

She understood his intention immediately, and moved to do as he asked. Within moments they had the gyrating, disoriented Nightsister deposited and sealed within the pod. Tenel Ka's hand hovered above the automatic jettison switch. Luke nodded.

With great satisfaction, she triggered the launch. With a *whoosh* and a *thump*, the escape pod containing Garowyn shot out into deep space.

"Master Skywallker," Tenel Ka said, her face serious, "I

believe I now understand how it might be possible, as you said, to . . . *turn* a situation."

Luke looked at her, blinked once in amazement, and laughed. "Tenel Ka," he said, "I believe you just made a joke. Jacen would be proud of you."

Later that day, when they dropped out of hyperspace and the autopilot alerted them that they were about to arrive at their destination, Luke and Tenel Ka sat in the cockpit looking vainly for a planet, a space station, *anything* on which they might land.

But they saw nothing.

Tenel Ka turned to Luke in confusion. "Could the autopilot have malfunctioned?" she asked. "Did we have the wrong coordinates?"

"No," he said, seeming calm and self-assured. "We must wait."

Then, as if a curtain had suddenly been drawn aside, they saw it: a space station. *A Shadow Academy*, Tenel Ka reminded herself. A spiked torus spinning in space, protected by exterior gun emplacements and crowned with several tall observation towers.

"It must have been cloaked," Luke said.

As they approached the Shadow Academy, docking-bay doors opened automatically, and Luke placed a reassuring hand on Tenel Ka's shoulder.

"The dark side is *not* stronger," he said.

Tenel Ka let out a long breath, and some of her tension drained away with it.

"This is a fact," she whispered.

20

DURING THE SHADOW Academy's sleep period, all students were locked in their individual chambers and told to rest and meditate, to recharge their energies for further strenuous exercises. It was just part of the Imperial rules, and most students followed them without question.

Jacen sat alone in his small cubicle, bruised and aching from the training ordeal. He dampened one of his socks and used it to soothe the many cuts and scrapes he had received from the sharp rocks and knives.

He and Jaina had requested simple pain relievers, but Tamith Kai had flatly refused, insisting that the aches would serve to toughen them up. Each twinge of pain was supposed to remind them of their failure to deflect a ball or stone. He used what he knew of the Force to dull the worst of the pain, but it still hurt.

Jacen sat cross-legged, trying furiously to figure out some escape before Brakiss launched another raid on Yavin 4 to grab more of Uncle Luke's trainees.

His sister Jaina was always best at making complicated plans. She understood how things worked, how pieces fit together. Jacen, on the other hand, who liked to live in the moment and enjoy what he was doing, was a bit more disorganized. He managed to get things done—but not always in the same order he had originally planned.

Maybe the most important step was to free Jaina and Lowie. After that, they could decide what to do next. Of course, the biggest question was *how* Jacen could free them all from their cells.

Then he remembered his Corusca gem.

Jacen nearly laughed out loud—why hadn't he thought of it before? He grabbed for his left boot, shook it, and was startled to hear nothing. Then he recalled he had put the stone in his other boot. He picked it up and dumped the precious jewel into his cupped hand. Smooth on one side, with sharp edges and facets on the other, the Corusca gem glowed with internal fire—trapped light from when it had formed deep in Yavin's core ages ago.

Lando Calrissian had said a Corusca gem could slice through transparisteel as easily as a laser through Sullustan jam. But then, Lando said a lot of things that couldn't entirely be believed. Jacen hoped this wasn't one of them.

Jacen held the jewel between his thumb and his first two fingers and went to the sealed door. When Tamith Kai and her Imperial forces had stormed GemDiver Station, they had used a large machine fitted with industrial-grade Corusca gems to cut through the armored walls. Surely Jacen's little gem could cut through a thin wall plate. . . .

He ran his fingers along the smooth metal near where the door sealed. Jacen wished he understood machinery and electronics like his sister did, but he would do his best.

He didn't think that he could cut through the whole door using only the strength in his fingers, but Jacen knew where the control panel was. Perhaps he could peel back this side of the plate, get to the wires, and somehow trigger the door to open—though he hadn't the slightest idea how to do it. Still, he took the gem, found where the control box should be, and probed lightly with the Force. He sensed a power source here, tangled controls. This was it.

Jacen drew a generous rectangle with the gem, easily scratching a thin white line in the metal plate. *A good start*, he thought.

Pressing harder this time, Jacen retraced the rectangle, feeling the sharp edge of the gem gouging deeper into the metal. After his third effort, his fingers hurt, but he could see that he had made a substantial cut through the plate. His pulse raced, and excitement gave him new energy. He forgot all about his aches and pains.

One side cut through and bent inward. Jacen gasped. *Almost there.* He sawed away at the long side of the rectangle. With a *clink*, the metal parted. The last two sides were easier, and he sliced through them quickly.

The metal rectangle slipped from Jacen's sore fingers and fell to the floor with a loud clatter. "Oh, blaster bolts!" he muttered. He was sure the other Shadow Academy students would wake up and that stormtroopers would come running.

But outside, the halls remained utterly silent, as if a cloth gag were bound around the station, muffling all sound. Everyone remained locked in their quarters. Only a few guards wandered the halls at night.

Jacen was safe for the time being. He peered into the hole he had cut, looking with dismay at the mass of wires and circuits that controlled the door. *Okay, what would Jaina do?* he wondered. He closed his eyes and let his mind open up, tracing the lines of the wires and circuits. Some ran to communications systems, or computer terminals mounted at regular intervals along the corridors, or lights, or thermostats. Some ran to alarms, and others . . . connected to the door mechanism!

Jacen took a steadying breath. *Now, what to do with those wires?* He probably needed to cross them, but in a particular way. There was nothing to do but try it.

With aching fingers, Jacen disconnected one of the wires in the cluster he had isolated and touched it to another, careful that the exposed, electrified ends didn't touch his bare skin. A little spark flashed, and the lights in his room flickered—but nothing else happened. He tried with the second wire and got no response at all.

Jacen hoped he wasn't setting off silent alarms in the guard stations. He sighed. What if none of this worked? Well, he reasoned, then he might have to slice directly through the door after all. He shook his stinging fingers, anticipating the pain. First, he decided, he would try the last set of wires.

As if sensing Jacen's impending despair, the door slid quietly open when he touched the wires together.

Jacen laughed aloud and looked out into the empty corridor. He glanced from side to side, but saw only a string of sealed, featureless doors. Glowpanels lit the metallic corridors at half illumination, conserving power during the academy's sleep period.

The door controls looked much easier from the outside, and he didn't think he would have any trouble freeing Jaina and Lowie—once he found them.

It proved less difficult than Jacen had feared. He had seen the corridors down which the guards usually led Jaina and Lowie, so he went in that direction, calling with his mind. *Jaina will be the easiest*, he thought. He tiptoed along, afraid that at any moment stormtroopers would come marching around the corner.

But the Shadow Academy remained silent and asleep.

Jaina, he thought. *Jaina!*

Jacen walked along, listening at each of the doors. He didn't want to cause too much of a disturbance, because the Dark Jedi students might sound an alarm if they noticed him.

At the seventh door he found her. Jacen sensed his sister, awake and excited, knowing he was out there. He worked the controls until her door slid open. Jaina burst out, hugging him. "I've been expecting you," she said.

"Used my Corusca gem," he explained, pointing toward his boot, where he had stashed the stone again.

Jaina nodded, as if she had known all along what her brother would do.

"We've got to find Lowie and free him, too," Jacen said.

"Of course," Jaina agreed. "We'll escape and warn Uncle Luke before Brakiss makes his raid on the Jedi academy."

"Right," Jacen said with a lopsided grin. "Uh, since I got us this far, I was hoping *you* could figure out the rest of the plan."

Jaina beamed at him as if he had paid her the highest compliment she could imagine. "Already have," she said. "What are we waiting for?"

They managed to find Lowie, who was excited to see them, and Em Teedee, who was not. "I feel obligated to warn you that I simply must sound an alarm," the translating droid said. "My duty is to the Empire now, and it's my responsibility—"

Jaina gave the little droid a rap with her knuckles. "If you make so much as a peep," she said, "we'll rewire your vocal circuits so that you talk backwards, and they'll toss you in the scrap heap."

"You wouldn't!" Em Teedee said in a huff.

"Wanna bet?" Jaina asked in a dangerously sweet voice.

Jacen stood next to her and glared at the miniaturized translating droid. Lowie added his own threatening growl.

"Oh, all right, all right," Em Teedee said. "But I submit to this only under stringent protest. The Empire is, after all, our friend."

Jaina snorted. "No it isn't. Think we may need to arrange for a complete brain wipe when we get you back to Yavin 4."

"Oh, dear me," Em Teedee said.

Jaina looked around, casting her gaze from one end of the silent corridor to the other. She rubbed her hands together and bit her lower lip, considering options. "All right, this is the plan." She pointed to one of the corridor terminals.

"Lowie she said, "can you use that computer to slice into the main station controls? I need you to drop the Shadow Academy's cloaking device, and also seal all the doors so that no one gets out of their quarters. No sense inviting trouble for ourselves."

Lowie made a sound of optimistic agreement.

"Lowbacca, you aren't capable of accomplishing all of that," Em Teedee said, "and I'm certain you know it." Lowie growled at him.

"If we can all get to the shuttle bay," Jaina continued, "I think I can pilot one of the ships out of here. I've trained in simulators for various craft, and you know I was ready to fly that TIE fighter before Qorl took it."

Lowie tapped the keyboard of the computer terminal with his long hairy fingers. He hunched low to stare at the screen, which was not mounted for someone of Wookiee stature. Lowie called up the screens he needed, showing the status of the Shadow Academy's shuttle bay.

"Perfect," Jaina said. "A new ship just came in, still powered up and ready to go. We'll take that one, as soon as Lowie locks everyone in their rooms."

Lowbacca grunted in agreement and kept working, but he soon encountered an impenetrable wall of security passwords. He groaned in frustration.

"Well, there now, you see?" Em Teedee said. "I told you you couldn't do it by yourself."

Lowie growled, but Jaina brightened as an idea struck her.

"He's right," she said. "But Em Teedee was reprogrammed by the Empire. Why not plug him into the main computer and let *him* get through for us?" She plucked the small translating droid from the clip at Lowbacca's waist and began opening Em Teedee's back access panel.

"I most certainly will not," Em Teedee said. "I simply couldn't. It would be disloyal to the Empire and completely inappropriate for me to—"

Lowie made a threatening sound, and Em Teedee fell silent.

Working rapidly, with nimble fingers, Jaina pulled wires, electrical leads, and input jacks from the droid's head case and plugged them into appropriate ports on the Shadow Academy's computer terminal.

"Oh, my," Em Teedee said. "Ah, this is much better. I can see so many things! I feel as if my brain is full to overflowing. A wealth of information awaits me—"

"The passwords, Em Teedee," Jaina said, reaching toward the recalcitrant droid.

"Oh, dear me, yes. Of course—the passwords!" Em Teedee said hastily. "But I remind you, I really shouldn't."

"Just do it," Jaina snapped.

"Ah, yes, here it is. But don't blame me if the whole lot of stormtroopers comes after you."

The screen winked, displaying the files Lowbacca had been trying to access. Jacen and Jaina sighed with relief, and Lowie made a pleased sound. His ginger-furred fingers were a blur as he descended rapidly through menu after menu, finally penetrating all the way into the station computer's main core.

With two swift commands Lowie shut down the Shadow Academy's cloaking device. Then, with a resounding *clunk* that echoed throughout the station, he closed and sealed every door except those the three of them would need to escape. He yowled in triumph.

Belatedly, the station alarms went off, screeching and grating with a harsh, piercing sound, unpleasant as only Imperial engineers could make it.

Lowie unplugged Em Teedee. "There, I tried to warn

you," the silvery droid said. "But you wouldn't listen, would you?"

21

BRAKISS SAT CONTEMPLATING in his dim office, long after the other workers had retired for the night. He reveled in the dramatic images on his walls: galactic disasters in progress, the fury of the universe unleashed like a storm around him—with Brakiss as its calm center, able to touch those immense forces but not be affected by them.

Brakiss had just written up the plans for a swift attack on Yavin 4 so that he could steal more of Master Skywalker's Jedi students. He had sent the encoded message deep into the Core Systems to the great Imperial leader, who had immediately approved his plans. The leader was eager to get more ready-chosen Jedi students to train as dark warriors.

The assault would occur in the next few days, while Skywalker was no doubt still reeling from the loss of the twins and the Wookiee, perhaps even away from Yavin 4 looking for them. Tamith Kai would go along for the assault. She needed the outlet to vent her anger, to drain some of the rage she kept bottled within herself. That way she could be more effective.

Brakiss stood and looked at the blindingly bright image of the Denarii Nova, two suns pouring fire onto each other. Something was bothering him. He couldn't quite put his finger on it. The day had gone routinely. The three young Jedi Knights were doing even better than he'd expected. But still Brakiss had a bad feeling, a low-level uneasiness.

He walked slowly out of his chambers, his silvery robes flickering around him like candlelight. He let the door of his office remain open as he turned to scrutinize the empty corridor. Everything was quiet, just as it should have been.

Brakiss frowned, decided he must be imagining things,

and turned back toward his office. But before he could get there, the door slammed shut of its own accord. Brakiss found himself trapped outside his office.

Up and down the corridor the few open doors also sealed themselves. He heard clicking sounds as locking mechanisms engaged all around the station.

Automatic alarms shrieked. Brakiss would not tolerate such an interruption in his routine. Someone would be punished for this. He held the storm inside himself and strode down the halls, intent on squashing the disturbance.

Jacen, Jaina, and Lowie rushed into the docking bay, tense and ready to fight their way out of the Shadow Academy.

A gleaming Imperial shuttle of unusual design sat in the middle of the brightly lit landing pad, still going through its shutdown procedures. Other TIE fighters and Skipray blastboats stood locked down and in various stages of maintenance. The alarms continued their deafening racket

Jacen saw movement in the shuttle and frantically gestured for the others to duck down, just in time to see two figures emerge from the entry ramp. One of the figures crouched and drew a lightsaber.

"Uncle Luke!" Jaina cried, springing to her feet.

The second figure, a fierce-looking girl, whirled, ready to attack. Her braided red-gold hair swept like a burst of flame across her gray eyes.

"And Tenel Ka!" Jacen said. "Hey, am I glad to see you!"

Lowie bellowed a delighted welcome.

"Well, it certainly is a relief to see familiar faces in the midst of all this infernal racket," Em Teedee said.

"All right, kids," Luke Skywalker said, "we came to rescue you—but since you managed to get yourselves this far, I guess we're ready to go. Right now."

Jaina issued a brisk report. "We managed to shut down the cloaking device, Uncle Luke. Sealed most of the doors on the station. Won't be many people coming after us, but we should get out of here as soon as we can."

"How will we get the sealed space doors open again?" Tenel Ka said, looking over her broad shoulders. "It will be difficult to open them without help from someone inside. Is this not a fact?"

Lowie answered her with an extended series of growls and snorts. He waved his lanky arms.

Em Teedee, his chrome back plate still rattling loose behind him, scolded, "No, you can*not* do it yourself, Lowbacca. You're getting delusions of grandeur again. It was *I* who helped bring down the Shadow Academy's defenses and . . . oh—oh dear, what have I done?"

"Maybe I can help," Jaina said. "Let's get into the shuttle cockpit. We'll try it from there."

Up in the control center for the docking bay, Qorl stood amazed as the unexpected alarms continued.

He watched the three young Jedi Knights rush into the large room below. The *Shadow Chaser* had just returned from a supply run to Dathomir, and a sandy-haired man emerged with a tough-looking young lady. Qorl recognized her as one of the Jedi students who had worked on his crashed TIE fighter back in the jungle.

As soon as the alarms sounded, Qorl knew that Jacen, Jaina, and Lowbacca were somehow behind the disturbance. The other Dark Jedi students were pleased to have an opportunity to increase their powers and appreciated their training, but Qorl had been certain these three would cause trouble—especially since Brakiss and Tamith Kai seemed determined to injure or kill them.

Qorl had been gravely disturbed at the supposed duel to the death between the holographically disguised brother and sister. He also knew the dangerous testing routine with flying stones and knives had already been responsible for the deaths of half a dozen promising Shadow Academy trainees.

He didn't agree with Brakiss's tactics, but Qorl was just a pilot; no one listened to his point of view, no matter how certain he was. Yet Qorl served his Empire, and he had to do what he knew was right.

He opened the comm channel and gruffly reported. "Master Brakiss, Tamith Kai—anyone who can hear me. The prisoners are attempting to escape. They are currently in the main docking bay. I believe they intend to steal the *Shadow Chaser*. All of my defenses are down because of computer failure. If you can offer assistance, please come to the main docking bay immediately."

Tamith Kai's violet eyes snapped open, and she leaped from her hard, uncomfortable bunk at the first sound of alarm. She came instantly awake, her mind burning with demands to know what was going on. Someone was threatening the Shadow Academy.

The Nightsister threw on her black cloak, which swirled around her with glittering silvery lines, like the trails of stars during a launch into hyperspace. She reached the door to her quarters, but it would not open. She pounded on it, punched the override controls, but the locking mechanisms remained engaged.

"Let me out!" she snarled. Tamith Kai worked the controls once more, again with no success. Her rage built within her. Something was happening, something terrible—and she knew the three kidnapped trainees were behind it all! They had caused more trouble than they were worth. The Shadow Academy could find so many other willing trainees in all the worlds of the galaxy that regardless of the talent of these three, their potential for disaster was too great.

She would destroy them once and for all, and then the Shadow Academy could settle back into its smooth, regular routine, with Tamith Kai dominating and Brakiss running the details. Then she could be happy again.

Her fingers coiled, and a smoky black electricity curled between them. "Out!" she roared. "I must get out!" Tamith Kai slashed with both of her hands in an opening gesture as she cried her command.

With an explosion of power, the doors bent backward, folding down in a burst of smoke and sparks from the sheared-off wiring in the controls. Then using her bare hands, she tore one of the heavy metal plates completely out of its tracks and tossed it with a loud *clonngg!* onto the floor. Tamith Kai stormed out, her eyes shimmering like violet lava.

Qorl's message came over the hall comm systems, and Tamith Kai did not let her anger slacken for an instant. *The docking bay.* She strode forward at high speed.

While Jacen, Jaina, and Lowie scrambled aboard the *Shadow Chaser*, Luke remained outside with Tenel Ka. He glanced back and shouted to the twins. "I need to know about this place. There's something familiar and . . . very wrong here."

"Yes," Jaina said. "Uncle Luke, the person running the Shadow Academy is—"

But Luke had become distracted—fascinated, really. He suddenly stood up straighter, his eyebrows drawing together. "Wait," he said. "I sense something. A presence I haven't felt in a long time."

He walked slowly across the bay and drew his lightsaber again, feeling a storm in the Force, a deadly conflict. As if in a trance, Luke strode toward one of the sealed red doors that led deeper into the academy station.

"Hey, Uncle Luke!" Jacen cried, but Luke held up a hand for the boy to wait.

They needed to escape soon—it was their only chance. They had to seize the moment. But Luke also had to *see*, had to know. Behind him, he heard the weapons systems of the *Shadow Chaser* powering up. The ship's external laser cannon turrets raised and locked into firing position.

When the red door slid open ahead of him, Luke Skywalker stood transfixed. He stared at the sculpture-handsome face of his former student.

"Brakiss!" he whispered in a voice that carried across the docking bay, even above the chaos of shrieking alarms.

Brakiss stood where he was with a faint smile. "Ah, Master Skywalker. So good of you to come. I thought I sensed you here on my station. Are you impressed at how well I have done for myself?"

Luke held his lightsaber out in front of him, but Brakiss remained outside in the comdor and did not step across the threshold.

"Oh, come now," Brakiss said with a dismissive wave, "if

you intended to kill me, you should have done it when I was a weak trainee. You knew I was an Imperial agent even then."

"I wanted to give you the chance to save yourself," Luke said.

"Always the optimist," Brakiss replied in an airy tone.

Luke felt cold inside. He didn't want to fight Brakiss, especially not now. They had little time. But didn't he have to confront his former student somehow—resolve their conflict?

They had to go *now*. He needed to escape with the kids before the Shadow Academy managed to get its defenses back on-line again.

Brakiss held out his soft, empty hands. "Come and get me, Master Skywalker—or are you a coward? Would your precious light side allow you to attack an unarmed man?"

"The Force is my ally, Brakiss," Luke said. "And you have learned to use it to your own ends. You are never unarmed, any more than I am."

"All right, have it your way," Brakiss said. He brushed the fabric of his shimmering robe and made ready to step forward. His eyes blazed now, as if he held the fury of the universe within him, ready to unleash it from his fingertips.

Just then, an explosion of hot energy streaked past Luke's head from behind and melted the door controls. With a second blast from the *Shadow Chaser*'s laser cannon, the controls were completely fried. The heavy metal plates slammed back into place, sealing Brakiss and Luke apart from each other.

"Uncle Luke, come on!" Jaina yelled from the ship. "We have to go."

Luke shuddered with stunned relief, turned, and sprinted back toward the shuttle. He knew it wasn't over between him and Brakiss, but that would have to wait for another time.

Jaina and Lowie and Em Teedee linked into the *Shadow Chaser*'s computers, trying to open the station's huge space door from within. While they worked, Tenel Ka raced around the docking bay, sealing all of the red doorways, making sure that none would open. The ominous man in the silvery robes had stalled Luke, and they couldn't afford another skirmish like that. Tenel Ka had to seal the doors, just in case a contingent of stormtroopers made its way to the docking bay.

Luke climbed into the shuttle. Tenel Ka sealed another metal door, then ran to the last one. Just as her fingers touched the controls, though, the door slid open. A tall, dark woman loomed in front of Tenel Ka, crackling with angry energy and ready to attack.

Tenel Ka looked up and instantly knew what this person was. "A Nightsister!" she hissed.

The dark woman glared down at her with a similar flash of recognition. "And you are from Dathomir, girl! I claim you. You are a fitting replacement for the three I am about to destroy."

Tenel Ka stood in front of the Nightsister, her arms and legs spread like a barrier. "You will have to get through me first."

The dark woman laughed. "If you insist." She struck with the Force, an invisible blow that nearly knocked Tenel Ka sideways—but the young woman deflected it and stood strong, lips clamping together in determination.

The Nightsister drew herself taller in surprise, looking like a black bird of prey. "Ah, so you are already familiar with the Force. That will make it easier for me to train you, to turn you."

Tenel Ka remained tense and rigid, glaring at her opponent. "This is not a fact. And I will not let you harm my friends."

The Nightsister seemed to snap as her anger came free of its delicate cage. "Then I won't hesitate to destroy you as well!" Her black robes rippled like a thunderstorm. Locking her violet gaze on Tenel Ka, she raised her clawed hands, fingers outspread, glossy dark hair crackling with static as her body charged with electrical power.

Tenel Ka stood directly in front of her, unflinching, as the dark Force built to a climax within the Nightsister.

Without warning, Tenel Ka lashed out with her foot, putting all of the strength of her muscular, athletic legs behind the kick. The sharp toe of her hard, scaled boot struck the Nightsister's unarmored kneecap. Tenel Ka distinctly heard the *crunch* of a breaking bone and tearing muscles as her blow struck home. The Nightsister shrieked and fell to the ground, writhing in agony.

Calm and self-satisfied, Tenel Ka stared down at her with cool gray eyes. "I never use the Force unless I have to," she said. "Sometimes old-fashioned methods are just as effective."

Leaving the Nightsister moaning on the floor, Tenel Ka jogged back toward the *Shadow Chaser*, where Luke was gesturing for her to hurry. She climbed aboard, and the ship doors sealed.

Alarms continued to sound, their clamor muffled inside the cockpit of the *Shadow Chaser*. Luke piloted the vehicle, raising it off the floor on its repulsorfields. Jaina and Lowie still worked desperately to open the heavy space doors.

With a loud *crrummp*, two sets of the red metal doors blasted open. Smoke from detonators curled out, and white-armored stormtroopers charged in, blasting at the shuttle.

"You'd better get that space door open," Luke said. "Soon."

Lowie yowled. "We're trying!" Jaina said, keying in a new command string, working even more furiously.

More stormtroopers came through. Blaster fire sprayed across the room. They could hear the splatter and boom of impacts. But the *Shadow Chaser*'s armor held.

"We've got company," Luke said, staring at the sealed bay doors. "We're out of time."

"I can't get the—," Jaina began, and suddenly the heavy doors cracked open, spreading wide for the *Shadow Chaser*. The atmosphere-containment field shimmered in front of the star-strewn blackness, but now the shuttle could launch into open space.

"Well, what are we waiting for?" Jaina said, trying to cover her confusion.

"Let's go!" Luke shouted, and punched the accelerators. Everyone grabbed the arms of their seats as the launch threw them back. The *Shadow Chaser* roared away from the Imperial station, leaving the huge, spiked structure uncloaked in space behind them.

Luke heaved a loud sigh of relief as he punched the escape coordinates into the navicomputer. "Let's get back to Yavin 4," he said.

None of the young Jedi Knights objected, and they surged into hyperspace.

"Good work, Jaina and Lowie," Luke finally said. "I didn't think you'd ever get that docking-bay door open."

Lowbacca mumbled something unintelligible, and Jaina fidgeted. "Uh, Uncle Luke," she said, "I kind of hate to mention this, but—we *didn't* get the door open."

Luke shrugged, not wanting to quibble. "Well, we owe our thanks to whoever did it."

Qorl stood by the docking-bay controls, watching the *Shadow Chaser* disappear. The escape left absolute turmoil in its wake as the Shadow Academy scrambled to regroup. Qorl touched the space door controls, smiled faintly to himself, and then closed the doors. He would, of course, never tell Brakiss or Tamith Kai.

Brakiss came into the control room next to Qorl, exhausted and troubled. "Is our cloaking shield up yet? We must get it working. The Rebels will no doubt send attack fleets in search of us. We'll have to relocate. That's why this station was designed to be mobile."

Brakiss drummed his fingertips on one of the control panels. "I don't know what I'm going to say to our great Imperial leader. He can trigger this station's self-destruct sequence at any time, if he's displeased."

Qorl nodded grimly. "Perhaps he won't be quite that displeased . . . this time."

Brakiss looked at him. "We can only hope."

Tamith Kai limped into the control chamber, utterly outraged. Her eyes still glowed with violet fire, and her hands were set in clawed curves, as if she wanted to shred hull plates with her fingernails. "So they've escaped! You let them get away?"

Brakiss looked at her mildly. "I didn't *let* them do anything, Tamith Kai. I don't see what more we could have done. Our duty now is to get away and plan our next step—because you can be sure there will be another opportunity."

Qorl powered up the station engines, and they began moving the Shadow Academy to a new hiding place.

22

JACEN AND JAINA crowded together, pushing closer to the transmission area in the Jedi academy's Comm Center as the image of Han and Leia came into focus. The twins cried out their greetings.

Han Solo laughed in delight. "Looks like I didn't have to come after you kids in the *Falcon* after all!"

"And I didn't have to mobilize the whole New Republic to rescue you." Leia beamed. "We got Luke's report yesterday. The scouts I had out searching for you kids are already looking for the Shadow Academy." In the background, Chewbacca roared a message in the Wookiee language to Lowie, who responded in kind.

In the Comm Center, Luke Skywalker stood next to Artoo-Detoo, letting the excited young Jedi Knights talk. Jacen's words tumbled out in a rush. "Lando Calrissian says something like this can never happen again. He's already working with his assistant Lobot to come up with refinements to GemDiver Station's security. I think he's even going to use Corusca gems somehow."

Luke spoke up. "Yes, but I doubt the Shadow Academy will come here again to look for new trainees. We know what Brakiss is up to now—I suspect he'll go somewhere else for potential new Dark Jedi."

"But we brought the Shadow Academy's best ship back with us," Jaina said. "And you should see the design. State-of-the-art. Not like any of the models in the manuals, Dad!"

Luke put a hand on her shoulder. "We need to offer it to the New Republic, Jaina. It isn't ours—"

Han interrupted. "Hey, Luke, you need us to send some mechanics over to check out the ship, try to figure out its design?"

Luke shrugged. "Go right ahead if you want, but I've got a skilled mechanic and an electronics specialist right here on Yavin 4, ready to start on the project right away—Jaina and Lowie."

Leia flashed a bright, warm smile. "All right, Luke. We'll send our engineers to study it, but you keep the ship there. Use it when you need to. You earned it rescuing Jacen, Jaina, and Lowie. Besides, you're an important part of the New Republic. We'll all feel better knowing you've got a safe, fast ship when you go running off across the galaxy—and don't tell me you've forgotten how to fly a fast ship!"

Luke gave an embarrassed chuckle. "No, I haven't forgotten—but I could still use the practice."

Jaina and Lowbacca sat in her quarters, tinkering with the holographic projector, making a coarse schematic of their new ship, the *Shadow Chaser*. The schematic was not as accurate as the one they had made of Lowie's T-23 skyhopper, but they would refine it as they learned more about the Imperial ship.

Lowie roared as the hologram lost its focus.

"Master Lowbacca says that he most fervently hopes a comet will crash into the vacation home of the designer of this subsystem," said Em Teedee from the clip on Lowie's belt.

Lowie growled down at the miniature translator droid. Em Teedee had been completely purged of his corrupted Imperial programming, and the irritating little droid was now back to his normal self.

"Well, how am *I* supposed to know that you don't wish me to translate Wookiee epithets?" the little droid said defensively. "Although you must admit, I certainly captured the feeling well. Why, think of all the idioms I have to parse during a single—"

Lowie switched Em Teedee off with a satisfied grunt.

* * *

Tenel Ka entered the Comm Center, feeling well rested. No nightmares had plagued her since her return to Yavin 4. She wondered what would happen now that a new order of Nightsisters had appeared on Dathomir, joining forces with the Empire, but at least they did not haunt her dreams.

Tenel Ka made contact with the Hapan Royal Household; she spoke to her parents, assured them that she was unharmed, and passed along greetings from the Singing Mountain Clan. Then, steeling herself for a set of imperious orders, she asked to speak with her grandmother, the Royal Matriarch.

When her grandmother's face appeared on the screen behind its customary half veil, her eyes carried a smile and something else Tenel Ka wasn't sure she could read—surprise?

"Thank you for remembering to call. My sources tell me I should be very proud of you," the Matriarch said, with what seemed to be genuine pleasure. "I'm sorry that my ambassador wasn't able to visit you. Now, I'm afraid the meeting will be delayed indefinitely. I was forced to send Yfra on an urgent errand to the Duros system."

Tenel Ka's mouth opened, but she could not think of a response.

"But you'll forgive a concerned grandmother if she tries to find a way to look out for her granddaughter from a distance, won't you? One or two unobtrusive guards in a nearby system, perhaps? I think that might be the best thing for both of us."

The image of her grandmother leaned forward to turn off the communication link, but just as the connection broke the Matriarch whispered, "Besides, I have a feeling you weren't terribly disappointed to miss Ambassador Yfra."

"This," Tenel Ka muttered, "is a fact." And she realized it was the first time in years that she had agreed with her grandmother.

Jacen stood atop the Great Temple on Yavin 4, waiting for Master Skywalker. In the aftermath of the morning's rainstorm, reflected orange light from the giant planet pierced the gray clouds overhead and gilded their edges with a warm glow. The light breeze ruffled his hair and spattered him with an occasional raindrop.

As much as he dreaded the reprimand Uncle Luke was almost certain to deliver, Jacen was glad to be back on the jungle moon. In the day since their return from the Shadow Academy, the Jedi Master had already spoken privately with Jaina and with Lowie. Though he had no idea what Luke had said to either of them, both had been quiet and reserved afterward.

And now it was his turn.

Jacen sensed Master Skywalker's presence even without seeing him as Luke came to stand quietly next to him. For a long time, neither said a word, as if by mutual agreement. Gradually Jacen relaxed. He was ready for anything the Jedi Master had to say to him.

Almost anything.

"Take this," Luke said, pressing a metallic cylinder into Jacen's hands. "Show me what you learned."

Surprised, Jacen looked down at Luke's lightsaber. The weapon was solid and heavy, its handle warm as his own skin. He hefted it, studied it, ran a finger along the ridges of its grip up to the ignition stud. His eyes closed. In his mind, he could hear the hum of the lightsaber, feel its pulsing rhythm as the weapon sliced through the air. . . .

Jacen opened his eyes and squared his shoulders. "This is what I learned," he said, handing the lightsaber back to the Jedi Master without igniting it. "You were right; I'm not ready. The weapon of the Jedi is not to be taken up lightly."

"Even so, you learned to use it. Didn't Brakiss teach you?"

Jacen nodded. "I'm physically capable. I know how to fight an opponent with it—but I'm not sure I'm ready mentally. Maybe I'm not mature enough emotionally."

"You didn't enjoy the fighting as much as you had thought you would?" Luke raised his eyebrows.

"Yes. No. Well, yes—I learned some things. . . . I'm just not sure they were the *right* things. A lightsaber isn't just some impressive tool to dazzle and amaze your friends. It's such a big responsibility. One mistake could get an innocent person killed."

Luke nodded, his blue eyes twinkling with understanding. "It sometimes feels like too great a responsibility even to me. But the Force guides us as we fight. Not simply how to defeat our enemies—but also to know when *not* to defeat them."

Their eyes locked. "Even if what our enemies teach or do is evil?" Jacen said.

Luke Skywalker's gaze did not waver. "No one is completely evil. Or completely good." He flashed a rueful smile. "At least nobody *I've* ever met."

"But Brakiss—" Jacen began.

"Brakiss passes the teachings of the dark side on to his students. You heard him teach. But a teacher is not always right. And because you thought for yourself, you knew not to believe him." Master Skywalker nodded approvingly.

Jacen thought this over. "Brakiss let me do what I wanted to do more than anything else: practice with a lightsaber. But I couldn't trust him. He was hoping to turn me to the dark side, to use me for the Empire. I *do* trust you, though. You were right about the lightsaber, and I'll wait until you think I'm ready."

Luke looked up toward the clouds, which were breaking up, letting more and more light through. "With the Shadow Academy out there, and the young Dark Jedi that Brakiss is training, I'm afraid that time will come all too soon."

THE LOST ONES

To our editor Ginjer Buchanan,
for her support and encouragement,
which made this entire project possible
in the first place, and for extending the series
to let us tell the whole story . . .
and for just being a really neat person.

acknowledgments

To Lillie E. Mitchell, for her fast and furious typing: Jonathan MacGregor Cowan, for being our test reader and providing youthful excitement; Karen Haber and Robert Silverberg, for allowing us to mangle their monickers (sort of); Sue Rostroni and Lucy Wilson at Lucasfilm Licensing, for their sharp eyes and helpful suggestions . . . and Norys Davila at Walt Disney World Celebrity Programs, for having such a nifty first name we couldn't resist using it.

1

AS THE JEWEL-GREEN moon of Yavin 4 dwindled behind them in the *Millennium Falcon*'s rear viewscreens, Jaina Solo gave a happy sigh. "Excited to be going back home, Jacen?" she asked, looking into the liquid brown eyes of her twin brother.

Jacen ran long fingers through his tousled brown curls. "Never thought I'd say it," he admitted, "but a month on Coruscant with Mom and Dad and our kid brother does sound kind of nice."

"Must be a sign of maturity," Jaina teased.

"Who, *me*?" Jacen said, pretending to take offense. "Nah." Then, as if to disprove her theory, he flashed a lopsided grin that made him look like a younger version of their father, Han Solo. "Want to hear a joke?"

Jaina rolled her eyes and tucked a strand of straight brown hair behind one ear to keep it away from her face. "Don't suppose you'd take no for an answer?" Then pretending to have a brilliant idea, she snapped her fingers. "Say, why don't you go up to the cockpit and tell it to Tenel Ka instead?"

She knew full well that the young warrior woman, one of their closest friends at the Jedi academy, had never even smiled—much less laughed—at Jacen's jokes, though he tried daily to coax a chuckle from her.

"I want you to be a test audience first," he said. "Then I'll go try it on Lowie—wherever he is. He's got a pretty good sense of humor for a Wookiee."

"Shouldn't be too hard to find him," Jaina said. "The *Fal-*

con's not *that* big, and you can be pretty sure he's somewhere near a computer."

"Hey, you're just trying to distract me from telling my joke," Jacen said. "You ready?"

Jaina heaved a long-suffering sisterly sigh. "All right, what's the joke?"

"Okay, how long does Uncle Luke need to sleep?"

She gave a puzzled frown. "You got me."

"One Jedi *night!*" He laughed out loud, proud of his joke.

Jaina gave a melodramatic groan. "I don't think even Lowie will laugh at that one."

Jacen looked crestfallen. "I thought it was one of my best jokes so far. I made it up myself." Then his face brightened. "Hey, I wonder if Zekk is still hanging around back on Coruscant. *He* always laughed at my jokes."

Jaina smiled at the mention of their mischievous friend, a street urchin who had been taken in and cared for by old Peckhum, the man who brought supplies to the Jedi academy. A couple of years older than the twins, Zekk had proven to be a resourceful scamp, despite his disadvantaged life. Jaina would sit and listen to Zekk for hours as he regaled her with stories of his childhood on Ennth and how, when the colony had been devastated by a natural disaster, he had escaped on the next supply ship.

Jaina had to admire Zekk's determination. The wild dark-haired boy never did anything unless he wanted to. In fact, when the captain of the rescue ship had suggested that Zekk might be better off in an orphanage or a foster home, Zekk had jumped ship to another outbound freighter at the very next stop and stowed away on it. From then on he had traveled from planet to planet, sometimes working as a cabin boy, sometimes stowing away, until one day he had met old Peckhum, who was on his way to Coruscant. Though both were independent, somehow a friendship had formed, and they had been together ever since.

"Okay, Zekk might laugh at your joke," Jaina agreed at last. "He has a strange sense of humor."

Leaving the Jedi academy far behind on Yavin 4, Jaina and Jacen watched the viewscreen in silence as the stars stretched into starlines and the *Millennium Falcon* flew into hyperspace, taking them toward Coruscant. Toward home.

Sitting at the hologame table in the rec area, Jacen studied the board. He racked his brains for a strategy to counter Lowie's previous gambit.

"It is your turn," Tenel Ka pointed out, her voice low and matter-of-fact.

Jacen had been hoping to impress his friends by winning a game or two, but he found it hard to concentrate with Tenel Ka beside him. She crossed her bare arms over her reptile-skin tunic, watching his every move. Her reddish-gold hair, tamed into numerous braids, dangled wildly around her head and shoulders every time she spoke or shifted position.

Across the table, Jaina stood behind Lowie and conferred with the ginger-furred Wookiee in a whisper, pointing from one holographic gamepiece to another. The tiny wriggling figures on the table seemed impatient for Jacen to make his next move. A thin film of perspiration formed on his forehead and upper lip. Jacen knew he didn't stand a chance against the computer whiz—especially not while Jaina was helping Lowie.

"We'll be coming out of hyperspace in about five standard minutes," Han Solo announced from the cockpit. "You kids ready?"

"Hey, Dad, can we try some target practice?" Jacen leaped to his feet, glad for the interruption. Finally, something he was good at!

Jacen loved this game their father had devised for them. Whenever he brought them back to Coruscant in the *Millennium Falcon*, Han let the twins sit in the two gun wells. As the ship approached orbit, Jacen and Jaina scanned for floating chunks of metal and debris left over from the space battles that had raged over Coruscant years before, during the overthrow of the Empire.

"We hardly ever find enough debris for both of us to shoot at," Jaina grumbled.

"Oh yeah?" Jacen said, giving her his most challenging smile. "You're just worried because last time I hit something and you didn't. I'm *sure* we're going to find some wreckage to shoot at today. I have a good feeling about this." He shrugged once. "But if you're just not up to it . . ."

Jaina's eyes narrowed as she accepted his challenge. A smile tugged at one corner of her mouth. "What are we waiting for?" she said. With that, she dashed toward one of the gun wells, leaving Jacen to scramble to the other. Tenel Ka followed him, while Lowie loped after Jaina, eager to help.

Behind them, the blurry monstrous figures on the hologame table hunkered down and waited for somebody to make a move.

Jacen settled into the overlarge seat of the bottom gun well. He strapped in and leaned forward to take the laser-cannon firing controls as Tenel Ka dropped into place beside him. Her granite-gray eyes narrowed, intent on the weaponry. "Watch that screen there," Jacen said. "Help me get a target. There's plenty of debris left, but it's all pretty small."

"Even small, such wreckage could be deadly to incoming ships," Tenel Ka said.

"This is a fact," Jacen answered with a grin, echoing his friend's often-used phrase. "That's why we clear it out every chance we get." Loud explosions sounded from the other gun well as Jaina began firing her quad lasers. Jacen heard a loud Wookiee roar of encouragement.

"Hey, how did she target so fast?" he said.

"Honing in," Tenel Ka said, pointing at glowing lines on the tracking screen.

"Oh! Well, I could fire too—if I was paying attention," Jacen said. He swung the four-barreled weapon into position, then watched the targeting cross move closer and closer. Maybe it was an old shielding plate from a blown-up Star Destroyer, or an empty cargo pod dumped by a fleeing smuggler. He tracked in closer. . . .

"Stay on target," Tenel Ka said. "Stay on target . . . fire!"

Jacen reacted instantly, squeezing the firing buttons, and all four laser cannons shot focused beams that vaporized the hunk of debris. "Yahoo!" he yelled. A similar whoop of delight came from the other gun well.

"It would appear that Jaina also hit her target," Tenel Ka said.

"Don't get cocky kids," Han shouted good-naturedly from the cockpit. His copilot Chewbacca roared agreement.

"Just making the galaxy safe for peaceful navigation, Dad," Jacen called.

"We're at a tie," Jaina said. "We need one more shot each. Please, Dad?"

"You twins are always at a tie," Han answered. "If I let you keep shooting until one of you scores and the other doesn't, we'll be circling the solar system for years. Come on back up to the cockpit. We're almost home."

As the *Millennium Falcon* settled onto a clear rooftop, Lowbacca unbuckled his crash restraints and groaned. The landing on Coruscant had been smooth, and he had enjoyed his time optimizing the *Falcon*'s computers—but he was anxious to get back into the open air. Even city air, as long as he could be high enough off the ground.

By the time Lowie reached the ship's exit ramp, Jacen and Jaina had managed to unfasten their crash webbing too. The twins sped past him down the ramp and into the waiting arms of their mother. Leia Organa Solo, the New Republic's Chief of State, stood on the landing platform with her younger son, Anakin Solo, and the golden protocol droid See-Threepio.

Lowie adjusted the miniaturized translating droid, Em Teedee, at his hip and made his way down the ramp, watching the close family scene with a certain amount of envy. Dark-haired Anakin hovered beside his two older siblings, asking occasional questions, his ice-blue eyes taking in everything. Leia, her long brown hair arranged in intricate coils, looked at all three of her children with obvious pride and affection. When Han Solo came out to join the reunion, the family erupted in another joyous burst of kisses and hugs and hair ruffling.

Lowie missed his family on Kashyyyk.

Jaina said, "Thanks for letting us bring our friends home with us for the visit, Mom."

"Your friends are always welcome here," their mother

replied. She stepped forward to greet Lowie with a warm smile, then bowed briefly to Tenel Ka, who had followed him down the ramp. "We're very honored to have you all here. Please, treat the palace as if it were your own home."

Though Lowie didn't say a word, Em Teedee spoke up at his waist, chiming in with a delighted voice. "Ah, See-Three-pio! My counterpart, my predecessor, my . . . *mentor*! I have many things to upload to you. You'll be most distressed to hear about some of the adventures I've had since Chewbacca first delivered me to the Jedi academy—"

"To be sure! A pleasure to see you again, Em Teedee," Threepio said. "I doubt, however, that your tribulations are anything compared to the heavy diplomatic responsibilities *I* have to bear here on Coruscant. You simply couldn't believe how easily offended some of these out-world ambassadors can be!"

As the two droids chattered along in near-identical voices, Lowie rolled his large Wookiee eyes. Chewbacca, having finished the *Falcon*'s shutdown procedures, came out to join his nephew just as Lowie handed Em Teedee over to See-Threepio so that the two could reminisce as "family" for a while.

Lowie heaved a small sigh, thinking of his homeworld of Kashyyyk, his parents, and his younger sister. His uncle placed a sympathetic hand on his hairy shoulder. Perhaps Chewbacca sensed Lowie's homesickness, because he immediately launched into a description in Wookiee language of the room he had picked for his nephew to sleep in—one of the highest rooms in the Imperial Palace. Though Lowie would see no treetops from his window, Chewbacca assured him that the heights were indeed breathtaking, which should make him feel comfortable and secure. Chewie had also seen to it that the room was furnished with trees and hammocks and lush green jungle plants.

It wasn't as good as visiting home, Chewbacca said, but it was a great place for a vacation.

Tenel Ka stared at the opulent room chosen for her by Leia Organa Solo. The furniture was beautifully carved, and the draperies and bed coverings were of the finest quality. The mattress looked soft and luxurious:

It felt like home in the Fountain Palace on Hapes. Tenel Ka shuddered. She was a princess of Hapes, since her father, the son of the former queen, a powerful matriarch, now ruled the Hapes cluster with his Dathomiran wife. But Tenel Ka had kept this fact hidden from her friends at the Jedi academy, preferring instead to follow her mother's heritage from wild Dathomir. This palace was a bit too much like home on the Hapes central world—and Tenel Ka was uncomfortable with such amenities right now.

"Ah," she said. "Aha."

Striding to the bed, she yanked the covers off and pulled the pad onto the polished stone floor. She squatted down on it and nodded with satisfaction. The room no longer seemed as posh and fluffy—therefore, it was much more comfortable, not to mention much more suitable for a tough warrior woman. This was a fact.

2

AS SHE TRIED to sleep, Jaina thought of how different Coruscant was from the thick jungles of Yavin 4. The planet-wide capital city bustled with an intensity and energy that filtered into every aspect of daily life. Unlike the tiny moon, which managed to still itself in the quiet hours before dawn, the New Republic's central world stayed awake all the time.

Her brother Jacen blinked his bleary brown eyes as he joined her in the dining area the next morning. Tenel Ka and Lowbacca had risen early and, already at work on their morning meals, greeted the twins as they arrived. The golden protocol droid See-Threepio hurried about, making sure the guests had a fine eating experience.

Lowie ate steaming pieces of heated (but still raw) red meat from a gold-etched plate frilled with sculptured loops;

Threepio had used the best diplomatic tableware and the choicest garnishes. The Wookiee youth, however, seemed to have trouble avoiding the decorative sprigs and delicate flowers that adorned the bloody meal. Tenel Ka, using a small dagger to poke at her plate, speared a piece of fruit.

"Ah, good morning, Mistress Jaina, Master Jacen," Threepio said. "Such a pleasure to have you home with us again."

Jaina glanced at the holographic window that stretched across the wall of the room—actually an image transmitted from one of the towers elsewhere in the great city. Because their mother was the important Chief of State, their family quarters were protected deep within the palace, without any real windows to the outside. Jaina knew that many other diplomats around the city were looking out their own false windows at the same projected image.

"Thanks, Threepio," Jacen said. "We've been looking forward to this vacation. Uncle Luke has been teaching us some terrific Jedi skills, but it can be exhausting."

The droid tapped his gold-plated hands together. "I am delighted to hear it, Master Jacen. Although I am naturally quite busy tutoring young Master Anakin, I have taken the liberty of setting up a fine curriculum of studies for you while you remain here on Coruscant. Your guests are more than welcome to attend classes as well. Oh, it will be just like old times!"

"Classes!" Jacen interrupted as he plopped down in a chair and began to shovel breakfast into his mouth. "You're joking, right?"

"Oh, no, Master Jacen," Threepio said sternly. "You mustn't neglect your studies."

"Sorry Threepio," Jaina said, "but we have other plans today."

Before the droid could advance his argument any further, the twins' mother came into the room. "Good morning, kids," Leia said.

Jaina smiled at her mother. Princess Leia looked as beautiful as in the old picture Jaina had seen from the Rebellion. Since that time, Leia had taken on extremely heavy political duties and devoted most of her waking hours—along with

quite a few of those she should have spent sleeping—to un-
tangling knots in the threads of diplomacy.

"What are you doing today, Mom?" Jaina asked.

Leia sighed and rolled her dark brown eyes in an expression that Jaina often unconsciously imitated. "I have a meeting with the Howler Tree People of Bendone. . . . they speak
a very strange language and need a team of translators. It'll
take me all morning long just to hold a conversation." She
closed her eyes and rubbed her fingertips at her temples.
"And their ultrasonic voices give me a headache!" Leia drew
a deep breath and forced a smile. "But it's part of the job. We
have to keep the New Republic strong. There are always
threats from the outside."

"This is a fact," Tenel Ka said gruffly. "We have seen the
threat of the Shadow Academy and the Second Imperium
firsthand." Lowbacca growled, clearly remembering the dark
and difficult time he and the twins had experienced aboard
the cloaked Imperial training station.

"Hey. I've got something that'll cheer you up, Mom,"
Jacen said, reaching into his pocket. "A present I kept for
you."

He held out the glittering corusca gem he had snagged
while using Lando Calrissian's gem-mining machinery deep
in the stormy atmosphere of the gas-giant Yavin.

Leia looked down at it, blinking in amazement. "Jacen,
that's a corusca gem! Is this the one you found at GemDiver
Station?"

He shrugged and looked pleased. "Yeah—and I used it to
cut my way free from my cell in the Shadow Academy.
Would you like to have it?"

Leia's expression showed how deeply moved she was, but
she closed her son's fingers around the valuable gem. "Just
having you offer it to me is a very special gift," she said. "But
I don't really need any more jewels or treasures. I'd like you
to keep it—find a special use for it. I'm sure you'll think of
something."

Jacen flushed with embarrassment, then turned an even
deeper red when she gave him a big hug.

Han Solo came into the cozy dining area from the family's

living quarters, freshly washed and wide awake. "So kids, what's up for you today?"

Jaina ran to give her father a hug. "Hi, Dad! We're going to spend some time catching up with our friend Zekk."

"That scruffy-looking teenaged junk hunter?" Han asked with a faint smile.

"He's *not* scruffy-looking!" Jaina said defensively.

"Hey, just kidding," Han said.

"Just make sure you don't get into trouble," Leia said.

"Trouble?" Jacen said, blinking his eyes in feigned innocence. "Us?"

Leia nodded. "Keep in mind that we're having a special diplomatic banquet tomorrow night. I don't want to have you stuck with a medical droid because of a sprained ankle—or worse."

Threepio interrupted as he tried to herd dark-haired Anakin off to a quiet room. "I do wish you'd let me keep them here to continue their studies, Mistress Leia. It would be ever so much safer." Anakin looked dejected that he couldn't go out on an adventure with his older brother and sister.

Em Teedee spoke up from Lowbacca's waist. "Well, you need have no fear for their safety, my conscientious colleague. I shall personally see to it that they behave with the utmost caution. You can count on me."

Lowbacca growled a comment, and Jaina didn't think the Wookiee was agreeing with the little translator droid.

In the open air Jaina waited next to Lowbacca, Tenel Ka, and Jacen as they stood in one of Coruscant's busy tourism information centers, a deck that jutted from the grandiose pyramid-shaped palace. Dignitaries and sightseers from across the galaxy came to the capital world to spend their credits visiting parks, museums, odd sculptures, and structures erected by ancient alien artisans.

A boxy brochure droid floated along on its repulsorlifts, babbling in an enthusiastic mechanical voice. It cheerfully listed the most wonderful sights to see, recommended eating establishments catering to various biochemistries, and gave instructions on how to arrange tours for all body types, atmosphere requirements, and languages.

Jaina fidgeted as she studied the bustling crowd—white-robed ambassadors, busy droids, and exotic creatures leashed to other strange creatures. She couldn't tell which were the masters and which the pets.

"So where is he?" Jacen said, putting his hands on his hips. His hair was tousled and his face flushed as he scanned the crowd for a familiar face.

The four young Jedi Knights stood under a sculpture of a gargoyle that broadcast shuttle arrival times from a speaker mounted in its stone mouth. Gazing up at the cloud-frothed sky, Jaina watched the silvery shapes of shuttles descending from orbit. She tried to amuse herself by identifying the vehicle types as they passed, but all the while she wondered what had delayed their friend Zekk. She checked her chronometer again and saw he was only about two standard minutes late. She was just anxious to see him.

Suddenly, a figure dropped directly in front of her from the gargoyle statue overhead—a wiry youth with shoulder-length hair one shade lighter than black. He wore a broad grin on his narrow face, and his sparkling green eyes, wide with delight, showed a darker corona surrounding the emerald irises. "Hi, guys!"

Jaina gasped, but Tenel Ka reacted with dizzying speed. In the fraction of a second following Zekk's landing, the warrior girl whipped out her fibercord rope and snapped a lasso around him, pulling the strand tight.

"Hey!" the boy cried. "Is this the way Jedi Knights greet people?"

Jacen laughed and slapped Tenel Ka on the back. "Good one!" he said. "Tenel Ka, meet our friend Zekk."

Tenel Ka blinked once. "It is a pleasure."

The wiry boy struggled against the restraining cords. "Likewise," he said sheepishly. "Now, if you wouldn't mind untying me?"

Tenel Ka flicked her wrist to release the fibercord.

While Zekk indignantly brushed himself off, Jaina introduced their Wookiee friend Lowbacca. Jaina grinned as she watched Zekk. Though the older boy had a slight build, he was tough as blaster-proof armor. Under the smudges of dirt and grime on his cheeks, she thought, he was probably rather nice-looking—but then, *she* wasn't one to talk about smudges on the face, was she?

Recovering himself, Zekk raised his eyebrows and flashed a roguish smile. "I've been waiting for you guys," he said. "We've got plenty of stuff to see and do . . . and I need your help to salvage something."

"Where are we headed?" Jacen asked.

Zekk grinned. "Someplace we're not supposed to go—of course."

Jaina laughed. "Well then, what are we waiting for?"

Jacen looked out at the sprawling city and thought of all the places he had yet to explore.

Coruscant had been the government world not only of the New Republic, but also of the Empire, and of the Old Republic before that. Skyscrapers covered virtually every open space, built higher and higher as the centuries passed and new governments moved in. The tallest buildings were kilometers high. Many had been destroyed during the bloody battles of the Rebellion and had recently been rebuilt by huge construction droids. Other parts of the planet-wide city remained a jumble of decay and wreckage, their abandoned lower levels and piled garbage forgotten over the years.

The buildings were so high that the gaps between them formed sheer canyons that vanished to a point in the dark depths where sunlight never penetrated. Catwalks and pedestrian tubes linked the buildings, weaving them together into a giant maze. The lower forty or fifty floors were generally restricted from normal traffic; only refugees and daring big-game hunters in search of monstrous urban scavenger beasts were willing to risk venturing into the shadowy underworld.

Like a native guide, Zekk led the four friends down connecting elevators, slide tubes, and rusty metal stairs, and across the catwalks from one building to another. Jacen followed, exhilarated. He wasn't sure he knew exactly where they were anymore, but he loved to explore new places, never knowing what sort of interesting plants or creatures he might find.

The skyscraper walls rose like glass-and-metal cliff faces, with only a narrow wedge of daylight shining from above. As Zekk took the companions farther down, the buildings seemed broader, the walls rougher. Mushy blobs of fungus grew from cracks in the massive construction blocks; fringed lichens, some glowing with phosphorescent light, caked the walls. Lowbacca looked decidedly uneasy, and Jacen remembered that the lanky Wookiee had grown up on Kashyyyk, where the deep forest underworld was an extremely dangerous place.

High overhead Jacen could hear the cries of sleek winged creatures—predatory hawk-bats that lived in the city on Coruscant. The breeze picked up, carrying with it heavy, warm scents of rotting garbage from far below. His stomach grew queasy, but he pressed on. Zekk didn't seem to notice. Tenel Ka, Lowie, and Jaina hurried behind them.

They proceeded across a roofed-in walkway where many of the transparisteel ceiling panels had been smashed out, leaving only a wire reinforcement mesh that whistled in the breezes. Jacen noted etched symbols along the walls, all of them vaguely threatening. Some reminded Jacen of curved knives and fanged mouths, but the most common design showed a sharp triangle surrounding a targeting cross. It looked to Jacen like the tip of an arrow heading straight between his eyes.

"Hey, Zekk, what's that design?" He pointed to the triangular symbol.

Frowning, Zekk glanced around them in all directions and then whispered, "It means we have to be very quiet down here and move as fast as we can. We don't want to go into any of these buildings."

"But why not?" Jacen asked.

"The Lost Ones," Zekk said. "It's a gang. They live down here—kids who ran away from home or were abandoned by their parents because they were so much trouble. Nasty types, mostly."

"Let's hope they stay lost," Jaina said.

Zekk glanced up, his forehead creased with troubled thoughts. "The Lost Ones might even be looking at us right now, but they've never managed to catch me yet," he said. "It's like a game between us."

"How have you managed to get away from them all the time?" Jaina whispered.

"I'm just good at it. Like I'm a good scavenger," Zekk answered, sounding cocky. "I may not be in training as a Jedi Knight, but I make do with what skills I've got. Just streetwise, I guess. But," he continued, "even though I have kind of an . . . understanding with them, I'd rather not push it. Especially not while I'm with the twin children of the Chief of State."

"This is a fact," Tenel Ka said grimly. She kept her hands close to her utility belt in case she needed to draw a weapon.

Zekk quickly ushered them through dilapidated corridors that were heavily decorated with the gang symbols. Jacen saw signs of recent habitation, wrappers from prepackaged food, bright metallic spots where salvaged equipment had been torn away from its housings.

At last they moved on to deeper levels. They all breathed more easily, although Zekk confessed even he had not fully explored this far down. "I think it's a shortcut," he said. "I need your help so I can recover something very valuable." He raised his dark eyebrows. "I think you'll like it—particularly you, Jacen."

Zekk made his living by scavenging: salvaging lost equipment, removing scraps of precious metal from abandoned dwellings. He found lost treasures to sell to inventors, spare parts to repair obsolete machines, trinkets that could be turned into souvenirs. He seemed to have a real skill for finding items that other scavengers had missed over the centuries, somehow knowing where to look, sometimes in the unlikeliest of places.

They descended an outer staircase, slick with damp moss from moisture trickling down the walls. Jacen had to squint just to see the steps. As they turned the corner of the building, Zekk stopped in surprise. In the dim light reflected from far above, Jacen could see a strange jumble protruding from the side of the building—smashed construction bricks, naked durasteel girders . . . and a crashed transport shuffle. From the drooping algae and fungus growing on its outer hull, the damaged shuffle appeared to have been there a long time.

"Wow!" Zekk said. "I didn't even know this was here." He hurried forward, edging his way along the damaged walkway. "I don't believe it. The salvage hasn't even been picked over. See— I'm lucky again!"

"That's an Old Republic craft," Jaina said. "At least seventy years old. They haven't used those in . . . I can't even remember. What a find!"

Tenel Ka and Lowie held the creaking ship steady as Zekk scrambled inside to look around. He poked into storage compartments, looking for valuables. "Plenty of components are still intact. Engine still looks good," he called. "Whoa, and here's the driver. I guess his parking permit ran out."

Jacen came up behind him to see a tattered skeleton strapped into the cockpit.

"Oh, do be careful," Em Teedee said from Lowbacca's waist, "Abandoned vehicles can be terribly dangerous—and you might get dirty as well."

"Was this what you wished to show us, Zekk?" Tenel Ka said.

The older boy stood, bumping his head on a bent girder that ran along the shuttle's ceiling. "No, no, this is a new discovery. I'll have to spend a lot more time down here." He grinned. Engine grease smudged his face, and his hands were grimy from digging through compartments. "I can get this stuff later. I need your help for something different. Let's go."

Zekk scrambled out of the shuttle wreckage and grasped the rusted handrail on the rickety walkway. He looked around to get his bearings, making certain he wouldn't forget the location of this prize. The skull of the unlucky pilot stared out at them through empty eye sockets.

"Looks like you really do know this place like the back of your hand," Jacen commented as Zekk led them elsewhere.

"I've had plenty of practice," Zekk said. "*Some* of us don't take regular trips off planet and go to diplomatic functions all the time. I have to amuse myself with what I can find."

It was midmorning by the time they reached Zekk's destination. The dark-haired boy rubbed his hands together in anticipation, and pointed far below. "Down there—can you see it?"

Jacen looked down, *down* over a ledge to see a rusted construction crawler latched to a wall about ten meters away . . . completely out of reach. The construction crawler was a crane-like mechanical apparatus that had once ridden tracks along the side of the building, scouring the walls clean, effecting repairs, applying duracrete sealant—but this contraption had frozen up and begun to decay at least a century ago. Its interlinked rusted braces were clogged with fuzzy growths of moss and fungus.

Jacen squinted again, wondering why the other boy meant to salvage parts from such an old machine—but then he saw the bushy mass, a tangle of uprooted wires and cables woven together, bristling with insulation material, torn strips of cloth, and plastic. It looked almost like a . . .

"It's a hawk-bat's nest," Zekk said. "Four eggs inside. I can see them from here, but I can't get down there by myself. If I can snatch even one of those eggs, I could sell it for enough credits to live on for a month."

"And you want *us* to help you get it?" Jaina asked.

"That's the idea," Zekk said. "Your friend Tenel Ka there has a pretty strong rope—as I found out! And some of you look like good climbers, especially that Wookiee."

Em Teedee shrilled, "Oh no, Lowbacca. You simply cannot climb down there! I absolutely forbid it." Lowie hadn't looked too eager at first, but the translating droid's admonishment only served to convince him otherwise. The Wookiee growled an agreement to Zekk's plan.

Tenel Ka attached her grappling hook to the side of the walkway. "I am a strong climber," she said. "This is a fact."

Zekk rubbed his hands together with delight. "Excellent."

"Let me get the eggs," Jacen said, eager to touch the smooth, warm shells, to study the nest configuration. "I've always wanted to see one up close." This was such a rare opportunity. Hawk-bats were common in the deep alleyways of Coruscant, but they were horrendously difficult to capture alive.

Pulling the fibercord taut, Tenel Ka wrapped her hands around it and began lowering herself to the old construction crawler. Jacen had seen her descend the walls of the Great Temple on Yavin 4, but now he watched with renewed amazement as she walked backward down the side of the building, relying only on the strength of her supple arms and muscular legs.

Jacen admired the girl from Dathomir—but he wished he could make her laugh. He had been telling Tenel Ka his best jokes for as long as he had known her, but he still hadn't managed to coax even the smallest smile from her. She seemed not to have a sense of humor, but he would keep trying.

Tenel Ka reached the construction crawler and anchored the fibercord, gesturing with her arm to summon him down. Jacen wrapped the cord around himself and started down the slick wall, trying to imitate Tenel Ka. He used the Force to keep his balance, nudging his feet when necessary and soon found himself standing beside Tenel Ka on the teetering platform.

"Piece of cake," he panted, brushing his hands together.

"No thank you," Tenel Ka said. "I am not hungry."

Jacen chuckled, but he knew the warrior girl didn't even realize she had made a joke.

Lowie slid down the fibercord with ease, while Em Teedee wailed all the way. "Oh, I can't watch! I'd rather switch off my optical sensors."

When they all stood on the creaking platform, Jacen bent over, straining to reach the tangled nest just below. "I'm going to climb down there," he said. "I'll pass the eggs up."

Before anyone could argue, he dropped between two thin girders, holding a crossbar to reach the piping brace that supported the odd nest. The eggs were brown, mottled with green, camouflaged as masonry covered with pale lichen. Each was about the size of Jacen's outspread hand; when he touched the warm shells, the texture was hard and rough, like rock. With the Force, he could sense the growing baby creature inside. Perhaps he could use the Force to levitate the prize up to his friends.

He smiled, tingly with wonder as he hefted one of the eggs. It wasn't heavy at all. As he touched a second egg, though, he heard a shrill shriek from above, coming closer.

Tenel Ka shouted a warning. "Look out, Jacen!"

Jacen looked up and saw the sleek form of the mother hawk-bat, swooping down at him and screaming in fury, metallic claws extended, wings studded with spikes. The hawk-bat's wing-span was about two meters. Its head consisted mostly of a horny beak with sharp ivory teeth, ready to tear a victim to shreds.

"Uh-oh," Jacen said.

Lowie bellowed in alarm. Tenel Ka grabbed for a throwing knife—but Jacen knew he couldn't wait for help.

The creature dove toward him like a missile, and Jacen closed his eyes to reach out with the Force. His special talent had always been with animals. He could communicate with them, sense their feelings and express his own to them. "It's all right," he whispered. "I'm sorry we were invading your nest. *Calm*. It's all right. *Peace*."

The hawk-bat pulled up from her dive and clutched one of the corroded lower crossbars with durasteel-hard claws. Jacen could hear the squeaking sound as the claws scraped rust off the metal, but he maintained his calm.

"We didn't mean to hurt your babies," he said. "We won't take them all. I need only one, and I promise you it'll be delivered to a fine and safe place . . . a beautiful zoo where it will be raised and cared for and admired by millions of people from across the galaxy."

The hawk-bat hissed and pushed her hard beak closer to Jacen, blowing foul breath from between sharp, teeth. He knew the hawk-bat was extremely skeptical, but Jacen projected images of a bright aviary, a place where the young hawk-bat would be fed delicacies all its life, where it could fly freely, yet never need to fear other predators or starvation . . . or being shot at by gang members. Jacen snatched the last vision—blurred figures of young humans shooting as she hunted between tall buildings—from the mother's mind.

This last fear convinced the mother, and she flapped her spiked leathery wings, backing away from the nest and leaving Jacen safe . . . for the moment. He grinned up at his friends.

Tenel Ka stood poised, dagger in hand, ready to jump down and fight. Jacen felt a pleasant warm glow to think that she was willing to defend him. He took the hawk-bat egg he was holding and used the Force to carefully levitate it into Jaina's hands. She cradled it, then handed it to Zekk.

"What did you do?" Zekk called.

"I made a deal with the hawk-bat," he said. "Let's go."

"But what about those other eggs?" Zekk said, holding his treasure with great amazement.

"You only get one," Jacen answered. "That was the deal. Now we'd better get out of here — and hurry." He scrambled up to join Lowie and Tenel Ka.

Lowie climbed the fibercord first, racing up the side of the building to the upper ledge. Jacen urged the others to greater speed, and finally, when they were all standing back on the walkway, Zekk said, "I thought you made a deal with the mother. Why do we have to hurry?"

Jacen continued to hustle them out of sight of the construction crawler. "Because hawk-bats have extremely short memories."

3

AS THE FIVE companions left the hawk-bat's nest behind, Jaina stuck close to Zekk. She watched the dark-haired boy move instinctively, hurrying through the maze of upper and lower walkways and cross-connecting bridges as he made a beeline back to his living quarters. The green-eyed boy beamed with self-congratulatory pride at the precious egg he held, as if it were a trophy he had hoped to win for a long time.

"Peckhum is going to be so pleased!" Zekk crowed, looking from Jaina to Jacen. "He'll know just what to do with it. He's got a line on everyone who's looking for anything." He glanced sidelong at Jacen again. "Don't worry about it. We'll find a good home for this baby, just like you promised, Jacen. It shouldn't be too hard for a professional zoologist to incubate this egg until it hatches."

Tenel Ka cleared her throat and said ominously, "*If* we bring the egg back intact."

Jaina suddenly noticed that they had returned to the abandoned levels emblazoned with gang graffiti. *The Lost Ones.*

The sharp corners of the cross in a triangle symbol seemed brighter now, as if freshly painted. Jaina wondered if the gang members could have marked their territory afresh in the short time since the young Jedi Knights had passed through. If the gang members kept such a careful eye out for everything, they might have spotted the five companions already.

Maybe they were watching from hidden, shadowy corners right now . . . .

Tenel Ka tensed and pulled out a small throwing knife, looking from side to side. She seemed alert, ready to spring at the first sign of danger, but Jaina didn't feel safe. With her Jedi senses, she felt a tingle down her spine.

"If the Lost Ones are so tough and powerful, how come we've never heard of them before?" Jacen looked around nervously in the creaking, musty buildings.

"Because you never come down here," Zekk answered. "Whenever we get together, you either have me come to the Imperial Palace or we meet in the safe upper levels. I'll bet your parents would blow their thrusters if they knew where we were right now."

"We can take care of ourselves," Tenel Ka said defensively, flashing her tiny dagger.

"Dear me, I shouldn't be so certain about that, if I were you," Em Teedee replied from Lowie's waist. The young Wookiee groaned.

Zekk smiled thinly. "Down here you can see how *I* live every day. I don't have anyone to wash my hands for me or cook my meals, you know. And I don't have the luxury of worrying about how to amuse myself. Every day is a search—I'm just lucky I have a special knack for finding things."

Jaina was surprised to hear a hint of resentment behind her friend's words. "Zekk, if you needed anything, you should have just asked. We could have found you new quarters, given you credits to spend—"

"Who said I wanted that?" he responded through clenched teeth. "I don't need charity. I've got my freedom here. I can do whatever I want. Besides, it's more satisfying to live by my own wits than to be pampered and coddled all the time."

Em Teedee piped up, "Well really, Master Zekk! It might interest you to learn that not *everyone* minds being pampered and coddled." Jaina ignored the translating droid and wondered if Zekk really meant what he said.

"Nothing personal," Zekk said with shrug. He looked up at the cross-in-triangle symbol. "Being a gang member doesn't impress me either. Their leader Norys—who's our age—is a big bully who likes to throw his weight around. I can run my way through the lower levels better than any of the Lost Ones, so he's been after me to join for a long time. He'd love to have me as his right-hand man, but I'm too independent for that. I work for myself."

They stood at the entrance to a sheer-walled building, near one end of a dilapidated covered walkway that extended to an adjacent skyscraper. More threatening gang symbols marked the inside walls. Half of the windows were broken, and confined breezes whispered through the walkway like voices warning them to go back.

Zekk looked behind him. "This building we're in is the headquarters of the Lost Ones. We're taking a pretty big risk being here." His emerald eyes sparkled. "Kind of exciting, isn't it?"

The building was large and dark, filled with cavernous spaces of empty meeting chambers, offices, and abandoned supply rooms. Jaina wondered if any record or blueprint of this ancient building still existed in the vast computer archives of the Imperial Information Center.

"I don't think you have to worry about Norys, though," Zekk said, raising his voice. "He talks big, but his ambitions are definitely low. He has no interest in becoming anything more than the biggest bully in a run-down section of a single building on an average planet in a big galaxy." Zekk's voice sounded taunting. "He'll never go anywhere, because his dreams are small."

Just then ceiling panels smashed down from above them, and a dozen wiry young men and women dropped to the floor. They looked scuffed and dirty, with hard, lean faces; each held an interesting cobbled-together weapon scavenged from sharp pieces of scrap.

"You trying to annoy me, trash collector?" the biggest burly young man said. His face was broad and dark, his eyes close-set, his teeth crooked as he ground his jaws together and spread his lips in a sneer.

"It's not polite to eavesdrop, Norys," Zekk said.

Then the gang leader's eyes fixed on the precious hawk-bat egg that Zekk cradled close to his chest. "What has the little trash collector found?" Norys said. "Hey, everybody! Looks like we're gonna have fresh eggs for morning meal."

Lowbacca growled loudly enough to startle the Lost Ones, baring his long Wookiee fangs. Zekk looked suddenly nervous, as if the valuable hawk-bat egg made him vulnerable in new ways.

"What do you want the egg for?" Jacen said.

"He only wants it because *I* want it," Zekk said. "He'll probably smash it, not knowing what it's worth."

Tenel Ka now held a throwing dagger at the ready in each hand. The Lost Ones looked at her and Lowie, then at the three seemingly easier targets of Zekk and the twins.

"In a case like this," Zekk said, moving slowly, extending the mottled egg gradually, as if reluctant to surrender it to the brawny gang member, "the most sensible idea is to . . . *run!*"

He whirled and dashed onto the rickety walkway. The vibration of his running knocked loose a broken wall plate, which dropped silently into the murky depths below. The young Jedi Knights reacted quickly and scrambled after their friend onto the covered bridge.

The gang members howled and gave pursuit, clattering their crude weapons against the walls.

Out in the middle of the dilapidated walkway Zekk suddenly pulled to a stop as a gang member—an angry young woman who looked even tougher than Tenel Ka—appeared from the opposite building and stood ominously at the far entrance.

"We're trapped," Jaina said with a hard gulp. This did not seem like a good place for a standoff.

Zekk looked back and forth, as if seeking inspiration in the middle of the swaying bridge. The cold wind sighed through the broken windows and gaps in the flooring. "Just to be fair," he said, crossing his arms with feigned good humor, "I'll let you guys solve this one. Got any ideas?"

Jaina tried to think of something she could do with what Uncle Luke had taught them at the Jedi academy. With uninterrupted concentration she could manipulate objects with the Force, but she couldn't think of any way her fledgling powers could help them escape.

Norys strode forward, his chest puffed with confidence. "Now give me that egg, trash collector, and maybe we won't throw you over the edge!"

Just then a screeching sound came from above, a blood-curdling animal shriek. A predator's heavy shadow swept like a dark blanket over the cracked windows of the walkway.

With another loud scream, the mother hawk-bat struck the side windows, smashing against the wire mesh that barely held the frames in place. She spat and hissed, her sharp beak ripping at the wires, her forked tongue thrashing as she dug her claws in, trying to get at Norys. The gang leader staggered backward with a surprised yelp.

Zekk protected the egg again, holding it to his chest. At the same time, Lowie—focusing on the lone woman guarding the opposite end of the walkway—let out a ferocious roar and charged forward.

"Oh, my!" Em Teedee squeaked. "Would anyone object if

I switched off my optical sensors again so I don't have to watch?"

Distracted by the attacking hawk-bat and startled by the snarling battering ram of Wookiee fur, the gang member backed off and leaped aside.

"Well, what are we waiting for?" Jaina cried. Zekk ducked low to protect the hawk-bat egg as he ran after her. Jacen followed them, while Tenel Ka turned once to threaten the Lost Ones with her throwing daggers before bringing up the rear; sprinting along on her muscular legs.

Seeing them escape, the mother hawk-bat shrieked one more time, then flew off, as if satisfied.

Zekk kept running while Norys yelled after them. "We'll catch you next time, trash collector. Do you hear me?" he shouted. "You'll join our gang—one way or another."

Zekk didn't respond as he led the young Jedi Knights though a maze of stairwells, slides, and lifts in the lower levels, climbing up to rickety catwalks, then higher to lighted levels. He was panting, but his flushed face wore a grin of exhilaration. Triumphant, Zekk cradled the hawk-bat egg close to his body.

"I thought you said hawk-bats had short-term memories," he gasped.

Jacen shrugged and looked sheepish. "Aren't you glad I was wrong?"

"Yes," Jaina said. "We all are."

"Come on," Zekk said. "Let's get this egg back home."

4

VORACIOUSLY HUNGRY AFTER their adventure, the four young Jedi Knights followed Zekk back to where he made his home. Since much of Coruscan's population had fled the capital world during the devastating battles of the Rebellion, many of the midlevel apartments had been left

empty but still serviceable. People scraped out a decent existence there without being forced to live in squalor far below
at the bottom levels.

For years, Zekk had shared quarters with old Peckhum.
The thin, gray-haired man had no particular career, but spent
his days doing odd jobs such as transporting cargo in his battered ship, the *Lightning Rod*, or performing whatever duties
the New Republic required. Zekk and the old supply runner
got along well and helped each other as if they were family,
providing mutual support, company, and a place to stay.

Zekk led the companions through dim corridors on the
way to his apartment. At the entrance Jaina saw that Peckhum had installed a new messaging center beside the door so
that visitors could leave videonotes if no one was home.

"We can kick back here for a while," Zekk said, tucking
the hawk-bat egg into the crook of his elbow as his nimble
fingers punched in an access code.

The metal door slid aside to reveal a paradise of junk—
rooms stacked high with salvaged items, partially restored
antiques, and strange gadgets whose original use had long
since been forgotten. A small sapphire-feathered bird flitted
around inside, but Jaina couldn't tell if the creature was a pet
or just some stray that had wandered in to look for nesting
materials.

A grizzled old man stood up from a rickety table where he
had been poring over manifest files on a scuffed datapad. He
had lank gray hair, a leathery face, and a broad smile—and
he very much needed a shave. "Ah, Zekk, you're back." He
looked past the teenager. "And you've brought guests. Hello,
my young Jedi friends."

Zekk sealed the door behind them, and Jacen immediately
began trying to catch the bird, while Tenel Ka poked around
suspiciously in the stacked cases and gadgets, as if attempting to uncover traps. Lowie sniffed at a cluttered jumble of
electronic equipment.

Zekk beamed proudly as he held out the mottled hawk-bat
egg. "Look at this prize!" he said. "How much do you think
we can get for it?"

Peckhum nodded with enthusiasm as he held out his

hands to take the egg gently in his grasp. "More than a hundred credits, I'd guess. Plenty of zoos and biological establishments are begging for a specimen like this."

Jacen said sternly, "Just make sure it goes to a good home. I made promises to its mother."

Peckhum laughed, shaking his bead. "I'll never understand you Jedi Knights. But I don't suppose that'll be too difficult," he said. "In fact, I think I'll even talk to your mother—I heard a rumor that the Chief of State was looking for some unusual zoological specimens."

Jacen blinked his eyes in astonishment. "*Our* mom wanted to collect weird animals? She could have just asked me. . . ."

Peckhum shrugged. "I didn't ask *why* she wanted it. I think it's for some sort of diplomatic gift. And I think this egg, with the proper incubating apparatus, might just do the trick!"

Jaina found a place to sit down, perching herself on a stack of recycled blankets that Peckhum no doubt intended to sell to some alien merchant. Zekk hurried off to prepare a quick lunch. "Last time we saw you, Peckhum," Jaina said conversationally, "you were cornered by a jungle monster on Yavin 4."

Peckhum laughed nervously at the memory "I haven't been that scared in a dozen years!" he said. "Let's hope your jungle moon gets a little more civilized."

"Are you making another supply run to the Jedi academy soon?" Jacen asked.

"No, I've been assigned to riding the mirrors up in Coruscant orbit," Peckhum said. "It's a lonely job, but the pay is good—and somebody's got to do it. Besides, it's relaxing . . . if you look at it that way."

Because so much of the surface of Coruscant was covered by cities, engineers had long ago found ways to make even the cold northern and southern latitudes more habitable. By focusing sunlight from huge orbiting mirrors, they could direct enough warmth to thaw land as far north as the arctic, so that millions upon millions could live even in Coruscant's less hospitable areas.

Jaina understood the engineering difficulties of operating the huge automated mirrors, of making sure that the beams of directed sunlight shone down on appropriate areas. The job was not unlike the ancient task of running a lighthouse on an ocean world, where people worked alone, ready for emergencies that rarely came.

"Such an austere assignment would provide a good environment for contemplation," Tenel Ka pointed out.

"It does that, all right," Peckhum said. "I just wish conditions weren't so . . . basic."

"What makes the mirror station so uncomfortable?" Jaina asked. "Don't you have entertainment systems and food-processing units up there?"

Peckhum snorted. "According to the design, yes. But they're all malfunctioning. The mirror stations were set up long ago, even before the Emperor took over. During the Imperial years, tiding the mirror station was a punishment assigned to stormtroopers who had disobeyed orders.

"Nowadays, the food-prep units, entertainment systems, temperature control systems—even the communication systems—all fritz out randomly. No repair tech is willing to go up and give the whole station an overhaul. The New Republic has so much other business that I'm afraid getting spiffy holovideo reception for the mirror station just isn't high on anyone's priority list."

Jaina pursed her lips and placed her chin in her hands. "Those symptoms you described sound familiar," she said. "Could be you need a new central multitasking unit. That might fix everything all at once."

Peckhum switched off his datapad and tucked it into a satchel hanging from the seat. "Don't I know it! But those units are expensive and hard to come by. I've requested a new system five times, and it's always been turned down. 'The resources of the New Republic are allocated according to greatest need,'" he said, as if quoting from a report. "My comfort isn't a great enough need." He scratched his stubbled chin. "Oh well, I'll survive. It's a job. Last month I used some of my own credits to get a handheld holoplayer to take up with me. It'll do."

Zekk came out of the kitchen area balancing a stack of self-heating ration cans in his arms. "I know where we can get a central multitasking unit!" He pressed his chin against the top can in the stack to hold them all in position. "Remember that old shuttle we found? Models like that had lots of subsystems. They must have had units to run everything."

"Sure did," Jaina said, nodding vigorously. "Those outdated passenger shuttles all had central multitasking units. They were cumbersome, but they worked."

Peckhum grinned, then frowned. "Well, I'm leaving tomorrow morning, and I'm not sure how I'd install one of those units myself, even if you did get it."

Zekk waved his hand in dismissal. "Relax, Peckhum—I'll get one for you by the time you return. I promise."

Jaina piped up, seeing an opportunity. "And maybe next time you go up to the mirror station, we could go along and help install it." Lowbacca bellowed his interest in the project as well.

Peckhum's eyes widened with surprised delight. "Well, I suppose that might work after all. Let's celebrate by eating lunch."

The old man swept unsorted debris from a low table, clearing a spot for Zekk to set down the stacked cans of food. The dark-haired boy studied them and passed out rations to everyone. Warm steam curled up from open lids as thermal units heated the contents.

Jaina sniffed at hers suspiciously, and Jacen poked into the goo, while Tenel Ka studied the label seriously. Lowie gave a doubtful growl.

"You needn't complain, Master Lowbacca," Em Teedee said. "I'm certain it's quite nutritious. See? The label bears the Imperial stamp of approval."

Zekk held up one of the cans. "These are old stormtrooper rations. We found an entire cache in one of the lower buildings. They don't taste like much, but they have all our nutritional requirements."

Tenel Ka dug in, grunting with satisfaction. "Quite acceptable," she said.

Jaina stirred the grayish puttylike substance, smiled as

Zekk dug in, then took a small bite herself. It didn't taste bad. In fact, it didn't taste like *anything*, so she ate courteously. When they had finished, she stood up, meeting Zekk's emerald-green gaze. "Want to join *us* for a meal next time?"

Zekk brightened. "Fine with me. When?"

"Well," Jaina said, biting her lower lip and considering, "since Peckhum is leaving you all alone, why don't you come to the Imperial Palace tomorrow night? We're taking a holiday with my parents in the morning, but we're having some sort of special banquet in the evening. Banquets are usually pretty boring, but I'm sure we could get you invited."

"Really?" Zekk said.

"Sure," Jaina answered.

"That's right," Jacen agreed. "We'll probably give Three-pio the time of his life tending to us."

5

FAT SNOWFLAKES FELL in skirling patterns of white against white. There was ice and snow as far as the eye could see on the frozen mountains of Coruscant's polar ice caps. Jaina's exhaled breath produced small puffs of fog in front of her face. Her nose and throat tingled with cold as she inhaled, reveling in the feeling. The crisp air was fresh and clean and delicious.

The tauntaun beneath her, however, smelled *bad*. The creature was supposed to be well behaved, but Jaina didn't think the Bothan stable manager at the polar corrals spent any more time training the wild arctic animals than he did bathing them.

The tauntaun was a white-furred reptile with curved horns jutting from its head. It ran on muscular three-toed hind legs designed to crunch across the snow at high speed. The animals were native to the ice world of Hoth, where the Rebel Alliance had long ago established a secret base. In recent years, though, an enterprising stable manager had transported a few of the beasts to Coruscant's ice caps, intending to offer tauntaun riding as an activity for winter-sports enthusiasts who came to the north pole. But the tauntauns had become surly and stubborn after being transplanted from their home, and Jaina couldn't see how riding one was supposed to be fun.

Her tauntaun fought the bit in its mouth as she tried to make it keep pace with Jacen and his mount. Anakin stayed closer to their father, who hung back next to Leia. Han Solo had claimed to be an expert rider of the uncooperative tauntauns, but Jaina giggled as she watched her father experience plenty of difficulty as they raced across the snows.

The part Jaina enjoyed most was just being able to spend a few hours away from the bustling city with her family, so they could be kids and their parents could be parents—if only for a little while.

Lowie had already made plans with his uncle Chewbacca, and See-Threepio had offered to spend the day showing Tenel Ka the finest obstacle courses and training facilities that Coruscant had to offer.

Before long, she and Jacen and their friends would have to return to the Jedi academy to continue their training, and Han and Leia would get back to their work building the New Republic.

For now, though, they were on vacation.

"Race you," Jacen called, hunching over his tauntaun.

Jaina took up the challenge instantly. "Well then, what are we waiting for?" She leaned forward and jabbed her heels into the side of the snow lizard.

But just as Jacen whooped his own challenge, his tauntaun stopped dead in its tracks and refused to go a centimeter farther.

Jaina's mount lurched forward at full speed, but she wasn't able to gloat over her victory in the race, because she had as much trouble getting her tauntaun to *stop* as Jacen had getting his to move.

"More soup?" Leia asked, huddling next to the thermal container on the snow.

Jaina shook her head. "Don't think I could eat another bite, Mom."

"Hey, I'd love some more," Jacen said.

"Me too," Anakin chimed in.

"Make that three hungry Solo men," Han Solo added with a lopsided grin, handing his soup cup to Leia. "Never could resist one of your packed lunches."

"Yeah, I can push food-prep buttons better than anyone you know," Leia said wryly.

Jaina sighed with contentment, glad just to relax. After the tauntaun riding, they had spent hours turbo-skiing, having snowball fights, and building cities in the snow. Now, seated on a thick slab of heat-reflective insulfoam, Jaina spread her arms wide, catching snowflakes on her gloved hands. "I wish we could do this more often," she said.

"Maybe we should," her mother replied.

Anakin slurped the last of his soup. "I'll be coming to the Jedi academy again soon," he said. "We can have more meals together then."

"Oh, that reminds me," Leia said. "Don't forget, I'm hosting a very important banquet tonight for the new ambassador from Karnak Alpha."

"Where's Karnak Alpha?" Jacen asked. "I don't think I've ever heard of it."

"Out beyond the Hapes Cluster near the Core Systems," his mother answered.

"Aren't there still some Imperial strongholds in the Core Systems?" asked Jaina.

"Sure are," Han Solo replied. "That's why your mother thinks this dinner is so important. You'll have to be on your best behavior."

Jacen groaned. "If it's so important, how come we have to be there?"

Leia smiled warmly. "I'd like you to meet the ambassador. Children play a very special part in the society of Karnak Alpha. They are seen as great treasures that grow richer every day. In Karnak society, the more children you have, the more status and honor you gain. Their government even has a children's council."

"Blaster bolts!" Jacen said. "I almost forgot. We invited Zekk over for evening meal tonight."

"Can he come to the banquet too, Mom?" Jaina asked.

Leia looked flustered, an expression Jaina did not often see on her mother's face. "Zekk? Your young friend from the streets?"

"Aren't you always saying that everyone is valuable, no matter what their background is?" Jaina put in, a little defensively.

"Yeeeesss . . . ," Leia said, drawing the word out.

"Please? If you say yes, I'll even let you braid my hair," Jaina offered hopefully. She glanced at her brothers, looking for support, and saw Anakin's face take on that peculiar measuring look it always did when he was solving a problem.

"If they value children so much, won't the ambassador be happy to have another kid join us?" Anakin said.

Leia's face cleared. "Yes, of course—that's right. Your friend Zekk is more than welcome to come. In fact, we'll invite Lowie and Tenel Ka too."

Jaina laughed with relief. "Great! I'll let them know as soon as we get back."

Jacen finished his soup and stood up. "Do we have to leave right away?"

Han consulted his chronometer. "No, we've got an hour or two yet."

"Well, in that case," Jacen said, "I'll race you all to those hills!"

Everyone laughed and dove for their turboskis.

6

AT THE APPOINTED hour that evening, Zekk arrived at the enormous palace and was ushered inside. New Republic guards checked his name against the approved-visitor list and let him proceed into the elegant corridors, with their high vaulted ceilings. Although he knew his way to Jacen and Jaina's quarters, the uniformed soldiers insisted on "escorting" him, which Zekk found somewhat intimidating.

His new formal clothes were stiff and exceedingly uncomfortable, but he knew that this dinner was an important occasion. He silently vowed not to embarrass anyone. He especially didn't want to disappoint the twins.

Before old Peckhum had departed for his lonely mirror-station duties, he'd helped Zekk select a few items of formal clothing, and the young man had also gone out trading, bartering some of his best trinkets and artifacts for a particularly slick jacket. Now he felt like a dandy as he rode the turbolift up to the higher levels and wound his way through the maze of corridors to the Chief of State's quarters.

The protocol droid See-Threepio met Zekk at the doorway and hustled him inside, dismissing the soldier escort. "Ah, there you are, young Master Zekk. We must hurry—you're late! We have preparations to make."

Zekk tugged at his uncomfortable formal suit. "What do you mean 'preparations'? I'm all ready, I'm dressed . . . what more could you want?"

Threepio tsked through his mouth speaker and brushed the front of Zekk's shirt. "Dear me. These clothes are indeed fine and they are most . . . *interesting*. According to my files they were quite fashionable some decades ago. Quite an historical find, I should say."

Zekk felt a stab of disappointment. He had worked so hard, doing his absolute best to prepare for this special event—and in the space of a few seconds the prissy droid had dismissed all of his efforts.

Leia Organa Solo hurried out of the back room, her dark eyes widening as she saw him.

"Oh . . . uh, hello Zekk. Glad you could make it." Her gaze seemed to dissect Zekk; he clenched his teeth and tried not to show any embarrassment, though he was sure his cheeks were flushed crimson. His fine suit now seemed as ridiculous to him as a clown's costume.

"I hope I'm not being too much of bother," he stammered. "I didn't mean for Jaina and Jacen to invite me—"

"Don't worry about it," Leia said quickly and smiled. "The ambassador from Karnak Alpha has brought her own brood of children. So please relax. Just do the best you can."

Threepio returned with a kit of grooming implements. "First, we'll comb your hair, young Master Zekk. Everything must be presentable. This is a matter of diplomatic pride for the New Republic, though I do wish I could have located those old files about the customs on Karnak Alpha. The place seems to have been forgotten by my protocol programmers." He fussed over Zekk's hair. "Dear me, you could certainly use a trim! Hmmmm, I wonder if we have time . . ."

Jaina and Jacen came out to greet their friend as he stood soundlessly enduring the golden droid's overattentive ministrations. Jacen's hair seemed awkwardly straight, his face scrubbed so clean that Zekk barely recognized the boy. "Hello, Zekk!" Jaina cried with sincere delight, but when she noticed his outfit she covered her mouth to stifle a giggle. He felt his cheeks burning with fresh shame.

When Zekk struggled against the buzzing device, Threepio said sternly, "I *am* a protocol droid, you know, fully trained in grooming techniques." Zekk didn't argue, but winced as Threepio cleared a snag in his dark hair.

"I'm not sure this is such a good idea," Zekk said. "I don't know anything about diplomacy. I don't know any manners or etiquette."

Jaina laughed. "That's not important. Just use your common sense and watch what the rest of us do. It's a big diplomatic banquet, and you have to follow all sorts of boring ceremonies—but the food's good. You'll enjoy it."

Zekk didn't point out that it was easy for Jaina to say such things, since she had been brought up in this high political society and trained in the proper responses for so many years that such actions were second nature to her. Zekk, though, had no such instruction. This whole dinner was going to be a disaster, he just knew it.

See-Threepio finally gave up on his attempts to comb out Zekk's hair and shook his gleaming head in exasperation. "Oh, dear. I have a bad feeling about this," he sighed. Zekk couldn't argue with him.

* * *

Tenel Ka followed the group as they filed toward the formal dining chamber, conscious of her every movement. This was an important diplomatic function, and she had been well tutored by her harsh grandmother in the plush courts of the Hapes Cluster. Tenel Ka was a royal princess, after all, the heir apparent to an entire cluster; but she avoided such nonsense and spent as much as time as possible training instead on her mother's austere world of Dathomir. Tenel Ka's Hapan grandmother strongly disapproved of the path that the princess had chosen to follow, but Tenel Ka had a mind of her own—as she frequently demonstrated.

Now she strode behind Jacen, Jaina, and Zekk, walking next to Lowbacca and the silent younger boy Anakin, as they hurried to the dining chamber. She wore a short, tight-fitting sheath of colorful reptilian hides, freshly oiled and polished so that they gleamed with her every movement. Her muscular arms and legs were bare, but she wore a flowing cape of deep forest green over her shoulders.

Tenel Ka had spent many months at the Jedi academy in the primitive jungles of Yavin 4, and before that she had lived in the cliff cities of the Singing Mountain Clan. It had been a long time since she'd been spoiled with luxuries, but she viewed the formal evening meal with the Karnak ambassador as another challenge to face.

Lowbacca had been shampooed and dried, his fur neatly combed so that he seemed much thinner than usual without his swirling hair sticking out in all directions. The black streak that swept back above his eyebrow had been slicked down, giving him a dashing appearance . . . for a Wookiee.

See-Threepio strutted ahead of Leia and Han as if he were an escort. New Republic guards stood beside the entrance to the great dining hall and swung the doors wide as they approached. Clasping Han Solo's arm, Leia walked in, regal in her fine white robes. Though small of stature, the Chief of State seemed full of energy and confidence, like a battery overcharged with power. Tenel Ka admired her.

Their timing was exactly right. As they passed into the dining hall from one end, the opposite entrance opened, and the ambassador from Karnak Alpha entered, followed by her train of eight children.

The ambassador was a haystack of tan hair, a mound of fur that grew so long that it obscured every other feature of her body. Not even the ambassador's eyes were visible peeping out from between the strands, as she scuttled forward on feet also hidden by her flowing tresses. The ambassador took her place at the head of the table beside the seat reserved for the Chief of State. Leia sat down, with her husband next to her.

The ambassador's children, all eight of them, were miniature versions of her, heaps of hair that bustled to their seats. The girls' fur was knotted into colorful ribbons, while the boys jingled with bells tied to strands of hair. All of them seemed well-groomed and impeccably behaved as they took their seats along one side of the table.

Tenel Ka was glad she had thought to braid colorful ribbons into her own red-gold hair. She had seen natives of Karnak Alpha during her time at the royal court of Hapes. The hairy creatures were shy and had some unusual customs, but they were relatively easygoing.

Tenel Ka sat beside Lowbacca, while Jacen and Jaina took their dark-haired friend Zekk to the front end of the long polished table. Their little brother Anakin, with his eerie ice-blue eyes, seemed content to sit anywhere they directed him, quietly waiting for his place between Lowbacca and Jacen.

See-Threepio moved up and down the line, fussing over items and reveling in his position. This type of duty was, after all, what a protocol droid was programmed for—not for bravery or adventure, but for intricate diplomatic functions.

In front of each gleaming plate sat a crystalline vase containing a cluster of fresh, rich-smelling greens, exotic plants taken from some of Coruscant's botanical gardens—interesting specimens that formed a lovely bouquet for each honored visitor.

Before the start of the meal, Leia gave a carefully rehearsed speech, welcoming the ambassador and expressing her wish for a long and fruitful relationship based on commerce, mutual respect, and support. She whispered to Threepio, and the droid disappeared into an alcove, only to reemerge a moment later carrying a small package. Tenel Ka immediately recognized an incubator sheath wrapped around a smooth ovoid object.

"Hey, that's the hawk-bat egg we rescued!" Jacen said, unable to stop himself.

Leia smiled and nodded. "Yes, and I suppose the ambassador may appreciate the gift even more, now that she knows it was found by the very children she is dining with."

The Karnak ambassador trembled with excitement, her long hair jiggling, as Leia explained. "Madam Ambassador, we know very little about your culture—but we do know that you have a great love for unusual zoological specimens. We have heard reports of your magnificent holographic dioramas and huge alternate-environment zoos where the animals don't even realize they are in a cage. As a diplomatic gift to you and your people, we present to you this rare and precious hawk-bat egg, one of the most difficult-to-catch creatures native to Imperial City. Very few of them are in captivity."

Delighted, the Karnak Alpha ambassador cooed. "This will surely be a wonderful addition to our rarities."

"But you have to take special care of it," Jacen chided. "I promised its mother personally!"

The hairy ambassador didn't seem to find the comment at all strange. "I give you my solemn promise." Then the ambassador responded with her own rehearsed speech, her mouth moving somewhere between the strands of fur as she echoed the sentiments Leia had expressed.

Meanwhile, her children, little wriggling piles of hair, sat impatient and hungry for the meal, while Jacen, Jaina, and the other young Jedi Knights similarly felt their stomachs growling. Han Solo squirmed restlessly beside Leia in his formal clothes, as if chafing under his stiff collar and his medals of military service. Tenel Ka felt sympathy for him.

See-Threepio came into the room, strutting beside a trundle droid that carried a beaten silver tray of ornate plates piled high with scrumptious-looking cuisine, beautifully garnished and displayed. Out of normal political courtesy, the golden droid marched toward the head of the table while Leia

and the Karnak ambassador made the appropriate apprecia-
tive sounds, showing how impressed they were with the ex-
quisite food.

Tenel Ka watched See-Threepio move directly toward the
ambassador, picking up one of the larger plates from the trundle droid's tray. She knew instantly that Threepio meant to
offer the first meal to the ambassador—which was a terribly
rude thing to do, according to Karnak custom.

In one quick, fluid motion she sprang to her feet and
called across the table. "Excuse me, See-Threepio," she said.
"If you would allow me?" She hurried to one end of the table
as the droid stopped, completely at a loss as to what to do.
One by one, Tenel Ka removed the plates from the tray and
reverently set them in front of each of the ambassador's children, starting with the smallest—and presumably the
youngest— furball.

Princess Leia looked at Tenel Ka, surprised but reserving
judgment. The Karnak ambassador made a motion that must
have been a bow of her head. "Why, thank you, young lady.
You do us a great honor. This is an unexpected observance of
our customs."

Tenel Ka nudged See-Threepio and moved him around to
the other side of the table, where she tapped Anakin on the
shoulder. She handed the boy a plate, then whispered into his
ear. Anakin—without argument or question—stood up, duti-
fully moved down the table, and presented the next plate of
food to the Karnak ambassador.

The ambassador chirped with surprise. "I am most honored, Chief of State," she said to Leia, "that you would
choose your youngest to serve me."

"I—thank you," Leia said, uncertain of what else to say.

Tenel Ka stood behind Leia, nodding. Her braided red-
gold hair fell forward. "Yes, Ambassador," she said. "We
wished to show you honor by respecting the customs of Karnak Alpha—that a young member of the household provides
for the guest's children, before a child of the host family
serves the most honored adult guest."

"I am most pleased," the ambassador said. "We shall have

a simple time making diplomatic treaties, if all members of the New Republic are so considerate of our customs."

Trembling with relief that she had averted what could have been a social gaffe for the Chief of State, Tenel Ka sat back down, while Jacen bent toward her, his brandy-brown eyes wide with astonishment. "How did you know that?" he said in a low whisper.

Tenel Ka shrugged beneath her reptilian armor. "It is . . . just something I learned," she said, and then fell silent, reluctant to reveal her royal upbringing, even to a good friend.

Even though Zekk sat back and remained quiet, he still felt uncomfortable. The meal tasted delicious, but each time he moved he was afraid that one of his gestures might offend someone or cause a diplomatic incident.

Threepio served the rest of the meals, and Zekk fell to eating with quiet attention, savoring the delicious food . . . though it was far richer than what he was accustomed to.

The salad in the crystal bowl in front of him was crunchy and strange—some of the leaves bitter, others stringy—but he had eaten far worse in his days of scavenging the streets. He had roasted rock slugs and eaten sliced duracrete fungus. These greens at least were fresh, and he relished them.

The conversation around the table seemed to be empty polite chitchat, and Zekk, feeling like an irrelevant guest, did his best to participate. He pushed aside the empty crystal bowl. "Delicious salad," he said. "I don't believe I've ever had greens like that." That sounded good, a complimentary but neutral statement—enough to show willingness to take part in the dinner conversation, yet nothing anyone could fault him for.

Suddenly he felt all eyes turned toward him. He looked down to see if he had spilled something down the front of his out-of-style jacket.

Jacen seemed full of disbelief. Tenel Ka made no sign that she had even heard Zekk's comment. Jaina nudged Zekk with her elbow in a teasing way. "That wasn't a *salad*," she whispered. "That's the *bouquet*. You weren't supposed to eat it."

Zekk listened in horror, but kept his face a careful mask.

See-Threepio spoke up from behind them. "Now then, Mistress Jaina, many plants are edible, including all of those within the bouquet. I'm certain there's been no harm—"

From the far end of the table Princess Leia cleared her throat. "I'm glad you liked the salad, Zekk," she said in a voice loud enough for everyone to hear, and pulled her crystal dish toward her. She selected a frilly purple-green leaf and stuffed it in her mouth, munching contentedly. Han Solo looked at his wife as if she had gone crazy, then jerked as if he had been kicked under the table. He too began to eat his bouquet. Jaina followed suit, and soon everyone at the table had devoured their "salads."

Zekk was mortified, though he tried not to show it. His manners were laughable, his clothing was outdated, and he had embarrassed everyone by eating something he should have known was a decoration. He wished he had never been invited to this banquet.

He endured the rest of the evening in simmering silence until the Karnak ambassador and her entourage of furball children finally departed, accompanied by the Chief of State and her husband.

When New Republic escorts came to return them to their rooms, Zekk decided to take the first opportunity to escape.

"Don't worry about tonight, Zekk," Jaina said in an understanding voice. "You're our friend. That's all that matters."

Zekk felt stung by her comment, by the fact that she had even needed to say such a thing. He didn't belong here. That truth was etched in burning letters in his brain. He should have known better, but he had pretended that he could fit in with such high-class friends.

When he slipped out the back door of the main dining hall, fully intending to walk too fast for even the rigid escorts to keep up with him, Jaina tried to stop him. "Wait!" she called. "We're still going to meet tomorrow, right? We promised to help you get that central multitasking unit for Peckhum."

Zekk didn't particularly want to go home, but he certainly

couldn't stay. He hurried out into the corridors without answering Jaina.

7

LATER THAT NIGHT, the bulk space cruiser *Adamant* lurched into the Coruscant system, heavily guarded by New Republic warships. The number of assault fighters bristling with turbolaser cannons that clustered around the supply cruiser hinted at the military importance of the cargo it carried.

Standing ready on the cruiser's command bridge, Admiral Ackbar remained tense despite the additional precautions that had been taken. The *Adamant* approached a docking zone near the Coruscant space stations, precisely according to schedule. The assault fighters powered down their weapons and split off as each squadron signaled farewell to the admiral, commander of the New Republic Fleet.

"Thanks for the escort," Ackbar said into the comm unit. "Coruscant security will take over from here." He switched off and paced the bridge. It had been a long haul, but the New Republic badly needed the modern hyperdrive cores and turbolaser battery emplacements his ship carried in its armored holds. The *Adamant* would deliver the components to the Kuat Drive Yards, where they would be installed in a new fleet of battleships. Ackbar had been charged with making a formal inspection tour—and he always relished the chance to be aboard a fine military ship.

Though the main threat from the evil Empire had ended, trouble still flared up in the non-allied systems. The fragile government, led by Chief of State Leia Organa Solo, had to be ready at all times with a force strong enough to ward off attacks from known or unknown enemies.

"Coruscant Central acknowledges our arrival," said the helmsman.

Admiral Ackbar nodded. "It'll be good to take some rest and recreation downside," he said, turning to the helmsman and staring with his round, fishy eyes. "Ever been to Coruscant for a furlough before, Lieutenant?"

The young man nodded. "Yes, sir. Several times. I know where there's this little rooftop cantina, a rotating restaurant that lets you look out across the whole city. They've got a keyboard player with ten tentacles. Boy, you should hear the music she makes!"

Admiral Ackbar chuckled just as the tactical officer turned from her station, her normally pale skin flushed as she shouted an alarm. "Admiral! An unidentified fleet just appeared off our starboard bow. Range is less than fifty kilometers and closing fast. They appear to be in an attack formation."

Ackbar whirled to look out the front viewports. "Attack formation?" he said. "But we're in the Coruscant protected zone, one of the most heavily guarded areas in the galaxy. Who could possibly attack us?" He saw the incoming fleet as it soared in like birds of prey, appearing out of nowhere. In the same moment, he felt the stunning blows from their ion cannons, which immediately crippled the *Adamant*'s defensive systems.

"Battle stations!" he cried in his gravelly voice as another thundering blow slammed into the side of the *Adamant*.

"Minor outer hull breach," the operations officer shouted. "Loss of pressure. Emergency bulkhead doors have closed."

"Transmit a distress signal," Ackbar yelled. "Request immediate assistance from Coruscant security. Now!"

"All weapons systems off-line," the tactical officer reported. "We can't even fire a shot. Engines are still undamaged, though—almost as if our attackers are trying *not* to target them."

"They want to steal this ship," Ackbar said as the cold realization struck him. "And its cargo."

The communications officer had begun transmitting a distress signal, but the round-faced young man looked up almost immediately, his cheeks pale. "Sir, communication systems are nonfunctional. We can't even request help."

Admiral Ackbar swallowed. Coruscant would note the attack and respond within minutes—but by then, he knew, it would be too late.

The enemy ships closed in.

The modified assault shuttle zeroed in on its target. At his controls the former TIE pilot Qorl guided the attack. He wore a black skull-like helmet that sealed against his skin and recirculated breathable air. The dark goggles covering his eyes transmitted important tactical data to his retinas.

He positioned the shuttle's circular cutting "mouth" attachment against the armor plating of the Rebel supply cruiser. The name *Adamant* had been stenciled on the side . . . *Adamant*, which meant impenetrable, unyielding. Qorl grunted to himself. The exceedingly tough cutting teeth were made from industrial-grade Corusca gems and could slice through any known substance. The Shadow Academy's takeover troops would be in control of the ship within moments.

Qorl punched an important-looking red button on the controls. It set the Corusca blades spinning, chewing, until the attachment had sliced out a large circle in the *Adamant*'s hull, opening a hole into the supply cruiser.

Qorl clenched the black-gloved hand of his bulky droid arm into a fist. His own arm had been crippled when his TIE fighter crashed on the jungle moon of Yavin 4, but Imperial engineers had replaced the twisted limb with a more powerful droid attachment. His strength had increased, though he could not feel anything with his new mechanical fingers.

Eager stormtroopers assembled in the boarding tube, holding their blaster rifles ready. Qorl knew that the supply cruiser's main defenses had been on the escort ships, the fourteen heavily armed corvettes, E-wings, and X-wings that had flanked the *Adamant* on its trip to Coruscant. The Rebels had become complacent at their capital world, though, and they had let their defenses lapse for just a moment. Qorl, lurking in his invisible hiding place, had seized that moment to strike.

"Airtight seal complete," a stormtrooper captain reported.

"Very well," Qorl said, standing from his command chair. "Begin the assault. We must be away from here within five standard minutes. We have no time for errors."

The sealed hatch of the boarding tube popped open, and the stormtroopers charged in, firing at anything that moved using only stun beams. They had no particular desire to avoid killing the *Adamant*'s crew, but deadly blaster bolts might cause irreparable damage to the bridge's control systems.

Some of the Rebel crew had taken shelter behind consoles. They fired at the stormtroopers, releasing wild bursts of energy. One trooper went down, a smoking hole in his white chest armor, making a gurgling sound that ended with a burst of static over his comm system.

Qorl marched in, holding a blaster pistol in his droid hand. The stormtroopers fired repeatedly. The Rebel helmsman went down, flying backwards as bolts of blue energy knocked him aside. A tactical officer screamed a challenge as she leaped from her position, shooting four times in quick succession. She killed two stormtroopers before she, too, was stunned.

Qorl strode forward, intent on the *Adamant*'s helm. He needed to get this ship moving soon. The dark goggles of his TIE helmet allowed little peripheral vision, and as he passed the command station, the Rebel commanding officer—a fish-faced Calamarian—leaped up and tackled him. Qorl's blaster pistol clattered to the floor.

The officer wrestled with Qorl, fighting with flipper hands, but the TIE pilot drove his powerful droid fist into the face of the alien, knocking him out cold. Qorl retrieved his blaster pistol and climbed to his feet, brushing off his black uniform.

A stormtrooper captain marched up to him smartly. "The bridge is secure, sir. Ready to move out."

Qorl sat down in the *Adamant*'s command chair. "Very well." He sealed his helmet and his padded suit for total containment, which would protect him from the rapid decompression when the assault ship detached itself from the hull. He hesitated. "Stuff these Rebels into an escape pod, and launch it."

"Save them, sir?" the trooper asked, perplexed. "We don't have much time."

"Then be quick about it!" Qorl snapped. Conflicting emotions warred within him. These were the enemy, and he had sworn to fight them—but the crew on this ship had battled valiantly, and he couldn't stomach letting them die as they lay there unconscious.

The stormtroopers paused for only a second, then hustled as they dragged the limp forms to the bridge escape pod and unceremoniously dumped them inside the defenseless craft. The stormtrooper captain sealed the hatch and punched the pod's external launch control. With a hiss from explosive bolts and a gush of compressed gases, the escape pod shot away.

Qorl studied the *Adamant*'s tactical station. Rebel defensive forces were finally on their way, streaking up out of orbit and heading toward the besieged supply ship. "Go!" he said to the troopers. "Take the assault shuttle and escape. I will meet you back at the base."

The stormtroopers hurried to the shark-mouthed assault shuttle and sealed the boarding hatch. Qorl braced himself as the modified ship detached itself, letting the contained atmosphere rush out of the bridge through the gaping hole, to space.

Secure in his suit, Qorl powered up all the engines. He fed in preprogrammed coordinates, and the *Adamant* lurched into motion. As the Rebel fleet zoomed in, Qorl followed his Imperial ships, carrying with him an incredible treasure that would help the Second Imperium gain its rightful place of military superiority.

The base was very close indeed.

Admiral Ackbar returned to consciousness, and found himself crammed with his crew inside an escape pod that whirled out of control through space. His head ached, and he felt as if a space mine had exploded inside his skull. His crew members groaned and stirred, coming awake. For some reason their lives had been spared. He wriggled his way over to one of the tiny viewports so he could watch for rescue craft.

As the escape pod spun about in a nauseating spiral, Admiral Ackbar saw his own ship from the outside. The hijacked space cruiser *Adamant* lumbered into motion and picked up speed as the Imperial fighters streaked ahead of it.

New Republic reinforcements headed on a direct path to recapture the precious weapons and supplies—but already Ackbar could see that the Imperial ships would be long gone by the time those reinforcements arrived.

Ackbar watched the *Adamant* vanish before the Coruscant ships came close enough to fire a shot. He wished he could just fall back into unconsciousness, but the splitting pain in his skull kept him wide awake.

8

AS ZEKK HURRIED through the night streets of Imperial City, heading away from the palace, he took back stairways and crossed alley catwalks, wanting to see no one. Overhead, blinking lights from shuttles taxiing across the atmosphere fought through a blurring mist of condensed moisture from roof exhaust vents. The city's myriad lights and its sprawling landscape of skyscrapers extending beyond the horizon taunted him with the knowledge that, despite the millions upon millions of inhabitants, he was totally alone.

After the evening's miserable escapades, he felt as if a marquee droid was hovering over his head, broadcasting to everyone that Zekk was a clumsy fool, an embarrassment to his friends. What had he been thinking—trying to fit in with important society, mingling with ambassadors and diplomats, making friends with the children of the Chief of State? Who was he to spend time with such people?

He looked at his feet for something to kick, finally spotted an empty beverage container, and lashed out with his boot, a boot he had spent time polishing so he would look good in front of his so-called friends. The container clattered and bounced against a duracrete wall, but to Zekk's frustration it refused to break.

He kept his gaze turned downward, to the shadows and the clusters of garbage in the gutter. He shuffled aimlessly, wandering the back streets, not caring where he might end up. The lower world of Coruscant was his home. He knew it well, and he could survive here—which was good, because it looked as if he would be stuck in this gloomy place for the rest of his life. There was no hope, no chance for advancement. He simply wasn't the equal of those people who could look forward to a bright future—people like Jaina and Jacen.

Zekk was a nobody.

He saw a group of merchants closing up their kiosks for the night, chatting cordially with the New Republic guards who patrolled the streets. Zekk didn't want to go near them, didn't want any company whatsoever. He slipped into a public turbolift and punched a button at random, descending nineteen floors and emerging in a dimmer section of the city.

Old Peckhum had already gone up to the mirror station on his tour of duty so even Zekk's home would be empty and uninviting. He'd have to spend the night alone, trying to keep amused with games or entertainment systems . . . but nothing sounded at all interesting.

He could wander around for as long as he liked, so he decided to enjoy it. No one would tell him to go to bed, no one would admonish him for going places where he wasn't allowed, no one would breathe down his neck.

He smiled thinly. *He* had a freedom Jaina and Jacen didn't have. When they were out exploring and having fun, the twins constantly checked their chronometers, making sure they would be back home at the appointed time, never making allowances for unexpected circumstances. They certainly didn't want to give their protocol droid a burned worry circuit by not following their explicit orders. The twins were prisoners to their own schedules.

What did it matter if Zekk didn't know all the manners a life in the diplomatic court required? *Who cared* if he didn't understand which eating implement to use, or what the appropriate phrase of gratitude was when speaking to an insectoid ambassador? He snorted with derision. He wouldn't want to live like Jaina and Jacen. No way!

As he wandered along the abandoned corridors, purposely scuffing his toes against the floor plates, he paid no attention to the thickening shadows, to the oppressive silence that surrounded him. He sniffed and clenched his teeth in remembered humiliation. He didn't care about any of that. Zekk was his own person, independent—just the way he liked it.

Overhead, the glowpanels flickered intermittently; those at the far end of the corridor had completely burned out. A skittering sound in the ceiling ducts signaled the passage of a large and clumsy rodent. Ahead he heard another rustling sound, something even bigger.

Zekk looked up with a gasp to see a tail figure, darker than the inky shadows, step out in front of him. "Well, what have we here?" a syrupy voice said, deep and powerful.

The figure stepped closer, and Zekk could see a tail woman with eyes that flashed a burning violet. She wore a glittering black cloak with shoulder spines like defensive armor. Long black hair flowed around her like wire-thin snakes. Her skin was pale, her lips a deep crimson. She tried to smile, but the expression looked foreign on her face.

"Greetings, young sir," she said, her voice oozing persuasion. "I require a moment of your time." When she stepped more fully into the light, Zekk noticed that the woman walked with a pronounced limp.

"I don't think so . . . ," he said, backing up and turning around just as two sinister figures emerged from the side corridors: a compact woman with light brown skin and wavy bronze hair and a shadow-faced young man with dark bushy eyebrows.

"Just one moment of your time, boy. Vilas and Garowyn here will make sure you don't do anything foolish," the dangerous-looking woman said. She limped closer to him. "I am Tamith Kai, and we need to perform a test on you. It won't hurt a bit." Zekk thought he detected a tone of disappointment in her voice.

The young man Vilas and the short, bronze-haired woman grabbed him from behind. Instantly, Zekk struggled, thrashing and shouting out loud. The strangers didn't seem bothered by how much noise he made, and Zekk knew with a sinking certainty that cries for help were not at all uncommon in these abandoned levels—although brave rescuers were.

Zekk tried to yank his arms free from the clawlike grasp of his captors, but to no avail. Tamith Kai withdrew a strange device from the black folds of her cape. Unraveling wires connected to a pair of flat crystalline paddles, she switched on an additional power grid. A high-pitched hum vibrated through the machine case.

"Leave me alone!" Zekk lashed backward with his foot, hoping to deliver a sharp blow to sensitive shins.

"Be careful," Tamith Kai said to her colleagues with a meaningful scowl. "Some of them can be dangerous when they kick."

She leaned closer and waved the humming crystal paddles around his body, scanning him. His heart pounding with fear, Zekk gritted his teeth and squeezed his emerald eyes shut. To his surprise, he felt no tingling energy; no burning analytical beam sliced through his skin.

Tamith Kai withdrew, and Garowyn and Vilas leaned over Zekk's bony shoulders to observe the readings. Still struggling, Zekk caught a glimpse of the glowing image, a colorful aura projected in a micro-hologram.

"Hmmm, surprising," Tamith Kai said. "Look at the power he has."

"A good find," Garowyn agreed. "Quite fortunate."

"Not fortunate for me!" Zekk snapped. "What do you want?"

"You'll be coming with us," Tamith Kai said. Her tone was filled with confidence, as if she didn't care about his objections.

"I'm not going *anywhere* with you!" Zekk shouted. "No matter what you found, I won't—"

"Oh, just stun him," Tamith Kai said impatiently, turning about on her stiff leg and limping back down the shadow-shrouded corridor. "He'll be easier to carry that way."

Vilas released his grip on the boy's arms, and Zekk tried to run, knowing this was his last chance . . . but arcs of blue

fire looped out, engulfing him and slamming him down into
unconsciousness.

9

JAINA STARED MOROSELY at her brothers. She bit her
lip, wondering what their mother would say when she got
back from seeing the Karnak Alpha ambassador to her quarters. She hoped Leia wasn't too upset with Zekk.

Jacen paced the living area, muttering to himself. "Blaster
bolts!" he said with a dramatic gesture. "Can you believe
Zekk thinking the bouquet was a salad? It's a good thing
Tenel Ka was there to head off that other problem. We still
probably made a terrible impression on the ambassador."

"I don't think it turned out so badly," Anakin said from
where he sat on a large cushion near the door. "Mom will
handle it. You'll see."

Jainia groaned. "Zekk probably feels terrible."

"We'll see him in the morning," Jacen said, "when we
help him look for that central multitasking unit. We can apologize to him then."

The door to their quarters swished open and Leia walked
in wearing a bemused expression. After a moment of anxious
silence, all three of her children spoke at once.

"I'm sorry, Mom. It's all my fault," Jaina blurted.

"Was the ambassador very angry?" Jacen asked.

"Where's Dad?" Anakin said.

The barrage of questions snapped Leia out of her daze.
"Nothing to be sorry for, Jaina," she said, giving her daughter a hug. "The ambassador says I've got three wonderful
children, and they have charming friends." She stooped to
smooth back Anakin's straight dark hair. "And to answer
your question, your father had begun discussing hyperspace
trade routes to Karnak Alpha with the ambassador, and de-

cided to stay for some business that was even more important."

Jaina blinked in surprise at this unexpected turn of events and sat down at one end of a long, cushioned repulsorseat. Leia sat down beside her, and Jacen settled next to his mother on the other end of the seat. Leia adjusted the repulsorseat's controls to a gentle rocking motion. Anakin dragged his floor cushion over to sit beside them, quiet and attentive.

Leia smiled down at her children. "The ambassador was certainly impressed by the number of young people we had invited to meet her at the dinner. She also said that any adult who was willing to break with her own social traditions just to make a child feel more comfortable should have no problem negotiating an alliance with Karnak Alpha. I'm glad you twins were here with us, rather than at the Jedi academy."

"That's great, Mom," said Jaina, snuggling deeper into the cushions.

"I learned something very important about myself tonight," Leia continued. "As your father and I walked the ambassador and her children back to their quarters, I realized that *my* kids were more important to me than any ambassador. When we got to their quarters, the ambassador said she was ready to discuss her planet's alliance with the New Republic. That's when I amazed even myself. I said I'd be happy to talk with her about it in the morning—but that for right now I needed to be with my children."

Jaina gave a low whistle. Her mother was always so wrapped up in her duties as Chief of State, such a response seemed inconceivable. "You didn't!"

Leia chuckled. "Yes I did, and you know what she said?" She sounded a bit surprised. "She said in that case she no longer had any doubts that we could form an alliance. Everything is all set."

"If everything's all set, why didn't Dad come back with you?" Anakin asked. "What other important business was there?"

"He offered to stay behind," Leia said, raising her eyebrows, "and tell the ambassador's children one of your favorite bedtime stories. Can you guess which one?"

Jacen, Jaina, and Anakin all murmured in unison, "The Little Lost Bantha Cub."

"Then you'll have to tell us a story too, Mom," Anakin said in a sleepy voice.

So she did.

10

THE NEXT MORNING, as they found their way through the streets, Jacen had an uneasy prickly feeling at the back of his neck, as if a trail of mermyns were crawling along his skin. Something felt wrong, but he couldn't quite put his finger on what it was. "Blaster bolts," he muttered.

For some reason they all seemed a bit jumpy today. Jaina had taken the lead, since she was most familiar with the way to Zekk's quarters. Jacen, on the other hand, always got lost. Tenel Ka followed Jaina in silence, her shoulders squared, her back rigid, while Jacen and Lowie brought up the rear.

They trooped through the ancient cramped alleyways of metal and stone. The lights were too dim in this area, and the air tasted of rusting metal and decay. Even the odors were unfamiliar and, to Wookiees at least—judging by the wrinkling of Lowie's nose—none too pleasant.

"Here we are," Jaina said, rounding a sharp corner into an even narrower passageway. She stopped at a low doorway and pressed the signal button. The indicator light flashed red, denying them access. Jaina bit her lower lip. "That's strange. Zekk said yesterday that he'd clear us for access."

"Perhaps he is more upset than we expected," Tenel Ka suggested.

"Maybe," Jaina agreed, "but not likely. Zekk doesn't break promises. We've had disagreements before, but . . ." Her voice trailed off.

When Lowbacca rumbled a comment, Em Teedee translated. "Master Lowbacca wonders if Master Zekk might not simply have stepped out for a morning constitutional. Or perhaps he decided to procure comestibles for morning meal."

"Yeah, that would be better than those stormtrooper rations he gave us last time," Jacen pointed out, feeling his stomach gurgle with distaste at the thought.

"He knew we were coming," Jaina said. "He should have been here."

"Let's wait for a while," Jacen suggested, sitting with crossed legs on the floor. "He'll probably turn up in a few minutes with some wild story."

"That would be just like him," Jaina agreed.

Jacen, knowing his sister was still worried, tried to sound as confident as possible. "He'll be back any minute—you'll see. In the meantime," he suggested brightly, "I've got some new jokes, if anybody wants to hear them."

The twins entertained the other young Jedi Knights with stories of Zekk's past adventures. Jacen told about the time Zekk climbed forty-two stories down an abandoned turbolift shaft because he saw something glittery and reflective by the glow of his pulsed-laser spotlight. Imagining treasures that grew more and more extravagant with each level he descended, Zekk discovered in the end that the shining object was merely a discarded foil wrapping stuck to the ooze dripping along the shaft wall.

Jaina shared a story about how Zekk reprogrammed a personal translating device for a group of snide reptilian tourists who had shoved him out of line for free samples of a new food product. Zekk changed their translator so that every time the reptilian tourists asked for directions to eating establishments or museums, they were instead guided to seedy gambling parlors or garbage-reprocessing stations.

"How simply dreadful!" Em Teedee commented.

Minutes crept by and became an hour, and still their friend did not return.

At last Jaina stood. "Something's wrong," she said, biting her lower lip. "Zekk's not coming."

Lowie growled and Em Teedee translated, "Master Lowbacca suggests that perhaps Master Zekk requires a certain amount of time to overcome his embarrassment. I don't suppose I'll ever understand human behavior," he added.

"Maybe," Jaina said, her face troubled and unconvinced.

"Hey, why don't we leave a videonote," Jacen suggested. "We'll try again tomorrow. How long can he stay mad at us?"

But the next day Zekk was still nowhere to be found. Jacen pressed the access request button beside Zekk's front door, but again there was no response. Old Peckhum would be returning from the mirror station soon, and he would come home to an empty apartment.

"I think it's time to start looking for Zekk," Jacen said, staring at the blank infopanel.

"Agreed," Tenel Ka said.

"Well then," Jaina said, rubbing her hands together briskly, "what are we waiting for? And if we still can't find him, we'll talk to Mom."

Leia Organa Solo seemed preoccupied and concerned as they entered her private office. Leia smiled at them and brushed a stray hair out of Jaina's eyes. "I'm glad you're here, kids. I wanted to show you something."

Before Jacen or Jaina could tell her about Zekk, Leia played a grainy long-range videoclip that showed Imperial attack vessels striking a New Republic military supply cruiser in space near Coruscant.

"That looks like the ship that kidnapped us from Lando's GemDiver Station!" Jaina cried.

Lowbacca growled in agreement.

Leia nodded. "I thought so, from your description —and now I can confirm it to Admiral Ackbar. This attack came two nights ago. We may have a real threat on our hands, right here on the capital world."

Jaina watched the videoclip again and frowned. "Something else isn't right about those images. I'm trying to figure out what. . . ."

Leia returned to her desk. "Admiral Ackbar and a handful of tactical experts are analyzing the footage, and they might want to ask you some questions. We're stepping up security against the very real possibility that we may see another Imperial attack."

After that news, when Jacen poured out the story of Zekk's disappearance, Leia didn't seem overly concerned. She let her gaze drift across all four of the young Jedi Knights standing in her office. "All right, let me ask you this: Who knows the city better, the four of you . . . or Zekk?"

"Well, Zekk does," Jacen answered in a hesitant voice. "But—"

"And if Zekk is upset and hiding somewhere," Leia continued, "is it any wonder that you haven't been able to find him?"

"But he wouldn't do that," Jaina objected. "He promised us."

"Well then," Leia said in a calm, reasonable voice, "maybe he's found that central multitasking unit already and Peckhum shuttled him up to the mirror station."

"But he would have left us a message." Jaina set her mouth in a stubborn line.

"She's right. Mom," Jacen spoke up. "Zekk may seem like a scamp, but he always does what he says he's going to do."

Leia swept her children with a skeptical look. "How many years have we known Zekk?"

Jaina shrugged. "About five, but what—"

"And in those years," Leia went on, "how many times has he just disappeared on some adventure, only to reappear about a month later?"

Jacen cleared his throat and shifted uncomfortably "Um, maybe half a dozen times."

"There. You see?" Leia said, as if that closed the matter.

"But those other times," Jacen pointed out, we didn't have plans to spend the day with him."

Leia sighed. "And those other times he wasn't upset over an embarrassing diplomatic dinner, either. Look, he's older than you are, and legally he can come and go as he pleases. But even if we knew for certain that he was missing—which we don't—there's very little we could do about it. The galaxy is a big place. Who knows where he might be?

"People turn up missing all the time, and we simply don't have the resources to look for everybody. Just this week I've had reports of at least three other teenagers missing in Imperial City alone. Why don't you wait and talk to Peckhum when he gets back tomorrow? Maybe he'll have some ideas." She herded them out of the room so she could get back to work.

"Right now I've got to get ready for my next meeting with the Karnak Alphan ambassador. And then I have to see the Howler Tree People again for a musical ceremony this afternoon. ... ." She rubbed her temples as if in anticipation of a headache. "I really do love my job—uh, most of it at least."

As they left Leia's office, Jacen groaned. "Mom doesn't believe there's even a problem."

"Then I guess we'll have to keep searching on our own," Jaina said.

Lowie growled agreement.

"It's all up to us," Jacen said, pounding a determined fist into his palm.

"This is a fact," said Tenel Ka.

11

AFTER WHAT SEEMED like an eternity, Zekk fought his way back to consciousness. He felt as if a million volts had shot through his body, short-circuiting half of his nerves and leaving his muscles tingly and twitching.

His head ached. The hard metal floor beneath his body oozed a cruel chill. The harsh white light hurt his eyes.

When he sat up, he had to blink away sparkling, colored spots. Waiting for his vision to focus, Zekk finally realized there was nothing to see—only blank, whitish-gray walls. He found a small speaker grille and the vent for an air-circulation system, but nothing else. He couldn't even find the door.

Zekk knew he must be in some kind of cell. He remembered struggling with the evil-looking people who had captured him in the lower city—a black-haired woman with violet eyes using a strange scanning device, and a dark young man who had stunned him. . . .

"Hey!" he yelled. His voice sounded rough and hoarse. "Hey! Where am I?" He got to his feet, swaying from dizziness, and made his way to the nearest wall. He hammered on the metal plates, shouting for attention. He worked his way around the small room, but found no door crack.

He stumbled to the speaker and shouted into it. "Somebody tell me what's going on. You have no right to take me prisoner!"

But in spite of his brave words, Zekk knew things that Jaina and Jacen, raised within the protective confines of the law and guarded by security forces all their lives, had never understood. Zekk knew that his "rights" wouldn't be protected if someone had the power to take them away. No one would fight for *him*. No one would send military fleets to rescue *him*. If Zekk disappeared, there would be no public outcry. Few people would even notice.

"Hey!" he shouted again, kicking at the wall. "Why am I a prisoner? Why do you want *me*?"

He whirled as he heard a whishing sound on the opposite side of the room. A smooth door slid aside to reveal a powerful-looking man flanked by stormtroopers. The man was tall and wore silvery robes. His hair was blond and neat, his face gentle and complacent. His exceedingly handsome features looked as finely made as a sculpture. The man's very presence exuded an aura of peace and calm.

"Aren't you overreacting a bit?" the man said. His rich voice hummed with power and charisma. "We came as soon as we realized you were awake. You could have hurt yourself by pounding so hard on the walls."

Zekk did not allow himself to relax. "I want to know why I'm here," he said. "Let me go. My friends will be looking for me."

"No they won't." The man shook his head. "We have enough information about you to know that. But don't worry."

"Don't worry?" Zekk sputtered. "How can you say—" He stopped short, as the man's words struck home. No, his friends wouldn't be looking for him, would they? He doubted Jaina and Jacen would want to be seen with him after the debacle of the diplomatic banquet. "What do you mean?" he asked in a subdued voice.

The man in the silvery robes gestured to the guards. The stormtroopers waited outside as the man entered the cell alone, sealing the door behind him. "I see they put you in our . . . least extravagant living quarters." He sighed. "We'll find you a more comfortable room as soon as possible."

"Who are you?" Zekk said, still not letting his guard down. "Why did you stun me?"

"My name is Brakiss, and I apologize for the . . . enthusiasm of my colleague Tamith Kai. But I do believe she authorized the use of force only because of your struggles. If you had cooperated, it could have been a much more pleasant experience."

"I didn't know being kidnapped was supposed to be 'pleasant,'" Zekk snarled.

"Kidnapped?" Brakiss said in feigned alarm. "Let's not jump to conclusions until we've got the full story."

"Then explain it to me," Zekk said.

"All right." Brakiss smiled. "Would you like any refreshments? Something warm to drink?"

"Just tell me what's going on," Zekk said.

Brakiss pressed his hands together. His silvery robes flickered around him like rippling water under a cloudy sky. "I have some news for you—good news, I hope you'll agree, although it may come as something of a shock."

"What?" Zekk asked, frowning skeptically.

"Are you aware that you have Jedi potential?" Zekk's green eyes widened. "Jedi—me? I think you've got the wrong person."

Brakiss grinned. "Fairly *strong* potential. We were surprised ourselves. Didn't your friends Jacen and Jaina tell you? Weren't you aware?"

"I don't have any Jedi potential," Zekk mumbled. "I couldn't have anything like that."

"And why not?" Brakiss asked, raising his eyebrows. He seemed so reasonable. He waited for Zekk to answer, and finally the boy looked down at his hands.

"Because I . . . I'm just a street kid. I'm a nobody. Jedi Knights are great protectors of the New Republic. They're powerful and . . ."

Brakiss nodded impatiently. "Yes they are—but the *potential* to be a Jedi has nothing to do with where you live or how you were raised. The Force knows no economic boundaries. Luke Skywalker himself was just the foster son of a moisture farmer.

"Why shouldn't a poor kid like you have just as much Jedi ability as, for instance, a politician's twin children who live in luxury with all their needs cared for? In fact," Brakiss said in a lower voice, "it could be that because your life has been so tough, your true potential as a Jedi has been honed even sharper than the potential of those pampered little brats."

"They're not brats," Zekk retorted. "They're my friends."

Brakiss dismissed his comment with a casual wave. "Whatever."

"How come I never knew about this? How come I never . . . felt anything?" Zekk asked. He realized suddenly what Tamith Kai had been scanning for with her strange electronic device.

Brakiss rocked back on his heels. "You might not know you had any Force talent if no one ever trained you. It's a simple enough thing to measure, though. If Jacen and Jaina were such close friends, I'm shocked to think that they never *bothered* to test you. Isn't it true that Master Skywalker is desperately on the lookout for more Jedi Knights?"

Zekk nodded uncomfortably.

"Well, if that's so," Brakiss continued, "why didn't they test everyone around them? Why would they just dismiss you out of hand, Zekk? I think they've shortchanged you; they probably never even *imagined* that a street kid, a lowborn scamp, would be worthy of Jedi training, no matter what his innate potential."

"That isn't it," Zekk muttered, but his words carried no strength.

"Have it your way." Brakiss shrugged.

Zekk looked away, though the featureless walls of the cell gave him nothing else to stare at. He waved a hand around to indicate the cold, close cell. "What is this place?" he asked, trying to change the subject.

"This place is the Shadow Academy," Brakiss said, and Zekk was startled to recognize the name of the hidden station where Jaina and Jacen had been held against their will. "I am in charge of training new Jedi for the Second Imperium. I use different methods than Master Skywalker follows at his Yavin 4 training center." Brakiss frowned sympathetically. "But then you wouldn't know, would you? Your friends never took you there." His voice turned up in a question. "Did they? Even for a visit?"

Zekk shook his head.

"Well, *I* am training new Jedi, powerful warriors to help bring back the glory and order of a new Empire. The Rebel Alliance is a criminal movement. You wouldn't understand that, because you're too young to remember what it was like under Emperor Palpatine."

"I hate the Empire!" Zekk said.

"No you don't," Brakiss assured him. "Your friends have *told* you to hate the Empire, but you never witnessed any of it firsthand. You've only seen their version of history. You realize, of course, that whichever government is in charge always makes the defeated enemy look like a monster. I will tell you the truth. The Empire had very little political chaos. Every person had opportunities. There were no gangs running wild through the streets of Coruscant. Everyone had a task to do, and they did it willingly.

"Besides, what does galactic politics have to do with you, young Zekk? You've never been concerned with such things. Would your life really change if the Chief of State were replaced by a different politician in a different Empire? If you work with us, on the other hand, your life could be much improved."

Zekk shook his head, clamping his teeth together. "I won't betray my friends," he growled.

"Your friends," Brakiss said. "Oh, yes . . . the ones who

never tested you for Jedi potential, the ones who only come to visit you when it fits into their social schedule. They're going to leave you behind, you know, as they find more 'important' work to do. They'll forget about you so fast you won't have time to blink."

"No," Zekk whispered. "No they won't."

"Tell me, what does the future hold for you?" Brakiss continued, his voice persuasive. "Certainly, you've made friends that move in rich and important circles—but will you ever be a part of that? Be honest with yourself."

Zekk didn't answer, though he knew the truth deep in his heart.

"You'll be scavenging for the rest of your years, selling trinkets to earn enough credits for your next meal. Do you really have any chance for power or glory or importance of your *own?*"

Again, Zekk refused to answer. Brakiss leaned forward, his beautifully chiseled features radiating kindness and concern. "I'm offering you that chance, boy. Are you brave enough to take it?"

Zekk searched for the strength to resist, focused on a thread of anger. "The same chance you offered to Jaina and Jacen? They told me how you kidnapped them, brought them to the Shadow Academy, and tortured them."

"Tortured them?" Brakiss laughed and shook his blond head. "I suppose after being pampered all their lives, a bit of hard work might *seem* like torture. I offered to train them to become powerful Jedi—I admit it was a mistake. We wanted young Jedi Knights to train, but the candidates we invited were too high-profile. The risk was greater than we had anticipated, and it called too much attention to our academy.

"So I decided to change my plan. As I told you, the Force moves as strongly within the less-fortunate as in those who are rich and powerful. Your social status doesn't concern me in the least, Zekk—only your talent and your willingness to develop it. Tamith Kai and I have decided to search among the lower levels of society for people whose potential is just as great as in those among the higher levels, and yet whose disappearance won't cause such a stir. People with the incentive to work with us."

Zekk scowled, but Brakiss's eyes blazed. "If you join us, I guarantee you the name of Zekk will never be ignored or forgotten."

The cell door opened again, and a stormtrooper held out a tray with steaming beverages and delicious-looking pastries. "Let's have a snack while we keep talking," Brakiss said. "I trust most of your questions have been answered, but feel free to ask anything else you wish."

Zekk realized that he was voraciously hungry, and he took three of the pastries, licking his lips as he ate them. He had never tasted anything so wonderful in his life.

The implications of Brakiss's words terrified him, but the questions about his future bubbled to the surface again and again in his mind. Although Zekk didn't want to admit it, he could not shake the feeling that Brakiss and his promises made a lot of sense.

As Brakiss sealed the door behind him on his way out, he turned to the stormtrooper guards in the hall. "See that the boy gets a nicer room, he said. "I don't think we'll have much trouble with him."

The master of the Shadow Academy glided down the corridor as the old TIE pilot marched up to report. Qorl was still in his black armored suit and cradled his skull-like helmet in his powerful droid arm. "The captured Rebel cruiser *Adamant* is now enclosed within our shields, Lord Brakiss," he said. "Its weaponry is being off-loaded even as we speak."

Brakiss smiled broadly "Excellent. Was it as big a shipment as we expected?"

Qorl nodded. "Affirmative, sir. The hyperdrive cores and turbolaser batteries will enable us to virtually double the Second Imperium's military strength. It was a wise move to strike now."

Brakiss folded his hands together, letting his flowing silvery sleeves swallow them up. "Most excellent. Everything is proceeding as planned. I will report to our Great Leader and tell him the good news. Before long, the Empire will shine again—and these Rebels can do nothing to prevent it."

12

"SHUTTLE *MOON DASH*, this is Coruscant Control Tower One. You are cleared to leave spacedock. Bay doors opening in Gamma Section."

Captain Narek-Ag opened her main comm channel. "Thank you, Tower One. This is shuttle *Moon Dash*, heading for Gamma bay doors with a full load of cargo." She switched off the comm unit and grinned conspiratorially at her copilot, Trebor. "A few more good payloads like this," she said, "and I may just ask you to marry me." Her hazel eyes held a teasing look.

Trebor grinned back, accustomed to his captain's sense of humor. "Keep making good business deals like this one, and I may just accept."

With the ease born of long practice, Narek guided her shuttle out of its docking bay in one of Coruscant's orbiting space stations. "Coordinates locked in?" she asked.

"Locked in and confirmed," her copilot answered the moment she finished speaking.

Narek chuckled as her shuttle streaked away from the spacedock. Accelerating through the inner Coruscant system, she calibrated their hyperspace path for Bespin, the next planet on their run. "You know, for a small-time operation—"

"—we're not half bad," Trebor finished for her.

"Not half bad," she echoed with a satisfied nod. "Calculating hyperspace path."

"Almost ready," Trebor said. "If we hurry, there might be enough time to deliver this cargo to Cloud City and still arrange for a second payload on the return trip. That would double our profit for this run."

A pleased smile spread across Narek's face. She flicked her auburn hair to one side. "I love it when you think like a businessman."

"Business*person*," Trebor corrected. "Approaching top acceleration. Prepare for jump to lightspeed."

Suddenly the *Moon Dash* lurched as if it had slammed into an impenetrable barrier. The tiny craft ricocheted, spinning uncontrollably. Alarms whooped and bright warning lights flashed across the control console.

"What was that?" Narek demanded, shaking her head to clear the blurry spots from her vision. She stared out the viewport at empty space.

"I don't know!" Trebor said. "Nothing showed up on the sensors. Nothing showed up on the sensors! It's supposed to be clear space!"

"Well, it's the *hardest* piece of clear space I've ever encountered," Narek-Ag shot back. "Damage report!"

"Not sure. Can you get us stabilized?" her copilot asked. "Okay, looks like we got a lower hull rupture. Awww, there goes all our cargo! Engines running beyond the red lines." He swallowed. "We are in deep trouble, lady."

Then, as if to emphasize Trebor's assessment, a shower of sparks erupted from the main guidance console. *Moon Dash* careened out of control.

"Emergency, Coruscant One! This is shuttle *Moon Dash*. We've struck unknown space debris," Trebor yelled into the comm unit. A burst of static from the speaker grille was accompanied by a squeal of feedback and another spray of sparks.

Narek-Ag coughed and tried to wave away the smoke. She flicked a pair of switches. "Aft-thrusters not responding," she said in a terse voice. "Still scanning the area— there's *nothing*. What did we smash into?"

"News ain't any better from where I sit," Trebor said. "Can't get much worse."

"It can't, huh? Well, it just did," Narek said with a hard gulp. "I guess I'd better ask you to marry me after all."

Trebor caught sight of the readout that had grabbed his captain's attention. He groaned aloud. An unstoppable chain reaction had begun to build inside their engine chambers like an avalanche of deadly energy. Within seconds, the *Moon Dash* would explode like a small supernova.

"Always wanted to get married out among the stars," he said. Tears stung his eyes. Probably from the acrid smoke, he thought. "Never had a better offer." He placed his hand over hers. "I accept . . . but I have to say that your timing stinks."

She squeezed his hand, then looked down at the panels. "Uh-oh! Hyperdrive engines are going crit—"

In space, the *Moon Dash* erupted in a silent shower of molten metal and flaming gases, fading to black.

Jaina paced the main living area of her family's quarters in the Imperial Palace like a caged jungle creature she had seen once in the Holographic Zoo for Extinct Animals. She hated inactivity. She wanted to *do* something.

Jacen and Tenel Ka had gone out again to look for Zekk, taking along See-Threepio and Anakin, while Lowie was off working with his uncle Chewbacca. When Jacen had pointed out that it would be a good idea for someone to stay behind in case Zekk or Peckhum tried to reach them, Jaina had reluctantly agreed to be the one.

She had finally broken down and tried to contact old Peckhum up in the mirror station, though he was due to return home that day. At his station holo panel, Peckhum had answered right away, but as she started to explain that Zekk had disappeared, the old man's fuzzy image quickly deteriorated. His response was all but drowned out by static. ". . . can't understand your . . . not receivi . . . transmission . . . returning tonight . . ."

The station's central multitasking unit was getting progressively worse, and communication wouldn't be possible until she saw Peckhum face-to-face.

By the time her mother came home for midday meal, Jaina was ready to scream from just sitting around. She was eager to talk, but Leia's face seemed tired and careworn, and Jaina decided it was best not to intrude on her mother's thoughts. She brought Leia a warm lunch from the processing station and sat down to eat beside her in silence.

A few minutes later Han Solo dashed in and rushed over to his wife. "I came as soon as I got your message. What is it?"

A grateful smile lifted the corners of Leia's mouth as she looked at her husband. "I need to get your opinion on something," she said. "Do you have time to sit down and eat with us?"

Han flashed her a roguish grin. "Midday meal with the two most beautiful women in the galaxy? Of course I've got time. What happened? Another disaster like the Imperial attack?" He helped himself to a bowl of warm Corellian stew.

"A disaster all right." Leia took a deep breath. "A shuttle blew up this morning just as it was leaving orbit."

Jaina looked up in surprise, but her father nodded. "Yeah, I heard about it an hour ago."

Leia's brows drew together in a frown of concentration. "No one seems to know what happened. What could have caused something like that?"

"Poor maintenance?" Jaina suggested. "Engine overload?"

Leia looked troubled again. "Coruscant One picked up a transmission just before the *Moon Dash* exploded. The captain seemed to think they'd run into something."

Han's eyebrows shot up. "Still in outer orbit, you mean? Any other ships around that weren't cleared for takeoff?"

"Noooo . . ." Leia said slowly.

"A space mine deliberately planted there? Or a piece of debris?"

Jaina's ears perked up. "We ran into a lot of debris on our way home this time, didn't we, Dad?"

Leia grimaced. "I was afraid of that. The Commissioner of Trade has taken this personally. He says that all the leftover wreckage in orbit over Coruscant has always been an accident waiting to happen. He insists that we give higher priority to plotting safer space lanes. We've mapped out some of the bigger pieces, but I think quite a few chunks escaped our surveys—and we haven't had time to check it. Some of that wreckage has been up there in orbit for decades."

Han pursed his lips. "These accidents are pretty rare, Leia. Let's not overreact."

"According to the *Moon Dash*'s transmissions, they never saw what hit them—and it wasn't on any map. The Commissioner considers this an important safety issue. I have to agree—in the wake of this accident, we need to do something about it."

"How much work would it be to map the orbits of the larger pieces of wreckage?" Han asked.

"Quite a bit. And time-consuming, too." Leia pinched the bridge of her nose as if she had suddenly been assailed by another headache. "I'm not even sure the New Republic has resources to commit to a project like that—"

"Maybe I could help," Jaina interrupted, fixing her interest on an idea that would take her mind off Zekk. "After all, Uncle Luke said we were supposed to choose a study project while we're away from the academy. Lowie and I could map the debris for you. It sounds like fun."

Jaina looked from the datapad to the computer screen, then at the holographic simulation. "Okay, this is the next trajectory, Lowie." She stretched, trying to loosen the knotted muscles in her shoulders, then rubbed her bleary eyes, but her vision did not clear. They had been at the task for hours. She couldn't imagine why she had ever thought it would be fun.

The lanky Wookiee carefully programmed the orbit she had indicated, and another glowing streak appeared on the holomap. Jaina groaned. "This may be an important job, but I sure thought it would be more interesting."

Lowie grumbled a reply, and Em Teedee translated. "Master Lowbacca maintains that—although plotting swarms of orbital debris never should have seemed an interesting project in the first place—schoolwork is rarely interesting. This job, at least, carries a certain amount of urgency." Lowie growled another comment. "Furthermore, he points out that the project is only approximately twelve percent complete, and he will be most gratified when it is finished."

Jaina sighed wearily and ran her hands through her

straight brown hair. "Well then," she said, "what are we waiting for?"

13

PECKHUM SHIFTED THE strap of the travel duffel to his other shoulder as he trudged away from the *Lightning Rod*'s low-rent docking station, where many smugglers and con artists also parked their ships. It was good to be back in the city, if only because the equipment *worked* in his apartment, which was more than he could say about the facilities aboard the mirror station.

Despite his heavy pack, the grizzled old man slid through the broad streets and narrow alleyways with unconscious ease, muttering to himself as he went. "'You'll just have to make do, Peckhum.' 'We've got procurement problems, Peckhum.' 'New equipment is expensive, Peckhum.' 'Central multitasking units don't grow on starflower vines, Peckhum.'" Scratching at his chin stubble with one hand, he continued to rant, as used to talking to himself as he was to talking to Zekk.

He growled. "You'd think they'd at least wait till I got off my ship to tell me the news. 'We tried to reach you, Peckhum, but we couldn't get through.' Serves 'em right, since they haven't fixed my comm system!" He shifted his duffel again. "'Your replacement was reassigned to an additional security detail due to the recent Imperial attack, Peckhum. We need you back at the station tomorrow, Peckhum.' Hah!"

He stomped ahead, hardly noticing the cheery merchants, the wide-eyed tourists, the self-absorbed civil servants. "I just wish the administrator in charge of the mirror station would stop sitting in his comfy office down here and go up for a field trip. Feed him some of the swill the food-prep units have been putting out and see how much *he* likes it! See how well *he'd* 'make do.'"

Peckhum turned a corner and made his way down the corridor toward his home. "If I waited for those bureaucrats to get something done, why, the whole station would fall apart." Then he smiled at the thought of Zekk's promise of a new central multitasking unit. "Sometimes you just gotta do things for yourself . . . with a little help from your friends."

Peckhum looked up with satisfaction to find himself at his door. He keyed in the unlocking code, and the door slid open with a *whoosh* of escaping air. The air smelled stale and musty, as if it had been recycled over and over again for days. He'd have to remind Zekk to let in some fresh air now and then.

He tossed his duffel inside the front entryway, as the door sealed itself behind him. No friendly voice rang out to greet him. "Hey, Zekk!" he called. The apartment seemed oppressively silent, so he raised his voice a bit. "After three days of breathing from bad tanks on the mirror station, even *this* air smells good, but . . ." He paused. There was no response. "Zekk?"

He looked around the cluttered main living area, then searched the food-prep chamber, Zekk's bedroom, even the refresher unit. All empty.

A concerned frown crinkled Peckhum's forehead. Zekk rarely went out when he knew Peckhum was returning from a job—especially not when he had promised to deliver a piece of scavenged equipment. But Peckhum saw no sign of the central multitasking unit. He would need it before the next morning's trip back up to the station.

He scratched his cheeks again and thought for a moment. Then he relaxed. "Of course," he said to himself, "the Solo kids."

Zekk's friends Jacen and Jaina would be on Coruscant for only a few weeks. They were probably all out somewhere, enjoying themselves, telling tall tales of their adventures on other planets. Glancing back, he noticed the winking light on the infopanel beside the front door. That meant some messages hadn't been picked up yet. Probably just Zekk letting him know where he and his friends were, Peckhum thought.

There were three messages in all. Peckhum reviewed

them. The first message showed the image of Jaina and Jacen Solo, standing with the other two young Jedi Knights.

"Hey, Zekk," Jacen said in his characteristically good-humored voice. "We came to go on the scavenger hunt with you for that unit Peckhum needs. It was this morning, wasn't it? We'll come by again tomorrow morning. Let us know if there's a change of plans."

As the next message played, Jaina Solo appeared, her hair straight and her expression concerned. "Zekk, it's us. Are you all right? We've been looking for you everywhere! I'm sorry if you still feel bad about the other night—it's okay, really. Can you call us when you get home?"

The final message showed Jaina again, her face anxious and drawn. She spoke slowly, as if each of her words stuck in her throat. "Zekk, are you upset about anything? We're all really . . . sorry if we said anything to make you feel uncomfortable at the banquet. If you've already found that central multitasking unit and you don't want to take us scavenger hunting with you right now, we'll understand. Please talk to us, if you get this message."

As Peckhum listened, his stomach contracted with dread. Something had to be wrong. He looked around again, seeing no signs that the boy had planned to leave. No messages. No notes.

That was unlike Zekk. He was more reliable than that. Others might brush him off as a young scoundrel or a street urchin, but Zekk knew his responsibilities well and always met them. He had promised Peckhum a new central multitasking unit, knowing how important it was to the mirror station. If Zekk told him he was going to do something, the boy did it. Always.

Sure, Zekk was an orphan, a joker, a teller of tall tales, an adventurer—but he had always been a good friend, and he had always been completely reliable.

Almost before he knew it, his decision was made. Stopping only to leave a brief videomessage for Zekk on the infopanel, just in case the boy came back, he headed out the door toward the palace.

*   *   *

"Hey, am I glad to see you?" Jacen said, opening the door to find Peckhum standing there bedraggled and distraught. "Do you know where Zekk is? Have you seen him? Have you heard from him?"

Peckhum's face gave Jacen his answer. "I was hoping maybe you'd have some news for *me*," the old spacer said.

Suddenly remembering his manners, Jacen gestured Peckhum inside. "Uh, sorry. Come on in. I'll get Jaina and the others."

His sister and Lowie were at work plotting orbital debris patterns in their holo simulation while Tenel Ka polished the weapons at her belt.

"Hey," Jacen said, "Peckhum's here, and he says he doesn't know where Zekk is either."

His sister's intent expression turned to one of concern. Lowie scrambled to his feet and pulled Jaina to hers. Back in the living area, all five of them reviewed a map of Imperial City bending over a projection while Tenel Ka indicated several highlighted blocks of skyscrapers. "We have searched this area near your home," she told Peckhum.

Jacen crowded next to the image. "And we went to some of the places Zekk took us when we were scavenger hunting," he added. "The ones we could find our way back to, that is."

Peckhum nodded, scratching at his stubble, a distracted look on his face.

"Anakin and Threepio even went to a couple of the places that Zekk had talked about—didn't find anything," Jaina said. "We'd hoped you could offer us some other suggestions about where to look."

Lowie rumbled a comment, and Em Teedee said, "Master Lowbacca wishes to point out that our lack of familiarity with the, shall we say, 'less savory' aspects of Imperial City is, perhaps, an impediment to our search." The Wookiee growled at this overblown translation, but made no further comment.

"He's right, you know," Jaina said. "We really only know the good parts of the city."

Tenel Ka added, "And we were not absolutely certain

until now that Zekk was missing. Your observations make it more definite."

"Hey, now that Peckhum's back, and we know for sure that Zekk's missing," Jacen said, "we can report his disappearance to security."

Peckhum looked up sharply. "No, not security. Zekk wouldn't want that."

"But he's missing," Jaina pleaded. "We *have* to find him."

Jacen was surprised to see tears spring to his sister's eyes.

"Yes," Peckhum agreed, "but Zekk has had a few . . . 'misunderstandings' with security before, and he wouldn't thank us for calling them in. Don't worry, though—I can probably think of a lot of places you wouldn't have known to check."

"Well," Jacen said reluctantly, "that means we'll have to keep searching by ourselves then, but your ideas will be a big help, Peckhum. I guess it's still up to us."

"Zekk is a tough kid," Peckhum pointed out with forced optimism. "He's been through a lot, and he can take care of himself." Then his voice dropped. "I sure hope he's all right."

14

INSIDE HIS PLUSH new quarters at the Shadow Academy, Zekk awoke feeling oddly refreshed and exhilarated. He had slept deeply and well, as if he had somehow needed recharging. He wondered if Brakiss had placed some sort of drug in his food. Even if that was the case, he thought, it was worth it, because he had never felt so alive or so enthusiastic.

He tried to stop thinking positively, tried to summon up some anger at being kidnapped and dragged off to the Imperial station. But Zekk could not deny that he was being treated with more respect than he had ever experienced before. He gradually began to think of this place as his *room* rather than as a *cell*.

He showered until his body tingled with warmth and cleanliness, then spent altogether more time getting ready than he should have. He didn't care, though. Let Brakiss wait. It would serve him right. Zekk didn't want to be here, no matter how much attention the leader of the Shadow Academy paid him.

He was concerned about old Peckhum and knew that his friend must be wild with worry for him by now. He was pretty sure that Jacen and Jaina would also have sounded the alarm. But Zekk guessed that Brakiss knew how to deal with that. Zekk just had to bide his time until he could come up with a plan.

While he showered, someone had taken his tattered clothes and replaced them with a new padded suit and polished leather armor, a sleek uniform that looked dark and dashing. He looked around for his old outfit, not wanting to accept more of the Second Imperium's hospitality than necessary, but he found nothing else to wear—and the fine new clothes fit perfectly. . . .

Zekk tried his door, expecting to find it sealed, and was surprised when it slid open at his command. He stepped out to find Brakiss waiting in the corridor. The calm man's silvery robes pooled around him, as if knit from shimmering shadows.

A smile crossed Brakiss's sculpture-perfect face. "Ah, young Zekk—are you ready to begin your training?"

"Not really," Zekk muttered, "but I don't suppose it makes any difference."

"It makes a difference," Brakiss said. "It means I haven't explained well enough just what I can do for you. But if you'll open a chink in the wall of your resistance—just to listen—perhaps you will be convinced."

"And what if I'm not convinced?" Zekk said with more defiance than he felt.

Brakiss shrugged. "Then I will have failed. What more can I say?"

Zekk didn't press the point, wondering if he would be killed if he didn't fall in with the plans of the Second Imperium.

"Come to my office," Brakiss said, and led the boy down the curving, smooth-walled corridors. They seemed to be alone, but Zekk noticed armed stormtroopers standing in doorways at rigid attention, ready to offer assistance if Brakiss encountered any problems. Zekk stifled a smile at the mere thought of *him* posing a threat to Brakiss.

The Academy leader's private chamber seemed as dark as space. The walls were made of black transparisteel, projecting images of cataclysmic astronomical events: flaming solar flares, collapsing stars, gushing lava fields. Zekk looked around in awe. These violent and dangerous images showed a harsher edge to the universe than the galactic tourism kiosks on Coruscant had.

"Sit down," Brakiss said in his calm, unemotional voice. Zekk, listening for any implied threat, realized that at this point resistance would be futile. He decided to save his struggles for later, when they might count for more.

Brakiss took his place behind his long polished desk, reached into a hidden drawer, and withdrew a small cylindrical flare stick. Gripping both ends in his fine, pale hands, he unscrewed the cylinder in the middle. When the two metal halves came apart, a brilliant blue-green flame spouted upward, shimmering and flickering, but giving off little heat. The cold fire, mirrored on the office walls, threw its washed-out light against the images of astronomical disasters.

"What are you doing?" Zekk asked.

On his desk Brakiss balanced the two halves of the flare stick against each other, forming a triangle. The pale flame curled upward, strong and steady.

"Look at the flame," Brakiss said. "This is an example of what you can do with your Force abilities. Manipulating fire is a simple thing, a good first test. You'll see what I mean if you try. Watch."

Brakiss crooked one finger, and his gaze took on a faraway look. The bright fire began to dance, swaying back and forth, writhing as if it were alive. It grew taller and thinner, a mere tendril, then spread out to become a sphere, like a small glowing sun.

"Once you've mastered the simple things," Brakiss said,

"you can try more amusing effects." He stretched the flame as if it were a rubber sheet, creating a contorted face with flashing eyes and gaping mouth. The face melted into the image of a dragon snapping its long head back and forth, then metamorphosed into a flickering portrait of Zekk himself, drawn in blue-green fire.

Zekk stared in fascination. He wondered if Jacen or Jaina could do anything like this.

Brakiss released his control and let the flame return to a small bright point glimmering on the flare stick. "Now you try it, Zekk. Just concentrate. Feel the fire, like flowing water, like paint. Use fingers in your mind to draw it into different shapes. Swirl it around. You'll get the feel of it."

Zekk leaned forward eagerly, then stopped himself. "Why should I cooperate? I'm not going to do any favors for the Second Imperium or the Shadow Academy—or for you."

Brakiss folded his smooth hands and smiled again. "I wouldn't want you to do it for me. Or for a government or institution you know little about. I'm asking you to do this for *yourself*. Haven't you always wanted to develop your skills, your talents? You have a rare ability. Why not take advantage of this opportunity—especially you, a person whose life has had, if I may say, too few advantages. Even if you return to your old life afterward, won't you be better off if you can use the Force, rather than relying on what you once thought of as a 'knack' for finding valuable objects?"

Brakiss leaned forward. "You are independent, Zekk. I see that. We're looking for independent people—people who can make their own decisions, who can succeed no matter how much their so-called friends expect them to fail. You have your chance, here, now. If you aren't interested in bettering yourself, if you don't bother to make the attempt, then you fail before you've even begun." The words were sharp, reprimanding, but they struck home.

"All right, I'll try it," Zekk said. "But don't expect much."

He squinted his green eyes and concentrated on the flame. Although he didn't know what he was doing, he tried different things, various ways of thinking. He stared directly at the flame, then saw it out of the corner of his eye, tried to imagine moving it, nudging it with invisible fingers of thought. He didn't know what he did or how to describe it—but the flame jumped!

"Good," Brakiss said. "Now try again."

Zekk concentrated, retracing the mental path he had taken before, and found it with less effort this time. The flame wavered, bent to one side, then jumped and stretched longer in the other direction. "I can do it!"

Brakiss reached forward and snapped the flare stick together again, extinguishing the flame. Immediately, Zekk felt a sharp disappointment. "Wait! Let me try it one more time."

"No," Brakiss said with a smile that was not unkind. "Not too much at once. Come with me to the docking bay. I need to show you something else."

Zekk licked his lips, feeling *hungry* somehow and followed Brakiss, trying to squelch his impatience to try again with the flame. His appetite had now been whetted—and part of him suspected that was exactly what the leader of the Shadow Academy had intended. . . .

Inside the hangar bay Qorl and a regiment of stormtroopers worked to unload the precious cargo they had stolen from the Rebel cruiser *Adamant*. Brakiss came in leading Zekk, who stared at all the ships stationed at the Shadow Academy.

"I wish I could show you our finest small ship, the *Shadow Chaser*," Brakiss said with a look of regret, "but Luke Skywalker took it when he charged in here to capture our trainees Jacen, Jaina, and Lowbacca."

Zekk scowled, but refrained from telling Brakiss that it served the Shadow Academy right, since they had kidnapped the three young Jedi first, for their own ends. He looked away.

Up in the control room overlooking the cavernous docking bay the black-haired Tamith Kai stood watching the activities through slitted violet eyes. Beside her were two dark allies from Dathomir, Vilas and Garowyn. Zekk flinched, his lips curling downward in anger as he noted that these were the ones who had stunned him and taken him from Imperial City.

"Pay them no mind," Brakiss said with a dismissive gesture. "They're jealous because of the attention I'm paying you."

Zekk felt a surprising flood of warmth and wondered if the comment was true, or just something Brakiss had said to make him feel more special.

One of the stormtroopers stopped in front of them and saluted. "I have an update for you, sir," he said to Brakiss. "Our repairs on the upper docking tower are almost complete. We should have it fully functional in two days."

"Good," Brakiss said, looking relieved. He explained to Zekk, "I still find it difficult to believe that a Rebel supply shuttle could have been so unfortunately clumsy as to smash right into the cloaked Shadow Academy! These Rebels cause damage even when they're not looking!"

Qorl hefted one of the small weapons cores from a sealed crate. Zekk guessed from the melted, blackened craters around the control panel that the stormtroopers must have used blasters to break the cyberlocks. The hyperdrive core was long and cylindrical, with yellows and oranges pulsing though translucent tubes where condensed spin-sealed tibanna gas had been charged to power the drives.

"These are fine new models, Lord Brakiss," the old TIE pilot said. "We can use them to power our weapons systems, or we can convert more of our fighters to lightspeed attack vessels, like my own former TIE fighter."

Brakiss nodded. "We must let our leader make that decision, but he will be greatly pleased to see this new increase in our military capabilities. Be careful with those components, though," he said sternly. "Make sure that not a single one gets damaged. We cannot afford to squander resources in the Second Imperium's quest to regain its rightful power."

Qorl nodded and turned away.

"You see, Zekk," Brakiss said, knitting his pale eyebrows together, "we are truly the underdogs in this struggle. Although our movement is small and somewhat hopeless—we know we're right. We are forced to fight for what is ours against a blundering New Republic that continually seeks to rewrite history and force its chaotic ways upon us all.

"We believe that can only lead to galactic anarchy, with everyone following their own ways, invading one another's territories, disturbing people, neither caring nor respecting the rule of order."

Zekk placed his hands on his leather-clad hips. "Okay, but what about freedom? I like being able to do what I want to do."

"We believe in freedom in the Second Imperium—truly we do," Brakiss said with great sincerity. "But there's a point at which *too much* freedom causes damage. The races of the galaxy need a road map, a framework of order and control, so they can go about their business and not destroy the dreams of others in their own pursuits.

"You are independent, Zekk. You know what you're doing. But think about all those aimless people displaced by the changes in the galaxy, beings who have nowhere to go, no dreams to follow, no goals . . . and no one to tell them what to do. You can help to change that."

Zekk wanted to disagree. Wanted to refute Brakiss's words, but he couldn't think of anything to say. He clamped his lips together. Even if he couldn't come up with any good arguments against what Brakiss said, he refused to agree openly.

"No need to give me your answer yet," Brakiss said in a patient voice. Then he withdrew the flare stick from the pocket of his robe. "Take as long as you need to think about what I've said. I'll show you back to your quarters now."

He handed the flare stick to Zekk who took it eagerly.

"Spend some time playing with this, if you'd like." Brakiss smiled. "And then we'll talk again."

15

JAINA SPREAD HER hands in confusion as Peckhum began to describe some of the places where Zekk might have gone. They could spend months combing the underworld of

Coruscant, even years, and still never find the dark-haired boy—especially if Zekk didn't want to be found.

"Hang on a second," she interrupted. "Aren't you going to be with us during the search?"

Peckhum shook his head. "New emergency schedule, thanks to that Imperial attack on the *Adamant*. I have to go right back up to the mirror station tomorrow. Thing is, I'm not sure how to keep the systems running without some major repairs. Now even my comm units are down. Fat lot of good I'd be if Coruscant Central calls a red alert. I sure wish I'd gotten that replacement multitasking unit Zekk promised."

Jaina felt a wash of indignant defensiveness on the young man's behalf. "You know Zekk would've brought it to you if he could."

Peckhum looked back at her with a mixture of surprise and amusement. "I won't argue with that," he said, "but I can't keep my mirror station running unless something gets fixed—pronto."

Lowie spoke through Em Teedee as the three other companions sat restlessly in the open area of Han and Leia's living quarters. "Oh, indeed," the miniature translating droid said. "That's a fine idea." Em Teedee's tinny voice caused the other young Jedi Knights to sit up straighter and look at Lowie. "Why, it doesn't even sound very dangerous."

"What doesn't?" Jaina asked.

"Master Lowbacca suggests that perhaps he and you, Mistress Jaina, along with his uncle Chewbacca—if we can convince him—might accompany Master Peckhum up to his mirror station to see if we can effect temporary repairs."

"That's a kind offer," Peckhum said, "but I don't see how much you could do without a new central multitasking unit."

Jacen snorted. "I can't remember the last time Jaina *wasn't* able to whip up some kind of solution. She could probably fix the whole place using nothing but her imagination."

"Thanks for the vote of confidence," Jaina growled at her brother. Then, knowing what Zekk would have done, she sighed in resignation and smiled at Peckhum. "He's right, you know. I'm sure we can repair enough subsystems to keep you going until we find Zekk. So what are we waiting for?"

"But why should you want to do that?" Peckhum asked.

"You need the help, don't you?" Jaina asked, momentarily confused. She didn't want to admit that Zekk was the real reason she was doing this. "Besides," she rushed on, we've been having trouble mapping debris paths in certain areas. Maybe we'll get a better perspective from orbit. Meanwhile, Jacen, Tenel Ka, Anakin, and Threepio can keep searching for Zekk down here in the places you suggest."

"All right," Peckhum said. "You've got me convinced, but will your parents agree to it?"

Lowie growled a comment. "Master Lowbacca is confident that he can use his powers of persuasion to convince his uncle Chewbacca to accompany us into orbit," Em Teedee said.

Jaina's eyes lit with confident enthusiasm. "If you can do that, Lowie, just leave my parents to me."

Jacen half-closed his eyes, reached out with the Force, and listened for any sign of Zekk in the deserted building. But he heard only the hollow echo of their footsteps as he and Tenel Ka walked through the gloomy corridor.

He clicked on his comlink. "Hey Anakin—it's Jacen."

"Go ahead," his younger brother answered, transmitting from another building.

"Heading into section seven on the map. Nothing to report so far."

"Okay," Anakin said. In the background, Jacen heard Threepio say in a dismayed voice, "I certainly hope we can locate Master Zekk soon. I'm sure I would much rather be at home than inspecting such . . . unsavory places!"

"I hope we find him soon, too," Jacen said, then clicked off and followed Tenel Ka down the empty hall on the seventy-ninth level of the crumbling building.

The floor was littered with old cartons, canisters, bits of plasteel, and other items too broken-down to be scavenged. Some dry leaves were scattered about as well—though how leaves had come to be in this building, nearly a kilometer below the upper greenhouse levels, Jacen had no idea.

A thin, icy breeze whistled through a crack in the wall, skittering the dead leaves across the floor. The breeze did nothing to dispel the odors of mildew and decay that hung around the old structure, but it did send a chill of apprehension up Jacen's spine. He let his eyes fall half closed again in concentration as he walked slowly along.

Suddenly, something light and warm touched his arm. Jacen's eyes flew open. Tenel Ka's hand rested on the sleeve of his jumpsuit. "I thought you might stumble," she said, pointing at a small pile of rubble ahead of them, where part of the ceiling had given way. In these old buildings, nothing was repaired unless someone planned to use the space. Floors and ceilings were no exception. If she hadn't stopped him, Jacen would have fallen on his face.

"Thanks," he said with a lopsided grin. "Nice to know you really care."

Tenel Ka blinked once. She stood still beside him, not rising to the bait—or perhaps not noticing it. "It is simpler to prevent an accident than to carry an injured companion."

That wasn't the response Jacen had been hoping for. "Well, hey, I'm glad you didn't have to strain any muscles," he said, kicking at the rocky debris with the toe of one boot and sending a cloud of dust into the air.

"It is not a question of strain." Tenel Ka coughed, but her voice remained detached and gruff. "I could lift you easily, should the need arise." She stepped around the rubble. "But I saw no need."

Jacen followed her, wondering why he always managed to make an idiot of himself in front of the calmly competent Tenel Ka. He grimaced. At least if he had twisted an ankle, he might have had the compensating pleasure of Tenel Ka's arm around him to help him out. . . .

Jacen shoved the surprising mental image aside, realizing that Tenel Ka would probably be aghast if she knew the turn his thoughts had taken. Besides, the only thing he should be thinking about right now was finding Zekk.

Using a map on their datapad, they tried to be methodical in their search, concentrating on buildings where old Peckhum said Zekk most often did his scavenging. Walking from one end of the building to another, each of them would reach out with Jedi senses, trying to find their friend, looking for any sign that he had been there.

Once they were convinced Zekk was not close, Jacen and Tenel Ka would take the stairs, a turbolift, or a chute-slide a few floors down, and begin a search of the next level. If they again found no trace of Zekk, they would move to the next likely location, using the aerial catwalks that bridged the gaps between buildings. Many of these walkways had not been repaired for hundreds of years, and they creaked as the two young Jedi crossed them.

Anakin and Threepio were doing the same in other buildings. Jacen's younger brother was absolutely delighted to have a break from the golden droid's daily tutoring.

As the day wore on, Jacen grew tired. The longer they spent in the murky lower reaches, the more uncomfortable he grew. A sense of urgency stabbed like a needle at the back of his mind. Zekk had been missing for days, and they had to find him—soon. Before long, it would be too late for the dark-haired boy. He wasn't really sure *why*, but he knew that it was true.

They searched dozens of buildings and crossed as many walkways, but found no clues. The deeper they descended, though, the more signs of life they found. Low life.

Creatures scuttled past them to hide in every shadowy corner. When corridors were too narrow for them to walk side by side, the two young Jedi took turns leading. Jacen watched Tenel Ka in the light of her glowrod as she headed down another cramped stairwell into the inky darkness. Her reddish-gold braids bounced slightly as she made her quiet descent.

At one point Tenel Ka faltered, then regained her footing and continued her smooth pace. "Broken stair," she said, turning to point out the rough area. "Be careful."

Just then a dark fluttering shape rose up behind Tenel Ka with a keening shriek. Instinctively, she whiled and lashed out at the thing, dropping her glowrod in the process—but the more Tenel Ka batted at the creature, the more frantically it shrieked and flapped about her head.

As soon as Jacen understood what was happening, he reacted. "Hold still!" he said, moving toward the squealing creature, which had managed to tangle itself in Tenel Ka's long braids. "It's probably scared of the light."

Tenel Ka instantly held still, though he knew it must have gone against her instincts. Jacen's thoughts reached out toward the struggling creature, sending soothing messages to it. Gradually, the winged rodent grew calmer and allowed Jacen to touch it. Careful not to make any startling movements, he gently disentangled its claws from Tenel Ka's hair. Then, still crooning reassurances to the agitated beast, he set it behind himself in the stairwell and backed away.

He picked up the fallen glowrod and returned it to Tenel Ka. "Hey, are you all right?" She nodded curtly, and Jacen suspected that she was embarrassed at having been unable to handle a small flying rodent without his assistance.

As they resumed their search, he tried to get her mind off the incident. "So, do you know why the bantha crossed the Dune Sea?"

"No," she said.

"To get to the other side!" He laughed out loud.

"Ah," Tenel Ka said, without even stopping to look at him. "Aha."

He had expected her to be more subdued after the encounter with the winged rodent, but she continued at her usual pace. Jacen began to wonder if anything could penetrate her cool confidence. Though part of him admired her fortitude, another part wished that she had been more impressed by the way he'd gallantly come to her rescue.

At the next walkway, it was Jacen's turn to go first. The rickety bridgework was littered with the usual debris of rocks and plasteel. It creaked when he stepped out onto it, high above the ground.

"Be careful," Tenel Ka said from behind him—completely unnecessarily, as far as he was concerned.

"I think we're getting close to that old crashed shuttle," he said, choosing to ignore her remark. "I'm pretty sure it's just on the other—" The walkway shuddered beneath him, and his heart gave a lurch as metal support struts sheared away with a shrieking noise. He grabbed the rusty rail.

"Hold still!" Tenel Ka called, but it was too late.

With a sound of popping bolts and twisting plasteel, the walkway sagged downward, split in the middle. As if in slow motion, Jacen watched large chunks fall away as the bridge floor beneath his feet tilted at a crazy angle.

A whizzing sounded in his ears, followed by a soft *clank*. He felt himself slide toward the deadly gap and he grasped the railing, but the corroded metal broke away in his hand. He yelled for help, reaching back for anything to hold on to—and felt a strong arm wrap around his waist, then found himself being swept forward. Almost before he realized what had happened, Tenel Ka had swung both of them across the chasm on her fibercord rope and deposited them onto a sturdy metal stairway on the opposite side.

With a creaking groan of protest, the remainder of the bridge gave way behind them and fell in ominous, eerie silence into the deep blackness below.

It wasn't until Tenel Ka released him that Jacen realized they had been clinging together for dear life. After what they had just been through, the metal stairway where Tenel Ka had anchored her rope seemed none too safe to Jacen. Nevertheless, the two young Jedi Knights stood in silence for a moment longer, staring down into the bottomless gap between the buildings.

"I guess we make a good team—always rescuing each other," Jacen said at last. "Thanks." Without waiting for an answer, he turned and climbed down a few steps to a building entrance. Once inside, he sank to the floor in relief, reveling in its comparative solidity.

Tenel Ka lowered herself shakily beside him. In the dim light, her face looked troubled and serious. "I was afraid I might lose a friend."

You almost did, thought Jacen ruefully. But instead he said, "Hey, I'm not *that* easy to get rid of."

Although she did not smile, Tenel Ka's mood lightened. "This is a fact."

* * *

They came upon the crashed shuttle less than ten minutes after they resumed their search. When they saw it, they both spoke at once.

"Zekk's been here," Jacen said. "Something is wrong," Tenel Ka said. Hearing her, Jacen realized that something was indeed wrong. Tenel Ka noticed his hesitation, and stepped forward. "It is my turn to go first. You may wait here, if you prefer."

"Not on your life," he shot back. "After all, I've got to stay close to you—just in case you need me to rescue you again."

"Ah," she said, raising a skeptical eyebrow. "Aha." She entered the shuttle, and Jacen heard her say, "It is all right. No one here."

Following her inside, Jacen saw that while the shuttle was unoccupied, someone had been there recently, picking out the remaining salvageable items. Tangles of wire and cable snaked across the dusty deck plates. Stripped bolts and broken fasteners lay strewn about. Several access panels gaped open, showing empty spaces that had once housed the shuttle's vital equipment.

"Looks like Zekk may have been scavenging here after all," Jacen said. "That's a good sign."

"Perhaps," Tenel Ka said, lifting a finger to trace the frighteningly familiar symbol that was etched with crude strokes into one of the access panels. "Or perhaps not."

Jacen looked at the fresh scratches that formed a triangle surrounding a cross—the threatening symbol of the Lost Ones gang. Jacen swallowed hard.

"Well," he said, "I guess we know where to look next."

16

STILL DEEPLY WORRIED about Zekk, old Peckhum piloted his battered supply ship, the *Lightning Rod*, out of its sheltered hangar. The New Republic would have provided him transportation if he'd requested it, but Peckhum liked to take his own ship, though even on its best days it functioned less reliably than the *Millennium Falcon*. And it had never been made to carry so many passengers.

Lowie crammed himself beside Jaina into the back compartment, his ginger-furred legs stiff and awkward as he maneuvered his lanky Wookiee body into a seat built for someone little more than half his size. Lowie wished he had the T-23 skyhopper his uncle Chewbacca had given him the day he started at the Jedi academy, but the small craft was still on Yavin 4.

Peckhum had cleared tools and cartons of junk from the *Lightning Rod*'s cockpit—he usually flew the ship alone—so that Chewbacca could ride in the copilot's seat. Chewbacca brought his own tool kit of battered hydrospanners and diagnostics, gadgets he used while working with Han Solo to keep the *Falcon* up and running . . . if just barely.

When the *Lightning Rod* received clearance from Coruscant Space Traffic Control, Peckhum angled upward through the misty clouds at high acceleration until the glowing atmosphere faded into the night of space. Lowie watched, bending his shoulders to stare out the front viewport as Peckhum maneuvered the ship into a high and stable orbit. The huge solar mirrors remained in position like a lake of silver, spreading a broad blanket of sunlight across the northern and southern regions of the metropolis-covered world.

Although the mirror station was temporarily empty because of the emergency switchover of caretakers, the critical solar mirrors could not be left untended. Peckhum's name was next on the roster, and he had to report for duty, whether or not Zekk had run away from home.

Peckhum brought the *Lightning Rod* to dock against the corroded old station, which looked like a tiny speck dangling beneath the kilometers-wide reflector. Chewbacca and Lowie blatted to each other in Wookiee language, expressing their admiration for the huge orbital mirror.

The thin silvery fabric was like an ocean of reflection, only a fraction of a millimeter thick. It would have been torn to shreds had it approached Coruscant's atmosphere, but in the stillness of space the mirror was thick enough. Space engineers had connected it to the dangling guidance station by dozens of fiber cables, gimbaled to attitude-control rockets that could direct the path of reflected sunlight onto the colder latitudes.

With the *Lightning Rod* docked, Peckhum opened the access hatch, which still bore markings from the Old Republic, and they all scrambled through into the austere station where they would spend the next few days.

"Well . . . isn't this cozy," Jaina said.

"According to my dictionary programming, I should think *cramped* is a better word," Em Teedee observed. "I *am* fluent in over six forms of communication, you know."

The metal ceiling was low and dark, strung with insulation-wrapped coolant tubes and wires running to control panels. A single chair sat in the middle of an observation bubble, surrounded by windows that looked down upon the glittering planet below. Old-style computer systems blinked with reluctant readiness, waiting for Peckhum to awaken standby routines and begin the tedious monitoring of the solar path.

Drawn by the spectacular view of space and the planet, Lowbacca went toward the observation dome. He grasped a cold metal pipe that thrust out from the curved wall and bent down to look at the huge ball of Coruscant. High clouds masked the daylight side of the planet, while the darkened hemisphere gleamed with millions upon millions of city lights that sparkled like colorful jewels in the night.

Lowie had seen planets from space before, but somehow it had never struck him how intimate the setting was. Here, high above the world, he felt a part of the universe and apart from it, a piece of the cosmos and an observer at the same time. It was strange to have such a perspective, and it made the galaxy seem both small and immensely large at the same time.

"Don't just stare, Lowie," Jaina urged. "We've got work to do. Our first priority should be to get those communication systems up and running."

Chewbacca roared his agreement, clapping a strong hand

on his nephew's hairy shoulder. Peckhum seemed to be working hard to keep his attention on the routine aboard the station, rather than letting his thoughts wander to Zekk. "I really appreciate what you're all doing," he said.

"Happy to help," Jaina offered as she knelt down to poke around in some control panels. "Lowie, you're good with computers. Give me a hand here."

"Oh, absolutely," Em Teedee said. "Master Lowbacca is exceedingly talented when it comes to electronic systems." Lowie growled a response, and the miniature translating droid answered, "Of *course* they already know that. I was simply reminding them."

"Could you please work on the comm systems first? When I try to transmit, all I can really manage is static," Peckhum said, hovering behind them as he pointed out problems.

Jaina's forehead furrowed with concentration. "Sounds like the power transmission is still working, but the voice synthesis encoders aren't doing their jobs."

With everyone standing around, the area was far too cramped to let Chewbacca push his way in, so the older Wookiee hung back and waited. Lowie suspected his uncle was amused to watch the two young protégés working so hard. Perhaps it reminded him of the way he and Han had worked together, fixing things again and again.

"Well," Jaina said, scratching her cheek and leaving a smear of grime from the corroded control panels, "I expect that by the end of today we'll have these comm systems up and running." She smiled brightly at Peckhum, and Lowie rumbled his agreement. "Just a stopgap measure, you understand, but they'll work."

Peckhum shrugged. "Better than what I've got now. I still wish we had that central multitasking unit," he said dejectedly. "Almost as much as I wish we knew what happened to Zekk."

"I'm sure he's all right," Jaina said, but Lowie knew that she was sure of no such thing.

As Jaina tinkered, Chewbacca went to a different part of the station and roared a suggestion. Lowie readily agreed.

Since it was getting toward time for midday meal, it seemed a very good idea to get the mirror station's foodprocessing units up and running. Lowie's appetite was already large, and his mouth watered as he thought of the excellent dishes they could create, even from the meager ration supplies on board.

Em Teedee tsked. "Really, Lowbacca! There you go again—always thinking with your stomach."

Chewbacca roared an annoyed challenge, and Em Teedee's voice became thinner, less emphatic. "You Wookiees," the miniaturized translating droid said in quiet exasperation, "you're all alike."

17

JACEN HAD GOTTEN distracted so many times during their scavenger hunt for the hawk-bat egg with Zekk that he would never have been able to retrace his steps through the labyrinth of Coruscant's lower levels. Tenel Ka, however, led the way with an unerring sense of direction . . . which didn't surprise Jacen a bit.

The buildings drew closer together, became more dilapidated, more ominous. The walls were dark and smeared with sickly discolored blotches that looked like centuries-old bloodstains. Jacen saw the ever-present cross-in-triangle gang symbol chiseled into the duracrete bricks or splashed on with bright, permanent pigments.

"Ah. Aha. We have found the territory claimed by the gang of the Lost Ones," Tenel Ka said, her senses sharpened like a hunter's blade.

Jacen swallowed. "Let's hope we find Zekk soon. I'd hate to overstay our welcome if that gang is in a bad mood again."

"I suspect they are always in a bad mood," she observed. "They may still be angry at us for escaping them before."

"Well, maybe they've got Zekk. We have to rescue him. That Norys guy seems like a bad customer."

Something skittered along the wall behind them, an ugly spider-roach dashing for cover in a clump of slimy moss. At any other time Jacen would have rushed to study the creature, but at the moment he just wanted to be back home and safe in his rooms.

Tenel Ka looked tall and brave as she marched down the enclosed corridor. Jacen wished fleetingly that he had his own light saber, like the one he had used at the Shadow Academy. He knew the Jedi weapons were dangerous and not for play, but right now he didn't want to *play* with one— he wanted it for genuine protection.

Jacen swallowed nervously and moved closer to the warrior girl, keeping his eyes on her dangling red-gold braids. Maybe humor would turn his thoughts from the sinister gang. "Hey, Tenel Ka—do you know the difference between an AT-AT and a stormtrooper on foot?"

Tenel Ka turned and gave him an odd look. "Of course I do."

He sighed. "It's a *joke*. What's the difference between an AT-AT and a stormtrooper on foot?"

"I am supposed to say 'I don't know'—this is correct?"

"Yeah, exactly," Jacen said.

"I don't know."

"One's an Imperial walker, and the other's a walking Imperial!"

Tenel Ka gave a sage nod. "Yes. Very humorous. Now let us continue our search." She narrowed her cool gray eyes as they approached a corner. "Zekk is your friend. You know him best. Reach out with your Jedi powers again to see if you can sense him. These corridors have many twists and turns."

Jacen nodded. He didn't think his powers were strong enough to locate any person specifically—he wasn't sure if even Uncle Luke could do that—but all he needed was a trickle of thought, an impression, a hunch. He and Tenel Ka were wandering blindly so far anyway, and the slightest inkling would increase their odds over pure luck.

As he concentrated and closed his eyes Jacen thought he felt a tingle, something that conjured up an impression of the dark-haired boy in his mind. He pointed the way before he could have second thoughts. Uncle Luke had always taught them to follow their Jedi instincts.

He hurried to keep up with Tenel Ka as they moved down one hall, then another. The old skyscraper seemed completely empty, oppressive in its silence despite the inhabited levels far above, but Jacen felt invisible eyes watching him from secret hiding places. He trusted his Jedi senses enough to guess that this was not just his imagination.

"We are getting closer, I think," Tenel Ka said.

They heard voices up ahead, and Jacen recognized the timbre of a clear, strong voice—a young man's voice—though he could hear none of the words. "That sounds like Zekk!" he whispered. "We've found him."

Filled with elation, suddenly dismissing all of his ominous thoughts, he rushed forward while Tenel Ka kept pace, advising caution. "Careful," she said just as Jacen turned another corner and ran into an echoing room filled with battered furniture, half-collapsed ceiling beams, and glowpanels wired to the walls as if someone had rigged them wherever it seemed most convenient to connect electrical power. Other doors leading from the large room were closed, some blocked by crates, others jammed on their hinges.

In the middle of the room Jacen saw a young man, emerald eyes glittering in the uncertain light of the haphazard glowpanels. It was Zekk. His hair, a shade lighter than black, was fastened at the nape of his neck with a leather thong instead of hanging free down to his shoulders. Jacen had never seen Zekk's hair like that. His friend's clothes were also different: clean, dark, padded, as if they were a uniform—and much more stylish than the suit he had worn to the diplomatic banquet for the ambassador from Kamak Alpha.

Sitting on chairs or sprawled on ragged cushions sat a dozen tough, hard-bitten kids, all in their middle to late teens. Most were boys, but the few girls looked wild and rugged enough to take Jacen apart piece by piece, like an obsolete droid.

The Lost Ones.

"Hey, Zekk!" Jacen cried. "Where have you been? We've all been worried!"

Startled from his speech, the dark-haired young man drew himself up, frowning at Jacen and Tenel Ka. His green eyes flashed with momentary surprise and delight, but he quickly masked the expression with a scowl. Zekk appeared to have aged a dozen years in the few days since his disappearance.

"Jacen, now isn't the time," he said in a rough voice.

A brawny boy with close-set eyes and thick eyebrows stood up, glaring. "I don't recall inviting you two." Jacen recognized the bully Norys.

Zekk gestured behind him to calm the burly gang leader. "Let me handle this." Anger showed clearly in Zekk's face as he shook his head at Jacen. "Why couldn't you have left me alone for just a little longer?"

Jacen scratched his tousled hair, completely baffled. When he stepped forward in confusion, Zekk flinched. "Go away," he whispered, "you'll ruin everything!"

The other Lost Ones stood up from their places like a pack of nek battle dogs zeroing in on a target. Jacen swallowed. Beside him, Tenel Ka placed a protective hand on his shoulder, in case they would be required to fight.

"Zekk, it's *us*," Jacen pleaded. "We aren't going to ruin anything—we're your friends."

Just then, one of the corroded doors at the far side of the chamber scraped open. "They are not your friends, young Lord Zekk," said a woman's voice, rich and low. "You know better than that now. They may *claim* to be your friends, but you've seen evidence of just how much they truly value you."

Jacen and Tenel Ka both whirled to see the ominous form of the black-cloaked Nightsister, with her static-charged ebony hair and blazing violet eyes. The upthrust spines on the shoulders of her cloak looked like spears. Two others dressed in similar fashion stood on either side of her: a young dark-haired man and a petite powerhouse of a woman, both of whom looked as rigid as the towering Nightsister herself.

"Tamith Kai . . . ," Jacen acknowledged. "Charming as usual, I see."

"And Garowyn. And Vilas," Tenel Ka said with an astonishing and unexpected expression—a feral smile—on her normally serious face. "So, how is your knee?" she asked Tamith Kai. Her grip on Jacen's shoulder felt tight enough to crack a bone.

The tall woman's face roiled with a thunderstorm of anger. Her wine-dark lips curled down, and she barely controlled her rage at being reminded of how Tenel Ka had humiliated her during the young Jedi Knights' escape from the Shadow Academy. "Jedi brats," she snarled, "you should learn when to leave well enough alone."

"And *you* should have figured out not to mess with us after the first time," Jacen responded in a challenging tone. "Zekk, what are you doing with these clowns? What sort of nonsense have they been telling you?"

Zekk seemed to waver for a moment, but his voice was strong. "They're offering us—all of us—an opportunity. A chance we never had before."

"Like what?" Jacen said, genuinely mystified. "What could these losers possibly offer you?"

"They're taking us back to the Shadow Academy to train us!" the burly gang leader, Norys, said. "Now we'll have our own shot at being powerful."

"But not everybody has Jedi potential," Jacen said reasonably, trying to keep Zekk talking until he or Tenel Ka could figure out what to do.

"*I* do. You would have known that if you'd bothered to test me," Zekk said defiantly. "And anybody who joins us but doesn't have the talent will be recruited into the Imperial military forces, given responsibilities and a chance for advancement in the Second Imperium."

"Oh, Zekk," Jacen said, shaking his head, "those are all lies designed to lure you into dropping your guard—"

"They are not lies!" Tamith Kai interrupted, her melodious voice holding the potential for deadliness. "We will keep our promises. You will all be given equal opportunities, without regard to your social status in the Rebel worlds. The Second Imperium won't judge who you are—only what you do for us."

"Zekk," Jacen cried, "how can you trust them? These are the people who kidnapped me and Jaina."

"Yes," Tamith Kai continued, "and we have learned our lesson. Highborn noble pups such as you are no more worthy of being Imperial Dark Jedi than any other student." Her violet eyes glared daggers at Tenel Ka.

"Zekk," Jacen whispered quickly, "this is your chance. Trust me on this: You're in great danger. You could escape now. Get away!"

But his formerly happy-go-lucky friend gave him a look that was somewhere between pity and a plea for understanding. Jacen thought he saw a glimpse of the deep sadness that touched the young man's heart.

Zekk said, "You don't understand, Jacen. You can't because you've always *had* too much. You've never wanted for anything. These people"—he gestured toward the evil Nightsister and her companions—"they're offering me something I never had in my old life. With them I have a chance to *be* someone."

"Not *much* of a chance, if they're the ones offering it," Jacen muttered.

Tenel Ka tensed, holding her hands at her utility belt, ready to draw a weapon.

One by one, each of the gang members stood and glared at the two young Jedi. The burly Norys and the other Lost Ones seemed to have been hypnotized, and Jacen wondered if Tamith Kai or the others were using some sort of Force trick to make them more susceptible to insidious suggestions.

Tenel Ka whispered, "Jacen, we must leave while we can still bring help."

Jacen tensed, ready to turn and run. He clicked on the comlink, hoping to signal Anakin and Threepio, but before he and Tenel Ka could sprint to the door, Vilas pulled out a blaster.

"We can't risk any more of your meddling," Garowyn said. "There's too much at stake."

Jacen and Tenel Ka managed to take a few running steps before stun bolts slammed into them from behind. They plunged headfirst into helpless unconsciousness.

18

BRAKISS SEALED THE locking mechanism on the door to his private office, changing the access code to make absolutely certain no one could disturb him. He wouldn't allow even Tamith Kai to eavesdrop on his special communications with the great Imperial Leader.

Brakiss always found inspiration on the walls of his Shadow Academy office, where the exploding stars, broken planets, and cascading glaciers reminded him of the fury locked within the universe. By using the dark side as his focus, Brakiss tapped into that incredible energy and used it for his own benefit, to help pave the way for the return of the Empire.

He set the glowpanels to low as he waited for the contact, checking his chronometer. Speaking with his ominously powerful leader filled Brakiss with both terror and awe, and he was forced to use a Jedi calming technique, though patience was very difficult.

The Great Leader of the Second Imperium had enormous burdens and responsibilities. He was frequently late for his scheduled communications—not that Brakiss would ever dare mention it. The Leader set his own schedule; Brakiss was merely the dutiful slave who knew his place in the grand scheme.

Just as the Rebels depended on the overestimated protection of their vaunted Jedi Knights, so the new Leader would have his own secret weapon: an army of Dark Jedi who could use the dark side of the Force to carve a broad place in history for the Second Imperium.

But Dark Jedi were notoriously dangerous and unstable, prone to delusions of grandeur. Realizing this risk, the Great Leader had taken precautions to protect *himself* from the Shadow Academy. The huge ring-shaped station was riddled with deadly explosives, detonators threaded through the life-support systems, the hull, and thousands of other places that Brakiss neither knew nor wanted to consider. The moment his Dark Jedi gave hints that they might get out of control, the Great Leader would detonate those explosives and end the experiment without remorse.

Brakiss had to show success after success to keep his powerful master happy—and the Shadow Academy had recently had several spectacular accomplishments indeed.

With a humming sound, the holographic generators in his sealed office activated, and Brakiss snapped to attention. The air shimmered in front of him as a massive image crystallized into focus, transmitted from some far-distant hiding place in the Core Systems. Static rippled along the edges of the gigantic cowled head that loomed over Brakiss, scowling down at him.

Brakiss instinctively averted his eyes, bowing his head in reverence. After performing the appropriate gestures of obeisance, he looked up into the face of the Great Leader of the Second Imperium—*the hooded, wrinkled form of Emperor Palpatine himself*!

Though the holographic image was fuzzy and fragmented from being transmitted across so many systems on the Holonet, through asteroid belts and solar flares and ion storms, the features of the sallow-faced Emperor were unmistakable. Brakiss looked adoringly at the harsh paternal figure. Here was the man who would make all star systems quake with terror until they learned to live again with respect and glory, in the Imperial way.

The Emperor's skin was ravaged with wrinkles brought on by too deep an immersion in the potent powers of evil. His yellow reptilian eyes blazed from hollowed sockets, and wattles on his neck hung down like the throat sac of a scrawny lizard.

Brakiss knew that the rest of the galaxy thought the Emperor had died many years ago, first in the explosion of the second Death Star, and then six years later in the destruction of the last of Palpatine's clones. But the Emperor's death *must* have been some kind of illusion, because Brakiss could see the transmission with his own eyes. He could not guess how the Emperor had survived, what sort of trick the great man had played on everyone—but with the Force, many things were possible.

Master Skywalker had taught him that.

When he finally spoke, the Emperor's voice was harsh and raspy. "So, Insignificant One, what is your report for today? More successes, I hope. I am tired of failures, Brakiss. I grow impatient to bring about my reign and the Second Imperium."

Brakiss bowed again. "Yes, my master. I have good news to report. We are sending along the hyperdrive cores and turbolaser batteries stolen from the Rebel supply ship, as you ordered. I think your glorious military machine will make efficient use of them."

"Yesss," Palpatine hissed.

Brakiss continued. "Here at the Shadow Academy your new force of Dark Jedi grows more powerful each day. I am particularly pleased that we have uncovered new candidates from the underworld of Imperial Center—exactly as you suspected, my master. No one will notice their disappearance, and we are free to turn them." "Yesss!" the Emperor said. "I told you it would be simpler to turn candidates whose lives held little hope. It is especially ironic to snatch them from under the very noses of the Rebel usurpers in the government."

Brakiss nodded. "Yes, indeed, my master. We merely offer the new candidates something they need—and they are desperate to take it from us."

"Ah," the image of the Emperor said. He seemed almost—*almost*—proud.

Brakiss drew a deep breath before continuing. "Naturally, many of these new candidates have no Jedi potential, but still they remain eager for opportunities. Therefore, we have begun training one group as elite stormtroopers. They know the underworld of Coruscant very well, and could prove to be effective spies or saboteurs, should we choose to employ them in such a fashion."

The projection of the Emperor nodded inside his cowl. "Agreed, Brakiss. Very good." A ripple of static flickered across the transmitted image, and the Emperor's voice wavered. "You shall survive another day."

"Yes, my master," Brakiss said.

The expression on the Emperor's ravaged face grew stern. "Don't disappoint me, Brakiss," he said. "I should be most displeased if I was forced to blow up your Shadow Academy."

Brakiss bowed low, and his silvery robes pooled around him. "I would be displeased as well," he said.

The holographic image of the Emperor shimmered, then broke into sparkles of static as the transmission cut off.

Brakiss felt himself trembling all over, as he did each time he spoke to the awesome Palpatine. Exhausted, he sat down again at his desk and began to review his next set of plans, obsessively careful not to allow any mistakes.

19

YOUNG ANAKIN SOLO stood next to the comm unit in the living area of his family's quarters, exhausted from his long and fruitless search, and worried about his brother Jacen. Staring at the darkened screen, he willed a message to come in from Jacen, but he knew that none would come—he could *feel* it.

He and Threepio had returned to their quarters an hour earlier after covering their assigned search locations, but they had heard no word from Jacen. And Anakin knew he couldn't delay any longer.

He turned and walked over to the wall, where the golden protocol droid sat enjoying the refreshment of a brief shutdown cycle. Ice-blue eyes looked into the droid's yellow optical sensors. Anakin gave the droid a tap. "Wake up, Threepio. We've waited long enough. Time to get help."

The optical sensors winked to life, and See-Threepio gave a start of surprise. "Dear me. I couldn't possibly have overslept, could I? I thought we agreed to rest two more cycles before going out to search again. And you have a lesson plan to—"

"I can sense that something is wrong," Anakin interrupted. "Jacen and Tenel Ka haven't come back."

"Well, if you ask me—"

"I didn't," Anakin cut in. "Try to signal them again with your mobile comlink connection."

"I'm sure they're quite all right, but I'll try." Threepio tilted his head sideways and stared off into space for a few seconds.

"Any response?" Anakin asked.

"No, Master Anakin," Threepio replied with greater concern in his voice. "None at all."

Just then Leia Organa Solo entered the room, smiling brightly at Anakin—then frowning. "Anakin, what's wrong?"

Anakin considered how much to tell his mother—after all, they had asked for her help earlier, but she had not believed Zekk's disappearance was anything serious. Now, though, maybe Leia would change her mind when she learned that Jacen and Tenel Ka had vanished as well. The young boy spilled the story rapidly, with Threepio adding sound effects and embellishing with unnecessary comments.

"Jacen would have answered our call if he could," Anakin said.

"Most certainly," See-Threepio added with enthusiasm. "Master Jacen may be somewhat disorganized, but he is *always* conscientious."

Her alarm growing visibly, Leia said, "He would answer—unless he's in trouble." She reached some sort of decision and snapped into action, demonstrating one of the qualities that made her a good Chief of State. "We've got to go find them. Tenel Ka wouldn't let Jacen do anything dangerous. But she probably doesn't think *anything* is dangerous."

Leia ran to a wall panel. "I'll summon a group of guards to go with us. Threepio, can you trace the location of Jacen's comlink?"

"Well, it's certainly not as precise a tracking system as I'd like, but I suppose that by sending a continuous signal and monitoring the feedback from the mobile comlink I could probably—"

"So how close can you get us?" Leia interrupted impatiently.

"I should be able to pinpoint the signal to within a radius of ten meters."

"Close enough," Leia said.

Anakin gave a sigh of relief. "Let's just hope both Jacen and Tenel Ka are still somewhere near the comlink."

"We'll worry about that when we get there," Leia said, grabbing a medkit and dashing toward the door. Guards rushed into position, still not clear on what the emergency was. "Let's go, Anakin. You're part of this rescue, too. Which way, Threepio?" Leia called.

The protocol droid followed as fast as his mechanical legs could move. "To your left, Mistress Leia. We'll need to find a turbolift and take it down forty-two levels."

Anakin tried to picture in his head where they were going, but with little success. "Maybe you'd better lead, Threepio."

Leia, the guards, and Anakin followed See-Threepio as he picked his way across another rickety walkway between two gigantic buildings. The protocol droid seemed to be enjoying his new importance immensely.

The buildings stretched out of sight above and below them. Once, at a spot where the side rail was missing, Anakin lost his footing and nearly fell off the bridge, but Leia instinctively grabbed him. She looked at her son with shock, then hugged him quickly. "Be careful," she urged. "We've *all* got to be careful."

Anakin shuddered. This area had not looked so dangerous on the map. As they homed in on the comlink signal, working through abandoned levels and empty, ominous halls, he noticed a design that appeared with increasing frequency on the grimy walls: an equilateral triangle surrounding a cross.

"I wonder what that symbol means," he said, pointing.

"I am fluent in over six million forms of communication," Threepio said. "Unfortunately, that design is not in any of my databanks. I'm afraid I cannot offer any enlightenment, Master Anakin."

Leia looked at the guards. "Do any of you recognize the symbol?"

One of them cleared his throat. "I believe it's a gang marking, Madam President. Several . . . unpleasant groups make a habit of living down in the untended lower levels of the city. They are very difficult to catch."

"I heard Zekk talking with Jacen and Jaina about a gang called the Lost Ones," Anakin supplied. "I think the gang wanted Zekk to become a member."

Leia's mouth formed a grim line, and she nodded, filing away the information for future reference. Right now, she just wanted to find Jacen and Tenel Ka.

See-Threepio paused to study his readings. "Oh, curse my inadequate sensors—I'm certain my counterpart Artoo-Detoo could have been much more accurate—but I believe that we are now within two hundred meters of their location."

As the group walked deeper into the dilapidated level, the hall became darker and darker. The guards held their weapons ready, glancing at each other uneasily. Leia held her chin up and bravely pushed ahead with greater speed. Three-pio increased the brightness of his optical sensors, shedding a soft yellow light directly ahead of them. Anakin kept his glowrod out and ready; it made him feel safer somehow, as if it were an imitation lightsaber.

Threepio made a sharp right turn into a low, narrow passageway, ducking under a half-fallen girder. Even Anakin had to stoop to get under it. "Are you *sure* this is the right direction, Threepio?"

"Oh yes, absolutely certain," Threepio replied. "Remember, we are following a direct path, homing in on the signal. Young Master Jacen may have taken a more roundabout way. We are within thirty meters now."

They finally emerged into a large, eerily lit room with flickering glowpanels mounted haphazardly on the walls. Anakin looked around at the set of rickety stairs leading nowhere, the food wrappers, cushions, and broken-down furniture, and the odd assortment of sealed doors on the other side of the room. "This must be the meeting place of the Lost Ones."

"Oh dear," Threepio said. "Didn't Master Zekk say those gang members were rather unpleasant sorts?"

The room was deathly silent, and the flickering lights made Anakin uneasy. The guards hesitated at the low doorway, pushing their weapon barrels inside. Even though the room was empty, Anakin sensed a lingering feeling of darkness as he entered and began to look around. He nearly jumped out of his skin when See-Threepio cried out, looking down at the floor in horror.

"It's all my fault!" Threepio wailed again. "Oh, curse the slowness of my processor. We should have come looking for them much sooner."

In a heartbeat Anakin had scrambled over the makeshift furnishings to where Threepio stood berating himself. Leia and the guards rushed over to join him.

Jacen and Tenel Ka lay crumpled on the floor, side by side, unconscious . . . or perhaps dead.

Quickly unstrapping the medkit, Leia pulled out a mini-diagnosticator and examined the two young Jedi Knights. "It's all right," she said. "They're alive—just knocked out." She ran her cool palm over Jacen's forehead, brushing aside his tousled hair.

Anakin and Leia slowly nursed the two back to consciousness. Jacen came around first, and Anakin could tell from the look in his brother's eyes that the news was grim.

"Are you all right?" Anakin asked. He shifted gears as he began to put the pieces of a puzzle together in his mind.

Jacen swallowed hard. "Tenel Ka? . . ." he asked, his voice shaky.

". . . is just fine," Leia said reassuringly. "Looks like you two got stunned. What happened?"

Jacen shivered, as though the room had suddenly become colder. "Tamith Kai was here—the Nightsister from the Shadow Academy—along with two of her friends." His brandy-brown eyes squeezed shut, as if he had just remembered something too painful to bear. He groaned. "And they've got Zekk! I think . . . I think he's gone over to the dark side."

Anakin's breath could not have come out in a greater rush if a bantha had just kicked him in the stomach.

"They're going to train him to be a Jedi," Jacen continued. "A Dark Jedi."

Tenel Ka grunted and sat up. "This is a fact."

"There were other kids here, too," Jacen said. "The Lost Ones. I think the Nightsisters took them all—to the Shadow Academy."

Leia shook her head, her dark eyes flashing. "I think it's about time we did something decisive about that Second Imperium," she said. "That's twice now they've hurt my children."

"Yes, indeed, Mistress Leia! That's all well and good, but we simply must get back home where it's safe," Threepio said in alarm. "Mistress Tenel Ka, are you capable of walking?"

Her granite-gray eyes narrowed, as if she suspected a veiled insult. "I could carry *you*, if I had to."

Jacen chuckled, then groaned as he held his aching head. "Yeah. I think she's just fine."

20

UP ON THE mirror station, Jaina worked with Lowie and Chewbacca to patch up as many of the worn-out subsystems as they could manage. After scraping together the few spare components they could find, they added their own ingenuity to come up with alternative solutions. Although it was impossible for them to program the food synthesizers to create anything remotely resembling gourmet fare, Lowie and Chewbacca did manage to produce a passable midday meal.

Jaina completed the task of reconnecting the communications systems, making it possible to send brief messages, though the transmissions were still plagued with bursts of static. Chewbacca set to work inspecting the life-support systems, the environmental controls, and the station beaters.

Peckhum watched, performing the few duties expected of him on his monitoring shift. He bubbled over with gratitude, emphasizing again and again how much he appreciated all the effort Jaina, Lowie, and Chewbacca were putting in on his behalf. "If I had waited for the New Republic to get around to fixing these things, Zekk would have been an old man by the time—" Peckhum broke off with a sad shake of his head.

With the major and obvious repairs completed, the young Jedi Knights had little to do while Chewbacca continued poking around. Lowbacca devoted his energies to finishing the orbital-debris plotting that he and Jaina had volunteered to do. Jaina had helped Lowie with the task, but tracking thousands of pieces of debris was just too daunting for her at the moment. Lowie, on the other hand, had extreme patience for a Wookiee, especially around computers. He diligently plotted one blip after another, noting the more dangerous space lanes in the heavily traveled orbits around the capital world.

Jaina glanced at Lowie's three-dimensional map, but soon turned back to the puzzling images on her own datapad. She reviewed file copies of the newsnet videoclips that showed the mysterious Imperial attack on the supply cruiser *Adamant*. On the day after the attack, she, Jacen, and Lowie had easily identified the modified assault shuttle, with its Corusca-gem teeth, recognizing the craft that had been used to kidnap them from Lando Calrissian's GemDiver Station.

Admiral Ackbar had verified their descriptions. The theft of military equipment was undoubtedly part of the evil work of the Shadow Academy. From Ackbar's description, Jaina knew that the Imperial in command of the attack had been none other than Qorl, the TIE pilot she and Jacen had tried to befriend near his crashed ship on Yavin 4.

She sighed and shook her head, watching the footage yet again. Jaina had hoped Qorl would see the error of his ways—and though the TIE pilot had trembled on the verge of surrender, the Imperial brainwashing had won out in the end. And now Qorl continued to cause trouble for the New Republic.

She replayed the videoclip of the *Adamant*'s capture a third time. The film, taken by New Republic forces as they'd rushed from Coruscant to defend the supply cruiser, had low resolution. But something about the clip bothered her in an indefinable way, as it had since the first time she'd seen it.

Jaina chewed on her lower lip. "Something just isn't right." She watched the shark-mouthed assault ship appear out of nowhere, while shots from the flanking Imperial ships took out the *Adamant*'s communication arrays and weapon systems. She turned her attention back to the replay—and suddenly sat up with a jolt. She had been watching Qorl's ship—but it was the *other* Imperial fighters that didn't fit.

"That's it!" she cried. "It can't be."

Chewbacca growled a question as he stood up from his cramped position in the control modules for the life-support systems. Jaina focused her attention on the images of the smaller ships, pointing. "I know my Imperial fighters," she said. "Dad taught me to identify every ship ever recorded . . . well, almost every one." She leaned closer to the image. "Those are short-range fighters." She jammed her finger at the image on the screen. "*Short-range* fighters! They had to come from somewhere nearby. Their base is close—hidden somewhere in this system!"

Chewbacca growled a surprised comment. Lowie, wedged into a chair built for humans with his knobby knees thrust high and his arms reaching almost to the ground, cradled his datapad in his lap, studying coordinates of the known items of space debris. He roared his own question, and waved the datapad in the air.

"Attention! Excuse me!" Em Teedee shrilled. "Master Lowbacca believes he has also found something of utmost importance, an inconsistency in the positions of orbital debris. I can't see it myself *since he hasn't shown me the data-pad*"—the miniature droid huffed—"but I trust it's something highly unusual for him to become so excited. You really must calm down, Master Lowbacca, and explain yourself."

Jaina rushed with Chewbacca to look at the thousands of dots plotted in the three-dimensional map of space around the planet Coruscant.

"That can't be right, either," Jaina said immediately. She was still puzzled by her own results, and now Lowie had made the mystery even deeper. "It's pretty much the opposite of what we expected."

Lowie barked his confirmation. Jaina sighed, biting her lower lip again. The entire reason for their mapping project had been to discover uncatalogued debris that posed a danger to navigation. Instead of revealing the uncharted hazard that had destroyed the *Moon Dash*, though, Lowie's map of space wreckage showed absolutely *nothing* in the marked zone. In fact, it was more like a forbidden area in space, an island empty of all known debris, as if somehow it had already been swept clear. But they knew the *Moon Dash* had struck something large enough to destroy it . . .

With a burst of static from the communications system, words filtered across the small, confined space. "Hello! Hello, Mirror Station? Can anyone hear me? Jaina, are you there?"

Peckhum perked up. "Well, now we're sure the communications system works."

"That sounded like Jacen!" Jaina rushed to the comm unit and flicked a switch, but was greeted by a flash of sparks from a burnt-out fuse. The sudden heat stung her fingertips. Scrambling, she yanked off the panel face and stared at the singed wires. She probed with the Force, following the path of the short circuit, and rapidly managed to hot-wire the damaged system well enough that she could answer her brother.

The speakers crackled back to life. "—are you there?

Jaina, answer me! This is important. We've found Zekk." A burst of static disrupted his next words. " . . . bad news . . ."

"Zekk!" Peckhum hurried forward, leaning over Jaina's shoulder. "Hello?" he shouted into the speaker. "Where is he? Is he all right?"

Jaina tossed her shoulder-length brown hair out of her eyes. "Wait. I haven't got the transmitter back on-line yet." She plucked out a melted cyberfuse and popped in a replacement yanked from her datapad. "That should do it," she said. "Okay, Jacen—we read you. Are we coming through?"

His voice came over the speakers, sizzling and broken. " . . . some disruption, but . . . understand you."

"What about Zekk?" she asked with an indrawn breath. "He's not? . . ."

"Dead?" Jacen finished for her. The transmission was clearer now, and his voice sounded stronger. "No. We found him—and then Tamith Kai and a couple of others from the Shadow Academy knocked us out."

"Tamith Kai!" Jaina gave a startled cry. Lowbacca roared, and even Em Teedee emitted a squeak of dismay. "But what would she be doing on—"

"They've recruited Zekk and a handful of the Lost Ones gang," Jacen said. "I don't know where they took him, but Zekk seemed to be with them willingly. Tamith Kai said she was going to train him to be a Dark Jedi! They're going to the Shadow Academy."

Lowie growled a curious question, but Jaina asked it without waiting for Em Teedee's translation. "But how *could* they train Zekk? He's not a Jedi—"

"Apparently he has the potential," Jacen said. "Remember, Uncle Luke found lots of candidates who never knew they could use the Force. Zekk had a knack for finding things to salvage, even in places where other people have scavenged already. We just never noticed, never put the pieces together."

Jaina hung her head, thinking of all the time they had spent with Zekk, all the fun they had had together, without her ever having recognized his true potential. "So where is he now?"

Jacen's voice became sad. "I don't know," he admitted. "They stunned me and Tenel Ka, then disappeared. Mom and Anakin came to find us, but that was hours ago. They've probably managed to get off planet by now. I have no idea where they might have gone."

Jaina covered her face with her hands. "Not you, Zekk. Not you!" Then she raised her tear-damp face and looked directly into Lowbacca's bright golden eyes. "The Shadow Academy!" she whispered. "Remember, the cloaking device makes the whole station invisible, like a hole in space—just like on your orbital map!"

He snarled in agreement. "Oh, my!" Em Teedee said, too flustered to provide a translation.

Jaina turned back to the comm system. "We know exactly where they are, Jacen." She glanced at Lowie's datapad and the projected map, zeroing in on the empty spot in space.

Jaina shouted into the voice pickup. "Tell Mom to contact Admiral Ackbar. We've got to mobilize the New Republic fleet. Lowie's going to send you some coordinates. We need to strike fast, before the Imperials realize we've caught them in the act."

"Great," Jacen said. "What are you going to do?"

Jaina smiled. "We're going to shine a little light on the subject."

Old Peckhum sat strapped into the command chair in the monitoring station as it dangled beneath the giant solar reflectors, working the outdated attitude adjustment controls. Jaina crouched over the chair, whispering excitedly into his ear. "Turn the mirrors," she said. "Turn, turn, turn!"

"I'm already beyond the maximums," Peckhum said in despair. His jaw was clenched, his neck muscles taut, and beads of sweat glistened on his brow. "These are delicate sheets of reflective material. We'll tear the solar mirrors if we whip 'em around too fast."

Jaina looked out the observation viewports, spotting the New Republic fleet launching from orbit and streaking toward their invisible target. Their weapons powered up as they homed in on the mysteriously empty zone. Before they arrived, Jaina and the others had to expose the Shadow Academy.

Lowie groaned a question, which Em Teedee translated. "Master Lowbacca wishes to inquire if the focusing apparatus has condensed the beam of reflected sunlight to its full-power configuration."

"That's for sure," Peckhum said. "Once we get this thing turned, we'll really make them hot under the collar."

Hanging in orbit over Coruscant, the big mirrors finally swung into position, focusing their bright beam of condensed sunlight into the empty void. The mirror beam cut a swath through space like a searchlight.

The light should have kept flying across the solar system, but when it struck the empty coordinates, space itself seemed to shimmer like golden smoke. The high-intensity flood of sunlight continued to bombard the cloaked area, finally overwhelming the invisibility shields around the Shadow Academy.

"There!" Jaina cried triumphantly.

The Imperial station rippled into view and then snapped into perfect focus, a large circular ring bristling with spiked gun emplacements and observation towers.

Lowie and Chewbacca roared in unison, and Jaina shook her head. "They were hiding right on our doorstep all along. That's why they could use short-range fighters to attack the *Adamant*. That's how Tamith Kai and her companions could slip down to the city and steal Zekk away."

"Zekk must be aboard the station then," Peckhum whispered. "That's where they've taken him."

"And the Lost Ones," Jaina added.

Chewbacca snarled, then pointed as the exposed Shadow Academy began to move. Thrusters along the equator of its donut shape burned blue-white on one side, nudging it away from the bright beam of concentrated sunlight.

"Turn the mirrors," Jaina said. "We can't let them get away before the ships arrive."

"Oh dear," Em Teedee said. "I do hope our fighters manage to apprehend that Shadow Academy. I'm still exceedingly vexed with them for reprogramming me when we were all taken prisoner there."

Peckhum punched new coordinates into the mirror directional systems, but the sudden acceleration and the change in direction proved too much for the already-stressed silvery sheeting. The long webs of cables that held the great mirror in position tore free, and a wide gash began to open up, spilling a seam of stars and black night through the glittering reflector.

"We can't hold it," Peckhum shouted. "It's too much!" He shook his head. "We could never target a moving object anyway." Then he looked up and moaned. "My mirrors!"

The Shadow Academy continued to accelerate, and Jaina watched the approach of Admiral Ackbar's vengeful fleet, silently urging them to greater speed. But she could see they would not arrive in time.

"The Shadow Academy must already have been preparing to leave," she said. "Of course. They've got Zekk and some other recruits. They've stolen a shipment of hyperdrive cores and turbolaser batteries. They were only increasing their danger by staying here."

Though its ringed shape made it appear unwieldy, the Shadow Academy picked up speed as it headed toward its appropriate hyperspace jump point.

The first of the New Republic ships soared ahead, firing laser bursts at the Shadow Academy. Several shots struck home, leaving dark blaster scoring on the outer hull; the intensity of the solar mirror must have burned out some shields.

Jaina reached out with her mind, searching for Zekk, still marveling at the thought that the handsome, dark-haired street boy might have the potential to be a Jedi Knight. Or a Dark Jedi. She muttered to herself, feeling guilty, "He was our friend, and we never even imagined he might become a Jedi, too. Now it's too late."

As the New Republic ships arrowed toward their target, firing numerous laser bursts, the Shadow Academy suddenly shot forward with a bright flash of light. Its acceleration

stretched space and bent starlines, then it vanished to its unknown hiding place deep in Imperial territory.

The Shadow Academy was gone. Again.

Jaina swallowed a lump in her throat. And this time the
Imperials had taken a friend with them.

21

AT THE OBSERVATION windows of the mirror station,
Jaina stood next to Lowie, her hands outstretched, as if she
were trying to pull back the vanished Shadow Academy—
and Zekk with it. But, with the exception of a few New Republic ships, the area where the Imperial space station had
disappeared remained stubbornly empty.

She let her arms fall back to her sides. Her eyes squeezed
shut against the un-Jainalike tears that had suddenly welled
up, and her mind sent out a silent cry. *Don't go, Zekk! Come
back.*

In stunned silence, Peckhum leaned against the station
wall next to her. His mirrors were damaged, and Zekk had
joined the fragments of the Empire. "He's gone," the old man
whispered.

When Lowie placed a sympathetic hand on her shoulder,
Jaina felt strength and optimism flow back into her, as soothing as cool water to her burning sorrow. Drawing a deep
breath, she searched the observation window again for any
sign of hope.

A new movement caught her eye. "There!" she said, turning to grab Lowie's hairy arm. "Did you see that?"

Peckhum squinted, and the young Wookiee gave an interrogative growl.

"What do you mean, 'See what?'" Jaina said. "Look—
something else is out there, right where the Shadow Academy was."

Lowie's rumbled reply sounded hesitant, but Em Teedee

piped up to translate. "Master Lowbacca is loath even to suggest the possibility, but might that not simply be a New Republic ship, or one of the pieces of debris you've been tracking?"

"Absolutely not," Jaina said stubbornly. "Besides, any debris with a path that intersected the Shadow Academy would have been destroyed already—just like that shuttle, the *Moon Dash*."

Peckhum hunched over the comm system "Strange. That object seems to be transmitting a pickup signal—if I read this correctly, that is."

Lowie's triumphant roar brought Chewbacca from the main stabilizer unit, where he had been attempting manual repairs to the mirror adjustment systems—to no avail.

"Not very big," Jaina said, studying the mirror station's crude scanners. "Small enough to be an escape pod, don't you think?"

Lowie looked up at his uncle, who rumbled negative.

"Looks more like a message canister to me," Peckhum said. "Speaking of which, the transmitters are working now, so why don't we send a message to the New Republic fleet? They'll pick it up, whatever it is."

"Well, then," Jaina said, "what are we waiting for? Let's raise Admiral Ackbar."

Lowie transmitted the message while Jaina stared at the screen, still hoping.

"Years ago, Uncle Luke told me about one of his first students, a young man named Kyp Durron, who managed to stow away in a message pod." Jaina sent her mind out toward the object, trying to gather tiny bits of information with the Force. But she felt nothing, sensed no presence of her dark-haired friend. She heard Lowie croon a sad note beside her, but even without his confirmation, she knew that they wouldn't find Zekk inside the message pod.

At least not alive.

Jaina bit her lip and tried to look over Peckhum's shoulder as he piloted his old ship, the *Lightning Rod*, back toward Coruscant. Her view was all but obscured by the hairy form of Chewbacca, who took up the copilot's seat and much of the area around it. Thinking about the retrieved message pod from the Shadow Academy—still sealed against the vacuum of space and possibly containing a message from Zekk— filled her with a sense of urgency.

She wished she could tell Chewie and Peckhum to hurry up, that they had to get back immediately so they could be on hand when the message pod was opened. But that would have been foolish, not to mention rude. The two of them seemed to understand her anxiety and had already pushed the *Lightning Rod* to the highest speed its safety limits would allow. In the compartment behind them, the engines made disconcerting clunking sounds. Jaina bit her lower lip.

Lowie sat in thoughtful silence beside her. Only the deep indentations left by his hairy fingers in the foam padding of the arm cushions told Jaina that the young Wookiee felt a tension similar to hers.

As they reentered the atmosphere, Jaina forced her eyes shut and practiced one of Uncle Luke's Jedi relaxation techniques. But it didn't seem to work.

Finally, a gentle thump and the diminishing whine of the *Lightning Rod*'s engines told her they had arrived at one of the landing pads in Imperial City.

Jaina jumped down onto the landing pad without waiting for the exit ramp to extend fully; she couldn't even remember having unfastened her crash webbing or opening the exit hatch. She immediately caught sight of her parents, brothers, and Tenel Ka, who were standing near another New Republic ship that had obviously just landed. The message pod from the Shadow Academy was already being unloaded. Jaina ran toward her family.

"Any sign of explosives or weapons?" Leia was asking Admiral Ackbar as he stood watching his troops perform their duties.

"Absolutely none. We scanned it," he said. "It's clean. No booby traps."

"What about biologicals?" Han asked. The admiral shook his fishlike head.

"Can't be anything dangerous in there," Jaina said, skidding to a stop beside her parents. "It's from Zekk—I can *feel* it."

Admiral Ackbar looked skeptical, but three young voices spoke up at once.

"Hey, she's right."

"I feel it too."

"This is a fact."

"Even so," the Calamarian admiral said, "in the interest of safety, perhaps we should—"

Unable to bear the suspense any longer, Jaina pushed past the two guards who stood between her and the capsule, and activated the message retrieval mechanism. With a small *whoosh* of depressurization, the double panels slid aside to reveal the contents—a device of some sort, a complicated jumble of knobby plasteel parts and cabling.

"What is that?" Leia asked in surprise.

"Stand back!" Ackbar shouted. The guards tensed, as if expecting an explosion.

Han glanced into the capsule and then looked over at Chewbacca and Peckhum, who had come to join them. "What do you think, Chewie?"

Chewbacca scratched his head and gave a couple of short, surprised-sounding barks.

"Yeah, looks like that to me, too," Han agreed.

"So what is it?" Jacen asked, exasperated at being unable to follow the interchange.

"A central multitasking unit, of course," Jaina whispered in amazement and delight. "From Zekk."

Jaina heard a satisfied grunt from behind her. Old Peckhum muttered, "Kid's never broken a promise to me yet."

Then, as if conjured by Peckhum's words, a holoprojector hummed to life. A tiny image of Zekk resolved itself in the air just above the message pod. Jaina bit down hard on her lip again as the tiny glowing form began to speak. "I'm doing this against the better judgment of my teachers here," Zekk said, "so I'll make this message brief.

"Peckhum, my friend, here's the central multitasking unit I promised you. You always expected only the best from me, and I always gave it. This must be hard for you, but I want you to know that no one has kidnapped me or brain-washed me.

"To Jacen and"—the tiny holographic image hesitated—"and Jaina, it turns out I do have Jedi potential after all. I'm going to make more out of myself than anyone imagined I could be. We were good friends, and I'd never want to hurt you. Sorry I messed up your mother's diplomatic banquet—but that's one reason I'm doing this. I have the chance to become something better—a chance that I was never given by anyone in the New Republic."

Jaina groaned and shut her eyes, but the image continued to speak.

"I know this is something you wouldn't approve of, but I'm doing it for *myself*. If I ever come back, I'll be someone you can all be proud of.

"Don't worry, Peckhum, I'll never let you down. You've been my truest friend, and if there's any way I *can* come back to you, I will."

When Jaina opened her eyes again the tiny image had faded into sparkles, but she wouldn't have been able to see it anyway through her tears.

22

THE HANGAR BAY at the base of the Great Temple on Yavin 4 was quiet and cool, welcoming the travelers back to the Jedi academy. The ship sighed as it settled down on the smooth floor. Luke Skywalker emerged from the hatch and stood in the shadows as his students climbed out after him.

In the days when the Great Temple had been a secret Rebel base on the jungle moon, the hangar bay had been a place of frantic activity, filled with X-wing fighters, noisy equipment, droids, fighter pilots, and miscellaneous weaponry. In recent years, however, this had been a peaceful place of Jedi contemplation.

Luke turned to watch the young Jedi Knights following him out of the *Shadow Chaser*, the sleek Imperial ship he and Tenel Ka had captured from the Shadow Academy while rescuing Jacen, Jaina, and Lowbacca. Luke's thoughts were as troubled as the faces of his young students descending the exit ramp.

With the help of the Shadow Academy, a group of renegades calling themselves the Second Imperium was mounting a serious threat against the shaky peace that had been built over the past two decades by the New Republic. They could all sense it, and the battle was brewing, a great battle that would decide the Fate of the galaxy.

The Shadow Academy had become more bold in searching for recruits with Jedi potential. In addition, it seemed to be welcoming trainees with no Jedi skills whatsoever—but why? And then there was the theft of hyper-drive cores and turbolaser batteries from the *Adamant*—components that could be used to build a powerful military fleet. Something big was going to happen—and soon. . . .

Luke had picked the kids up from Coruscant, which had given him an opportunity to see his sister Leia and learn more about the newest Imperial threat to the New Republic. Since then, none of the young Jedi Knights had spoken much, each lost in private thoughts. Now they had arrived back on the jungle moon, where the other students were still training, bringing back the powerful force of Jedi Knights to help strengthen the New Republic. The new government was going to need its Force-trained defenders soon.

Bright sunlight streamed through the broad door of the hangar, bathing the entire bay in light and shadow. Clean shadows. Luke looked up at the sunlight glinting off the burnished quantum armor on the *Shadow Chaser*.

"The *Shadow Chaser* is still a beautiful ship." Jaina's voice cut into Luke Skywalker's thoughts. "Look at those lines, the curves."

"And at least it's one powerful ship the Shadow Academy doesn't have anymore," Jacen added, coming to stand beside them.

Luke nodded. "But it also shows us what our enemies are

capable of building. Think of what they can do with that large shipment of hyper-drive cores and turbolaser batteries they just stole."

Lowie grunted agreement. "This is a fact," Tenel Ka said.

Luke turned and strode through the open hangar bay doors, and the young Jedi Knights followed him out into the humid sunlight. Droplets of morning dew still sparkled on the Massassi trees and climbing ferns. The jungle air was filled with the scent of sweet growing things and the croaking, rustling, and twittering sounds of exuberant life.

Jacen's forehead was creased, as if by the weight of his thoughts. He turned and glanced back into the dimness of the hangar bay, catching sight of the *Shadow Chaser*. He sighed, then finally said what was on his mind. "I still can't believe that Zekk willingly chose to go to the dark side," he said. "Uncle Luke, what are we going to do about him? What did we do wrong? He was our friend, and now he's joined the enemy."

Jaina spoke through gritted teeth. "It's our fault for not showing him that he was just as important as anyone else. We didn't even realize he had Jedi potential. It's our fault," she repeated.

Lowie started to snarl a reply, then quickly reached toward his belt and turned off Em Teedee before the little droid could offer a translation.

"It's not so simple to tell who has Jedi potential and who doesn't," Luke said, sensing Jaina's despair and self-reproach. "Especially if they don't know it themselves. Even Darth Vader had no idea that your mother Leia had Jedi potential, though he spent quite a lot of time near her. You can't blame yourself, Jaina."

Tenel Ka spoke up, a distant look in her cool gray eyes. "Zekk made his own choice for his own reasons," she said. "We all do."

"But how could he betray us like that?" Jacen asked

Jaina winced at the word. "He can't betray us!" Her voice was hot with the strength of her emotions. "He won't—he promised. And he'll be back. I know it."

"The pull of the dark side is strong," Luke answered. "It's

possible to turn away from it, but the price is always high. It cost your grandfather his life. . . .

"But there's always hope—for Zekk, even for Brakiss. We have no way of knowing. One thing I do know, though." Luke turned his face toward the sunlight and enjoyed the feeling of the free breeze ruffling his hair. "The forces of darkness are gearing up for a full-scale war."

"Do we have to just wait for them to make the next move?" Jacen asked. "Can't we try to prepare ourselves for the coming fight?"

Luke looked with pride at each of the young Jedi Knights. "Yes, we can. A great battle is coming," he said, his voice tinged with both sadness and hope. "The Jedi Knights—all of us—have no choice but to prepare for it."

About the Authors

KEVIN J. ANDERSON and REBECCA MOESTA are the authors of all fourteen volumes of the *Star Wars: Young Jedi Knights* series. Working together, they have also written for *Star Trek*, *Titan A.E.*, *Starcraft*, as well as original short stories. In addition to many other *Star Wars* novels, Kevin is the author of an epic science fiction series, which begins with *Hidden Empire* and *A Forest of Stars*, and original novels *Captain Nemo* and *Hopscotch*. With Brian Herbert, he has completed six prequel novels to the science fiction classic *Dune*. Rebecca has written three volumes in the *Junior Jedi Knights* series and *Buffy the Vampire Slayer: Little Things*. More information can be found on their website, www.wordfire.com.